Hell's Mouth

KEVIN KNUCKEY

**Grosvenor House
Publishing Limited**

The right of Kevin Knuckey to be identified as the author of this
work has been asserted in accordance with Section 78
of the Copyright, Designs and Patents Act 1988

This book is published by
Grosvenor House Publishing Ltd
Link House
140 The Broadway, Tolworth, Surrey, KT6 7HT.
www.grosvenorhousepublishing.co.uk

This book is a work of fiction. Any resemblance to
people or events, past or present, is purely coincidental.

A CIP record for this book
is available from the British Library

ISBN 978-1-80381-113-0
eBook ISBN 978-1-80381-114-7

Dedication

To Elayne, Caitlin, and Jacob
You made this take so much longer

Acknowledgements

I'd like to give my special thanks to the following people, who have all in some way helped in bringing this book into existence.

To my wife and children for putting up with my mood swings when I faced interruptions (largely from them). Okay, the outbursts weren't quite on the scale of Jack Torrance, but at least I still have somebody to aspire to.

To my friend, Eve Potts, for accepting the arduous task of becoming my first reader. Also, thanks to fellow author, A P Bateman, whose advice as somebody who has achieved great success in the world I intend to operate in is hugely appreciated.

Thank you to my English lecturer, Becky Rose, who not only inspired me with her exuberance and charisma, but also helped me to realise I could accomplish things my dumbass previous self could not even conceive.

I am eternally grateful to the whole team at Grosvenor House Publishing Ltd. And in particular to Tanis Eve, my Publishing Administrator, whose expertise and guidance has made what can be an intimidating experience as uncomplicated and enjoyable as possible.

And finally, thanks to Pappa Pete, aka Taggy. From another realm you helped bring this book to life.

CHAPTER ONE

When Andrew Tredinnick reported his wife missing at just after one in the morning, he really did not expect to be stood where he was now. Seven hours later – though time seemed to hold no bearing at that moment; seven hours, seven minutes, a lifetime? But here he was. Ageing red Ibiza in front of him. Hell's Mouth's familiar yet harrowing roar rampaging over the scrub and the rain-slicked surface of the North Cliffs coastal road.

Of course, his call was not taken seriously: a grown woman out for the evening with her mates, said she'd be home around ten o'clock. Only a few hours late. *'Probably gone back to a girlfriend's house to keep the night alive,'* the voice on the other end of the phone had said. *Probably shagging someone else* is what the mind behind the voice would have bet on.

'Alive', great choice of words, Andrew thought bitterly.

Well, they appeared to be taking it seriously now.

It was her car, Shona's, definitely her car. The faded yellow *Baby on Board* sign, still hanging crudely askew in the rear window, even though the only baby they had had together was now six years old. The rear window wiper rubber split and hanging from halfway down the blade, sticking to the wet boot, a drowned dog that won't be wagging its tail for this owner again. The number plate, fine dark cracks spreading like cobwebs from old and brittle screw holes. The faded paint on the plastic bumper, turned a mottled shade of pink by years of sun, rain, and salty Cornish air, peeling to its black base in several places.

Shona, always too sentimental to let go of the heap of shit.

Pulsating lights from the roof of a marked police car parked up close to the front of *the heap* made every drop of the February drizzle enveloping the hatchback dance in a blue-red frenzied discotheque.

Unaware of his own movements, Andrew's feet dragged him forward. Slowly, inch by inch, they pulled him numbly past his wife's unoccupied vehicle. Arm outstretched, he ran the tips of his fingers along the painted panelling; an attempt to steady himself? To convince himself that it was real? Or preferably, not real. Who knows? Drifting along the cold hard surface, his fingertips sent countless blood-red tears cascading down the door panels, stream upon stream amassing at the bottom and turning black as they left cold metal and found colder asphalt.

Stopping at the front end of the car, his feet crunched in the debris of the layby as he turned ninety degrees to his right, where Shona's Seat met nose-to-nose with the Focus estate, its blue lettering prominent on the bonnet. For just a moment the intimate positioning of the two vehicles reminded Andrew of that wacky Beetle from those seventies' films, flashing his headlights, flirting with his new love interest.

Another printed text that demanded Andrew's attention. Rising on a weather-worn wooden post in the hedge, in line with the gap between the two stationary vehicles, a pair of rusty old screws not quite enough to stop it rattling in the swirling wind, was a metal plate. Andrew was held in a trancelike state by the bold printed words projecting from it:

TALK TO US
If things are getting to you

This open invitation was followed by a telephone number, stating that it was 'FREE' to call around the clock. There was also a childlike white line drawing of an old telephone, a round-dial-and-cradle type landline with a coiled wire that Andrew's youngest child would probably not recognise as a phone. Funny, this part of the cliff road was littered with these little green signs. *Plenty of signs*, Andrew thought, *but never a fucking phone.*

Did Shona make a call? Certainly not to me. Why the fuck didn't she call me?

He had been here a lot over the years; with Shona, with his ex-wife, Alison.

Why here again?

Hell's Mouth; infamous countywide; heck, countrywide even. Forever lying in wait, one eye open if it slept, never ceasing its call. Sometimes it is just a low moan: Sometimes – when it is at its angriest – it's an overbearing series of explosions that resonate for miles across the fields and shaking the leaves in the nearby woodlands. And sooner or later someone will answer. Someone always gave themselves in sacrifice sooner or later, quenching but never eliminating its thirsty baying for blood.

Andrew was snapped out of his melancholy hypnosis. A sudden whip of wind sent rain plastering hard against the blindingly yellow jacket of a police officer, crackling like fireworks on the weatherproof material. The officer was mid-conversation with a guy dressed in tatty blue overalls, strapped, corded and pulleyed up to the hilt. One of the coastguard rescue team; it didn't take a genius to figure that out, and to know that this guy had seen sights over the years that some can't even imagine. Both men were using low voices, both had their heads down shielding their faces from the increasing downpour that went pretty much unnoticed by Andrew until that moment.

Straps – as Andrew named him in his head – turned a glance in his direction. Andrew noted the deep creases on his forehead, crow's feet at the corners of his eyes and fissures down his cheeks. *Hard paper round.* Blotchy red patches of dry, irritated skin flanked both sides of his nose, and sore-looking cracks gathered where his earlobes joined the sides of his face. Salt and pepper flecked his unkempt stubble up to and covering parts of his prominent cheekbones, along with miniscule flakes of skin from his weathered face. *Clearly no stranger to the elements.* He and Andrew locked eyes, just for a split second but long enough for Andrew to read the involuntary look of pity in them.

Had they found something?

The rescue worker quickly lowered his gaze, dropped his right shoulder and limped across the road, over the sodden ground and up to the cliff edge. Back to the sobering task of searching for the rock-torn and wave-beaten, lifeless remnants of a recently vibrant young woman.

Andrew wanted to follow him. To go beyond him. To lean, let go, feel oblivion. To feel nothing else ever again.

Closing his eyes as a wave of nausea assaulted him, Andrew's head was thrown into an audial kaleidoscope, all sound violently coming and going as the swirling gusts slung them from one direction to another, before slinging them back again. Waves smashed on rock; the coastguard helicopter thrummed in mind-splitting pulses; a rescue boat buzzed from an unseen lower realm; rain slashed; seabirds screamed.

Andrew stepped light-footed and dizzily into the road. A sharp blast of a car horn startled him out of his narcosis. Of course, there was no need to close the road for a 'jumper'. Just another slab of meat, taking the plunge and serving themselves as the main course for a hungry sea, leaving an evanescent stain on this supposed area of *outstanding natural beauty*.

Andrew stopped dead. The car, pulling out only a slight amount to narrowly miss his toes, came to an abrupt halt at his feet. A loathsome look was clinically executed by the baseball-capped driver, followed by a complementary air five-knuckle-shuffle. The piece of shit behind the wheel was in his early thirties – at Andrew's best and semi distracted guess (let's face it, his mind was on other things). He was scrawny and had scrappy little curls of brownie-ginger attempting to form a beard around his pointy weasel-like muzzle. A small crucifix tattoo was visible on his neck. Nicotine-stained teeth, crooked as ripped up floorboards, were revealed by his threatening snarl.

Occupying the passenger seat – and several inches either side – a huge woman sat deadpan; *Jesus,* Andrew thought, *it's almost like she's vacuum-packed in.* He nearly managed a smile at his witty observation, despite the solemnness of the present situation. The woman's soulless black eyes were locked on the road ahead.

Behind her, a kid of an age you would imagine would be gazing in fascination at the spectacle of the circling helicopter flying low over full-scale action on the clifftop, sat instead with his young eyes on Andrew. Raising his fist, the kid slowly extended his middle finger upwards and pressed his hand hard against the interior of the window. The pressure on the glass flattened his skin, turning the colourless flesh even milkier. Set below his scruffy mop of ginger hair in the lower parameter of his freckly moon of a face, the corners of his lipless mouth curled upwards in a sardonic smile.

Definitely his father's son, poor bastard.

With that last glimpse of the little shit, so destined for a life of conflict, crime and waste-of-time correctional methods, dad-of-the-year upped the revs. Dropping the clutch, he sprayed Andrew's shoes and lower legs with a shower of grit and road crud; fumes from the big boar exhaust of the old Golf filling his lungs with pungent acridity. Andrew watched as it pulled away; black paint, blacked out rear window, and novelty stickers he may never forget: the improbable '*Clunge Magnet*' and the ironic '*No Fat Chicks!*'

Turning his head to see what the copper made of all this, Andrew realised that it was close to *sweet FA*. The police constable opened the driver door of his squad car, slid in behind the wheel and placed a plastic evidence bag – containing solely a note retrieved from Shona's dashboard, scribbled by a shaky distressed hand – onto the passenger seat. Then he shut the door against the elements, leaned back, fought in his pocket for his mobile phone, and tapped away at the screen. Raising the phone to his ear, the PC waited a few seconds before speaking into it.

If you saw the PC laugh, like Andrew did, you wouldn't need to be a detective to work out that he had better things to do, better places to be, and better people to be there with. Odds on, this call was not work-related. Rubbing his clean-shaven chin, rearranging his windblown blond hair in the rear-view mirror, jiggling his genitals into a more comfortable and less constrained position. Talking to a mate about where he and *the boys* were going to watch the lunchtime kick-off, perhaps? Or to some lucky lady about where he's taking her later, if he ever gets off this cockblocking shift?

5

Andrew, less than slightly amused by what he was witnessing, had to turn away. He felt the warm, tightening beginnings of rage building from the pit of his stomach, like a jet engine ramping up furiously before take-off. Being neither the time nor the place for a confrontation, and deciding that in reality he had no idea who the young PC may be talking to, or about what, Andrew headed across the road. This time, he made sure he wasn't about to get his ass mowed down by another passing ASBO family.

Upon reaching the opposite side of the road the ground turned soft underfoot, making for unsteady treading. The short path from the road to the fenced-off cliff edge was boggy at the start, turning to a stinking sodden mat of dead grass and weeds as it first dipped and then rose.

Straps was on the other side of the low one-beamed fence when Andrew arrived, no more than a foot from the drop. He was stood with two colleagues of the same attire. One of which – a tall man, athletic build just about distinguishable through the rescue gear, silver hair and sun-browned but still smooth skin – was talking into a hand-held radio. His voice was authoritative, though his dress being akin to his companions made it impossible for the untrained eye to tell his rank or stature within the team.

Straps lifted his head towards the tall guy, 'That's the husband.'

Lowering his radio, the tall one turned a knob, silencing the equipment. Switching the black box between hands, the man extended his now free right to Andrew, leaning over the fence as he did so. He seemed to have to lower himself a great deal to reach Andrew's level. Must be at least six-foot-five. Andrew was a six-footer himself, but this guy was on a slight mound of higher, lumpy ground. It made Andrew feel diminished in his presence.

'Mr Tredinnick? I'm John Cole.'

Andrew received his hand. Cole's grip was firm and reassuring; his own, limp and submissive.

'I appreciate the distress this situation must be causing you, but please rest assured that we have the best teams working together here and we're doing everything we can.'

The sense of humility radiating from Cole's cool blue eyes was a total contradiction to the bellowing of the ocean below and behind him. It totally caught Andrew off-guard. Those piercing eyes opened him up to a level he was not comfortable with, his usual mask, used for concealing his emotions, completely and helplessly extirpated by them.

'I don't know what to do,' Andrew replied weakly, unaware that he was even going to open his mouth.

'At the moment the best thing you can do is go and get some coffee in you,' Cole advised. 'The café across the road doesn't open for another hour, but the owner's inside and said we are welcome to use the facilities. He'll sort you out with a hot drink.'

'I need to be here for her,' a pause. 'For when she…'

'We'll know where to find you if your wife needs you, Mr Tredinnick.' The inarguable authority returned to Cole's voice. 'You're not dressed for this weather. For now, the best thing you can do is go inside and let us do what we need to do.'

Andrew made to step over the fence. Immediately Cole's hand was on his shoulder, gentle yet utterly persuasive.

'You don't need to put yourself in danger any more than *we* need you to, Mr Tredinnick,' Cole asserted. 'We have enough to focus our efforts on right now.'

Cole raised his eyes in the direction of the café, a clear, but implicit, instruction for Andrew to head that way.

Point taken, that's exactly what he did.

He made his way back down the slope, slipping on the soaking ground on more than one occasion, brown hair blackened by rain, sticking to his forehead. The noise from the commotion that surrounded him disintegrated: waves lapped rather than smashed; the rotor blades of the helicopter turned from bedlam to a buzz, like it had suddenly become an insignificant insect, a lowly fly. The outboard motor noise from the small craft all but disappeared completely. Furious wind had dipped to a whisper; rain tickled; gulls no longer cried. Human voices died. Andrew sunk to the ground as his world turned black.

***

7

Miniature clouds of dust, licked up by the gentle breeze, danced their way lazily through the gloom over a crushed-stone car park, fading like ghosts as they rose into the night-darkened sky. The hostile weather from earlier had moved on, leaving a weary Hell's Mouth to rest at tranquil ease. The road lay dormant and empty, a winding lace as black as jet, cut off into nothingness east and west.

Blue and white police tape fluttered and tickled against the cold metal bodywork of a motionless, abandoned red hatchback in a roadside layby.

Fine scratching noises headed across the asphalt, Canidae claws clicking and scraping on the hard surface. Two globes flashed a brilliant yellow-green as moonlight struggled free from cloud before being drowned out once more. Trotting the short climb up the damp footpath, the vixen caught sight of a large shape in front of her. Suspicious and a little wary of the unexpected intrusion, she darted to the left, following the narrow path as it hugged the coastline.

The shape was perched on a chunky beam of fencing, situated at the gaping mouth of a compounded stone, earth, and rock drop. Not too many years previously, a huge rock fall approximately fifty yards from where the shape now sat, sent tens-of-thousands of tonnes of cliff face crashing into the sea. The lonely figure thought about that at this moment, wondering, even hoping a little, if it might happen again. Right now. Right at his feet.

When Andrew came around earlier, he was in the café with a small crowd around him. Police, a couple of rescue workers, others he had no idea who they were or why they were there. Other than being caked in mud, and obtaining a small cut on his right cheekbone, he was given the all-clear. No headache; no blurred vision; sound.

The painfully long hours since then had been a succession of comings and goings, but mainly goings. Wind dwindled to a breeze. Rain drifted away. Daylight dulled. Coastguards departed. Police departed. The cluster of noisy bystanders departed. Darkness arrived. Shona remained unfound.

The search had been called off.

What the hell do I tell the kids?

Andrew raised himself off the low fence and took a tentative step forward, the brush shapeshifting under the unexpected pressure of his feet. Would throwing himself off be easier than telling the children? Probably. Could he leave them without him *and* Shona? Kerenza had had no contact with her father since before Andrew was even on the scene, and Cameron's mum (Andrew's first wife) went years ago; at this very spot. Then there was Merryn, she would lose both mummy and daddy in one single day. So, probably not.

He looked down. The normally mesmeric sapphire blue had now turned a cataclysmic, bloodcurdling sea of oil.

CHAPTER TWO

'Eat your breakfast, Merryn, honey,' said Andrew. 'We need to be leaving soon.' He let out a low sigh. She was such a dawdler in the mornings.

'I feel sick.'

'No you don't,' he returned. 'You feel fine and you're going to school. I've got work and there's no one here to look after you.'

'You work here, and mummy wouldn't make me go.'

'Mummy's not here, sweetheart. You know that.'

A surge of pain stabbed Andrew straight through the heart every time he said this. He downed his cup of still-too-hot coffee, in the hope that the serpent burn moving down his throat and chest would detract from the mental anguish. Sadly, although physical pain is most often temporary, the same cannot be said for the psychological hurt caused by remembering a lost loved one.

'They pick on me!' Merryn threw this revelation out there with an emphatic fold of the arms, more comical than dramatic.

'Who?' Andrew threw back. 'The other kids? Why would they do that?'

'Cos I don't have a mummy,' Merryn lowered her head to hide the trace of tears welling in her eyes. Her long mousy-brown hair slid from behind her left ear, falling into her cereal.

Seven months had passed since mummy went out with her friends and did not come back.

Andrew reached forward and gently removed his young daughter's hair from her bowl, letting it fall onto the kitchen table.

'You do have a mummy,' he said gently. 'She just had to go to Heaven and wait for us there for a while.'

'Where is Heaven, Daddy?' Merryn raised her head and looked at him inquisitively, a look that always made Andrew dread what he would answer – never really being one to think before opening one's mouth, and prone to digging a deep whole even deeper with every stumbled word. No shovel required. Just keep talking.

'Up past the clouds, somewhere,' Andrew started to squirm away, uncomfortable with where his detective of a daughter would take this line of questioning next. He didn't believe in Heaven, or in *God*, any more than he believed in Father fucking Christmas, the Easter Bunny or pestilential Cornish Peskies! He was also pretty sure that if any of that shit *was* real, Shona, as a non-believer herself, would almost certainly be unwelcome *upstairs*. Especially after checking out of our mortal realm completely of her own accord. No, just as in the wee-small hours or that stormy February morning, she was heading down.

'In Space?' Merryn wrinkled her nose up, clearly doubtful and expecting something more substantial.

'Kind of,' Andrew returned in a cagey manner.

'So, she's always in the dark!'

'What? No, of course not; what kind of heaven would that be?' Feeling flustered now.

'But Space is *always* dark,' Merryn persisted. 'I've seen it on TV loads of times. Everything's black.'

She had him on the ropes now. Round one and cornered, ducking and diving fruitless, gaining him nothing but a black eye and a bloody, swollen lip. *Think man, think!*

'Time to go. Get your shoes on, squirt, we're leaving in thirty seconds.' *That's it? That's the best you've got?*

Squirt. Merryn hated it when he called her that. For a six-and-a-half-year-old she felt extremely grown up, and *squirt* was a sure-fire way to make her feel miniscule and babyish. Still, she got up, pushing her chair forcibly away from the table with the backs of her knees. The *vvvrrrpppp*-ing sound of wooden legs grinding against porcelain flooring sent a grating shudder down Andrew's spine. Merryn stomped off with a dramatic, Miss Piggy-esque flick of her hair

– accompanied with a 'hmph' – satisfied that she had annoyed her father with her actions.

Five minutes later, not the thirty seconds as foretold, Andrew was sliding his key into the lock on the front door of Sea Glass Cottage; their 'forever home'. He did this with such painful gradualness that he could hear and feel every nickel-plated brass tooth of the key biting into place within the lock's internal mechanism. This was the way he always left home now, delaying the moment where he would need to turn and face the drive; the two-car drive that now rarely housed more than one four-wheeled tenant – his deep grey Nissan crossover.

It had always been the way that Andrew would park closest to the exit of their slim driveway. Usually, Shona would park closest to the cottage that they had shared for the final seven years of her life.

As soon as they discovered that Shona was pregnant (after getting over the initial sucker punch to the gut, of course), the decision was made that they needed to look for somewhere a little bigger to live. A teenage girl would not want to share with a baby sister, understandably. It had never been their intention to fall pregnant; Andrew had Cameron, Shona had Kerenza (both from previous marriages), and let's not forget, they had each other. And that was enough. They *were* careful, but life has its innovative way of throwing little surprises at us all, doesn't it? Sometimes they are for the better, sometimes for the worse, but no one can deny the fact that they happen.

About five months before baby Merryn was scheduled to arrive, they found Sea Glass Cottage; a gorgeous, characterful property just a three- or four-minute walk from Trevaunance Cove; an idyllic bay of rock and sand and a once-upon-a-time harbour, its wall now lying in ruin, arcing out to sea like a sleeping whale. The cottage itself was set nicely back from the road, ideal for the kids to safely enjoy the substantial garden. Upstairs, the interior had the four bedrooms that they were looking for, and a family bathroom. Downstairs, enough space for them to not be under each other's feet, but not too much for them to feel overwhelmed.

They were doing well back then. Andrew's art was selling to rich Londoners, to adorn their holiday homes or swanky apartments back in the big city. And Shona was climbing the ladder with determined ease at the bank.

The house was perfect.

Except for one thing.

The previous owner had – as Andrew liked to say – gone *Bodmin*. Out-of-county folk may refer to this as insane; or loopy; or cuckoo; batshit; demented; crazy nuts bonkers. Call it what you will, to Andrew it was always *Bodmin*, on account of the infamous asylum that was founded in Bodmin (surprise) way back in the early eighteen-hundreds. For *'private patients'* and *'pauper lunatics',* according to media with no care for discretion. Where the previous owner actually ended up (that site now converted to office buildings) never once concerned Andrew.

As a result of the poor old chap's departure from senility, the place was a mess that no one cared to sort before the sale. The limited number of stud walls were as holed and as yellow as Swiss cheese; lino was lifting in the kitchen, the small downstairs toilet, and the bathroom. The front room carpet was stained an orangey-brown and stunk of piss. Mouse droppings infested everywhere you dared to look: floors, work surfaces, window sills. The ceilings were black and sagging in most rooms. The kitchen units, damp and swollen, doors hanging – or at least where they weren't missing completely. There was even what looked like human faeces, dried and welded to the carpet behind the living room's sole piece of furniture, a torn sofa covered in crude and X-rated marker pen drawings. Very imaginative, it had to be said. So many ways to depict breasts or penises.

Still, there was nothing that Andrew and Shona could not achieve together. And about three months before baby Merryn was born, they were handed the keys.

It was all-hands-on-deck. Every spare minute that they had, and every spare penny for that matter, was utilised in the renovation. Friends chipped in with their time and varying skillsets. Tradespeople were in and out like a fiddler's elbow. Hell, even Cameron managed to pick up a broom towards the end.

Hard work and a huge strain at the time. Looking back now, Andrew was drowned in nostalgia. He could see Shona nearing the end of the 'big project'. Almost midnight, a halo of warm yellow light radiating around her from the table lamp (temporarily standing on the bare chipboard floor), roller in hand, dark hair in a ponytail tied with a white polka dotted red scarf. Speckles of pale emulsion stood out on her dark fringe and lay just about visible on her light cheeks. Her heavily pregnant belly was putting a palpable strain on her blue denim maternity dungarees.

Andrew remembered thinking that she had never looked sexier than she did that night. And that night, even though his body ached and craved for a deep sleep to swallow its ailments forever, closing the doors of time once and for all; and no matter how heavily pregnant she had ballooned, he showed her exactly how sexy he thought she was. Taking her on that very floor, decorator's dust puffing up in scant plumes around them.

Merryn waited patiently, watching her daddy from the back seat of the crossover, accepting the likely outcome of her being late for school. She didn't know where he went when he stalled like this, but it didn't worry her. She knew he always came back in the end.

The click-click-click of a stone caught in tyre-tread rolling by brought Andrew back to the here-and-now. He turned and lowered himself from the doorstep, feet crunching down onto the gravel drive. The scuffling of foot traffic kicking at the gravel had, over time, covered the indentations once made by Shona's much loved old banger. Andrew though, as vehemently as he avoided parking in Shona's space, also avoided walking across it. He opted instead to use the grass that flanked the drive – the grass now turning dead and yellow under his repeated passage. Pretending the little red Ibiza still lay in its homely bed was just one of the self-taught coping mechanisms he applied, denying certain elements of the past, picking and choosing reality as easy as flicking through television channels.

Reaching his Qashqai, Andrew opened the door. Easing in behind the steering wheel, he depressed the clutch and hit the 'START/STOP' button.

Ten minutes later, he was watching his youngest bounce and skip merrily along the school pavement in front of him. He offered a *hiya* to the people he knew, acknowledged the ones he didn't with a smile or a nod of the head. Most of the latter handed back uneasy half-smiles and lowered their gaze to the floor as they passed; *that's him... why did she do something like that...maybe it was something to do with him...you never know what goes on behind closed doors...*

Andrew Tredinnick was no stranger to persecutory glances; had in fact become accustomed to them. He'd been sucking them up for years before Shona made like a wave and crashed against the rocks – I mean, it hadn't been the first time, let's be honest.

Arriving at the classroom door, he raised a hand in greeting to Merryn's teacher, who was listening distractedly to an animated young mum and looking like she couldn't wait for the conversation to be over.

'See ya later, squirt,' he said, kissing the top of Merryn's fuzzy head and ushering her through the door.

'Don't call me that,' Merryn returned with an assertive and oddly adult voice.

'Love you.'

'Love you too, Daddy.'

Andrew turned and headed back toward the car park, hoping for as little contact as possible with any other living soul during the short commute. All he wanted was to get back home, conceal himself in the solitary bliss of his studio – an outhouse lovingly created with his own gifted hands, complete with kettle; beer fridge; spirits shelf (for artistic purposes, not human consumption); hammock; favourite aging brown leather armchair; and the tools of his trade. Also, a wall-and-a-half full of his *Angry Work*: work that had not sold and had been unceremoniously rejected by galleries. Black twisted trees with dead black roots exposed; black seas furious under anthracite skies; black blood gushing from gaping wounds in charcoal cliff-faces. An expression of his emotions on canvas. Yep, a lot of black.

Social avoidance turned out to be a lot easier than expected, although really it was inevitable for someone with his position in the rumour mill. All Andrew had to do was stare at the floor the whole way back to the car. Passers-by were pleased, relieved even, to escape his attention.

He made it to his *studio*. Did some thinkin'. Did some drinkin'. He was awakened an unknown number of hours later by a shrill chirping sound. Its intensity heightened as it ricocheted from the bare, buffed cement floor, the painted walls and the galvanised roof.

Being dragged excruciatingly from his slumber, and completely against his will, Andrew finally cottoned on to where the relentless sound was emanating from. The room was near-dark, a combination of only one small window and him not bothering to turn on any of the lights; not ideal for work but that had never been on the agenda for today. Old dust from the crumbling leather armchair filled his nostrils and his mouth – tasting as old funeral parlours might – as he stirred and shuffled, trying to spot the lit-up screen of his phone.

The chirping stopped, filling the room with silence for only five seconds before firing up again.

There you are.

Pressing the 'answer' icon without saying a word into it, he raised it to his sleepy head.

'Hello, Mr Tredinnick?' a female voice seeped out of the phone.

'Last time I checked.' Andrew arched his back, wincing at the pain and regretting crashing in the armchair, rather than the hammock.

'Mr Tredinnick, this is Miss Sanders, from the school. I was hoping we could have a chat about Merryn when you collect her this afternoon?'

'Yeah, no, sorry. I've got a lot on later, so I'm going to have to grab and go,' Andrew exaggerated. Bung in the oven tea for three hardly portrayed a busy finish to the day. Maybe he would sort some food for himself after, really put a strain on the to-do list, though he'd most likely fill the hole with some of good ol' Arth Guinness' finest.

'I understand that you have a lot on, but it's important that you can make some time to meet with the Headteacher and myself. We have...' a moment of nervous silence as Miss Sanders decided how much to disclose over the phone, '...concerns over Merryn's behaviour. I know that your family is going through a very difficult time, but___'

'What about her behaviour?' Andrew fired back, bluntly cutting of Miss Sanders, midsentence.

'Mr Tredinnick, I'm sure you can appreciate that it is better for all parties if we talk about this in person,' starting to sound more confident. 'We are expecting a backlash from some of the other parents over the upset and distress that Merryn has caused today. We need them to know that we, as a school, are responding appropriately to the situation and keeping their children safe when they are under our supervision.' Miss Sanders' voice wavered slightly at this last statement, allowing just a hint of emotion to creep through.

Upset and distress? 'What situation?' Andrew queried. 'Are these the same kids that are picking on her?' Anger was more than just creeping into him, it was like a flame licking its way along a shining trail of fuel, heading right for the pumps, *lick, lick, BOOM!*

'If Merryn feels she is being picked on, I sincerely apologise and we will look into it,' Miss Sanders assured. 'We take allegations of bullying very seriously. I must point out however, that this has not been brought to our attention, and we have seen no signs of note.'

Andrew sank back in his favourite leather armchair, rubbing his burning eyes with a grubby thumb and forefinger. 'I'm not getting off the phone until you get to the point.'

'Okay. We think that Merryn would benefit from spending some time with a child counsellor,' she said, with anxious uncertainty in her voice. 'We believe that she needs a little help in understanding and coming to terms with the differences between life,' a painful pause, 'And death.'

What the fuck? 'Understanding life and *death*? Her mum threw herself off a cliff, for fuck's sake. She *was* alive, and *now* she's dead! How's that for understanding?' A swarm of guilt and regret stabbed Andrew right through his breastbone. Miss Sanders did not deserve to be spoken to like that. He wanted desperately to apologise, yet shame had devoured him, strangulating his vocal cords.

As cold and hard as deep ocean stone, Miss Sanders' reply was so concise and unexpected that Andrew could not mutter a word, even if he had wanted to.

'Mr Tredinnick, Merryn had a dead bird in her lunchbox today.' Silence on the other end of the line. 'And that's really only half the story.'

CHAPTER THREE

Tinkering gently against the rim of the glass tumbler like the tubes of a brass wind chime playing in the breeze, the shaky hand tasked with pouring steadied as two clear objects came to rest together. An *oh-so-sweet* glug of golden spirit rose to fill the pourer's ears. At the tipping back of the bottle, the heavenly sound was cut short, replaced with a high-pitched screech as bottleneck slid from vessel. A protesting squeak followed as the cork stopper was forced to resume its place at the glistening opening of the sixteen-year-old single malt. Turning to resume his own place – nestled blissfully alone in his hammock – Andrew left the bottle on his worktable.

After a brief pause for thought, he swivelled, took back custody of the discarded bottle with a determined vigour, and carried it over to the sling he planned to fall asleep in. Andrew could not care less if he drank himself into a coma, as long as he woke up with the grade-A hangover he was about to work so hard to construct.

As the edge of the glass brushed his bottom lip, the warm and welcoming scent of his finest Scotch drifted like a debauchery spectre towards his nostrils.

The moment was shattered by an unwanted knock at the door. Despite the lack of verbal response from him, the rickety old wooden slats started creeping open.

'Hi. I heard what happened at school today,' Kerenza's soft face and long blonde hair appeared through the darkness of the opening. 'Wanna talk about it?'

'What I want,' Andrew replied, nonchalantly, 'Is to forget about it.'

'And drink yourself unconscious in the process?'

Andrew looked at Kerenza, wanting so much to tell her to fuck off, but knowing how important to the family she was right now. She was the glue stopping them from breaking apart. He lowered his head, ashamed that hurling abuse at his stepdaughter had even crossed his mind.

Sensing his submission, Kerenza pushed the door further and took a tentative step into the dimly lit room, closing the door behind her. The makeshift studio was a mass of shady corners and lurking shadows; the room's only light coming from a shade bare lamp on a battle-scarred square pine table. The odours of the room were a stifling, toxic mix of solvents, damp and decay. *Might want to open the door again before I pass out.* After a moment to compose herself and make sure that that was not going to happen, she surveyed the worktable. Empty or near empty paint tubes; filthy rags; a broken craft-knife blade; an empty bottle of whisky.

'Somebody's thirsty,' She muttered.

'It's old,' Andrew replied, defensively.

'None of *my* business, I guess.'

A few tense seconds passed with the pair of them locking eyes. A stand-off. Inevitably, Andrew was the first to lower his weapons.

Crossing the room and carefully navigating each footfall in the dimness, Kerenza skirted around torn canvasses displaying meaningless splashes and strikes of acrylic paint. She pulled a dust covered chair from against the wall, placing it a few feet from Andrew. After a quick pat-down of the filthy surface, she sat down to face him. Andrew did the gentlemanly thing and looked away as she slowly crossed her legs, her pleated skirt inching up her nylon covered thighs.

'I spoke to her,' she moved on, regaining Andrew's focus. 'She said someone else must've put it there.'

'And what do you think?' Andrew questioned before taking another sip of his Scotch.

'I think she's a mixed up girl who needs you in there,' Kerenza said. 'Not hiding in your grubby little shed getting paralytic.'

Leaning forward, she took the tumbler from his hand and raised it to her slightly parted lips, necking the intoxicating liquid.

'That's eighty quid a bottle!' Andrew wailed, sounding pathetically childlike.

'Then you'd better learn to paint properly again so you can afford another one,' Kerenza just about managed to croak in reply, the whisky alight like petroleum in her throat. 'God, it tastes like shit.'

Her welling eyes sparkled in the jaundiced glow of the table-lamp as her smooth glazed lips curled at one corner in a cocksure smile. She stood and handed Andrew his empty glass.

'Come in, sober up and get some sleep,' she instructed. 'Talk to Merryn in the morning.'

Kerenza leaned over, kissed Andrew lightly on his unshaven cheek and headed for the door. 'She needs you,' she said upon reaching it, brandishing him a smile more sorrowful now than cocksure.

'Ten minutes. Okay?' Andrew responded, looking at his empty glass on the table.

She studied him, her expression doubtful. Turning her back to him, she left the building, the draft from the closing door sending dust and debris scurrying across the floor. Andrew watched as the door clicked shut, half expecting the latch to flick up again as another lecture leapt into Kerenza's mind.

It didn't.

He realised that this both pleased and disappointed him concurrently. He refilled his glass, swung a leg over the side of the hammock and gave the floor a gentle nudge with the tip of his shoe. Leaning back and swinging in the gloom, he thought of how she had grown up, taking responsibility for the family and keeping everyone on track. He thought about how he was failing to do the same.

CHAPTER FOUR

Lounging back listlessly against his stack of old and thinning pillows, Cameron plucked absent minded at the cherry-red Gibson hollow body resting idly on his skinny, but toned, midsection. One grey-green eye, lined with a fine black crescent, stared at nothing at all on the wall facing him. The other eye lay hidden under the fall of his jet black, sloping fringe. The set of his mouth displayed a straight-lined contented smile.

Downstairs, voices muffled through his bedroom floor from the kitchen. He could hear *dad-of-the-year* (who finally came skulking in not long after the sun had crept over the hilly side of the valley) talking to Merryn. Something about *'life'*, and *'happiness'*, and *'love'*, and *blah blah fucking blah...*

And a hamster? Cute. Best keep it out of Exit's way.

The bird. Ah the bird. Now that worked a fucking treat, no arguments. *Dad* thinking that the nasty little bullies at school put it there. Teachers thinking Merryn did, and that she was both mentally and emotionally unstable...Peachy!

Cameron had barely gotten around to congratulating himself on that one, had not even granted himself a little celebratory wank; a situation he would rectify shortly. He deserved to be rewarded, surely?

The bird itself was pure chance. Luck *sweet* luck. Well, not for the bird, obviously; singing joyously one minute, and the next...well. Cameron spotted it just sitting there in the tree outside of his open bedroom window, tweeting its annoying happy little tweet. He, she, it, whatever the fuck it was (Cameron was no expert in the sexing of animals) needed to be shut up.

In the top drawer of his bedside cabinet was the catapult he used to take fishing with him when he was younger. Leaning slowly to the side, he slid the drawer open and lifted it out. Fumbling at some change in his pocket, Cam pulled out a penny. Not the usual choice of ammunition, but from fifteen feet away he didn't think that mattered, he hadn't fired the thing for so long, he convinced himself that the shot would miss by a country mile.

He was wrong.

With a swish and a slap of elastic, a rustle of leaves and a puff of tiny grey-blue feathers, the chirping little bastard chirped no more.

The assassin made his way downstairs to gloat over his kill. Darting as nimbly as a ninja through the living room, the small hallway and the sun-filled kitchen, he sprang out into the fresh air and made his way to the tree that had once been the stage for a merrily singing dickie-bird. Looking down at the grassy ground, pride swelled and turned his cheeks a pinkish red.

'Fuckin' headshot!'

He stooped and collected the fruits of his labour in his eager hands, marvelling at the warmth and the lightness of the headless cadaver. He was sure he could feel a gentle twitching.

Cameron's mind was blitzing through all the possibilities. What to do, what to do? One idea stood prominent, claiming pole position with ease. He made his way back inside with his trophy.

Placing...it? No. Jack. Cameron went to school with a Jack and he hated the prick; would love, in fact, to see Jack's head smashed into a million different pieces, splinters of bone and splashes of brain and blood creating the only epitaph a shit like that deserves.

He placed *Jack* on a chopping board that was conveniently left on the kitchen worktop. Having no intention of chopping Jack up, but needing both hands free to rummage through the wall units, Cameron was hopeful that somebody would soon use the chopping board, without cleaning it first. The thought gave him a giddy feeling in the pit of his stomach.

There you are. The second cupboard up for inspection offered the perfect item. Removing one from the plastic packaging and placing it between his teeth, he picked up Jack and made his way back upstairs.

The final item Cameron needed, the Scarlet to his Rhett, was in his little sister's bedroom, lying handily in the middle of the floor, oversized rubbery red lips smiling up at him.

Plucking the cocktail stick from his mouth, inserting it into the hard rubber of the Jade the Bratz' decapitated head was an arduous task, although much satisfaction was gained from removing the head from the little tart's body. Sliding the stick down through the frayed and bloody stump of Jack's neck, however, well that was as easy as one, two, three.

Cam held his creation at arm's length in front of his face, studying it with vainglorious pride. Jack was now *Jadenstein*, and he looked so much prettier for it.

A sudden burst of birdsong snapped Cameron out of his reverie and dragged him back to the here-and-now. His eyes darted to the tree outside of his bedroom window, where he expected to see his own interpretation on Mary Shelley's brainchild staring back at him. A ridiculous thought. Jack/Jade was now the school's property, not that they appreciated it. Wondering what had become of it, he felt a weird sort of father/son-daughter connection to the freak.

Stupid. The random song was being sung by some random bird in the tree that sometimes kept him awake on stormy coastal nights, whispering its whispers, rustling its taunts and creaking its obscenities.

The cheery chirping did nothing to rouse Exit Wounds, who was sleeping contentedly, draped across one of Cameron's legs towards the bottom of the bed.

Bought for him a couple of years after the birth of his little sister Merryn, amid concerns that Cameron was distancing himself from everyone and everything, spending every spare minute shut up in his room, his dad and step-mum felt the need to give him a sense of responsibility, as well as some companionship. Cameron spent days arguing with Andrew and Shona over the name. Explaining that *Exit Wounds* was purely paying homage to the musical eminence of

Placebo, Andrew and Shona just couldn't help expressing their own valueless and tedious views.

'*Exit Wounds is a bit morbid,*' Shona had declared. '*How about Smoky?*' It was more an instruction than a question.

'*Or Blacky?*' Andrew rather predictably chipped in.

How about you shove it up your asses you boring old twats?

So, as arguments often turn out between adults and children, Smoky it was – in front of them, anyway.

Cameron lay back, sniggering to himself, wondering if cats could suffer split personality disorder, or dissociative identity disorder, or whatever the fuck they labelled it now.

'Better show my face,' he said, as much to himself as to the sleeping feline.

Dropping his strumming arm off the bed towards his amplifier, Cameron fumbled at the landscape of controls. Finding the *Volume* and *gain* knobs and cranking them up to full, he lifted his arm again, before thrashing down hard on the open strings.

Exit Wounds damn near shit himself. Springing up onto all-fours, claws like protruding missiles embedded themselves into the tight flesh of Cameron's shin.

'AHH FUCK!' he shouted, more to the four walls than the dopey cat.

The intended effect of the deafening outburst was to warn everyone downstairs that he was coming; not that he gave a rat's ass if they were talking about him. He just did not want to hear what they had to say. Of course, he also did it to annoy them.

After stroking Exit Wounds and reassuring the wired feline that there were no hard feelings, Cameron rolled up the leg of his jeans. Seven of the ten front claws found puncturing purchase.

'Good effort,' he offered, dabbing an index finger on each droplet of claret and raising it to his mouth. The coppery richness of the vital fluid was a taste to be cherished.

Cameron rolled the leg down once he had satisfied his thirst, then headed down to enjoy the thrills and delights of family life.

Standing open, the front door allowed the mild September air spill in. Hidden beneath the pleasant outdoor scents that greeted his senses, a stale and unsavoury undertow lurked.

'You need a shower,' Cameron said, looking at his dad.

'Not now, Cam,' intervened Kerenza. 'He doesn't need this.'

'He smells like Raymond!' Cameron flashed her his smile, its abundance of charm somehow equal to its conflicting abundance of Machiavellianism. An enticing, winning smile.

Kerenza gave a coy smirk in return, also a winner in Cameron's book. But it was his father that answered.

'I'll have a shower dreckly. And hello to you too, by the way, it's good to see courtesy is still high on your list of attributes,' and turning to Merryn, 'You finish your breakfast while I scrub up, squirt. Then we'll go shopping.'

Andrew bowed and kissed Merryn on the top of her head.

Jesus Christ, thought Cameron, *any closer and the little shit'll get pissed.* It took a gargantuan effort, but for once he managed to keep his mouth shut. Merryn barely seemed to notice the intoxicating odour however, flashing an addictively beautiful and excited grin back. It stretched so wide her stretched face must have been in danger of splitting.

'You coming, Cam?' Andrew asked.

'No ta, I have an etiquette tutorial to attend.'

'Suit yourself,' Andrew said, turning to leave the room.

Quiet fell temporarily in the glowing kitchen, the only sound the sporadic chink of Merryn's spoon against her retro Rice Krispies bowl. Snap, Crackle and Pop laughed heartily on the white, ceramic exterior. Cameron made his way over to Kerenza, winning smile emblazoned on his face again.

'Woss on, sweet cheeks?'

'You seriously think I'm going to talk to you after that display towards your dad?' Her tone mocked annoyance, her eyes said otherwise.

'Stay here with me when they go,' Cameron insisted.

'Thanks, but it's a *no* from me,' Kerenza said, crushing his enthusiasm. 'I'm going hamster shopping with them. You should come, too, it'll be fun.'

'About as much fun as cauterizing my own asshole. No, I'll be staying home and doing some weed, sure you wanna miss out?' Cameron was working his smile, but the raised eyebrows and sternly folded arms suggested the resistance was strong this morning.

'What's "doing some weed"?' Merryn's sweet-as-honey voice interrupted.

'*Weeding!*' Cameron snapped back. 'It helps the garden. Doing some *weeding* gives the flowers more room to grow.

'You said "weed",' Merryn argued. 'Not weed*ing*. I heard you.'

'You heard wrong you little turd!' Cameron barked back at his baby sister in a tone that Merryn had heard before, a tone that did not invite a response.

'Go out and do some weeding if you must, Cam,' Kerenza interjected upon seeing Merryn's cereal bowl had been drained of its stock. 'But leave her alone. Merrsie, pop your bowl in the sink and we'll get ready to go. Today's going to be a fun day.'

With that, the two of them left the room, a buoyant spring in their step bearing them away. Cameron was left alone to listen to the entrails of their girlie conversation fading away in the other room.

CHAPTER FIVE

A click, click, click rattled across the floor, slowing, then upping the tempo again. The furry new edition to the Tredinnick family found its stride. Giggling hysterically, Merryn watched as it scooted around in the plastic sphere.

It's actually been a good day, Andrew thought. *First one for a long time.*

Harvey swivelled and started off in another direction, the rhythmic click, click on the oak floor speeding up again, before stopping abruptly with a *clunk* as the ball hit the slate edge of the fire hearth. Merryn erupted with laughter, rolling around and hugging her ribs as Harvey toppled over, appearing confused as he regained his footing. Twitching his fishing wire whiskers at the air, he methodically plotted his next move.

Seeing her this happy for the first time since her mummy left them almost reduced Andrew to tears. The one thought that he could concentrate on enough not to cry was, *where the hell did she get the name, Harvey?*

Looking down, Andrew saw that Harvey was now at his feet, sat on his hindquarters looking up at him, rubbing his head from ears to his nose with one forepaw. Harvey set his black beadlike eyes on Andrew's big brown ones, a quizzical expression as if reading his thoughts and answering, *I've no idea, mate.*

Kerenza, who was sat on the sofa tapping away at the keys on her purple laptop, stopped and took in the situation: Merryn laughing her head off; Andrew, appearing to be fighting away emotions but smiling all the same. Could there really be a way out of this dark and consuming shaft? Was there a chance at a good life again? *Doubtful.*

The moment of reflection was cut short by the crisp sound of Dave Gilmour's Les Paul Goldtop ringing out "Another Brick in the Wall." The display on Andrew's mobile lit up BARRY CALLING. He picked up his phone, swiped the ANSWER button with the thumb of his right hand and greeted the caller.

'Bazza!' Andrew blurted, knowing how much Barry hated this pet-name.

'Andr…how's…ing?' Barry's broken up butt-licking tone stammered through. 'I got…ad…'

'Hold on a sec,' Andrew replied, getting up from his recliner chair. 'I'll go outside, granite walls in a valley are crap bed buddies.'

Merryn gave Andrew a scolding glare for his obscene use of language. 'Daddy, not in front of Harvey!'

Kerenza laughed and gave Merryn an exaggerated, flabbergasted look, shaking her head.

As Andrew made his way out of the back door, Cameron entered from the hallway at the bottom of the stairs. To the cynically minded, this would have looked like a deliberately timed move, but Cameron neither knew, nor cared, whether his dad was in the room or not when he decided to vacate his citadel of solitude. Coming down in search of Exit Wounds, he wondered hopefully if the feline would be down here taking a carnivorous interest in Harry, or Henry, Herpes, what-ever-the-fuck Merryn had decided to call the stinking little rodent.

A few moments earlier, Cameron was lying on his bed, hand in his tight button fly jeans – made even tighter by the throbbing in his cacks – thinking of his stepsister's not-too-small and not-too-big, perfectly formed titties. His attentions were dragged out of his fantasy by the annoying rolling sound that drifted up the stairs and along the landing. Instead of envisaging the sweet, soft curves of the forbidden fruit, he envisaged the little furry meal-for-one circling the living room, this way that way forward back; and Exit Wounds, lurking, eyeballing, murder in his luminous yellow wildcat eyes and licking his lips in anticipation.

In reality, what the boy saw when he got downstairs filled his heart with despondency, a despondency he knew would soon blacken to rage. Rolling? Check. This way that way forward back? Check. Exit Wounds? Stretched out on the rug in front of the unlit open fire, lazily watching the alien newcomer's ridiculous antics. Exit's head turned slowly from left-to-right, right-to-left. Just a cool cat at Centre Court, Wimbledon. The stupid piece of vermin even rolled into the cat's outstretched belly, and all the pussy did was look at it with vague disdain on his face.

Get back to licking your own butthole you dopey cunt! Cameron's mind hissed.

Outside, mobile signal stronger but still not great, Andrew tried to process the information being directed to him from the other end of the phone.

'I don't get it, I thought it was a dead-cert,' Andrew exclaimed.

'Bottom line is they just don't like what you're producing at this time.'

'At this time?' Andrew quizzed. 'I can fetch out some older stuff.'

'Older stuff,' Barry flummoxed. 'Can you hear yourself? You're not fucking Rembrandt. They don't want your *old* stuff anymore than I want a thirty-stone missus with halitosis and a penchant for blue cheese and pickled onions!'

Andrew had never met Barry's wife, so little did he know that Barry was describing that very woman with his brutal statement.

'Look, Andrew,' he said, his tone gentler. 'I'm going to be honest with you, not just as your agent but as a friend. Your work has not been great for a while now___'

Andrew tried to vent a response that just crept out in a choked whimper.

'No no, hear me out,' Barry insisted. 'I've known you for what, ten years now?' He didn't wait for a confirmation. 'Things have been bad for you; the worst. But they said they can't find any meaning to your work, and that sums up how I've been feeling about it recently.'

Silence on the other end of the line.

'You still there, buddy?'

'Yeah,' came meekly back at him, lacking the usual self-assuredness.

'Buddy, take a break, yeah? Go away if you can. Shona's parents would have the kids for you, wouldn't they?' Barry didn't give a chance for a response. 'Come back when you're ready. You know where to find me. Okay?'

Andrew killed the call without further comment. Standing on the spot for several minutes, taking in the cool evening air and gazing at the stars in the cloudless sky, he wished to the god he did not believe in that Shona had not have been so selfish.

Kerenza had noted the change in his mood as soon as he walked back in: slumped shoulders; lowered head; the antithesis of the person who had taken the call. Her lecherous stepbrother had once again retired to his pit, seemingly disappointed with the lack of attention he had received from the blonde on the sofa. This was a good thing, it meant that she could probe into the nature of the phone call without Cam's snidey and unnecessary comments.

'I think Harvey's just about ready for bed, Merrsie,' Kerenza almost crooned. 'Pop him back up in his house and then you can go brush your teeth.'

'But you said I could have a hot chocolate,' the youngster protested.

'Okay then, monkey,' Kerenza bartered. 'Put him to bed, get your jammies on and I'll make it when you get back. Leave your teeth until after.'

Springing to her feet, Merryn wrapped her arms around Kerenza and caressed her in a loving hug. Letting go, she grabbed Harvey's ball and tucked it into the crook of an arm before trotting upstairs.

The display of happy affection did little to raise Andrew's spirits. He had collapsed back into his recliner and sat morosely eying up nothing on the floor. Deep in thought, he wondered whether once you hit rock bottom, it would be possible to fall right through and keep descending forever. An eternity of getting lower and lower, beyond the realms of human imagination.

Kerenza said mildly, 'Care to share?'

Andrew thought about this for a few seconds, then without looking up, 'They're not exhibiting my work. Said it's crap.'

'I doubt they said *that*.' Kerenza's reply came as the voice-of-reason.

'Not in so many words,' Andrew conceded. 'But it's the same result.' He looked up at Kerenza for the first time since walking back in, annoyed with the interrogation.

Okay, maybe *interrogation* was a bit harsh, but it miffed him how someone so young could be so indomitable.

Bottom line is, she cared.

'I need a drink,' he said, knowing deep down that this would get him nowhere.

'Good timing,' Kerenza said, cheerily. 'I'm making hot chocolate in a minute.'

'That's not a drink,' Andrew sighed.

'It's the *only* drink you need right now. Was there anything else, or just your work is "crap"?'

'I think I got dropped by my agent as well. Or I dropped him, I can't quite work it out.'

'Barry's a waste of space,' said Kerenza, bluntly. 'Think about it. You've done some amazing work in the past, and what major exhibitions has he landed you? A lepper can count them on one hand.'

Atrociously expressed, but she may have a point, Andrew thought, struggling not to blush at the *'amazing work'* comment. Regardless, his mood remained sombre.

'I'm going out to the studio,' he said, as he heard little footsteps on the stairs.

'No you're not,' Kerenza corrected with authority. 'You're going to enjoy a hot drink with your two favourite girls. And then you're going to read Merryn a bedtime story.'

'I'm not sure I'm___'

'In the mood?' Kerenza finished his sentence for him. 'Not your call. I can't remember the last time you read to her, and besides, no one reads *Captain Duck* quite as good as you.'

'I suppose you're right, there,' Andrew agreed, with a mock modesty and a captivating grin. 'Never know, it may just cheer me up.'

'I believe it may,' Kerenza said, returning a smile. Behind it was a hidden doubt. A doubt that he would not end up in the studio that night, after the lights were out and Sea Glass Cottage had fallen silent, save for the gentle breathing of his sleeping family.

CHAPTER SIX

There was no reunion for Andrew and his old pal, Jock, in the studio that night. After reading the story to Merryn (applying his vast skill set of voice-over caricature genius, who upon hearing them, most people thought sounded remarkably alike), he tucked her up in bed and turned in himself. The sound of the bedroom door latch dropping down into its cradle was caramel sweet, smothering everything else out and delivering a complete and perfect peace, like the ethereal silence you get when you kill the power supply to a long-running vacuum cleaner.

Enjoying the rarely chartered recluse-state he fell to unconsciousness, drifting in and out of it for most of the next day. He ventured past the threshold of the bedroom door purely for the essentials. Coffee and bathroom breaks. During one comatose visit to the land of nod, he had even managed to sleep through Merryn being collected. Each fortnightly Sunday Shona's parents, Judith and Angus, would pick up their youngest granddaughter and take her out for the day, treating her to this and that, and an ice-cream here or there.

Andrew was convinced they were seeking to emulate a previous life with a young Shona, his assumptions based on the fact they never used to take Merryn out before their own daughter died.

They'll be pissed at me for not being up and making sure she was ready and presentable, thought Andrew, *another nail in the parental coffin of one Andrew Tredinnick.*

Other than bringing to life the great boating adventure of Duck, Sheep, Frog and Goat, Andrew had struggled to be there for his youngest and most vulnerable offspring.

He enjoyed that book because of Merryn's clear enjoyment of it. Other than that, he was not a *reader* at all.

Shona was though.

Always had her head in a *'good'* book. Always encouraging him to do the same. Well, *encourage?* Andrew would see it as *bang on about.* 'Escapism' was Shona's word for it. She said that books were a window into another world. That you could just jump in and live other people's lives, see the world through another's eyes.

'And the real beauty is,' she used to say, *'you can jump right out of it again just by folding the corner of the page and closing the cover.'* Something you couldn't do to your own story if things got too much. *'The ghosts always linger a while,'* he remembered her telling him, referring to the characters. *'It's all they* can *do when they have such a story to tell. But in the end their haunting turns to taunting, and you're desperate to pick it up again.'*

Christ he missed her. Missed her quirky little way of putting things. Missed the shit she could babble on about for hour after unrelenting hour.

She was still pestering him about reading now, even from beyond the grave. On his bedside cabinet sat a novel that Shona had read. Insisting he would *'love it!'* she had left it there, and it had not moved in the months since. He looked at the artwork on the cover: alluring yellow-gold sunset with devilish, fiery yellow eyes looking from the tiger stripe sky, down onto a boy in a boat with the unlikeliest of feline companions.

'I've seen that on the cover of a DVD,' he had said at the time. *'I'll just watch it.'*

'Sacrilege!' Shona had insisted. *'You'll get so much more from the book.'*

Lying on the bed, back in the present, Andrew picked up the book. Fanning through the pages, a musty richness drifted up towards his face, cooling and welcoming. The aroma was divine, full of the promise of fresh rains falling on a scorched earth. A new beginning. Why he felt that, he could not explain to himself. Perhaps this was part of the *'escapism'* that Shona was trying so hard to convince him of.

He looked at the ghost-folds of Shona's previous stopping points. *That'll drive me crazy if I read this,* he thought. Being a bit of a perfectionist he appreciated the cleanness of a dead-flat page. Shona, on the other hand, had some innocent little oddities from her school days that never left her. So, not willing to add to the tatty madness in the top corners, he reached forward to open the top drawer of the cabinet – getting his finger caught in the petit 'D' shaped handle, as was standard practice for him. After massaging his finger better in his mouth, he prepared to tackle the confusion held within.

This was his pocket-emptying drawer. One that every self-respecting *real* man has, and that may be seen as unnecessary and drive many women insane. Ready to rummage through the mass of screwed-up receipts, discarded crisp packets, chocolate wrappers and car park tickets, he realised the perfect thing was sat on the top of the pile. Clearly left in the drawer to surprise him, confident that he would eventually open it, was a straight piece of paper: a pastel yellow Post-it note.

Written upon its matt surface in Shona's *Get the Point* capitalised scrawl, were two words. READ IT, followed by not one, not two, but three exclamation marks. Underneath the text, a big 'X' symbolised a kiss.

There's my bookmark. 'Thanks, hon,' he said to the empty room.

Andrew made himself comfortable on the bed, and for the first time for as long as he could remember, he started to read a proper *grownup's* book.

An unknown number of hours later, Andrew was roused by the sound of heavy rubber crunched slowly over the gravel drive. There followed the cushioned *fwump* of two car doors in quick succession. Soon after, a third door could be heard. Adjusting his sleep strained eyes, Andrew saw the Bengal tiger looking back at him from the cover of the closed book. Next to it lay the homeless READ IT!!! bookmark. *Shit.*

Three sets of footsteps, two pairs slow and heavy, one pair lighter and nimble, drifted through the open window. His bedside clock informed him that it just passed four-thirty in the afternoon. Otherwise known as time-to-go-down-and-face-the-in-laws.

'I wish you'd park closer to the dwelling, Andrew, my ankles struggle enough without adding extra miles, especially of this terrain,' Judith carped on, her tone as brash as ever. 'I'll pay for it later. I'm supposed to be quizzing with the girls tonight and I'll be a swollen, hobbling mess!'

Angus will pay for it later, with your incessant moaning, Andrew thought, *and you and your cronies haven't been* girls *since before the first flushable shitter was patented.* Okay, that may have been a slight exaggeration, but what's a few hundred years between frenemies?

'Judith. Nice to see you,' he said instead, with a smile that took way too much effort to construct, especially on a day of rest.

'It's good to see you out of bed,' Judith barked back, her roller-curled fringe bouncing irritatingly up and down her powdered forehead in time with her sharp jaw movements. 'What were you thinking,' she raved on. 'You have responsibilities.'

Bitch just can't help herself.

Running over from the car, Merryn threw her arms around Andrew's legs. A new cuddly unicorn swung from her right hand. Its glorious rainbow-coloured tail and mane swished silkily in the gentle flutter of wind. Andrew placed his hands on her head and messed her hair up, affectionately.

'I missed you, Daddy.'

'I missed you too, squirt, and I bet a certain furry little fella by the name of *Harvey* did, too. Why don't you go check on him and I'll be in in a minute?'

Merryn beamed happily, 'Can Nanny and Pappy come in and see him? I got a unicorn.'

'That's cool, hon,' Andrew grinned, referring to the unicorn. 'Course they can. Run on in and bring him down,' he said, through pursed lips.

She ran in excitedly, new unicorn air-galloping at waist-height beside her.

'Right, you two,' Angus broke the silence, not knowing and having no intention to find out how long the Mexican stand-off would last. 'No need to hang around on the doorstep; let's get in and see the new arrival.'

Stepping aside, Andrew gestured to the door. As Judith reached the step, he held out a helping hand for the poor old woman and all her ailments. It was met, and declined, with a stifled grunt and an upturning of her lancelike nose. He gestured for Angus to follow. Angus did so with a grateful smile, stopping to place his hand on Andrew's shoulder.

'It's good to see you, pally, you're looking well.' You're coming out *yewer*.

*You can take the man out of Scotland...*Andrew mused. Several decades had passed since Angus made the move south of the border, but it did little to soften that fine accent.

'Right back at ya,' Andrew replied, turning to follow the big brick-wall of a man through the doorway.

Andrew had always liked Angus. A *do anything for anyone* kind of guy. One-woman man all his life, which in any case takes dedication, but this *one* woman in particular? Jesus. His hardworking life still showed in his broad, muscular shoulders, and in the shovel-like hand that had recently landed on Andrew's comparatively scant shoulder with a deadening clap. In retirement, all this big man wanted was an easy life, as chilled and as conflict-free as possible. Which contributed heavily and showed through in the placidity of Angus' character, a quality that Andrew admired very much.

As he followed Angus in, Andrew marvelled at the shininess of his completely bald head; a lighthouse beaming from a hulk of rock. Hearing Judith ratchet on about dirty dishes, and crumbs, and animal smells, Andrew new that he was staring at some pretty damning evidence – living with this particular woman had been far from a carefree joyride.

CHAPTER SEVEN

Waking early to the warbling alarm of her smart speaker, Kerenza showered, dressed, and headed downstairs. Accepting the gruelling events of yesterday would leave Andrew sulking again, she had planned to make up a packed lunch for Merryn before catching the bus to school.

Hearing much of the one-sided conversation that flowed like poison, Kerenza had tried and failed in mammoth proportions to stop her gran's relentless onslaught. The old woman was on form, with sharp remarks tearing like rusty razor blades, and her clawing raven's beak pecking continually.

Retiring mentally exhausted, she would guess that her stepdad would be cowering in his room this morning.

On arriving in the kitchen, she found Cameron already there. Leaning casually on the worktop, he blew into a cup of coffee. The strong aroma trailed over to her in misty tendrils of steam. The pair shared some small talk, leaving out much of the detail from last night's discussions, and questions such as *where the hell Cameron had been until the break of the day?* Cunningly, sensing a use for the boy and the possibility of making the morning easier on herself, Kerenza reeled him in with an irresistible grin and listed off instructions.

'Cheese and cucumber sandwiches; Bear Fruit; apple; carrot sticks.'

'Carrot sticks?' he said in disgust.

'Yes, carrot sticks. You know how to peel and cut a carrot I take it?'

Bit harsh, Cameron thought. 'Yes Miss!'

'P.E. kit.'

'Check!'

'She can have crumpets for breakfast, not too much spread though,' Kerenza continued. 'She'd eat the whole tub if you let her. Make sure she brushes her teeth, *and* uses toothpaste!'

'Anything else, *Kaiser?*'

'Very funny,' Kerenza said, without humour. 'Show 'n' Tell; she needs to take her drawing and the story she wrote, *not* the actual Harvey, as she will probably try to convince you.'

'I'm not fucking stup___'

'And be nice to her,' she said, cutting off any desires for an argument.

'Wait, What? Why would you say that?' asked Cameron, looking hurt at the implication written in her steely glare.

'Because you can be an asshole,' said Kerenza, matter-of-factly.

Then, moving in close and rising on her tiptoes, she kissed him briefly on the cheek, the corner of her mouth deliberately brushing the corner of his. Cameron instantly felt a tingle in his balls, spreading like an invasive army of ants. Moving in for round two, he parted his lips. Quick as a flash, Kerenza spun on her feet and floated to the door. Turning back at him with the sexiest smile on her face, she gave a *tough-titties* finger.

'Good luck,' she laughed, and then she was gone.

Silence filled the suddenly lonely kitchen.

Cameron made his way to the bottom of the stairs and called up to Merryn, checking that she was cleaning her teeth. The youngster confirmed that she had already done so.

Bathroom's empty, Cameron thought with a wide smirk on his face. *Just enough time to sort out this throbbing. Prick-teasing bitch.* He bounded up the stairs, flung the bathroom door shut behind him and grabbed a handful of tissue. His racing mind had barely lifted her exquisite, nylon-clad ass onto the kitchen worktop before he was spent.

***

A scattering of browning leaves tickled along the road in the tailing September breeze, though the majority of trees held resiliently to a lush green plumage, standing firm against the caressing fingers of early autumn. It always seemed the way that children would be suppressed by dull, wet weather in the summer holidays. As soon as playtime was over and they had to return to school, nonetheless, the sun would return to the sky for a few glorious, mocking weeks, seeing out the season with a cheeky smile.

Walking side-by-side (or skipping, in Merryn's case) through the shadows of the beach road, she asked in a tone that was perhaps chirpier that the topic warranted, 'Am I going to live with Nanny and Pappy?'

'What?' Cameron replied, surprised at the question. 'No, why would you ask that?'

'I heard Nanny last night,' Merryn expanded. 'She said that Daddy was…income…incumpy___'

'Incompetent?' Cameron offered.

'Yes,' Merryn confirmed. 'Incumpentent! She told Daddy that's what he was, and it would be better if I lived with her and Pappy.'

'Well, she's wrong,' Cameron said bluntly, and then, testing the water a bit, 'You wouldn't wanna live with them, would you?'

Cameron reached an arm out, guiding Merryn in closer to the hedge as the sound of a car's engine approached from the rear. The driver gave a *thank you* wave as they passed. Cameron only nodded a *whatever*.

'No way,' Merryn continued as they stepped back into the road. 'Nanny stinks of flowers,' holding her nose and screwing her face up. 'I think it must be her soap. Besides, at home I've got you, and Daddy, and Krenny, and Harvey, and Smoky…'

Such a nerd. 'Well, don't worry,' Cameron said with reassuring confidence. 'We like living with you too much to let that old bat have you.'

The two figures carried on walking, flickering between brightness and shadow as the low morning sun danced between the branches of flanking trees. After a few moments, Cameron noticed that something had changed. The tap-tap-scuff, tap-tap-scuff had ceased. Merryn was no longer skipping merrily by his side. Stopping, he turned to face the way they had come from. Fifteen yards or so back down the road, Merryn stood in stare. The thing that demanded her attention was an old cottage tucked behind an overgrown and unattended garden. Pacing back to stand beside his little sister, he put a comforting hand between her young, prominent shoulder blades. He knew the feelings this place evoked, parasitically crawling over a person's skin as they passed by. He knew the stories that floated around, as stories do in any village with gossips to start the rumour mill churning, and kids to exaggerate upon it.

'Problem, Mez?' He asked mildly.

No immediate answer from the girl who was dumbstruck in a trance.

Past the rustic yet robust Cornish-stone wall that stood four-feet tall, just back from the road – an assault of weeds and dead vegetation shooting between the cracks and crevasses where colourful wildflowers should be boasting their last flourish of the year – was tangle of twisted and taunting trees. Their roots burst from the earth like the bony limbs of skeletal corpses. Beyond, through encompassing thickets of brambles and bracken, stood an empty shell.

Soulless and smashed, a cycloptic black-eye window stared down from the upper floor. Below, a frayed door devoid of its once bright white paint sat askew on its hinges, inside of a dilapidated entry-porch-come-summerhouse. At either side of the door, tall sash windows were covered from the inside with what looked like old, sun kissed estate agent's *For Sale* signs. Nothing revealed what lay behind them.

Anyone desperate enough to see inside – and believe me, they existed – would need to undertake the treacherous mission of climbing the rotting wooden frame of the summerhouse. Heading to its deathly centre they would hope to steal a glimpse through the lone top window, praying the decaying structure refrained from opening its hollow mouth. To open it would be to condemn them to an Accident and Emergency visit.

Like Stevie Dunn. Cameron recalled his old mate disappearing from view amidst the din of cracking wood and shattering glass.

A broken ankle and a six-inch laceration to his right calf were all he got for his troubles. *Idiot didn't even make it to the window.*

Cameron felt a light quiver through the back of Merryn's cardigan.

'Earth to Mez,' he said, cupping his free hand around his mouth, mimicking the voice from a walkie-talkie.

'Is the story true?' she asked, returning to this planet.

'Which one?' he said. 'There are so many.'

'The one about his family; did they…die?' Merryn gave another shudder as the 'D' word managed to fumble its way between her innocent lips.

'Yeah,' Cameron sighed. 'A few years ago, now.'

'Even the children?' Merryn asked timidly, with what the tale-tellers around here called *The Murder House* looking back at her from its singular dark eye.

''Fraid so, kiddo,' Cameron looked down at her pale, upset face. 'They were asleep. It didn't hurt. They wouldn't even have known it was happening.'

Clouds drowned out the sun, casting a timely and menacing dull hew over the derelict property before them. Cameron tried nudging Merryn to move on, but she stood firm. He knew there was more coming.

'Did *he* kill them? That's what Billy Eden says.'

'Billy's wrong, Merryn,' Cameron assured. 'It was an accident, a horrible one but an accident all the same. I'm sure he misses them a lot. Come on, we gotta move.'

'What about animals?' Merryn went on. 'Billy says he kills them, too.'

Cameron though for a moment. He'd been nice to his little sister all morning, so nice it was giving him a headache. Time to strike a teensy bit of fear into her.

'Oh, that bit's true,' he said with a satisfied grin that she didn't look up to see. 'I've seen them hanging from bits of fishing wire in his garden. Birds; ferrets; cats.'

'What if he gets Harvey?' Merryn shrieked, suddenly terrified.

'I'm sure that won't happen,' Cameron said. 'Harvey isn't exactly an out-door kind of animal. 'Smoky, though?' He did not like to talk about his own faithful friend like this, but knowing how Merryn loved Smoky so, he could not resist unsettling her for the day. 'Now get a wriggle on, vamoose!'

Turning away from *'The Murder House'*, the duo continued on their way.

Through the jungle of garden, along a path that ran alongside the rundown cottage and past its moss-green wall, lay an entanglement of rear garden. Unnoticed by any living soul, a pair of colourless eyes observed the road. Bordered with thick, wiry ashen eyebrows, the eyes watched on as two kids, a late-teen and an infant, gawked at his property. An angry curl formed at the mouth below grimy bearded jowls.

Raymond was skilled in reading body language. He had had plenty of experience from studying the suspicious looks he received. Strangers, and often non-strangers, would scurry to the other side of the road whenever they were on a collision course with him. But a mind reader he was not. If he *had* been, he would have known that this particular late-teen – a tall, skinny lad, irritatingly floppy dark fringe desperately in need of a pair of shears, a wannabe Rockstar character that he had seen around the village – was walking away smugly, thinking about all of the wonderful things that carbon monoxide poisoning had done.

CHAPTER EIGHT

Making his way down through the estate that spread from the school grounds, Cameron lapped up the glorious morning. So far, it had given him the satisfaction of unnerving his little sister and given him a subtle taste of his stepsister's sweet Chapstick. Deciding to take an alternative route, he headed down a tight little rat-run that wound its way behind one of the village's numerous public houses. He was the man of the hour; I mean seriously, the sprog would not have made it to school if it had not been for him. The pub, however, was not his intended destination. Obviously. They weren't serving alcohol at this time of morning. No; his chosen destination was the bakery past the end of the narrow byroad.

Every superhero deserved a meaty treat.

The dilemma that lay ahead, and he hoped for it to be the most taxing decision of the day, was which of the fat-*as* sausage rolls to go with? Lamb and mint, or pork and chilli?

Jesus, life can be so tough.

Settling for both, he paid up and headed home through the quiet, secluded trees of Stippy Stappy. Eating both on the way, and regretting it after, Cameron lay flaked out on his bed. His default position.

Trickling through the open window, a warm breeze tickled its way across his slender body. Gently, the breeze hinted that the last remnants of this year's sunshine needed a slightly more active attention. Fighting his lethargy, he would take a spin on his KMX 125cc before his shift at the hospital was due to commence. The North Cliff's coast road was calling. His *go-to*. His dark star.

Exit Wounds was soundo, slumped comatose across Cameron's amplifier.

Bollocks.

'Can't very well be scaring you to death, can I, Ex?' he said to the sleeping cat. 'Can't make Mez think Raymundo's gonna get ya if I kill you myself.'

His usual head-splitting thrash at the open strings, overdrive cranked to the full designed to piss his dad off, would have to wait. For now.

Exit Wounds, oblivious to his master's conversation, continued to sleep soundly as Cameron pulled himself to his feet and left the room.

On any normal occasion, Cameron would pull his motorbike backwards along the narrow gravel walkway that skirted around the side of the cottage. Positioning it to face the exit of the driveway, he would proceed to kick it into life and pull away leaving all of the family bullshit behind him.

Today was different. Today, his pathetic waste-of-space father was couped up in his bedroom, directly above the KMX's little wooden lean-to. In light of this, after Cameron pulled the bike out, he spun it around and rolled it backwards, back into its store. Being several inches taller than the lean-to, he had to crouch when hoisting himself uncomfortably onto the seat. Satisfied that he was positioned to avoid decapitation by lintel upon exit, he stamped the bike into life, pulled hard on the throttle and released the clutch, leaving Sea Glass Cottage in the scream of an engine and a spray of gravel and grit. All that was left to tell of his presence was a hazy cloud of blue fumes and a dirty tear in the Earth.

Less than thirty minutes later, a lone figure sat in the brush at the pinnacle of Hell's Mouth's cracked, eroding lips. Eleanor watched him suspiciously as she drew nearer, ambling her way through rises and falls of the lumpy coastal path. The sound of the sea was mellow today, foam fizzing over the protruding rocks, no raucous crashing against the foot of the cliffs. Match this with the late September sunshine (extra layers were still needed, of course, especially at Eleanor's age) and everything was splendid.

Except for this youth. He looked sombre, and that was worrying. There were few reasons for a young and sombre person to be here – In Eleanor's sceptical mind, at least – and the most prominent of those reasons had a very negative conclusion.

Lily scampered along two feet in front of Eleanor's cautious feet, stopping every few seconds as she stumbled on the scent of a previous four-legged passer-by. Forever thinking the worst, Eleanor always kept the retractable lead short on this part of walk. Of course, it meant that Lily could often end up under her feet, but that was preferable to the little hound having more freedom and making a spur of the moment dash close to the edge.

It was at this point, the direct centre of the gaping mouth, that Eleanor would stop and take in the rugged beauty of the county's northern limit before turning back toward home. Being well into her seventies did not stop her completing this walk of some seven miles here-and-back every day (barring when the wind was too threatening). She would listen to the thrum of the stirring waters below, inhaling the fresh scents of sea-salt and gorse flowers (when they were in bloom). She would watch the fulmars sailing on currents of air, rising and falling with spread wings as constant as a Catherine Wheel, calling gayly to each other. On very rare occasions, if Lady Luck was smiling fortuitously upon her, she would spot a peregrine falcon searching for prey with clinical eyes.

The days of this old woman being brave enough to lean over the edge of the precipice, taking in the plummeting cliff face, had long since departed. This upset her, though she was thankful that she still had the strength to make her way here.

Looking at the lone figure hunched some fifty yards further along the path disconcerted her. His black clothing reminded her of those goths that you sometimes see around, or on television; there was even one in her favourite soap opera. The impression she had of them – until coming across the chirpy one on the box – was that they were moody, depressed, and unapproachable. Combining the characteristics with the dark history of this stunning setting left Eleanor feeling unsettled and fearful. Not fearful for herself, but for this young man she was watching closely. Today she would cast her apprehensions aside and walk further than she had done for years.

'Come on Lily, my darlin',' she said, giving the lead a gentle flick and proceeding further.

Sticking fast at first, Lily gave a confused look in the direction of home. A real slave to routine and a creature of habit, was the little Westie.

'Lily, this way,' Eleanor said, with a *no arguments* edge in her voice, giving slightly more insistent tug on the lead.

After a few seconds of deliberation, Lily gave in and trotted up behind her trusty two-legged companion.

Getting closer, she made contact with his cool, calculating green eyes, Panthera looking and black rimmed. They gave him an androgynous appearance, reinforced by sharp facial features. His left hand rested on a dark, round shape. Eleanor managed to make the shape out to be a motorbike helmet. She questioned whether approaching the youth had been the wrong decision. Well, you hear such stories about bikers, don't you?

Was it too late to turn back and head in the direction of home, of *sanctuary*?

'Morning,' the youth beamed at her.

Yes, it was.

Eleanor was suddenly struck by the young man's dazzling smile. The figure she was so wary of moments ago had transformed into a handsome, charismatic gentleman.

'Mornin' my luvver,' Eleanor returned, suddenly taken giddy. 'Boodiful day.'

Cameron's smile widened (though how that was possible, Eleanor could not understand), amused by the strength of the old bird's Cornish accent. A Cornishman himself, he would love for such obvious origins to come forth in his dialect. Unfortunately for him, though, years of English invasion had diluted his own accent down to just a light southwestern twang.

'Fine day for a walk, don't ya think?' He offered, still sporting the charm-offensive smile.

'O'ess,' Eleanor loosened. 'Juss thawd I'd pop along and check yer awl-right?'

'Never better,' Cameron grinned. 'Just enjoying my favourite spot in the world.'

''Tis luvly innut,' Eleanor concurred. 'Perfect fer just *chillaxing*' she continued, pleased with her down-with-the-kids persona. 'You sure yer okay, bein' on yer own an' that?'

Cameron knew what the nosey old cow was getting at. Offering that killer smile, he said, 'I'm not on my own. My memories are here with me,' he looked out to sea thoughtfully. 'Chopper.'

'*Chopper?*' Eleanor quizzed.

'Yeah, *Chopper*,' Cameron enjoyed seeing the confusion on the old woman's face, like he was talking an alien language. 'You know the one. Stephen King. The scrap yard owner's trusty hound. *Sick balls, Chopper*! No?'

'I'm afraid you've lost me, my boy.'

'Never mind,' Cameron smiled, hiding his exasperation well. 'I highly recommend it. I used to walk my Chopper around here; named him after the dog in that book.'

'That's nice,' Eleanor returned, not knowing what else to say; an unusual concept for her.

'Mongrel,' Cameron darted an accusatory look at her.

'I beg your pardon?' Eleanor said, flummoxed.

'Chopper.' Cameron went on. 'Mixed breed. Dunno what shot the muck in what. Not like your beautiful boy.' he nodded down at Lily.

'Oh. Girl,' the woman returned.

'Huh?

'Lily's a girl,' her smile wavering a little.

'Oh, right. Girl,' *sanctimonious bitch*, thought Cameron. 'Anyway, where was I? Oh yeah. Chopper loved it here. To me there was nothing better than getting my Chopper out and letting him run free.'

'Run free? Here?' Eleanor was struck back, horrified.

'Yep, he used to love chasing the seagulls, daft ol' bugger,' Cameron motioned to the open air above Hell's Mouth, enjoying watching the stupid old woman's face plummet. 'I used to just sit and wait for him over at the café, like, letting Chopper do his own thing.'

The elderly lady really did not like what the youth was saying, did not like the way his dazzling smile had taken on a demonic hue. Despite the desperate need to flee the situation, she stood glued to the spot. It was as if her aging feet had taken root in the impenetrable rock below.

'So,' Cameron persevered. 'One day, I finished my latte, and he still hadn't come back. Which was weird cos he always made it back before I was done.' Cameron paused for effect. 'I came over here and couldn't see him. I was manic, shouting to anyone and everyone "have you seen my Chopper? Have you seen my Chopper?" People just backed away from me, acted like I was nuts,' He now focused on the old woman's eyes. 'Have you ever had anyone do that to you? Treat you like you were a freak?'

'Uh___'

'Probably not,' Cameron cut the faffing old fucker off. 'Bit of a looker, truth be told; you know, age aside and all that. More likely to look at you like they wanna bone, rather than like you're a freak. Yeah,' he mused, 'Not bad at all. I bet you've had more than your fair share of Chopper over the years. You single?'

Eleanor couldn't construct an answer. Her mouth hung open in disgust. Her feet even less able to turn and dash away than before.

'Actually, don't answer that. Relationship status means nothing to me when I've got my eyes on some *sweet, sweet honey*,'

Fuck me this is fun, Cameron thought, *think I'm actually getting a stalk on.* 'Anyway, where was I? Oh yeah. So, I finally plucked up the courage to edge towards the fence, that one down there. I remember taking a breath; it was spring, and the air was so fresh I felt ice-burns in my lungs. I leaned over, looked down, and there he was. I couldn't see his fur, used to be beigey- blonde, like the bog roll puppy, you know the one?' He didn't wait for a response; he was in *the zone*.

'What I could see was what came out: blood and guts all over the rocks. Bluey intestines like a long run of sausages the butcher hadn't twirled and chopped yet. Even saw his brains where his happy little skull had split in two. The impact pretty much turned the fucker inside out.' He paused and looked at her with a growing smirk and a glint in his piercing eyes. 'Still, he died doing what he loved. Chasing birds.'

Finally, having heard enough, Eleanor forced herself to move. Tearing the roots that had previously anchored her feet she turned, pulling violently at Lily's lead.

Cameron watched her scrambling away in the direction she had wandered over from, the gentle wind flicking up her floral dress as she almost lost her footing on the crumbly surface. He couldn't help but notice the tops of her tan knee-length stockings. Pale skin mapped with heavy blue veins charted above them. Cameron gave an appreciative whistle and laughed. Why wouldn't he laugh? He was delighted with his own ingenuity. He'd never even had a dog.

In contrast to his joy, Eleanor stumble-rushed away, fearful that she may never be able to enjoy these walks with little Lily again.

CHAPTER NINE

Muffled scuffling noises floated up from the kitchen, followed by the *clash* of a baking tray being laid by a heavy hand on the granite worksurface. A cushioned *thwump* signalled what was likely the fridge or freezer door being swung shut, again by a heavy hand.

And whistling.

Unusually good mood for Cameron, Kerenza thought.

She had been sitting on her bed reading up on *crime and punishment in Britain c1000 – present*, the gunpowder plot of 1605, to be precise (an uncanny coincidence, she would later consider). So, the clattering from downstairs offered a welcomed intervention.

She pulled her dressing gown from the corner of her tall mirror and shrouded her shoulders, her straight blonde hair flowing like water from opened floodgates as she pulled it from the back. The gown's baby-pink fluffy texture was a stark contrast to the grey camo bed-gear Kerenza had underneath, giving her the look of a G.I. Joe in drag. I cannot even describe what the red *All-Stars* she donned added to the look, but that is the eclectic attire she arrived downstairs in less than a minute later.

'Yo, I'm making pizza, d'you want some?' It was not Cameron, but Andrew who had been making the noise, and now his casual tone had not even a hint of the *'yeah, sorry, I know I've been hiding away for days and leaving everything to you, but…'*

'Just a slice, if there's any going spare,' Kerenza replied, bemused.

'Wouldn't have offered if there wasn't,' Andrew pointed out. 'Where's Cam?' He pulled open a bright red door on the front of the range and slid the pizza in.

'Evening shift,' Kerenza said, perplexed with this total change of character from the last Andrew she encountered to this one. The change was so drastic that her mind more than touched on the possibility of it being chemically induced.

'Evening shift?' Andrew queried. 'Doesn't that finish at half-seven? That's three hours ago.'

'Yeah well, he's been getting home late for months now. Who knows what he gets up to?' Her tone was more of accusive than questioning.

'True,' Andrew agreed, peeling the seal from a bottle of Chateauneuf-du-Pape. 'Tipple?' he angled the bottle towards her.

'No, ta,' she said. 'Not on a school night.'

'You sound like your mum,' he said. 'And Merryn, where's she?'

Is he taking the piss? Kerenza asked herself. 'In bed. It's half-past-ten, as you know. I read her a bedtime story, though I think she was hoping you'd started a little routine going.'

Andrew was reading now: body language. Arms folded, leaning on the door frame, left foot crossed over right. Scalding, simmering countenance. A black mamba, ready to strike.

'Okay, okay,' he pleaded. 'Look, I'll read her one tomorrow. Promise.'

'Well, I hope for her sake you do; she doesn't say it, but she suffers when you're not around. I know cos I'm around to see it.'

Ouch, Andrew thought, *kick me in the nuts why don't you? They're right here with bells on; fill your boots.*

'Look, this is a new start, 'kay? I'm gonna eat this, take my vino to the studio and create my greatest masterpiece yet.' He tried to sound upbeat. 'One so good it won't even be worth the satisfaction of ramming it up pompous Barry's podgy ass!

'Then, in the morning, I'll make Merrs her breakfast, take her to school, pick her up again, cook her tea, read her a bedtime story, tuck her in...all that jazz. You'll see.'

'I'd better see,' Kerenza sighed. 'I'm going to bed.'

'What about your piz___'

He didn't bother finishing. Kerenza had already disappeared from sight.

Twenty minutes had passed. Andrew stood on the doorstep, the glow through the glass in the kitchen door silhouetting his frame. The bottle of Chateauneuf hung from his right hand. Darkness lay ahead.

The pizza tasted good. Deep pan double pepperoni. Hell, given the high spirits he had entered the evening in, and the hunger he felt in the depths of his stomach (he could not remember when he last ate), deep pan double dog shit would not have tasted bad.

Now however, as the reality of his neglect had been spelled out for him in guilt inducing font, he felt the grips of another slump gripping into his flesh like talons, pulling him to the pits of Hell.

Taking a step into the garden, he was lost to the gloom. Another step forward and the security light pinged into life, bathing him in a yellow glow. Andrew headed for his makeshift studio, smiling at the old familiar creak of the door as he flicked the latch up and nudged it open. Strong odours laced with nostalgia hit him: oils; acrylics; cleaning spirits. To him, this is what *coming home* smelled like.

Another homecoming essential, scarcely viewable until he clicked the small dim light above the door on, was the welcoming sight of his trusty hammock, lying empty and calling out for a catch-up.

'Hello, beautiful,' he cooed to the vacant netting.

Blocking his path to the hammock were two canvases that bared no significance. He kicked them out of the way like discarded litter, one tearing across the skin and the other's frame voicing a hefty wooden *crack* as they hit the wall. Reaching his haven, Andrew lowered himself into the coarse netting, careful not to spill a drop form the open wine bottle he was nursing. He gave the floor a gentle kick with the tip of one hanging foot, hoping to rock steadily into nirvana.

Feeling like little time had passed, Andrew, raising the bottle to his lips, was surprised to find the reservoir had dried up. He realised with dismay that time had indeed escaped him somewhere. Huffing with disappointment, he swung his leg back over the side and, gingerly as not to unbalance the hammock, got himself to standing.

Gazing from left to right, he assessed the one-room studio. Taking in the corpses of old work strewn across the floor on the far side, he saw work long dead, life never even beginning to forge its way in. These were the ones to gather first. He would force purpose into them, determined to accomplish that much, at least. Andrew picked them up and placed them neatly along the floor, propping them against the back wall before collecting the few pieces of work that he had deemed worthy of exhibiting – the ones the experts had concluded were, in truth, quite shit.

The dead work accumulated nicely, a row of headstones against the surrounding wall of a cemetery.

Turning his back on this Halloween scene, he faced the opposite wall, the one containing a small, elevated window. Below it: the angry work. Arguably some of the most expressive paintings he had ever unleashed. These paintings (or lashings) took several minutes to amble from one studio wall to the other. But the end result was the same. They had joined the amassing tombstones, ghosts of paintings past.

A new start, the voice in his head insisted.

For his next trick, Andrew headed for the vintage wooden filing cabinet, in which he stored a range of tools and utensils, and a bottle of homemade whisky from his mate, Dave. This was for emergency purposes only. *No time like the presence*. Andrew had never told Dave that it was only for emergencies, being a sucker for other people's feelings. But the truth was, it tasted like shit and was strong enough to have you performing *the Birdie Song* in your birthday suit after only three shots.

Removing the part bottle (taste was irrelevant at this moment, but potency was everything), and his cooking blowtorch, he pulled out a third item. A long, dry rag.

A new start.

Backing as close as he could to the window wall and unscrewing the cap of the emergency whisky, Andrew proceeded to stuff the scrap of rag into its open neck.

'A moment of quiet reflection please.' Andrew felt like a priest at a funeral for Cornwall's most unwanted. Holding the fused bottle in his left hand (*sorry, Big Dave*) and the blowtorch in his right, he slid the thumb of the latter across the safety switch. *Click*. Realising he needed two free hands to fire the blowtorch, one for the gas and one for the spark, he placed the moonshine between his knees and clamped the bottle tight. Now fired up, he lit the rag, suddenly grasping this was apt to burn his balls off. *Of all the dumbass ideas, Andy boy...*his mind reprimanded.

Working fast (I mean let's face it, what choice did he have?), Andrew killed the gas and dropped the blowtorch on the dusty floor. Grabbing the ticking timebomb in his now-free right hand, he slung it at the centre of the wall above the canvases. A ball of flame turned the room an angry orange, blooming and abating at the speed of a lighthouse beacon. The heat was uncomfortable at first but lowered as welcoming as a good pub's open fireplace on a damp winter's night.

The canvases took to flame like a duck to water, helped by the paints which bubbled and cracked upon heating, an orchestra of relief and reprieve.

A new start.

Intoxicating odours hit the circulatory system like heroin. Andrew recognised with bliss as his old life burned, the flames dancing like a depiction from a Satanic horror film, that he had found his nirvana.

Watching the blaze with a lunatic obsession as tendrils coursed their way up the wall, Andrew raised his gaze. There it was, as clear as daylight now that his masterplan was in irreversible operation yet going unnoticed in the previously shadowed room and his delirium. The long shelf high on the wall. Oils; white spirits; pure turpentine; distilled turpentine; rectified spirit of turpentine. *How many fucking turpentines?* Solvent and thinner; solvent and thinner; countless cans of universal refill for his accomplice, the blowtorch.

As the flames raced up and made light work of the shelf's soft and oily wooden underside, Andrew had time for one last conscious thought.

Fuck!

***

As the KMX's small engine buzzed away beneath Cameron down Quay Road, an orange glow was growing in the darkness. It domed high beyond a row of detached bungalows he was approaching, radiating an apocalyptic light through the trees that encroached the dwellings from the rear. Cameron knew immediately that it was coming from home. Drawing back hard on the throttle, his white knuckles popped in a death-grip.

The narrow right-hander of the drive hurtled towards him. Too fast, he comprehended, when there was no time to react. The KMX's rear tyre slid out from underneath, sending boy and bike skimming through a shower of gravel and grit. Leaving the drive, they tore across the lawn in unison.

Looking up as he finally came to a stop on the soft ground, Cameron spotted Kerenza running barefoot and awkwardly across the stony drive towards his dad's studio; the source, he now saw, of the flames.

'*Cameron, your Dad's in there!*' she screamed when she saw the dazed heap on the floor. The rear wheel of the motorbike continued to spin wildly.

The enormity of what his stepsister screamed took a moment to set in. Then he was springing to his feet, ignoring as best he could the pain in his lower right leg where a later check would reveal a red area of flayed skin. A closer look at the studio revealed jagged shards of broken glass, blackened at their lethal edges. The building's lone window was no longer in residence. Flames darted through the roof towards the rear, Spanish flamenco dancers licking and flicking at the night sky, in dresses of reds, oranges, yellows, greens and blues.

Normally, Cameron would stop to enjoy such and enthralling spectacle. Bask in its hellish heat. But not today. Without an ounce of consideration for the closed wooden door that had stood firm and filled the entry alcove for years, he darted straight at it, bursting through as though it was mere paper. Kerenza would never forget the superhero demeanour he displayed in that heartbeat of a moment.

The door parted company with its hinges in a spray of splinters, landing on the floor with a clatter that was all but drowned out by the roaring flames. To his left was a burning wreck of God-only-knew what; the ceiling burnt through and partially collapsed. *If he's under there he can stay there!*

A quick scan of the room informed Cameron that he would not have to fight his way through any flames. Huddled motionless under the blown window, looking as dead as any dead thing could, was his father. The man who had always been there for him, no matter how much Cameron had thrown it back in his face.

Cameron shot in the unmoving form's direction, smashing his hip on the corner of the battered table. He narrowly avoided being thrown off balance and landing on the person he'd come to rescue. Instead, he came to a crunching stop on his knees, pain roaring up and through his jarred back, only centimetres from Andrew. He grabbed his old man by the shirt front, dragged him up and slung the lifeless corpse over his shoulder, noticing for the first time how skeletal the old boy had become.

Toxic fumes were doing a real number on Cameron now, his head was spinning, and he was coughing near to the point of puking. Determined but exhausted, he trudged over cracked and deformed pots and chunks of charred wood, finally making it through the opening where the creaky door once stood.

Outside, the fresh air hit him like a brick, momentarily taking his breath away. He struggled over the drive, right leg dragging behind him, and gently lowered his dad down onto the small patch of grass outside the kitchen window. His motorbike lay just off to the side, its rear wheel no longer spinning, as inert as Andrew.

'He's___a_gonner,' Cameron gasped through short, sharp intakes of chill night air.

Kerenza collapsed to her knees at Andrew's side, tears streaming from her haunted eyes.

By this point, a neighbour had arrived at the scene – a chubby guy in his mid-to-late fifties – short of breath as he went to his knees beside Kerenza. He informed Cameron that he had phoned for an ambulance and for a fire engine. Both were on their way. Cameron only stood, unable to conjure up any words, taking in as much cold air as he could in an attempt to soothe his burning lungs.

The neighbour leant forward, placing the side of his head on Andrew's narrow chest. Next, he raised his ear to the blackened sooty face. 'Well I'll be buggered,' the neighbour blurted out zealously. 'He's only bloody-well breathin'!'

Kerenza put a hand lightly on Andrew's chest, detecting the weakest of rises and the shallowest of falls. The sound of distant sirens trickled into the air, and the night-darkened trees that flanked Quay Road illuminated a pulsing blue. She dared to believe that everything was going to be okay.

CHAPTER TEN

Kerenza sat isolated and numb in the deserted sanctum of the living room. Even the small electrical conversation of the lamp seemed miles away.

Andrew had survived the blast without even the most minor burns, which was astonishing given the state of the former studio he was hauled from by his son, riding in like Street Hawk and bursting from the flames like Kurt Russell. The true extent of his injuries, however, was of serious concern. The trauma caused to his brain as the blast's sheer force smashed his head backwards against the block wall, would not be truly known until the swelling abated.

A coup and a contrecoup traumatic brain injury, *TBI*, Cameron had explained to her. Informing her that *'the coup,'* which he pronounced *coo*, *'was inflicted on the back of his brain, at the site of the initial impact.'* He elucidated this with way too much arrogance in medical knowledge for a hospital cleaner. *'The contrecoup,'* he went on over the phone. *'Occurred to the frontal lobe, where his brain flew back and hit the front of his skull directly opposite the crash site. Bang bang.'*

Kerenza had envisaged a marble being shaken in a bean tin. The thought gave her a cold shiver.

Her stepfather had spent two days in an induced coma, allowing the swelling on his brain to reduce with as little stress caused as possible. Cameron explained how they had likely used a barbiturate drug to induce the coma, probably pentobarbital or thiopental; and warfarin to thin the blood. A blood clot could kill him, the boy informed Kerenza. Sniggering on the other end of the line, he added, *'Or worse.'*

Kerenza had wondered after this discussion if Cameron's drug knowledge may be cause for alarm. His duties at the hospital included the occasional stint in the pharmacy, and his eyes shimmered with deviancy whenever he touched upon the subject.

Her darling stepbrother then fantasised a dark and dismal prognosis.

'He may not be able to walk again. He could be a complete vegetable. How will you feel if he can't remember your name?' Cameron did not expect an answer, so therefore did not wait for one. *'You may even have to spoon-feed him. I say "you" cos there's no fucking way I'm doing it; fuck that for a game of soldiers! And change his shit and piss filled boxers. If that's a frequent occurrence he may end up with a colostomy bag; fancy changing that baby, do ya? Carrying it 'round like sausages in gravy.'*

Fortunately, this was all just Cameron being a wind-up. That's the kind of prick he could be when he wanted – which was often, as it happens. Kerenza could not shake that niggling feeling that he was getting off on this in a very unhealthy manner.

The truth of the matter was that the doctors treating Andrew were delighted with his progress. His prognosis was as good as could be hoped for. Although obviously disorientated and confused when he came to – I defy anyone not to be, when placed in his shoes – he soon understood who he was, where he was, why he was here. He remembered his date of birth and where he lived, what year it was, and the names of his children. He even remembered that the current prime minister was an overweight, porridge faced, fuzzy blonde-haired bumbling buffoon.

He recalled the fire, too, though he claimed to have no recollection as to how it started. Andrew stressed fervently, however, that it was completely accidental.

On top of that, and with considerable pain, he remembered that his wife would not be here to meet him when he was discharged.

The swelling in his brain had shrunk like a cheap balloon from a child's party. Andrew was able to stand – aided at first, flanked on each side by a female physiotherapist; one of which a hot redhead with delicate porcelain skin, eyes as clear green as Caribbean waters; the other would look at home in the defensive line of the Chicago Bears.

In no time at all he was putting one foot in front of the other, and as a result of this remarkable recovery (doctor's words, not his), he was able to continue his recuperation at home as from the next day. Provided Cam could pick him up.

Please say he's got the brains to bring my car, Andrew thought, *and not that frigging boneshaker.*

Cameron, as it happens, was nowhere to be seen. Being otherwise engaged in something far too important to let his silenced phone interrupt, he had no idea that his father was being discharged.

The clock crept past ten at night. Kerenza had challenged Cameron recently as to the nature of his nocturnal behaviour. The answer to where he had been, was delivered simple and dismissive.

'Just out.'

This was like a sledgehammer to Kerenza's gut. Whilst not letting him have his wicked way in their budding relationship, she did believe he may genuinely be into her.

There were boys at school *into* her; for sure there were. Long blonde hair, naturally straight like an extravagant silk scarf; clear and intelligent blue eyes; a toothbrush commercial of perfectly straight, white teeth; slim and very leggy. She had no idea how many of those *boys* went home and relieved themselves after a lesson or two spent in the same classroom as her each day, and she certainly had no idea that one of the girls in her friendship group often did the same. Boys, they were, nonetheless. Immature boneheads, playing at being big men.

There was one older boy on the scene; had been for a few weeks now. The same age as Cameron in fact, and there lay the problem. The boy and Cameron had *'history'* apparently.

Her mind drifted back to Cameron. Older, still immature, but with a kind of cultivated charm. A dark intensity to his demeanour; mysterious; *equipped* came as a dreamy afterthought. Kerenza knew this last trait because he seemed to enjoy changing with his bedroom door open when he knew it was just the two of them in the house, standing butt-naked for an unnecessary length – pardon the pun – of time, deliberating what to wear and changing his mind more than a woman. So far, despite all the advances of her stepbrother, Kerenza had not given Cameron *the goods*. She had her reasons, one of which was not the stepbrother/stepsister thing one might expect. That aside, she knew that she would have to stop *dangling the carrot* – whoops, there we go again – eventually, and go that extra step if she wanted to stop this particular fish from falling off the hook.

It had just been the two of them since the night of the fire. Merryn, who had somehow slept through the commotion, thanks to a combination of being around the back of the cottage and having to catch up after several restless nights plagued with nasty dreams, had been picked up in the wee-small hours by her nanny and pappy. Despite Kerenza's protests and vows that she would do the school runs and the cooking for as long as it takes, they, or rather *Judith*, had insisted upon taking their youngest granddaughter. Cameron was delighted with this outcome, but Kerenza's nose was knocked seriously out of joint. She had been *mum* to the family for over half-a-year, how *dare* that pushy bitch assume that Kerenza was not up to the task.

As she sat deep in thought, curled up under her duvet on the sofa in the glow of a tall lamp and nursing a glass of Pimm's with an unopened book on her lap; she heard the faint but unmistakeable rattle of a motorbike. Cameron's now scratched and scraped motorbike, to be exact. She liked the way that Cameron made out that his *mean-machine* was the bee's knees. Rather than bees, Kerenza always thought that it sounded more like wasps in a beer can.

The front door opened and clapped shut, followed by the clatter and scratch of keys being thrown onto the kitchen's stone worktop. She did not look up, but noticed the room darken as his frame filled the doorway. Cameron swaggered in and slung himself into the recliner, four-pack of cyder hanging from one finger.

Silence.

'Not talking to me?' he mocked, his tone put-out.

'Reading,' came the muted reply, as she pulled the book open.

He eyed her up and down. *No flesh on show, bummer.* 'Jilly Cooper? Getting in the mood?'

'You wish,' Kerenza smirked, still looking down. 'Animal Farm.'

'Whao-ho-ho! You dirty little bitch. You can forget about getting Henry involved. I'm not having him tubed up my poopshoot for anyone, and I doubt very much that you want him ferreting 'round up yer chuff.' Cameron laughed at his own hilarity.

See, immature.

'George Orwell, you dick!' Kerenza exasperated. 'The Russian Revolution, Stalin, dictatorship and all. Your tiny little mind wouldn't begin to understand. And its Harvey,' she added finally.

'I thought you said it was George?'

'The hamster, you twat, not the author.'

'Oh,' Cameron paused for a moment. 'Got pigs in?'

'Yes,' Kerenza puffed, 'but not in the w___'

'I arrest my case,' Cameron cut in, victorious.

A few moments passed; Kerenza pretending to read her book, Cameron imagining dragging her into a barn and beating her back doors in. A clock ticked. The fridge's low hum floated through from the kitchen. A car passed outside.

It was Kerenza that reignited the conversation. 'Dad's coming home in the morning. You need to pick him up.'

This was clearly not up for negotiation, but noticing that she referred to him as *dad*, and not *your dad*, like normal, sparked a pang of jealousy. 'Unlucky. I've pulled the early shift. I don't finish 'til one.'

Kerenza was a little frustrated by the *hardman* attitude. 'Oh good, you'll already be there.'

'Can't see him enjoying the back of my bike,' he put in as a counterargument.

'You can take his car,' Kerenza had put her book down and made her way over to the recliner. She sat down on the arm and placed her hand lightly on Cameron's thigh. 'Without you, he'd be dead,' she pointed out, while Cameron's mind was racing to the hand near his groin. 'That's got to mean something to you. What you did. *He's* got to mean something.'

'Maybe I've just got other plans for him.'

'It's just you and me here, you can stop giving it the biggen now,' Kerenza stated, slightly peeved with his attitude. 'Let go of the past, it wasn't his fault.'

'He should've noticed,' Cameron said, indignantly.

'Shhh,' she soothed. 'Don't get yourself worked up.'

Kerenza moved her face slowly towards his and gently kissed him on the cheek. Cameron turned his head to face her, drinking in her cool blue eyes. They glistened as reimagined images of his past toiled with her emotions. Sensing her guard was lowered, he chanced to return the kiss, expecting her to pull away. She didn't. Instead, she slowly opened her mouth, letting her tongue do the talking. Cameron took it in, savouring the sweet taste of Pimm's.

How does she always get served? Tits I s'pose, I never had tits at that age and I never got served.

Attempting to dictate the play, he placed his hand her leg, feeling no resistance. That was all the encouragement Cameron needed. Pushing further, he slid his hand up around the curve of her hip. Kerenza kept on devouring him, praying he wouldn't notice her lack of experience.

No worries on that score, he was in the zone and desperate to strike while the iron was hot. His hand continued along its explorative path, coursing around to her front and fondling at the bottom of her tee shirt. He slipped his hand inside the fabric, feeling a shiver from Kerenza but still no resistance. Tracing a path up her firm belly, his hand came to rest on a fist-sized breast. Cameron could feel the padding in her bra, but the firmness behind it confirmed she had everything in its right place. Running the tips of his fingers lightly over the soft fabric ignited an intense heat in the nervous but anticipating girl. The boy with the winning smile could feel every goosebump as he touched upon her heavenly flesh.

Breaking away, Kerenza brought the kiss to an abrupt end. Disappointment flooded Cameron's heart. He could feel its deadened thud beating inside him. The disappointment was short lived. She eased herself to a standing position and held out an inviting hand. His heart jumped to a gallop as he took the hand, grinning like a Halloween jack-o'-lantern. As Kerenza pulled at him gently, Cameron almost floated out of the recliner. They headed for the stairs.

CHAPTER ELEVEN

In the middle of a thick, biscuit-coloured carpet, surrounded by a battlefield of plastic pieces, a young boy sat with a partially assembled X-Wing cradled in his hands. His dark mop of hair hung before his eyes as he slouched head down, trying to the best of his abilities to finish the construction. The instructions had been cast aside as soon as he realised his first mistake, but with the picture on the box to compare to he could see that it was far from a disaster. It would fly in his hand just as well.

His mother's voice was ringing though from the kitchen. She was on the phone to a friend, clearly ranting about his father. The everyday teatime smells of fishfingers, chips and beans that seemed to vent from each house, intoxicating the airspace above the entire estate, drifted through with her cutting tones. *'I can't,'* she said, sounding like a hissing python. *'He's "working" late, and I'm stuck with the boy again.'*

Even now, all these years later when he thought really hard, he could not recall one single occasion where his mother referred to him as *her son*, or even by his name. It was always *the boy*, or *him*.

There was a heavy clack as the phone handset was restored to its cradle on the kitchen wall. Entering the front room, her eyes beady and sharp like as buzzard's, red dress complimenting her dangerous mood, she looked threateningly at him.

'You see my life, boy?' she said, leaning over him, glowering. *'You see how you've taken* everything *from me? I can't even have friends anymore, and it's all because of you. Tiny, pathetic little you, causing an endless river of trouble.'*

Fear forbade him from answering his senior, as it always did in these situations.

The simmering demon with orange-fire hair – pulled back so hard the face below appeared angular and wooden, like some malevolent puppet villain – went on. *'Another night out with the girls missed. And for WHAT?'* She stooped further, right into his face so he could nearly taste the stale cigarettes that dominated her breath. It made the boy think of the fire-breathing dragon from the story he liked. Smaug. That's who his mother was.

'I'll tell you for what. *For you, you little brat,'* she sneered. *'Always you.'*

In a flash her hand darted down, grabbing the skin on the side of his chest and giving it a hard pinch. As quick as the initial movement, her reptilian fingers let go. She stepped back slowly with a macabre smile on her face, spotting the satisfying watery drop that darkened the carpet as it landed.

'Quit your snivelling you whinging little sod. You're the lucky one. It's me who's life's been ruined.'

Her bird of prey eyes homed in on a lone piece of plastic resting a few inches from the rest of the scattering. The clear cockpit of the X-Wing. A dismal smile lit her face and she raised one heeled shoe over it.

The boy managed to speak for the first time in this encounter. *'Please don't, mum,'* his tears running faster. *'Dad bought it for me.'*

'Screw your dad,' she whispered.

I wish you didn't do that in the first place, the boy kept in his head, not daring to let it tumble out of his mouth.

Coming down in slow motion, the windscreen gave with a heart-breaking crack.

'Oops. How clumsy of you,' she said. *'And I know how much you want to tell your precious* daddy *about this, but I wouldn't if I were you.'*

Stepping away from him towards the kitchen doorway, absorbing the tortured look of agony on his face, Alison reached back to the work surface, where her searching hand located a packet of cigarettes. She pulled one out, along with her lighter, and placing the stick between her red painted lips she flicked the wheel with a purposeful thumb.

Inhaling, and exhaling a puff of blue smoke, not breaking eye contact with her inconvenient child, she said, *'Because if you do, you'll feel the burn again.'*

As the hot end of the cigarette glowed bright in her black pupils, Cameron thought he could see Hell in his mother's demonic eyes.

CHAPTER TWELVE

An Atmosphere as uncomfortable as a bath of discarded hypodermic needles filled the room. Words on the tips of usually free flowing tongues fell into throats of obscurity as their masters sat with the day's dying light struggling through the window. Outside, leaves tittered and chattered on the old tree, whilst inside, the only audible sounds were the tinkering of stainless steel knives and forks against porcelain, and that dull buzz of the fridge. The warm, welcoming aromas of tomato and garlic hung in contradiction of the cold, uneasy aura.

'This is amazing,' Andrew said, knowing that somebody had to say something. The sudden voice came like a klaxon through a fog.

'Thanks,' Kerenza replied, relieved that someone had finally braved to break the silence. 'I know how much you used to like Mum's. And okay, mine doesn't live up to that,' she said modestly, 'But I thought you could do with a treat.'

'Anything's better than hospital food,' Andrew said.

'Wow, there's a compliment for you,' Cameron sarcastically chimed in.

'That's not what I meant,' exclaimed Andrew.

'So, you don't think it's better than hospital food,' Cameron threw back.

'That's enough,' Kerenza said. 'Dad, you don't___'

'No, seriously,' Andrew placed his hand on the back of Kerenza's as it lay dormant on the table. 'Your mum's spag bol *was* the best, but I think we can say second best now.'

Cameron opened his mouth, stuck out his tongue and aimed two fingers at the back of his throat, mocking the corniness of Andrew's comment. Kerenza, on the hand, enjoyed the compliment, even though her gut warned her of the possible white lie lurking in his words.

Noticing that all the plates were clear, *maybe not such a white lie after all*, she delegated the task of washing up to Cameron. His first reaction, as predictable as his eyes being on her ass whenever she bent over, was to protest. One stern, teacherly look from Kerenza was authoritative enough for him to backdown.

Stepfather and stepdaughter made small talk across the table as Cameron huffed and tutted through his chores. When he had finished, Kerenza offered coffees. It was a 'yes' from the man sat at the table, having not had a *proper* coffee for days also, but the son had other plans.

'I thought you wanted my help upstairs?'

'Hmm? Nope, don't think so,' Kerenza replied, doing her best to remain composed.

'That's what you said earlier. Something about homework?' Cameron could usually act well, his ability to feign a deadpan seriousness capable of pulling the wool over the sharpest supersleuth's eyes. Usually. This performance, however, was bordering on pathetic.

Not so sharp when the little doggy wants his belly rubbed, Kerenza told herself with some amusement.

'No,' she said, enjoying watching his face crumble like a gingerbread house at the epicentre of an earthquake. 'I checked online. I'm all caught up.'

'Whatever,' Cameron said, shooting a wounded look in her direction.

He made for the door, confirmed that his dad was not looking, and gave her a good, hard squeeze on an ass cheek as he passed. *Like a puppet on a string*, Kerenza mused, enjoying the sport.

Pouring coffees, she took up both cups. Andrew and herself retired to the comfort of the living room. She put his coffee on the low table next to the recliner and lowered herself onto the sofa, lifting her feet up and hugging her mug.

Knowing that something would be needed to fill any uncomfortable silence, she fumbled for TV remote and hit the standby button. The black screen illuminated into life on channel three, where a dark-haired weathergirl informed them that tomorrow was changeable – the buzzword as far as the forecast was concerned these days – but the weekend promised sunshine and temperatures above average for this time of year. Andrew stared fixatedly at her lavish raven hair and thought of Shona.

Remembering the previous life they all shared together made him want nothing more than to return to those days.

'How long until Merryn comes home?' Andrew asked Kerenza, an audible pained edge to his voice.

'Don't worry, Gran and Grandad are bringing her over to see you tomorrow. After school,' Kerenza tried to sound reassuring.

'Bringing her to see me?' he said, seeming agitated. 'They'll be leaving her here. Right?' His breathing became erratic, his face reddening in anger.

'Easy,' Kerenza soothed, moving over to and taking his head into her shoulder. 'It's okay, she's fine. But she'll stay with them again tomorrow night.' She could feel him shaking under her hand. 'We all just need to make sure you're good. And besides, you need to be taking it easy. Merryn doesn't do easy, does she? She does loud and hyper.' Kerenza tried to add a humorous quality. 'Things will be back to normal soon; we just have to be patient.'

Kerenza deliberated over the ease at which Andrew had grown angry, how unlike the easy-going Andrew she knew that was. Cameron had warned her that an ineptitude to control aggression was a common side effect for people who had survived a trauma to the brain. She hoped with all her heart that this was just a minor bump in the road, an obstacle that is well behind you when you get to the end of the street. When Andrew arrived home, he had seemed so, *so normal*. God, she hated using that word, like he was now *abnormal*.

Trying hard, Kerenza pushed at the niggling demons that played with her mind.

'She's really okay?' He was regaining some composure, his breath returning to its naturally steady pattern.

'Yes. She's fine.'

'And they're definitely bringing her home tomorrow?'

'Yes. After school.' Kerenza took a deep breath that didn't go unnoticed by the man in her embrace. 'But___'

'But what?' he fired back, pulling away from her and staring up, desperately.

'Gran will ask? Her and grandad need to know. I need to know. Why did you do it?' She thought hard to hold back an inevitable liquid breach of her defenceless eyes.

'Because it was all shit,' Andrew answered, nonplussed.

'You should have spoken to someone. You should've spoken to *me*!'

'What could you have done about it?' he said, genuine confusion hazing his expression.

'I could've helped, I could___'

'You can't even paint,' he said, laughing now. 'No offence, of course.'

'*What*,' Kerenza blurted out, exasperated. 'This is about *painting*?'

'What the hell else would it be about?' still laughing. 'Wait, you didn't think___'

'Yes,' she snapped back. 'I thought you tried to fucking *kill* yourself!'

Andrew was in hysterics now. 'Why would I want to do that? And even if I did, why would I choose to burn to death? That's gotta be one of the *worst* ways to go,' he said, burying his head in his palms, trying to muffle his chortles into extinction.

Succeeding – or almost – he uncovered his face and went on. 'Sorry, sorry. I only wanted to get rid of that crap I can't believe I produced. Next thing I know, I'm waking up in a jungle of wires under a canopy of fluid bags.' He paused briefly, pondering. 'Must've screwed that up, an' all.'

'Yes, you did,' said Kerenza, in disbelief. 'And you left me an emotional wreck in the process. Do you know how hard I've tried to get this family through since...' she didn't need to state since when. 'She's my mum and I can't even grieve, for fear of this family imploding.'

'Alright,' Andrew replied, face glowing in embarrassment. 'Cool your jets, kiddo.' He wrapped his arms around her, crushing her in a warm hug. 'I'm sorry. I've been so consumed by self-pity, I didn't even stop to think what you might be going through.'

Kerenza lowered her head onto the top of his, snivelling quietly. Andrew kept his grip, allowing her time to cry it out.

CHAPTER THIRTEEN

Judith Ballantyne sat across the table with her head cocked slightly in the air, beady eyes looking down her upturned beak at her son-in-law. He looked small and pathetic under her scrutinising glare.

Andrew looked up at her timidly. *My God I hate that face,* he thought.

The atmosphere in the kitchen was as fresh as a rugby team's changing room. Giggles drifted through from the living room as Merryn rolled around on the floor, synchronising her turns with Harvey in his clear plastic ball.

I'm stuck in Digory Kirke's musty old wardrobe, and if I could just break through, I'd be in Narnia with them.

The wait for someone to say something had a sense of impending doom, like sitting anticipative in the relative's room for some doctor to visit after a crisis in resus. Angus examined his grubby fingernails, digging at them absently with a thumb. Andrew had both hands wrapped around his untouched cup of coffee, only vaguely aware that there was little warmth coming through the ceramic anymore. Kerenza was by his side. Knowing that she had his back was a relief, he needed someone in his corner. Someone to help him face down *the Terminator.* The cyborg wore a deep pink hat, akin in style to what the Queen would don. But that was not fooling Andrew. *Piss her off enough,* he mused with a smirk, *and one of those calculating eyes will glow red. TARGET ACQUIRED.*

'Something amusing you, Andrew Tredinnick?' she glowered. Her Headmistress tone sounded almost comical.

'No. Yeah. No, it's nothing,' Andrew said, fighting to erase the grin from his face.

'Nothing indeed,' said Judith. 'Well, the whole tale seems like poppycock to me, nothing but impetuous fabrication.'

'You know what he's like, Gran,' Kerenza cut in from beside him. 'He could do with instructions on how to get out of bed safely in the mornings.'

'Oi!' Andrew shot her a betrayed look.

Kerenza raised her eyebrows at him, *tell-me-I'm-wrong*.

Judith was thinking quite the same thing, only with more than just a sprinkle of spite added. She had never wanted *her* Shona to get involved with the *arty-type*: dossers, drifters, vagabonds. Dreamers. Not the level-headed kind of man that could provide her daughter with a secure and prosperous future. I mean, most artists only started making money when they were six-feet under, right? No, that would not do for her precious little princess.

Shona had often wondered if Judith would still have considered her precious if she had known about her inner rebel, one that Shona kept locked away from her mother. Judith and her *must appear aristocratic in front of the neighbours* persona. My God, that woman's heart would shatter into a million little pieces if she knew an ounce of the shit Shona would get up to when she was younger.

But the little girl would always be precious, the only child that Judith and Angus Ballantyne had brought into the world. To Judith Ballantyne, sexual intercourse was strictly for reproductive purposes, not to be taken lightly, and certainly not for eroticism or carnal pleasures. It was a dirty and ungodly act. Providing her husband with one child, to Judith, was fulfilment of her marital obligation. The fact that Angus had also wanted a son, someone to keep the family name passing down the line through time, had no bearing with Judith. Occasionally, when Angus dared to mention the possibility of trying for another, he was shot down with the pains and dangers of childbirth.

'You know the hell *I went through, Angus!'* she would revel in reminding him, *'How could you even think of endangering me like that again?'*

Regretfully, Angus eventually gave up on the matter, accepting that reasoning with his wife was like trying to steal a great white shark's lunch. Instead, he conceded the fact that, for now and forever more, he would have to live a life of sworn celibacy.

In the present moment, Judith sat unmoving. Her vulture death-stare eagerly anticipated the man opposite, awaiting his unavoidable change from conscious to carrion. The version of events that Andrew had recently fed her would seem entirely ludicrous to any rational mind, but she conceded that they may be utterly feasible where this waste of space was concerned.

So, Andrew had been using his blowtorch on an acrylic pour – a trial medium for him – bringing the light base colours through a level of deep reds and blacks that had been applied over the top. Noticing that a patch of canvas was bare, he set the torch aside to free his hands and grab a cup of acrylic that had not quite been emptied. Knowing he would use the blowtorch in a few seconds time, he did not bother to kill the flame. Then, right on cue, the comedy moment. Returning to the table, an unnoticed shoelace free and flicking around like a lethal serpent, Andrew planted one heavy foot on it. Suddenly, face moving toward the table edge at an alarming rate, the luxury of time to throw a defensive arm forward evaporated. That was it. Bang. Goodnight Vienna.

Days later, he awoke in a hospital bed. The flaming torch had hit the floor nanoseconds after his head hit the table. The dusty sheets on which the phosphorescent blue flame came to rest were the perfect conductor. The rest, as they say, was history. Inevitably, the hungry flames crept and crawled in search of a greater fuel source: a shelf full of flammable liquids.

Andrew would never underestimate how lucky he was that Cameron had shown up when he did, heroically hoisting him over one shoulder and carrying him out of his catastrophically ill-fated yet completely accidental situation.

I'm also lucky that Cameron isn't here now, Andrew thought, *he'd probably tell them it was all a load of bollocks. To see me squirm if nothing else. All for shits and giggles.*

'Well,' Judith finally continued, still peering down her nose at him. 'This goes against my better judgment, but given how utterly outlandish your little story sounds, it may just be true.'

Internally breathing a simultaneously sigh of relief, Andrew and Kerenza battled the intense urge to look at each other.

'But I will be keeping a close eye on you, Andrew,' Judith went on. 'My main priority is my little Merryn.'

'*My*, little Merryn,' Andrew dared challenge.

'My main priority is *my* little Merryn,' the bitch reiterated. 'She can stay here tonight. But if I think she is in harm's way again because of your sheer incompetence, no matter how minor, I'll be back here as quick as you can say *social services*. And I *will* take her with me.'

There was an anxious moment where no one dared respond. Andrew had to pinch himself, *did she just say Merryn can stay?* After thirty seconds or so of hostile silence, Judith took the victory. She pushed her chair back on the tiled floor, the reverberation finding a new level of decibels under the enormity of her weight, sending shudders through the silent congregation. Standing, the table she used for support gave a tormented wobble large enough to lap cold coffee over Andrew's knuckles from the cup cradled in his grasping hands.

'Angus, we're leaving.'

Angus rose to his feet, giving Andrew a sympathetic raise of the eyebrows. Then he made his way through to the living room to say goodbye to Merryn. When he returned to the kitchen, he kissed Kerenza's cheek and gave her a hug, which she returned.

'Take care, Grandad. Love you.'

'Love you too, sweetie,' the big man replied. 'Keep looking after this lot, you're doing a great job. You know where I am if you need me.'

Then, the two of them were gone, disappearing like phantoms from the glow of the security light. Andrew and Kerenza relaxed a little as they heard the thud of one car door closing, then another. The cough of an engine reaffirmed their freedom.

The joyful sound of Merryn's laughter continued to drift through from the living room as though nothing had happened.

***

Cameron had spent the previous hour sat on the stubbly chin of Hell's Mouth. A dull pain across his back informed him he had rested against the timber railing for too long. The backs of his trousers were still damp from sitting with his feet hovering over the business end of the cliff. Tonight, he had contemplated the future. His next steps.

Almost home now, zipping down Quay Road, he squinted against a pair of oncoming headlights. Slowing to a stop, he let the lights pass. Turning his head to look back, he could just make out the last three letters of Angus and Judith's registration plate in the glow provided by the tiny surrounding white bulbs. The car's interior was filled with blackness, affording him with not so much as a snip of the figures inside. As a result, Cameron could not make out if his half-sister was in the back or not.

He hoped that she was.

CHAPTER FOURTEEN

Studying shards of golden light reaching across the dew-glistening garden instilled an uncharacteristic optimism into Cameron. The summer's refusal to depart had him fantasizing of chugging cyder in the warm evening glow. Hell, it was only morning but the temptation to act on that now was strong.

'We should have a barbie,' he said, his back to the room. 'Few more days and all we'll get for months will be crappy mizzle and gales.'

Andrew sat at the table making light work of a small breakfast. He looked towards the window, through dancing orbs of dust and fibres as they caught in shafts of light cast by the window blind. *Looks like an office*, he thought, wondering why they did not plump something more traditional, something more sympathetic to the cottage's rustic charm.

'Have some crumpets,' Andrew said. 'I saved you a couple.'

'Breakfast is for pussies,' Cameron told his dad, seemingly having the reply already in the bank.

Andrew ignored this petty act of insubordination. It had been a good week, and nothing was going to spoil that. Not even the goading comments of a nineteen-year-old with a flourishing attitude problem.

Merryn was happy and the school-week had sailed by without incident. Andrew was Andrew again, not even the hint of a headache. Kerenza and Cameron were being civil. Scrap that, they were being actively friendly towards each other. Normally, Cameron would offer snide criticism of Kerenza's cooking, or about how she was turning into an old biddy mollycoddling everyone. It would be nice if they could continue the courtesies through the weekend; enjoy the moment as a family.

'A barbeque sounds a good idea,' said Andrew. 'Make the most of the weather while we've got it.'

'Awesome,' Cameron beamed. 'I'll get the supplies in.'

'I don't think so, buddy. If you got the supplies, the so-called barbeque would consist of four burgers (without baps), a crate of Rattler and a bottle of cheap vodka.'

'I don't see anything wrong with that,' laughed Cameron.

Andrew joined in, realising what an unusual sound it was coming from his son. He could not remember when he last heard genuine laughter from him.

'But whatever,' Cameron said. 'It's up to you guys. I'm off out, I got some business to attend to.'

'Is it reasonable for me to ask *what* business?'

'Nope,' Cameron replied with a smirk. 'It's *reasonable* for you to keep your nose out of my fucking business.'

'Language! What's going on?' asked Kerenza entering the room.

'Nothing much,' Andrew replied. 'Just MI5 here off on another secret mission. Got any plans for this morning?'

'Just a bit of homework to catch up on; nothing major.'

Cameron drew a 'square' sign in the air, index fingers starting together, working away, down, and meeting in the middle again. *Ah, there's the Cam we know and love,* thought Andrew, catching site of the gesture.

Kerenza returned the compliment with a well-choreographed raise of her right hand and smooth extension of its middle finger.

Normal service resumed. 'Good,' Andrew interrupted the childish formalities. 'Crack on with that now, then grab your sister. We're going shopping.'

***

Sitting with his back propped against the gnarly unmoving trunk of the old tree, six-string lounging contentedly across his lap, Cameron kept a keen eye on the girls. Dark fringe hiding one lens of his sunglasses, the other lens stealthily kept his leering intent inconspicuous. It was Kerenza in particular that commanded his attention. Her blonde hair flailing, long smooth legs protruding from the hem of small denim shorts, their every movement sending his body rigid.

Merryn capitalised on being the shortest in their game of Swingball, sending the fluorescent yellow tennis ball high towards her opponents, hitting it up from near ground level, whether she decided to go left or right. With natural ease, she inflicted headshot upon headshot on the other two girls.

Suffering most of the devastating blows, though she took them well, was Kerenza's friend, Grace. Kerenza tracked the orbiting yellow sphere as it hurtled this way and that, gauging its line of travel – happy to let her little sister get the better of her, but not prepared to be destroyed by her. Grace, on the other hand, caught herself out whilst shifting sideways glances at her friend's darkly intriguing brother under the tree.

Behind the barbeque, Andrew stood as head chef. He appeared as a mirage in the shimmering waves heat from the hot coals. The custodian of the cooking: turning sausages, flipping burgers and making sure not to dry out Kerenza's preferred salmon fillet that was sat snugly wrapped in kitchen foil. Reaching out, he lifted his lager from next to the rack. Condensation like a misty winter drizzle on the cold bottle surrendered to gravity, running down the angle of the glowing, green translucent surface and dripping onto the hot ashes in a series of satisfying puff-sizzles.

Cameron slouched absorbing the situation while feeling slightly annoyed that Kerenza had invited a new player into their bubble. He spotted Exit Wounds lying lackadaisically on the grass not far from the Swingball players, eying up Harvey. Yes, even that Russian rodent was invited to this event, safe in his protective plastic world, of course.

Keep looking puddy cat, just give me the nod and he's all yours, a la flambè.

The food went down a storm, as the opulent scents of the cooking had promised. Charred coals mingled with sweet and succulent meats, temporarily replaced the decaying odours of the partially standing studio that remained lingering in the still air. Andrew was the undeclared King of the Barbie, executing the cuisine with a modest perfection, and he assured Kerenza and Grace that their first ever attempt at homemade coleslaw and potato salad were the best he had ever tasted. He believed it, too.

'Oi, stop being so unsociable,' Andrew called over to Cameron from the garden table, raising an unopened beer bottle in invitation.

Why not? Cameron thought, *enjoy the vista better from there.*

He leaned forward and placed his acoustic against the trunk of the tree. Grabbing his cyders and his bottle of vodka, he made his way over to join his old man.

'They're having fun.'

'Certainly looks like it,' Cameron replied, taking a seat and staring slyly at Kerenza rear-end.

'You should join in,' Andrew suggested.

'Don't be a dick.'

'No need for that,' said Andrew, defensively. 'It was only a suggestion.'

'Well then I *suggest* you stop suggesting,' advised Cameron. 'Seriously, me? Swingball?'

'Yeah, maybe you're right. Not really your thing, you know, fun and all that.'

Cameron opened the beer offered by his dad and took a swig. Grace took another knock on the head as she watched him with inquisitive fascination, the other two girls erupting with laughter. Cameron didn't notice at first, his mind on other things.

After another thirty minutes of forced pleasantries the light began to fade, pulling a cool blanket over the garden. The girls packed in their game and Kerenza told Merryn to take Harvey in. She picked him up in the sphere without protest.

'Maybe we should go in, too,' Andrew said, whilst struggling to his feet.

'If you're cold you could always start another fire,' Cameron said, dryly.

Kerenza shot him a smouldering look of smoky disapproval, so dangerous that Cameron could almost feel a heat from it.

'What, too soon?' he shrugged.

'You're funny,' sniggered Andrew. 'Girls, you coming in?'

Merryn followed her daddy, and after Kerenza glowered at Cameron for a couple of awkward seconds, she and Grace headed in the same direction.

Shit, thought Cameron.

The best part of an hour later, the boy stood and walked over to the remains of the studio. He took a piss against its smoke-blackened wall. Looking up to the sky, he took in a couple lungs of chilled salty air. An onshore breeze, light earlier but now starting to gather pace, brought aromas of the beach flooding up to Sea Glass Cottage. As he took another gulp, Cameron could just about taste the slimy algae that clung to the rocks of the old harbour wall that had fallen into the sea just shy of a hundred years ago. The wall a metaphor for his life if he could not sort his shit out.

One day he would be with Kerenza, with everyone who once knew them out of the way and nobody knowing the private and rather unfortunate stepbrother/stepsister detail. Everything would be perfect.

Placing the fingertips of his right hand on the sooty wall of the studio, he steadied himself against the broiling combination of excessive alcohol and excessive oxygen. After composing his dizzy head, he started back towards the house. Disappointed, he spotted a light coming from Kerenza's bedroom Window.

Andrew was alone in the living room, feet up in his recliner. Cameron held out a bottle to him, which was accepted with a smile and a nod.

'What the fuck are you watching?' Cameron asked as he looked at the screen, face screwed up.

'Some film. This Kraut's a surgeon who likes to sew people together,' Andrew stated like it was a perfectly normal pastime.

'German,' Cameron returned.

'No, it's in English.'

'German, not Kraut. Idiot,' Cameron smarted. 'Kraut's not been fashionable for quite some time now. Political correctness and all that bollocks. Sew them together?'

'Yeah,' said Andrew. 'Cakehole to asshole, like.'

'You're shitting me,' Cameron quizzed, in disbelief.

'That's what she said.' The two of them shared a laugh at that quip.

'Well, you'd better hope Merryn doesn't come down and see it,' Cameron said, dumping himself onto the sofa.

'No worries on that front,' said Andrew. 'She's soundo. The girls knackered her out.'

After a moment of silence, digesting what the television was showing him, Cameron apologised for his earlier indiscretion. 'You know it was meant as a joke.'

'Yeah, well,' Andrew sighed. 'Some jokes just aren't funny. Particularly yours.'

This last comment Andrew offered with a grin, which Cameron returned, conceding that his dad may have a point.

On the screen, a bloke and two women crawled along the floor like a slow-moving steam train, searching for an escape from the mad surgeon's lair. The first woman's face was nuzzled in the leading guy's ass-crack, connecting stitches bandaged over. *Least he's thought about the spread of infection,* Cam thought to himself. The second woman's face was positioned in the same fashion, only to the first woman. *Talk about fucked up.*

'That's enough excitement for me,' said Cameron, lifting himself from his seat. He grabbed the remainder of his Rattlers. 'I'm turning in. And now might be the time to turn that over, I can hear movement upstairs.'

'Good call,' Andrew said, reaching for the remote. 'Night, Cam.'

'Night.'

Cameron passed the two girls on the stairs, making sure to stop and let them by, brandishing them with the bad luck that superstition had born into existence. Kerenza gave him a friendly elbow to the ribs, while Grace offered a meek thank-you nod before darting her gaze to the steps below, her dark brown fringe waving and springing against her forehead. Her cheeks glowed a dusky pink.

'No troubles, Bubbles,' he said, and grinned at the nervous giggle that issued form the girl.

Entering his bedroom and closing the door behind him, Cameron opted not to turn the light on. He had heard the car pull up at the end of the drive and stood back unobservable in the black hole of the window, watching on as the two girls exited the door below and faded slowly out of the reaching beam of the security light. The motor was killed, followed shortly after by the death of the red rear lights. A figure emerged from the driver's door. Tall, well-built, wearing light shorts that stopped at the knees, and a tight, plain white tee shirt.

Little innocent Gracie likes the big fellas, does she? Cameron mused. *That fucker's likely to split her in two.*

Grace reached the parked car – a sporty, silver saloon, dropped on its nuts – and opened the passenger door without making to get in. Biggun carried on walking until he reached the end-post of their garden fence. The tree outside of Cameron's window that had supported his body only a few hours previously had now become his nemesis, its foliage obscuring the stranger's face.

Why was Kerenza walking towards him?

This soon became evident to Cameron with sickening clarity. His stepsister stopped at the guy's feet and lifted her head towards him. Her blonde hair fell further down her back, a tantalising waterfall go golden honey. As this new imposter leaned down to kiss Kerenza grotesquely on the mouth, the tree shifted its allegiance once more, this time playing whistle-blower. Shifting in a gust of wind, the shielding cluster of leaves parted like stage curtains for the opening scene.

Jack.

CHAPTER FIFTEEN

Plodding into the kitchen, lethargic and hungover, Cameron's usually pale complexion had taken on an almost translucent vampiresque hue. The ethanol reek of his breath could bring a tear to the eye of even the hardiest of onion sellers.

Kerenza looked up from her laptop and gave an unsympathetic smile. 'Ooh, looking good, Bro.'

'And what exactly do I need to look good for, *Sis*?' he sneered back.

'Chill out, I was only messing.'

'I could not give a rat's ass what___'

'Whoa, simmer down, teasy bugger,' Andrew intervened. 'There's fresh coffee on the top, think you might need some. I was beginning to doubt you'd ever surface.'

'It's Sunday, Dickwad,' Cameron stated. 'Day of rest.'

He didn't need to be told there was coffee on the top, the thick, rich smell clogging the air was so intense that it made him want to retch. He screwed his nose up and looked back at Kerenza, who kept her focus on him just long enough for Cameron to catch her blistering stare, before returning her attention to whatever she was streaming.

'I'm good, ta. I've got to go out, anyway.'

'On your bike?' replied Andrew. 'That's not a good idea, bud, you'll still be over the limit.'

'Relax, I'm only going up to the village,' Cameron said with a stretch and a yawn. 'Walkin's good, right? That's what old farts like you usually say.'

'Well, there's a first,' Andrew sniggered. 'Take your key, *Bradbury*, we're taking Merryn to the animal park and getting an ice cream. We may not be here when you get back.'

'Whatever,' Cameron said, as he reached the door. Turning back to give Kerenza one last glance, he hoped to see her watching him. She wasn't. He stepped out into the bright daylight, focussing on his breathing to suppress his anger, and closed the door behind him.

Andrew and Kerenza gave each other a bemused *oh-well-what-can-you-do* look in the moment of silence that followed, before an audible cuss broke through the thick granite walls. Some crunching footsteps later the door was flung open.

'Who's the funny fucker?' Cameron demanded as he stood with his left hand clasped around the neck of his guitar.

'What the hell's wrong with you?' Kerenza asked, baffled by the sudden outburst.

'Don't act dumb,' he ranted. 'I know it was one of you twats!'

'That's enough!' Andrew cut in. 'I've got no idea what you're on about, but you can't talk to your sister like that.'

'She's *not* my sister,' Cameron argued, eyes blazing like a feral cat.

'Fine, *step*sister, whatever. You still don't talk to her like that.' Andrew was on his feet now, facing his son down.

Cameron lunged the acoustic forward. 'I'll talk how I fucking want until you tell me which one of you nicked my string.'

Both Andrew and Kerenza had to stifle a laugh from this development which neither one of them could have predicted.

'Oh, this is just a big fucking joke to you two, isn't it?' continued Cameron, incensed.

'Seriously…mate,' Andrew struggled to draw breath. 'You're demented!'

'Demented? You can see it's gone, right? You can see I'm not imagining it?' Cameron shoved the guitar in Andrew's face, so close that Andrew caught the faint scent of barbeque coals circling around in its hollow body.

'Yes, it's gone, but,' he struggled for a reasonable suggestion or explanation, settling on, 'Could it just have snapped?'

'No! It couldn't just have snapped, you cock. It would still be hanging off it if it did.'

Andrew conceded this point, standing down and returning to his chair thoroughly flummoxed. He looked towards Kerenza in amused disbelief.

'Krenz, did you take the string?' he asked, his voice sensible and impartial.

'No, Dad,' Kerenza replied in a blasé manner. 'What about you?'

'Afraid not. Don't know what Merryn's guitar skills are like though.'

The childish pricks shared another laugh. *Keep fucking laughing, pops,* Cameron thought. Kerenza wasn't out of the woods yet, but she was much easier to forgive than his father, just one flash of cleavage and she would be back in favour.

'It's a conspiracy,' said Cameron. 'I will find out who did this. May take a while, but you can bet your life I will.'

Cameron clapped the guitar down on the table and stormed back out into the late morning sun, slamming the door behind him this time with an earthmoving crash.

This hissy-fit was too much for Kerenza and Andrew. The silence borne of the slamming door broke instantly as their laughter filled the void; laughter that amplified when they heard the shout of *'PISS OFF'* reverberate through the walls.

CHAPTER SIXTEEN

Unseasonable warmth beat down from the sky above. Shadows cast by the thin strands of cloud ran like a herd of zebra through the wavering grass, transforming strips of the small glade from lime green to emerald.

This display of nature's pyrotechnics was going unwitnessed by Andrew. His colours transfigured instead from blush, to salmon, to rouge as he sat on a bench, head back and eyes closed. The pores on his face drank in the solar rays fervidly. Happy sounds of children playing on the modest range of apparatus (Merryn's distinctive jubilant giggling easy to pick out in the crowd) had left him contented and light of heart.

The smell: not quite so palatable. That distinctive aroma that comes as standard with pigs wafted over from his right. Piglets grunted away, play-fighting with their siblings, battling for space on the teats of the huge sow, who lay indifferently on the dusty ground. The sour tang of countryside scent emanating from the nearby dairy herd did little to help the air quality, but what can you say? best ice cream in the county as far as Andrew was concerned.

'This seat taken?'

Flicking his eyes open, alert like a rabbit under the passing shadow of a hawk, Andrew took in the vague outline of a female figure stood before him. Gradually, his vision acclimatised to the sudden change in light condition.

The figure waited patiently for her question to be answered, head silhouetted by the soaring sun.

'Miss Sanders?'

'Please, we're not in school now. It's Alycia. I only wear my *teacher's* hat on weekdays.'

'No, course. Please,' Andrew gestured to the vacant space at his side.

'Perfect weather for a snooze on a park bench, wouldn't you say?' said Alycia, shuffling from one cheek to the other in search of comfort on the hard, slatted surface.

'What? I wasn't snoozing,' Andrew protested, embarrassed and defensive.

'It's not a crime,' she said, giving him a wry smile. 'Most of us have done it at some point, only not with a half-finished tub of ice cream on our lap.' She spotted his confused expression and suggestively dipped her eyes down to his legs.

'Ahh, balls!' Andrew exclaimed, noticing the tilted container and the spreading pool of blackcurrant and clotted cream flavoured delights soaking into his jeans.

Alycia laughed without the slightest hint of mock in her demeanour, pulling a pack of tissues from her bag. 'Here you go,' she said, plucking a couple from the pack and handing them over.

'Thanks,' said Andrew. 'Where would we be without a lady's handbag? They seem to contain everything from the brilliantly useful to the dreadfully useless.'

'I'm in a good mood,' said Alycia. 'So I'll take that as a compliment, and not as the sexist remark it sounded like.'

'Thanks,' said Andrew. 'What are you doing here?' he asked rather stupidly as he went to work on his little accident.

'Um, we teachers are allowed a life outside of school, you know. Which includes things like bringing my daughter to the park for a treat and a much-needed runout.'

'Daughter? I never knew.'

'Well, it's not a secret, I just don't broadcast it. Accusations of *'class favourite'* and that sort of thing,' she replied, her tone cheerful. 'She's in my class this year. Darcy. Just over there playing with your Merryn.' Alycia pointed to the sit-on toy diggers in the sandpit.

Andrew spotted Merryn operating one faded and flaky red metal digger, while a mini version of Miss Sanders – same curls, only darker; same copper skin – controlled another.

'So, how come the *'Miss'* asked Andrew, berating himself internally for the invasiveness of the question.

'I would have thought that was obvious. It's *'Miss'* because there's no Mr.' Alycia did not appear negatively affected by the subject and carried on in her normal happy manner. 'Never has been. Well, that is to say, when I told him I was pregnant he promptly gave me two choices: get rid of the baby, or he walks. I chose. He walked.'

'I'm sorry,' said Andrew, seriously regretting the question.

'Don't be. I'm not,' Alycia replied, with an assured smile. 'Every day when I look at Darcy, I'm reminded that I made the right choice. The only choice.'

Andrew thought to ask if there had been anyone since, before deciding that was none of his business and he had already pried too much. Looking over at the girls, he saw Kerenza sat next to the sandpit, face turned in his direction. She looked away when they made eye contact. Leaning towards the girls, she mouthed something that made both younger girls erupt with laughter.

Alycia smiled. 'You're lucky to have her.'

'Who?' Andrew quizzed. 'Kerenza?'

'Yes. Merryn talks about her *all* the time. She looks up to her.'

'Yeah, she's great with her.' Andrew pondered over a thought and added, 'With all of us. She had to grow up quick. So quick that I rather selfishly forgot that she's been going through hell, too.'

'I'm sure she doesn't think badly of you for that.'

'I hope not,' Andrew sighed, thoughtful.

The girls suddenly ran past, high on life and vocally letting every living soul within half-a-mile hear it.

'We're going to see the piglets,' Kerenza said as she followed the girls. 'Hiya, you alright?' she said to Miss Sanders.

'Hi. Good thanks; and yourself?'

'Perfect thanks. A bit out-of-breath keeping up with these little livewires. I seriously need to get back in shape,' she mused.

'You're being modest,' said Alycia. 'You look in great shape, doesn't she?' She looked to Andrew for confirmation.

'Uh, yeah,' Andrew fumbled feeling slightly awkward and looking at Kerenza. 'You do.'

'Thanks,' replied Kerenza. Feeling the colour rise in her cheeks, she decided it was time to scarper.

'So, Merryn has a new hamster,' Alycia said to Andrew, absently watching Kerenza heading after the girls.

'Uh-huh, we got it after the, uh, you know. The bird thing,' said Andrew, cagily.

'And how's that working out?'

'Good,' Andrew replied, wondering if this conversation was developing into an interrogation. Was she suddenly *Miss Sanders* again? sat behind her desk while he sat before it, small even on an undersized year-two pupil's chair. 'Really good, actually. Harvey, his name is. Merryn absolutely adores him.'

'Tell me about it,' Alycia chuckled. 'Her free-drawing book is full of hamster pictures and "I heart Harvey's." And there have been no more *incidents* that I know of, so it would appear you made a really smart move.'

'First time in a while,' Andrew said, sounding more than just a little sorry for himself.

'You've been through a severely traumatic time. You're only human,' Alycia reassured, soothingly. 'Trust me, Merryn's happy again. Kerenza certainly seems happy. Which says to me that you're doing a great job.'

'Do you really mean that?'

Alycia exhaled, smiling gently, and pointed over to the pig pen. Three figures stood leaning on its surrounding fence, one at ground level, two stood elevated on the bottom rail. All three pointing, chatting, giggling, having fun.

'Does that look like you're not?' she asked in seriousness.

Andrew took in the scene, and the kind words Alycia had spoken to him. He allowed himself a proud – but still not entirely convinced – smile.

They sat together in comfortable silence for several minutes, listening to the soft breeze fluttering through the overgrown weeds of the calves' paddock behind them. The ratcheting knees of the grasshoppers called, and the extravagantly ugly turkey to their left gobbled erratically.

Alycia eventually broke the peace. 'You ok?' She placed a concerned hand on Andrew's shoulder – a motion not missed by Kerenza.

'Perfect,' he replied.

Removing her hand, Alycia leaned forward. Ruffling the golden-brown coils of her fringe with glossy plumb nails, she made her apologies.

'I'm going to have to love you and leave you, I'm afraid. I have a mountain of marking to do this afternoon. It was nice chatting with you, Merryn's dad.'

'Andrew,' he corrected.

'Andrew,' Alycia confirmed.

'Marking? On a Sunday?'

'It's not all nine-to-three-fifteen and more week's holiday than you can count on a Camborne native's fingers, you know!'

'Whoa, that's not very PC,' said Andrew, slightly taken aback. 'Especially for a teacher.'

'I told you, I'm not a teacher today. Having loads of marking to do doesn't change that.' Alycia smiled, flashing him a cocky wink.

'Hopefully see you around?' he said.

'I'm sure you will. It's a small village, and I do teach your daughter.' She smiled and turned away. 'Darcy-doo, come on lovey.'

Andrew watched as Darcy clasped the hand offered by her mum as she passed the pigpen. Both mother and daughter skipped cutely towards the car park.

Alycia was the first woman in the village since the gossip mill had spun into life that had approached him of her own accord, making an effort to speak, rather than pass by inconspicuously.

CHAPTER SEVENTEEN

With a gentle click, the front door – still in one piece despite the assault inflicted upon it earlier that day – closed softly. The same old annoying monotonous buzz of the fridge-freezer, and steady thrum of the range cooker were the only audible sounds. Standing on the rough coco-fibre 'Welcome' mat, an intruder with malice in mind listened attentively for any signs of life within the property.

No muffled bullshit chatter taking like an ear infection from another room. No footsteps forcing a groan from the floorboards above. No crappy R&B music emanating from Kerenza's room.

The car had disappeared from the drive, apparently taking the entire human occupancy of Sea Glass Cottage with it for the ride.

Entering the long and spacious-yet-cosy living room, the ticking of the wall clock seemed a summons, ushering the condemned to the eagerly anticipated spectacle of a public hanging.

Walking to the bottom of the stairs, loitering, listening.

Nothing.

Nothing, that is, but the plastic squeaking and scraping of a rotating wheel under rodent paws.

One black trainer alighted the first stair, silently. The squeaking continued as the next silent foot motioned forward. Left followed right followed left. After what seemed an age to the impatient visitor, like exaggerated slow-motion footage a B-rated horror movie might offer, the figure reached the pinnacle of the staircase. Looking to his right, he spotted the open door of the bedroom belonging to the straw-haired scatterbrain.

'Harvey... *oh Harvey*,' his teasing voice called. 'Time to shut you up, you aggravating, cock-sucking, buck-toothed Siberian rat.'

Entering the bedroom, Cameron paused to make sure that the erratic spinning of the wheel *was* the only sound he could hear; no running motors or grinding tyres, no chatting voices. Bundles of soft toys eyed the boy suspiciously.

Unfortunately for Harvey there was no other sound, and the array of teddies and animals would never speak of what they were about to witness.

Cameron reached the cage. Crouching down, hands on knees, he inched his face closer to the hamster.

'That wheel's a waste of time, little man,' he said to the creature. 'Want a real reason to run? Yes? Well, isn't that just peachy. I'm the man who can make that happen for you.'

As if completely compelled by the offer, Harvey jumped from his wheel and slinked his little, furry brown body towards the face. Raising himself on his haunches, he twitched his fine white whiskers. His black pearl eyes studied the huge thing crouched before him.

Cameron let a laughing puff out from his nose, amused by the unquestioning compliance.

'You,' he said, 'Are a fucking idiot.'

Harvey, with impeccable comic timing, nodded his tiny, pointed head forward in agreement.

'Well, least you know it, I suppose.'

Reaching forward in a slow and steady, almost teasing motion, Cameron worked the latch with a thumb and forefinger. There was a tantalising *tink* as the steel caged door lifted and swung slowly open.

Cameron smiled blithely at a job-well-done, straightened up, turned, and left the room that little Merryn shared with her pet and loving friend, Harvey.

Upon entering his own bedroom, Cameron looked over Exit Wounds' three favourite spots: on the end of the bed; the windowsill; and finally, the amplifier. Sadly, the bloodthirsty huntsman was not in attendance. This disappointed Cameron deeply. He so wanted to tell the black fur clad ninja about his exploits, about the sport waiting to ensue across the landing.

Disappointment? Yes. Dejection? No. Exit would sniff Harvey-cock-knocker out from a country mile away. All was well. Just a matter of time. The next anyone would see of that goofy twat would be the little brownie-beige sack of his stomach, tacked with drying blood and lying without a host on the carpet. Cameron had witnessed from other kills that *that* bit was always left over. He neither knew nor cared why, as long as he got to see this one.

Maybe I'll find it first, Cameron surmised, *then I can make chilli con carne for Dad and the girls, with an extra kidney bean that's better than all the other kidney beans in the tin.* He began to salivate at the idea, greedily yearning for it to pan out precisely this way. *A little game of Russian Roulette, only rather than a lone bullet, a Russian Rodent's last piece of remaining offal instead.*

Cameron threw himself on the bed, covers bursting up around him, contented as a schoolboy finding his first discarded porno mag in a hedgerow.

He awoke an unknown amount of time later to an ear-splitting scream. In his confused, half-asleep state, Cameron wondered what in the world could have brought such terror to a person, to force that pitch on an otherwise tranquil Sunday afternoon here on the listless, off-season Beach Road.

A baleful smile grew on his sadistic chops as the world trudged back into focus, recollection working in his mind.

Quick work, Exit, me ol' pal.

Staving off the feeling of elation and trying to hold onto to at least an ounce of composure, Cameron got up. He glanced expeditiously into his mirror, making sure his false-concern countenance was passable. Of course it was, his duplicity was staggering.

Mask on, he rushed to the source of the screaming: Merryn's bedroom.

Thunderous footsteps boomed up the staircase and Andrew appeared at its summit, so fast it seemed he arrived ahead of the noise created by his heavy footsteps. Kerenza arrived a split second later, like the two were bound by a tow rope.

Awesome, Cam delighted. *Full house.*

Merryn came darting out of her room and threw herself at her daddy, screams turning to sobs as she clung to him as desperately as a limpet to a rock. Andrew tried his best to sooth her, smoothing his hand down her mousy-brown hair in reassuring strokes. Motioning with his head, he silently instructed Cameron to go and look in her bedroom. Cameron did this eagerly, a fervent desire to observe the destruction one small kitty could cause to a helpless, pathetic ball of fur. *I tawt I taw a putty tat*, he thought, stifling laughter.

He studied the floor. Zip, nada. No carcass; no bone fragments; no hair; no guts; and ultimately, no glory. The only thing out of place on the baby-pink carpet, a Charlie and Lola book lying in abandonment, open and face down.

He leaned back through the doorway. Obtaining Andrew's attention, he lowered his dark eyebrows in a clueless expression.

'Settle down, squirt,' Andrew said quietly. 'What's got you all scared?'

'Sss, ssp,' Merryn stuttered, snivelling into her dad's midriff. 'Spider.'

'*SPIDER!*' Cameron demanded, looking back into his little sister's bedroom, eyes fixing on the hamster's cage. The steel wire door was latched closed. Harvey slept in a curled ball nuzzled into his bed of shredded paper, belly gently rising and falling with each tiny breath.

Andrew couldn't help but laugh. 'All this for a little spider? It's probably more afraid of you than you are of it.'

'It's the biggest I ever seed,' Merryn exclaimed, pulling her head back to look desperately at her father. 'It ran under my bed.'

Andrew wiped a salty tear from her cheek with the pad of a thumb. 'Okay, okay. Cam, think you can handle it, superhero?'

Cameron sighed, offering no sign that he was going to cooperate.

Kerenza said, 'Want me to do it, Scaredy-Cat?' Her voice was heavily mocking.

'Grow up, retard!' Cameron snapped back. He disappeared into Merryn's room. Thirty seconds later he re-emerged with one fist clenched, heading to the bathroom. His leg deliberately barged

Andrew's side as he passed. The next sound to be heard, other than his footsteps and Merryn's shallow sobs, was the rushing water of the cistern, carrying an eight-legged terror off to the sewers.

'Not too big to flush then?' Andrew asked with a grin.

'No bigger than a penny,' replied Cameron, his face a picture of annoyance.

'You killed it?' Merryn trilled, sounding even more upset.

Can't fucking win, thought Cameron. 'Don't worry, it'll live,' he told her. 'Next time you wash your hands it'll climb up through the plughole and bite your finger off.'

'That's not helpful,' Kerenza reprimanded.

Cameron made his way bullishly down the stairs, almost knocking Kerenza over in the process.

'Watch it!' She blared.

She watched him with exasperated eyes until he reached the bottom of the stairs, where he turned and flipped her the bird.

Disappearing from sight, Cameron contemplated his next move. Could he get away with opening the furry little bastard's cage again? Probably not. Too obvious. He needed a plan *B*. But that was okay, there was always plenty of fun to be had in concocting ways to fuck people over. Hell, it could often provide almost as much enjoyment as the *act* itself. Almost, but not quite. Nothing could really live up to the allure of an anguished face when a cleverly devised plan transfigured into a gloriously executed reality.

Moments later the deadened clap of the front door hitting the jam came reverberating up the stairs. All three of the figures on the landing jerked simultaneously.

Andrew looked bemusedly at Kerenza. 'Gonna need a rubber door after today. Coffee?'

'Yeah, sounds good?'

'Cherry Bakewell from the posh one in town, or cheap instant?'

'Deffo the cherry,' Kerenza replied, with a smile broadening on her face. 'Gimme five and I'll be down. Hey, Merr the bear, we didn't feed your little friend this morning. I'll get the grub ready; you go fill his water bottle up.'

The girls trotted off happily to do their duties, the neurotic antics they had just witnessed soon fading into forgotten, irrelevant history. Andrew headed back down the stairs, wincing at the pain in his knees. Still riddled with aches and pains after his unfortunate stunt in the studio, and a tapestry of bruises covering his body, he guessed it may be a while before he was his true self again.

When he arrived in the quiet kitchen, he went through the motions in a contented daze. As the kettle tickled and tinkered on the range's hotplate, he gazed out at the low bank of grey clouds amassing over the garden. The covering darkened the tops of the trees to a silhouette black. Losing its light early, the departing day left sombre shadowy spectres over the land.

In defiance of the darkening gloom, cheerful footsteps danced through the ceiling. The cheerful noises from above – along with the chance-meeting that afternoon – afforded him the realisation that, although he thought his whole life had been stolen from him that dirty, deplorable day back in February, there was still a hope that he would live again. Just maybe, he would not have to trudge through a meaningless existence.

Low at first but steadily increasing, the tinnitus whistle of the kettle wrestled Andrew from his reverie. He moved away from the window and lifted the kettle from the hotplate, placing it on the worn and faded red cast iron cooling rack. He poured the boiled water into the cafetiere, a sweet cherry aroma started to dominate the homely kitchen.

Resuming his previous pastime of gazing dreamily out of the window, Andrew took in the transitioning of day to night. Threatening winter appeared to literally leap-frog autumn and bully the tired summer into submission. Anthracite clouds had gained in velocity across the sky. Leaves that waltzed a lethargic emerald green mere hours before, now blackened and upped the tempo to a passionate Paso Doble.

Above the rustle of leaves on the trees and the bountiful bushes of the cottage's garden, the rolling waves of Trevaunance Cove could now be heard, a charging cavalry galloping in and storming the shores from the North Atlantic Ocean.

Didn't hear about this coming in, Andrew contemplated. *Really should watch more* news *and* factual, *rather than people being stitched together ass-to-face by a crazy German.*

Not so deep in his conscious mind, however, he knew this thought would not morph into actuality. He decided long ago that fictional horror and fantasy was so much easier to deal with than arduous fact and reality.

Jesus, man. No wonder Cam's turning weird, with me as a role-mo___

'Boo!' Kerenza's voice sprang from the cavity behind him, striking at his consciousness like a funnel-web spider.

'Bloody hell!' Andrew snapped, whirling around. 'You scared the life out of me.'

The two girls were both sitting at the table, eyeing him with amused expressions. Merryn had her rosy cheeks resting in her hands, a neat line of white teeth visible between pink grinning lips.

'When did you pair sneak in?'

'About ten minutes ago,' answered Kerenza, casting a forbidding glance at her half-sister.

'One minute ago,' Merryn argued.

'Shush, you,' Kerenza scolded in jest. 'You can't keep quiet about anything, can you?'

Merryn gave an embarrassed giggle, burrowing her chin into her chest.

'Not from your old man, can you, squirt.'

'I will if you keep calling me *that*,' Merryn chastised back, folding her arms and slamming them against her belly.

Andrew apologised with a gentle bear hug and kissed the spongy hair at the top of her head. Releasing his youngest from his grip, he poured two coffees, and a hot chocolate for Merryn.

'I've gotta say, guys,' Andrew said as he added milk to Kerenza's coffee, 'I can*not* be bothered to cook tonight; question is, Chinese or Indian?'

A sudden fizzing sound interrupted the conversation, causing every pair of eyes to dart towards the darkening window. A heavy spray of droplets rapidly coated the outside of the pane, cascading down in waterfalls. In a flash of fireworks, the droplets lit and sparkled golden as a single headlight fired across the glass, turning blood-red as a brake light followed. In an instant, the scene dragged Andrew harrowingly back to that February morning, when analogous claret flowed in vertical torrents over the panels of his wife's abandoned Ibiza.

'Chinese,' said Kerenza, reclaiming his attention. 'You don't wanna be going Perran in this.'

'And I don't like Injun,' Merryn added.

'You like their chicken and chips,' Andrew counteracted. Looking over to Kerenza, now. 'And I don't mind going there, it's not far.'

'Well, I'm happy with eith___'

'*WHAT THE FUCK?*' came a shout, as the door crashed open.

'Whoa, no '*F*' words,' Andrew warned, as Cam stood wringing wet and dripping water all over the floor.

'Shit, sorry, didn't see her there,' Cameron said as his gaze found Merryn. The young girl sat at the table bulging eyes, both hands covering her mouth in shock.

'And no '*S*' words either,' said Andrew in despair.

'Bollocks okay?' Cameron asked sincerely.

Andrew chose not to answer that one, opting instead to ask the topical question. 'Indian or Chinese?'

'Not Chinky.'

'Charming,' said Andrew. 'Indian it is then. 'We'll phone them through. Merrs, I'll pick up your Chinese on the way back though.'

CHAPTER EIGHTEEN

Twenty minutes later, Andrew ran hunched over with one soaked arm shielding his face. The driving rain delivered a constant assault, leaving rivers flanking the roadsides and drenching his legs as he misjudged the leap to the opposing pavement.

Only two weeks ago, this seasonal getaway buzzed and flourished with migrating sunseekers. Summer air had hung heavy with the scent of factor thirty and countless varieties of ice creams and sorbets. Every voice boasted thick, out-of-county accents: Scousers; Mancunians; Brummies; Cockneys, all descending to the beach, the streets, and the bars.

Everywhere you looked was shorts, sunglasses and sandals. Wetsuits and women in skimpy bikini tops (some of them little more than thin connecting string and small triangles of spandex just big enough to modestly cover their nipples).

Apart from the obvious – gender – there had been two other defining body types on show: the trim and sculptured bronze – men and women alike – mostly covered in dark, cultural tattoos; and the pale and waxy crew, with massive, hairy bellies overhanging Hawaiian-themed board shorts of varying pineapple, flamingo and palm tree designs. Each step taken rippled their guts like pizza dough (men and women again alike). Sunburned shoulders the colour of cooked lobsters seemed ready to split and perish on many, straining under the slightest movement as if butterfly wings were about to break free of the dry casing, metamorphosing these human larvae.

Just two weeks before, you could walk no further than ten metres along the crowded street without some gobby little brat near taking your eye out with the bamboo handle from a fishing net or scraping your knee with the sharp edge of a cheap, plastic bucket.

The next thing you feel is the slap of a bellyboard as some kid span to look greedily into a shop window like it's Willy fucking Wonka's or something. Parents would mouth off at them, occasionally clapping the palm of a hand across the back of their head for an accumulation of *can I haves*.

Now though, holiday season had come to its abrupt annual termination. All was as it would remain until the Easter break of next year: a dormant, desolate and forlorn ghost town, the spirits of summers past being flushed down the storm drains as the bitter, lashing rains washed the streets clean. The echoes of shrill children's laughter and joyful sunshine screams. The *chinks* of glasses and bottles from beer gardens as crowds merrily toasted the days of their lives. The deep boom of live music and the cheers of partying people. All of that, now falling into the Perrancoombe Stream, hastily being dragged out to sea, submerging, and drowning in a watery grave.

Many of the buildings lay abandoned and shuttered this evening. Those without shutters stood solemnly with vacant black glazed eyes scrutinising anything that moved. The sweet ice cream fragrances of raspberry, blackcurrant, toffee apple and salted caramel, had been superseded by the claggy, gritty odour of fresh rain on sun-scorched tarmac; a smell that had always tormented Andrew's olfaction, though for some reason had given Shona a peculiar sort of satisfaction.

Reaching the door to his preferred Indian restaurant – this slight strip of a coastal tourist town somehow managed to harbour two, even throughout the desperate and dreary off-seasons – Andrew clutched the cold, wet handle of the uPVC door. In his hand it felt frozen and slick, like a dead fish from a crate of ice.

Instantaneously upon entering, seductive fragrances and warm air welcomed him, embracing like the arms of a long-lost lover. He had always been drawn to the more authentic and less contemporary vibe offered at this restaurant.

Shaking himself like a wet dog in the entry porch, Andrew made his way through the next glass panelled door, leaving dark impressions on the deep red, regal carpet as he went.

Culinary perfumes hit him with divine intensity: cardamom; cumin; coriander; chilli; turmeric; tandoori marinade, all combining to make the restaurant's array of sauces a behemoth from the Indian subcontinent. The scents forbade entry to the pungent, grimy stench issuing from the pavements outside.

Looking ahead, Andrew's clearing vision was met by the familiar dark complexion and welcoming smile of one of the waiters. A tall man, well built with a ring of silver hair around the back and sides of his substantial head. The light above reflected glaringly off the bald top of his head. The only thing giving more shine on his person were his black shoes, highly polished to a military standard.

Andrew scanned the surrounding area. To his right, a couple – late sixties or early seventies, at a guess – were the only patrons currently in attendance. Few others would brave going out on such a grim night. They looked to be enjoying the exclusivity of the setting. Newly retired, maybe, down for a break after the hordes of holidaymakers had made their mass exodus.

Loves old dream, Andrew mused.

He salivated at the site of the well-stocked table that stood between the old romantics. Chunks of meat sat in a rich dark sauce, dark green chillies showing here and there; naan breads; onion bhajis; pakoras and samosas. *Bloody hell they're making the most of this!* A wine glass and a beer glass sat next to the bounteous plates of food, both half-full, *like their outlook on life, no doubt.*

Mesmerised, Andrew watched the two-way flow of traffic on the beer glass, condensation running down the outside while bubbles navigated their way up through its golden interior.

'Good evening, Mr Tredinnick,' came the voice of the waiter in his smooth, rounded Bangladeshi accent.

'It is now,' said Andrew, returning the smile.

'It's good to see you again. Such pleasant weather you've brought with you, too.'

They shared a laugh and the usual small-talk, before the waiter turned for the kitchen to fetch the order.

As Andrew waited patiently, he took in a statue on a countertop in the waiting area. The Hindu Goddess – which one, Andrew would not profess to know – eyed him in unmoving silence. Although the colours of India had always enticed him, along with the noise and the hustle and bustle as busy streets accommodated various celebrations, Andrew had a limited knowledge of the religions and the cultures. Shona was more enthralled, however, and had made a conscious effort to read up on rituals of the country. A visit to India floated high on her bucket list.

That bucket's been well and truly kicked, Andrew rued, closing his eyes with a slight shudder.

'Sir? Your order.'

Rolling his head to the voice and opening his eyes, Andrew spied the full carrier of mouth-watering delights. He took the bag, the two men giving their *thanks* and offering their *see-you-again-soons.* Andrew then headed back out into the hostile night.

The B3285 from Perranporth to St. Agnes was a far cry from a great road, at the best of times. The usual decision of threading the passenger seatbelt through the handle of takeaway bag and clipping it in proved to be a sensible one. Embarking on the steep, curving climb (a feature of so many coastal towns and villages), the road straightens, filling you with a false impression of openness and encouraging the heavy footed to go for it. And that is exactly what Andrew would do whenever he was alone in the car, provided there was no doddery old fart in front of him holding the world up.

Driving conditions never entered the equation.

Swinging the wheel as the relative straightness turned to canned spaghetti, he would tackle a sharp right vigorously into a dip. Then, with a reverse throw of steering wheel, the car would sway like a tugboat, bend after dizzying bend. Here, unsuspecting speeders can swiftly find themselves stoved into a rugged Cornish hedge, or maybe even in a garden belonging to one of the sparsely situated houses that bordered the roadside.

It was on that first sharp left, with whipping rain lashing at the crossover's windscreen, that Andrew's screeching nearside tyre tore into it. Unseen in the darkness, headlights failing to differentiate one wet surface from another, a huge dark puddle breached almost half of the road. Wrestling the steering wheel from his grip, standing water sucked the vehicle in, sending the Nissan careering towards a curbed grass verge.

Regaining enough purchase to reverse the lock at the vital moment, Andrew managed to cut back and enter the proceeding sharp right. Both front tyres howled like their lives depended on it, stress and strain close to overpowering them. They held as the road briefly slimmed to single-track. Constellations flashed up on the windscreen as a hundred-thousand droplets lit under the glare of oncoming headlights, appearing as sudden as a lightning strike. Andrew stabbed desperately at the central pedal. Brake callipers applied urgent pressure to the four sets of pads, clamping them to vented cast iron discs.

Correcting the oversteer, he married the direction of the wheels with the road. Flooring the accelerator, Andrew avoided the oppositions wing mirror by mere millimetres as he shot off.

Once the devilish glow of brake lights disappeared behind another bend, Andrew eased his foot off from the throttle a touch. He glanced over at the passenger seat, confirming that the Indian takeaway had survived. Now, just to make it home in one piece and enjoy it.

Decelerating down into the village – *Twenty is Plenty*, the signs confirmed – he rolled the Nissan towards a mini roundabout. On his right, the Tappy, with its burnt orange façade and its flamboyant foliage, glowed welcomingly with tropical promise. The outer decking was empty of drinkers for the first time that Andrew could remember (during opening hours, anyway), and the array of lights twinkled and sparkled on the road's black and aqueous surface.

Straight ahead, looming over the faded white paint of the roundabout, the Chinese restaurant and takeaway looked down from its lofty perch.

'Thank the Lord I have to pass it,' Andrew laughed, admitting to himself that he had completely forgotten about Merryn's food.

Once collected, he skipped down the shiny, wet steps and returned to his car. Reversing out of the parking space with a bump from the raised platform, he pulled slowly forward, took the hairpin left, and headed behind the restaurant and down Quay Road.

Darkness consumed the way ahead. Manually flicking the headlights on to full-beam – believing that his own reactions were sharper than the automobile's automatic sensors – a hulking figure was instantly illuminated only yards in front of him.

The figure – a man, Andrew assumed by the character's build – flung an arm up over his face; possibly shielding his eyes from the blinding lights; possibly because he thought that the vehicle would strike him. Whether he thought his arm would help fend off the block of metal, or whether he just did not want to witness his own demise, is anybody's guess. He wore a thick jacket that ran down to his knees, his clothing so wet that every item looked heavy as stone. A bulky hood obscured the already limited amount of face that Andrew was able to glimpse around the raised arm. All that could be seen of its features was one reddened eye peering through the crook of their elbow.

With less than a second to spare, Andrew jerked the steering wheel – for what felt like the hundredth time this evening – and narrowly avoiding killing the scruffy looking lump of pedestrian.

Continuing the steady descent towards the ocean, Andrew strained his eyes at the rear-view mirror, hoping to clarify its emptiness. He was unable to fathom why he so desperately wanted to avoid viewing the stranger's face.

It must have been the eye. I mean, no one in their right mind would want to face the scrutinising stare of someone they had almost smashed into an early grave. *But that one red eye.* And to Andrew, it *was* red, not just bloodshot but pure, demonic *red*. A ridiculous notion, he knew that; but Andrew believed real malevolence pulsated at its core.

In the pissing, miserable, persistent rain, Raymond stood watching the dark body and diminishing rear lights of the arty-farty asshole's vehicle. The vehicle that almost ended him so conclusively, meandered down the road, fading from sight but not from mind. He smiled wildly throughout the short ordeal.

CHAPTER NINETEEN

A smug detective interrogated some halfwit in a drab interview room on the television screen. Andrew, Cameron and Kerenza sprawled out uncomfortably on the living room furniture, only half taking in the drama, wishing they had learned lessons in the past with regards to overeating.

The figure in the road repeatedly pushed his grotesque form to the forefront of Andrew's consciousness. Though he could not quite discern why, he avoided explaining what had happened to the others.

Thud.

Upstairs, Merryn bounded around, supposedly getting ready for bed. *'School in the morning,'* Andrew and Kerenza had reminded her, more than once each.

Thud.

'Where's that banging coming from?' Kerenza asked the other two.

'That rat, upstairs,' Cameron replied, uninterested.

'Harvey doesn't make that noise,' Kerenza pointed out.

'Not *that* rat, the other one,' said Cameron.

'Be nice to your sister,' warned Andrew, without any real conviction.

'*Be nice to your sister,*' squeaked Cameron, nasally.

'Grow up,' Kerenza said. *Thud.* 'There it goes again!'

Andrew said, 'Cam, turn the telly down a mo.'

Cameron let out a sigh that pleaded *get off my case*, yet he complied with the request.

'Merrs, you okay up there, honey?' Andrew called up to the ceiling.

'Yes, Daddy,' the muffled response came through the floor.

'Are you making that banging noise?' Andrew kept his voice raised.

'No-oh.'

Andrew turned his attention from the ceiling to Kerenza, creasing his face up, looking baffled.

Thud.

Cameron was about to re-thumb the remote control's mute button and fire the sound back into life, but stopped mid-motion as he now heard it for himself.

Thud.

Thud.

Thinking for a second, remote paused in suspension, he decided to fire the sound back anyway.

Kerenza continued on the subject. 'I think it's coming from the window. Behind you, Cam.'

'You might be right,' replied Andrew. 'It's shut, though. And the curtain isn't moving.'

'If you two fannies are so worried about it,' Cameron interjected, 'Go and have a look, rather than sitting here shitting yourselves?'

'I don't see you rushing to check, hard man!' Kerenza said, lowering herself to Cameron's level with the name calling.

'I'm not rushing cos I don't give a fuck what it is,' he said.

Thud.

'Give it a rest, you two,' urged Andrew. 'I'll go!'

'You stay put,' Kerenza ordered, 'I'll look, I'm getting up to get a drink anyway.'

'D'ya wanna grab the poker, Wonder Woman?' asked Cameron, nodding towards the open fireplace. 'You never know who could be there looking in at you. Maybe Raymondo's heard you're the village bike and he's come for a ride.'

'That's enough!' Andrew raised his voice again, this time at his son.

'Fuck off, you vile little creature,' Kerenza snapped at Cameron, apologising to her stepdad immediately for her foul language.

'No need to apologise,' said Andrew.' That was out of order.'

Thud.

Kerenza stopped for a few seconds, hands on curtains whilst taking a deep breath, doubting her own fortitude. What if there was a face looking back at her from the other side of the glass; the dirty, stormy night running in wet tendrils down its ugly features? She'd seen an old horror film from the eighties (long before she was born, so the visual effects were questionable in her critic's mind, but it was one of those films that, once seen, you would never forget). In that film, hordes of decomposing, murderous pirates came out of a thick fog that rolled in from the sea, just like the fogs that sometimes descended on this very property. They would hack the residents of the coastal town to pieces with swords and hooks. Anyone who got in their way was dispatched with the bloodiest of ease. Obviously, it was farfetched, inconceivable bullshit, but…but.

Thud.

Living in this unlit valley during a storm can shepherd one's rationale completely into doubt. If there was a fog outside the window when she braved herself to pull the curtains open, or even a light sea mist for that matter, it may just be enough to send her into hysterics.

Sensing his stepsister's discomfort at completing such a straightforward task, and putting aside the current feelings of bitterness he harboured for her, Cameron sprang to his feet.

'Right, ya fuckin' dildo,' he sneered. 'You grab that one, I'll get this one,' he said, taking the right curtain out of her hand. 'On three, okay?'

Kerenza started as another *thud* issued from directly behind the curtains. 'Okay,' she said, her voice faint, sounding as if it came from another room.

'Okay. One…'

A nod of her blonde head confirmed that it was okay to continue the count.

'Two…'

Thud.

A look of uncertainty was replicated on each face as they eyed each other.

'Three.'

Cameron held off momentarily, waiting anxiously for the first move to come from Kerenza.

She remained frozen, looking at him with those gorgeously seductive, clear-blue eyes.

'Fuck this,' he said, fighting himself from their magnetism. He grabbed the other curtain from her hand and flung them theatrically open.

At first, all they could see in the black sections of the sash window were their own reflections, the individual sections of glass like a sliding puzzle that had been solved but offered only half the picture. As their vision redirected its focus and transfixed the confusion of reflections and lights, shadows started to take shape.

A fine, vertical line of silvery steel moved pendulum-like in the wind, flashing at varying heights as light from the curtainless window caught and lost its cutting path.

Bewilderment swamped Cameron's mind as it struggled to process the information relayed from his ocular senses. His facial expression displayed his clear incomprehension. The shining metal line was his missing guitar string. But what was it doing there?

As his eyes became more acclimatised to the conditions, through the murky gloom Cameron could just make out that the string was nailed to a tree branch at the rear of the cottage. Following it down, it seemed to disappear into nothingness.

Wrong. Not *nothingness.*

Materialising out of the black hole world beyond the glass, was a form, elongated and limp. Soggy, rain caked black fur plastered a lifeless carcass; its only movements induced by the current climate.

Another gust of wind came, bringing the hanging monstrosity closer to the water-streaked windowpanes.

Thud.

The thing backed away again, pivoting slightly on its axis, and headed back to the glass.

Thud.

This time, as it hit the unmoving barrier with the same deadened noise that they had been hearing for some time now, Cameron could see the faded, accusing yellow eyes of Exit Wounds looking back at him.

As the hard-man fought to repress a rising rage that burned like ulcers in his gut, Kerenza reached a hand to his, covering her mouth with her other. Her baby finger made a fleeting contact with the soft pad on the side of his left hand. He pulled away. Clenching his fists, his eyes simmered red with rage.

CHAPTER TWENTY

Drizzling rain came down slow and thick. It was times like these – plodding along and skirting the range of puddles as best she could whilst holding her jacket over her head – that Grace wished she didn't live within walking distance of school. She tried her best to ignore the passing busses taking dry kids home, keeping her focus on the sodden pavement below her feet.

A tinny buzz rattled past, decreasing in pitch as a motorbike churned up the grass verge and mounted the pavement. It came skidding to a stop ten yards in front of her. Instantly, Grace recognised both bike and rider. Shyly, she put her face back to the floor and squeezed past him, making the passage look more difficult than it was.

'Oi!' the rider called out.

Grace turned as the lad on the motorbike removed his helmet. 'Oh, hiya.'

'Thought it was you,' said Cameron. 'Recognise those legs anywhere.' His grin oozed hunger and intent.

'You know you're not allowed that thing on the pavement?' she returned, cheeks starting to blush.

'This? It's a cycle path. I'm on a cycle.'

'Right. Well, see ya,' she said, turning away.

'Wait up,' Cameron called, reaching behind him and working on a bungee elastic. Bringing his arm back around, Grace could see that he was clutching a spare helmet.

'It's only a five-minute walk,' Grace informed him.

'And it's a thirty second ride,' he returned. 'Course, could be longer, if you're up for it?'

Grace eyed him, wishing she could gain an insight into the dastardly workings of his brain. She had every notion that the *'longer one'* had nothing to do with the bike. In the end she convinced herself that he would not be interested in her *that* way. After too long of hanging around with the popular blonde, playing second fiddle, more or less, Grace's opinion of herself was low where *boys* were concerned. *Though he did mention my legs,* she thought hopefully.

'You're not getting any drier,' Cameron prompted, snapping her out of her reverie.

'The thirty seconds will do,' she said, spotting what she hoped was a camouflaged look of disappointment on his face. 'For now.'

She lowered her jacket back into its intended position, grabbed the helmet and slipped it on. As she climbed onto the back of the bike, Cameron felt an instant pang in his groin. She slid one narrow thigh either side of his and wrapped her arms around his waist. After enjoying the feeling for a brief moment, he checked his mirror, tapped the bike into gear, and shot back over the low verge into the flow of traffic.

As he took a left into Grace's estate, he pulled up on the side of the road and asked which way. Like he didn't know. Truth is, he'd already done a recce of the area, knowing that somewhere around here he would spot a certain silver saloon, de-badged and dropped to the floor.

'Next right, next left,' came the muffled voice from inside the helmet behind him.

He pulled out again, zipped through the right-turn, then the left. Stopping again outside of her driveway, he cut the power and removed his helmet.

'Vibrations make you cream yer knickers?' Cameron asked, as Grace struggled off the back of his seat.

'No, but thanks for checking,' she smiled back, taking off her helmet and handing it to him.

'I didn't, I just asked,' he said. 'I can check?'

'I think I'll be fine,' she was blushing heavily now, her breath erratic. 'Thanks, though; for the ride I mean.'

Securing the helmet with the bungee once more, he turned back to Grace, who had resumed using her coat as a shield for her dark hair.

'Thanks. Is that it?' he asked earnestly.

'What else?' Grace asked, a nervous waver issuing with her voice.

Cameron turned his face slightly away from her and tapped his cheek twice with a forefinger. Grace breathed a quiet laughter through her nose as she cottoned onto the meaning of the gesture. Leaning in, she gave him the peck he was after.

'See ya 'round,' he said, charming her with his smile before covering his head again with the helmet. Kickstarting the KMX back to life, he shouted over the revs, *Same time tomorrow.*

Before Grace could respond, he released the clutch and spun the bike around, leaving a circle of rubber on the wet surface of the road before zooming off. She stood in the rain, grinning and breathing deeply, watching him until he disappeared around the bend.

Once the bike was out of site, she turned and ran up the drive with her face to the floor and her soaked jacket flying like a cape above her head. Through the door and up the stairs, she was wondering how much to tell her friend, Kerenza. Just about the lift? Or the flirting as well? The kiss on the cheek? Maybe not *that* bit; it was just a peck, after all.

'What were you doing with him?

Jack was stood between his bedroom door and hers, barring her way to sanctuary. His arms were folded, his lips pressed firmly in a tight seam, unimpressed.

'With who?' Grace asked, already kicking herself for such a lame response.

'Don't be stupid, Grace, Tredinnick?'

'It's pissing down with rain. He was passing and offered me a lift. So I took it.'

'Always carry a spare helmet, does he?'

'How should I know?' said Grace. 'Anyway, what are you getting at?' She thought she already knew the answer to that.

'He passed you, by chance, and coincidently had a spare to get you on that piece of shit?' Jack's chest was starting to heave now as he grilled her.

'It's not a piece of shit,' she huffed back, unsure why she was so quick to defend it.

'He's trouble. You're not hanging around with him.'

Finding a rare inner bravery way beyond her meek and mousy persona, Grace straightened herself into a challenging, defiant posture. 'You don't even know him, you haven't seen him for years. And you don't get to make that decision!'

'I know him well enough to know he's the same *wanker* he was in school!' Jack barked at her.

Grace had heard enough. She shoved her way past her brother with some effort – the size difference was quite staggering. Flinging her bedroom door open, she flew through and slammed it shut behind her. Jack stood riveted to the floor, face red and nostrils flaring.

CHAPTER TWENTY-ONE

Clawing around in her bag next to the busy A390, Grace fished out her mobile phone. Time check: 15:47.

She had finished school over twenty minutes ago but hadn't been concerned with heading home: the promise of second outing on the older lad's motorbike was too much to not get more than just a little excited over.

Having observed the time, however, she was beginning to feel a touch on the foolish side. As if Cameron would really be interested in her, I mean seriously: arms and legs as skinny as pipe cleaner, only thankfully not so furry; chicken fillet breasts; ghostly pale skin; dishevelled brunette hair, kept short to give the impression of it being better maintained; and a frenzy of freckles, the ground zero appearance at least detracting from how corpse-white the girl's complexion really is.

Only minor scatterings of kids were in close proximity – the club and detention skippers, the dossers with no real reason to rush on home, the smokers hanging around in sooty clouds of aerosol.

Anyone who caught a school bus was already well on their way home. On spotting the cream and blue coach with *208* printed on card in the windscreen, Grace turned her back and busied herself with nothing in her bag, hoping not to get collared by Kerenza. She had decided to tell her friend about the lift but had scrimped on both detail of that trip, and the prospect of hooking up again today. The fact that the boy in question was her besties stepbrother made Grace feel a little awkward. Also, something about Cameron kept her on edge; made her feel tense. It was a *good* tense, nonetheless, tense all the same. So, unsure of how he would react to her being loose lipped, remaining quiet had seemed for the best.

Another press at the side of her phone, waking up the sleeping screen. 15:56.

Stood up.

Returning her mobile to the bag at her feet, contemplating the lonely walk home and the sombre thoughts that would fill her head in the silence of her bedroom, a tell-tale rattle of a bike engine came from behind. Raising her head, fringe flicking in her eyes as it caught in the breeze, Grace peered along the road in the direction she had come from. To her relief, along with the dawning realisation of exactly how much she had wanted this, a familiar rider approached.

'Was beginning to think you found something better to do,' she said, as the motorbike came to rest next to her. 'I was about to give up on you and go home.'

'And cry?' Cameron smiled at her, cockily.

'Not that *that's* any of your business, but no. You're not that much of a catch.'

Cameron spotted what he hoped was a playful look in her eyes. 'Nothing better to do than you,' he returned, pleased to acknowledge the white behind the freckles turn a firestorm red. 'Any time you need to be home by?'

'Not really,' Grace said, turning her attention to the floor whilst trying to compose herself.

'Good,' he said, reaching for the spare helmet before lifting it towards her. 'Hop on.'

After shouldering her bag and slipping the helmet on – burning up as Cameron gently adjusted its strap for her – she did just that.

'What do I hold on to?' Grace asked. 'Your bag's kind of in the way.'

'Stick your thumbs through me belt loops. You can press your fingers down for grip, but don't let'em stray mind; I'm shy.'

'Shut up are you shy!' she blurted, taken aback by her own sudden confidence. She took advantage of this unusual moment of self-assuredness and threaded her thumbs through the loops of his jeans, letting her fingers nestle his groin.

The air was cool as they headed up the bypass, but the low sun to their left made the temperature bearable.

Carrying on, Cameron weaving through traffic on the single lane carriageway, they arrived at Chiverton Roundabout. The way was busy as always, forcing the couple to wait, and wait, and wait some more as the heavy stream of traffic from the A30 launched onto the roundabout, barring their passage. Finally, Cameron took his chance, pulling back hard on the KMX's throttle and darting through a tiny gap in front of a haulage truck. The bike's front tyre briefly left the surface of the road. Panicked, Grace jammed her fingers into Cameron as she fought against sliding from the rear of the seat and ending up as roadkill. The bright orange front of the tractor unit steamed closer; a glaring wall of steel pressing unstoppably on, air-horns blaring.

'*ARE YOU TRYING TO KILL ME?*' Grace screamed at the back of Cameron's head when they were safely past the truck's devouring metal jaws.

Cameron laughed, shouting back, '*SEE A HOLE, GOTTA FILL IT!*'

He exited the roundabout taking the St. Agnes turn, both rider and passenger leaning heavily to the left as he kept the speed high.

'You're not taking me to your house?' Grace asked, slightly concerned but also thankful that they both still had their lives intact.

'Chill,' he assured, trying to get his breathing under control. 'Gonna shoot off down the coast road.'

Although she had moved to Cornwall when she was too young to remember, Grace had never been down this stretch of the coast road. As they reached Atlantic View, she felt momentarily compelled to hold her breath, taken aback by the sight of the land falling away below them. Gorse and stony debris cascaded an ungaugable depth to quaint village, where beyond a series of white breakers charged through a deep blue rolling carpet, coming to rest in a splash on the sandy shoreline.

Turning a sharp left, the severity of the terrain forced Grace to ignore Cameron's impeding bag. She wrapped her arms around his middle, entwining her fingers as best she could. Fearful of being thrown over the front of the bike as the cracked and potholed road plummeted down into a valley, she closed her eyes, tight.

Cameron had finally reduced his speed, which was a blessing as far as Grace was concerned. She would never tell him – as that would not be cool – that there were several moments (one of which being whilst her eyes were bulging at the sight of the menacing black grill on the massive orange truck hurtling towards them) when she felt certain she would fill his spare helmet with vomit.

Reaching the base of the valley, Cameron leaned into a righthander. Correcting the angle of the bike, they began to ascend the other side.

They passed through another coastal village, this one complete with a harbour and a beach. After another nauseous moment, (this time down to a foul odour lingering around the place like an eggy fart in an elevator, rather than Cam's riding style), they climbed again. Soon becoming open and barren, the land spread out around them, appearing as vast and dramatic as a fantasy novel's landscape. Cameron once again put the bike's Hymenoptera-sounding engine through its paces.

Minutes later, they slowed passing a roadside café with a gritty car park. It looked strange and foreboding to Grace, hunkered alone in this desolate landscape. She was unnerved to realise that Cameron was swinging into a layby just beyond the building. Kicking down the stand, he silenced its insectile buzz.

'Off ya get, sweet cheeks,' Cameron said, patting Grace on the outside of her thigh as it rested against his own. 'We're here.'

'Where's *here*?' she replied, slightly on edge, head turning slowly from side to side.

'Never been to Hell's Mouth before?' Cameron asked.

'Hell's Mouth? You've brought me to Hell's Mouth?' Grace queried. 'Why, exactly?'

'It's romantic.'

'Romantic? Don't people come here to top themselves?'

'Amongst other things,' he grinned. 'Come on, we're going up there.' Cameron pointed up and to the right, where the cliff seemed to reach its crescendo.

He set off across the road, bag over one angular shoulder and helmet hanging at his side clutched in his left hand. Grace watched him reach the other side and trudge into the tufts of scrub, thinking how he looked the unlikeliest of hikers. Against her better judgement, she followed him over.

Cameron led the way up a narrow dirt path that cut off at the centre of what Grace assumed was the *Mouth* part, giving the option to head west or east. Both directions hugged the gaping crescent of cliff. Grace looked with trepidation at a low fence running along between the pathway – now only a few inches wide in places and consisting of what seemed a mixture of slightly sludgy sand and earth – and the drop. Fighting against the strong urge to turn around, she resisted, *don't want to look chicken*. She rested her knees against the sturdy, or at least what she hoped was sturdy, wooden bar. Leaning steadily forward, she afforded herself a breath-taking vista of a churning watery world below. Instantaneously, her brain was dizzied by the magnitude of the drop, though the foaming surf had an overwhelming mesmeric effect on her. As the sea tumbled and turned, a monstrous voice rumbled up and out of the mouth's rocky windpipe, reverberating in her head like thick blood pulsing rapidly though her cranial arteries.

In a flash she was lunging forward, the inadequate fencing too low to stay her. Grace was unable to throw herself back to safety, or even catch her balance.

'*SAVED YOUR LIFE!*' Cameron blared out as he grabbed the back of her jacket two-handed, shoving her forward before snapping her back again.

It took just a petrifying second for Grace's brain to discern what had just happened, but her lungs felt they had stopped breathing for an eternity.

'*YOU FUCKING BASTARD!*' she screamed at him, driving both clenched fists into his chest.

Cameron grabbed her wrists before a repeat impact hit home, laughing like a child might as a mate slipped from their pushbike saddle, agonisingly crunching their nuts on the frame as a result.

'Nice. Real funny!' Grace exclaimed, hurt and venomous eyes burning holes into his. Her heart was beating furiously within her tight ribcage.

'Simmer down. I was only messin' with ya,' Cameron said, not daring to release the agitated cobra neck he restrained in each hand.

A tense and almost passionate moment of silence hung between them. Grace finally broke it.

'I hate you!' she said, quietly and unconvincing.

'No you don't,' Cameron countered. 'If I let go of your claws, are you gonna play nice, pussycat?'

Taking her failure to answer as a positive response, he let go of her wrists and turned away from her.

They trundled on again along the narrow, irregular coast path, zigzagging as best they could to avoid twisting their ankles on scattered rocks and shallow pits. Grace lost her footing several times, flat-bottomed shoes slipping on ground that had not yet gotten over yesterday's deluge. The first time, Cameron's reactions had been akin to that of a light flyweight boxer, twisting as he threw out a hand and grabbing hers confidently. It was at that point, as Cameron moved to pull his hand away, that Grace tightened her grip and held on for the rest of the short stroll.

'This'll do,' said Cameron, leaving the path and stepping onto clumpy, grassy ground. He pulled her closer to the cliff edge.

Releasing her hand, he dropped to the floor. He shifted on his bony ass to get comfortable, gazing out to sea; nothing but the blue of the Atlantic and intermittent thin wisps of white cloud disappearing off to the horizon.

Grace noticed for the first time that there was no fence here.

'Is it safe?' she asked with a minor hesitancy in her voice.

'Yeah, totally,' he said, patting the springy grass next to him in invitation.

'We'll get soaked.'

'Nah, wind's been good here today and we're as high as we can get.' He gave her a reassuring smile, patting the ground once again. 'Park.'

'And you're sure it's safe?'

'Yes!'

She took a step forward and lowered herself to sitting next to him.

'I mean,' Cameron said, 'There was a landslide here a few days ago, but…'

Grace took his crooked, one-sided smile as a sign that he was messing with her head again.

Several minutes passed without a word, the only sounds being raucous sea and the shrill cries of the gulls. Sitting calmly, Grace noticed the coolness of the air and gave a little shiver, which didn't go unnoticed. Cameron lifted his left arm up and held it at ninety degrees to his body. After a dubious look of careful consideration, Grace remained as she was.

'D'ya want warmin' up or not?' he asked. 'No one here but you and me.'

That's what worries me, she thought, still thinking about the truck and his little prank at the fence. *Oh well, got to roll the dice sometimes. Odds or evens.*

She shuffled sideways and eased herself slowly under his welcoming arm. Despite the unease he had filled her with at times today, his hold felt like sanctuary. As she nestled in closer to his warmth, she envisaged steaming cups of soup on grey, wintry afternoons, with homely fragrances wafting up as raindrops tapped and trickled down the window. His deodorant was strong but not unpleasant. She liked it but couldn't place the brand. All she felt sure of was that it wasn't Lynx, like every boy at school lagged themselves in to toxifying levels. This, in her eyes, set him apart from the rest.

'Better?' Cameron asked her.

'Yeah,' came a timid reply. 'Thanks.' She gave him a smile that he took to mean he may be off the hook for his earlier indiscretion.

'Almost forgot,' he smiled back. 'I got something else to warm us up.'

Well, I guess that rules out you trying to get my clothes off, Grace thought, a little unsettled by the contrasting mixture of relief and disappointment she felt in equal measures.

Cameron leaned forward – not removing his arm from around her narrow frame – and fumbled the zip of his rucksack with his free hand. Once an adequate opening had been awkwardly established, he reached in. Searching blindly around in its dark cavity, he muttered something inaudible and fished out a large bottle of vodka.

Cameron clasped the bottle between his knees and broke the seal. 'You can have most of it, obviously, seeing as you're riding shotgun.'

'You trying to get me drunk?' Grace challenged.

'Do I need to?' Cameron smiled. He liked answering a question with a question; an effective way to avoid giving an answer.

Smirking back but saying nothing, she took the bottle, raised it to her wind-reddened lips and tipped her head back. A hot freeze alighted her throat and she stubbornly fought off the rising need to cough.

Cameron watched as the colour rose in her speckled cheeks and the sun glowed through her hair. Colours of orange and copper danced enchantingly over her darker base layer.

Shit.

Actually fancying her was never on the agenda, but that familiar tingling in his scrotum defied all choice in the matter.

Lowering her head and the bottle in perfect synchronicity, Grace handed the vodka back and wiped the moisture from her lips with the back of a cold hand, before slipping it behind him. His eyes never left hers as he took the bottle and glugged a mouthful, jammed it back between his knees and replaced the cap. Its dry scraping sound as it threaded its way down seemed enhanced as all his senses came alive with impeccable vividness.

He was still transfixed when she asked if he was okay. Cameron deflected the question again, only this time applying a different method. Leaning forward, penetrating eyes blazing, he placed his spirit-seared lips to hers.

Grace opened her mouth marginally, deepened the kiss. Closing her eyes, she let her tongue explore him as the vodka after-burn emanating from both mouths came together in a volcanic explosion. Moving his free hand closer, Cameron fumbled and found the opening at the bottom of Grace's untucked shirt. His touch was ice-cold as his fingertips made light contact with her bare skin. Having never had a boy place his hand in her midriff area before, Grace was too rapt in the moment to care. As Cameron slowly raised his hand, his fingers caught at Grace's pronounced lower rib.

Jesus, what the fuck is wrong with me? Cameron thought.

Skinny girls were never really his thing, yet at this point he was held hypnotised by the rises and falls of the terrain as her smooth skin clung tightly to the interior xylophone-like structure.

With a gargantuan effort, Cameron whipped his hand back from under the thin material, just as the extent of his middle finger brushed the synthetic fabric of Grace's bra.

'Sorry,' he said. He turned his head sharply away to gaze over the glistening water, unscrewing the cap from the bottle once more. 'Got a bit carried away.'

Grace plucked the vodka form his hand after he had taken a swig. 'It's okay,' she assured him, before placing her own stimulated lips to the bottle.

After adjudging her wait for an answer to be in vain, she leaned her head into the crook of Cameron's neck. He indulged in the scent of the sea spray particles floating in the air around them, mingled the sweetened coconut aroma of the shampoo in her waving cropped hair.

Both finding a distant point on the horizon to pay only casual attention to, using each other's bodies for warmth and support, the pair neither moved nor made a sound for the next thirty minutes.

Though in relationship terms they were effectively new acquaintances, the comfort in their lengthy silence was something that other couples may take years to achieve, if they ever could at all.

CHAPTER TWENTY-TWO

Darkness settled as a heavy veil over Cameron as he sat alone on the grassy clifftop; the same patch where he had sat only hours earlier with a slender-framed girl nestled into him. The bottle of vodka lay spent between his legs, its emptiness a metaphor for sentiments he now harboured.

He wished deeply that he did not have let her go. Sitting solitarily at the top of this infamous one way drop to the end of everything, this entrance to Hell, was doing him no good at all.

But…she had to go.

Mentioning Kerenza's mum had been the start of it. Although Grace knew that Shona had committed suicide by jumping from a cliff, she had never felt it necessary to force the terrible details from her grieving friend. Details, namely, the two *w's*. The *h* was covered; how. As for the *why* and the *where*, well that could just rest with the woman involved.

So, when Cameron covered the *where* without prompt, Grace had understandably found it a little disturbing.

'*Possibly at the fence where you leaned over, possibly right in front of us. I mean, this is the highest point, so it would make sense,*' is what he informed her.

Her noticeable tensing under his arm was a cue for him to stop. A cue he missed. So, not obliviously, but uncontrollably, he went on to the *how*. If the tide was out, her body would explode on impact with the rocks below, offal spilling out and steaming in the coolness of the early morning like minestrone soup, blah blah blah, sticking and drying out on the boulders, blah, ripped apart and feasted upon by the birdlife. He had gotten that nugget of information on good authority, so he had told her; knew one of the guys on the recovery team. Not from that day, but from other recovery missions.

That was when she asked him to take her home, using the excuse that her dad would be wondering where she was.

What the fuck did you go in with all the morbid shit for? Fucking dickhead.

Cameron had then angled for sympathy to get Grace back onside, offering a peek through the tiniest of windows at a vulnerability that guys like him would commonly keep under lock and key, fearing the mortal cost of any predator sensing weakness.

'I need to come here. It's too hectic at home to feel close to Shona. It's like this is the only place I can feel like she's still around. She was much more of a mum to me than the evil bitch *that dragged me up.'*

Grace loosened under his arm, looking into his eyes as liquid formed and glinted like drops of dew at the lower lids of her own.

She placed a hand to his face and gently kissed his lips, holding the contact just long enough to taste their saltiness from the clinging sea air. The kiss acted like a silent mutual agreement that that subject was, for the moment at least, closed.

That was a result. Everything was peachy again, and most importantly to Cameron, Grace would be leaving here under his terms, and not her own. Total control.

The swirling, strengthening wind licked up a fine haze of briny moisture. Chilling his face and his hands, it snapped him out of his meditation, awakening him to the fact that he was still alone.

Soon enough, memories of his mother came rolling into his mind like the waves below, beating against his brain as they thumped at the impenetrable rocks.

His brain, however, was not impenetrable. Constructed simply of soft matter, its attempts to fend off the sight of his mother were hopeless. The scars that his mother's *'moments of frustration'* left behind, both mental and physical, were here to stay.

Pinching him and telling him that he's ruined her life – *'Sorry, Cammie, Mummy had a moment of frustration.'* Clamping his nostrils between thumb and index finger, pressing her thin painted lips to his and exhaling plumes of cigarette smoke directly down his throat, until his coughing fit forced him free from her clutches – *'Sorry, Cammie, you know how you make Mummy have moments of frustration.'*

On one of those occasions, she had neglected to wipe the incriminating smears of lipstick from Cameron's face before Andrew arrived home. The man was obviously intrigued by the origin of such markings. In answer, the poisonous bitch reeled off a tale about how Cameron like to kiss his mum way too much, and that the filthy little pervert would need that disgusting behaviour slapping out of him.

Andrew, of course, would never condone slapping a child, though he was open to discussing alternative ways of handling such issues. *If* it persisted.

The boy, on the other hand, was assured that *Mummy* would squeeze his teeny-tiny balls (again), only this time she would not stop until they popped out their shrivelled little bag. All he had to do, to avoid losing his walnuts, was confirm her story if and when asked about it.

Neither Alison nor Cameron knew back then that it would be the last time she ever threatened to squeeze his teeny-tiny balls.

On the evening of the lipstick saga, the grownups had their serious *grownups chat*. Cameron had crept quietly from his bedroom to where the landing met the top of the stairs, hoping to listen in on anything else his mother might say about him. Leaning forward with extreme caution to spy a glimpse of proceedings, he peered through the banister's uprights. The lower halves of both parents came into view. They were sat on armchairs opposite each other, with a low mahogany coffee table between them. An opened bottle of red wine and two partially filled glasses occupied the table, along with the television remote, some unopened envelopes, a lighter and a packet of the revolting woman's ghastly cancer sticks.

He heard his mother's raspy smoker's voice first, telling his dad of what a nightmare their son had become; how he needed constant supervision, how he would lash out at her whenever she attempted to stop his inappropriate acts of affection. And how, in an act of defiance, he would proceed to break, or make as to break something to provoke a reaction from her. He was calculating, aiming to force her into taking action against him that she might later regret.

She never did, though. It took all of her resolve, but she never resorted to using physical punishment on her son. Even on the occasions where the little demon tried to slap or bite her.

Salt water trickled down Cameron's face and onto his top lip as Alison poured Andrew another glass of deep-red lies from the bottle.

Andrew sat thinking how his boy needed serious help, how they must have somehow failed him as parents.

Alison went on. *'And you don't help when it comes to The Boy's behavioural issues. He needs his father,'* she declared, her voice sharp with spite. *'You're never around to deal with him.'* This, Cameron would discover, would be the only honest part of her plea. *'Or to give me a break,'* she continued. *'God knows, I need a life, too.'*

Cameron saw his dad lean forward and place a tentative hand on the woman's knee.

'I know,' he confirmed. *'I'm so sorry. I have to step up and start putting the two of you first. Starting now. I'll cook for you tomorrow night, something posh for when Cammie's gone to bed. And you can see if any of the girls are free on Saturday, have a night out. I'll stay home, so no need for a babysitter.'*

Cameron saw his mum's hand landing on the back of his dad's, stroking and caressing. He could hear her gentle sobs. The snivelling sound made him wish that she would just disappear and leave him and his dad alone, forever.

'Sunday we could go for a walk,' Andrews's voice was warm and soothing. *'Just the three of us, take in a bit of the coast path. We can stop at Chapel Porth on the way back, get one of those* Hedgehogs *that you find so irresistible.'*

Alison gave a timid laugh at the suggestion and whispered an *'Okay.'*

Andrew leaned forward and Cameron heard the hideous wet sound of a kiss. One of their last. After sneaking back to bed, betrayed, hurt and angry, his parents finished the last of the bottle and did the same. That night Cameron heard the gross panting and puffing sounds that had not come through the wall for a long time. That was the very last time they made *those* noises together.

Alison Tredinnick did get to the coast on that warm and sunny Sunday. Thanks to an unwitnessed timely nudge from her young son, however, as she leaned over the gaping cavern of Hell's Mouth to look for seals, she never did get the promised *Hedgehog* ice cream that she was so looking forward to.

CHAPTER TWENTY-THREE

Mr Grayson stood with his backside propped against his desk, arms folded, and wiry eyebrows raised in bemusement. His eyes lay fixated on one student in particular.

Is this what my life has amounted to?

He'd been talking for fifteen minutes straight (or what may as well have been fifteen days), about the basics of trigonometry. Trig was a branch of mathematics Grayson thought he would never tire of. Explaining it to these deadheads, however, awoke in him the startling realisation that he was boring, his job was shite, and that at the age of fifty-two he had casually wasted his one-time-only existence.

Other children in the class took in his buffaloed expression and turned their heads towards the object of his nonplussed gaze. A few sniggers escaped around the classroom, yet the girl with the mobile phone in her hand remained blissfully unaware.

Grayson sighed, shook his head, and wondered behind his desk, where he procured a steel one-meter ruler. *Much more persuasive than the old wooden crap*, he reflected, turning it over in his hand, admiring its sheen. He resembled a samurai warrior wielding a good blade for the first time. Grayson allowed himself a smile. It was a rare thing for him these days, to smile, and the kids may have found it unsettling were his back not to them, but Mr Grayson compelled it to fade before he turned to face the girl.

Still the phone sat loosely in her hands, which both pleased and infuriated him as he made his way towards her. Unsure of what was going to happen, the sniggers and titters doing the rounds were strangulated into an anxious silence.

The silly old bastard's finally flipped, was the communal thought of the students.

As he stood in front of the girl's table, still with no sign that he had been noticed, Grayson raised the ruler high above his head, stopping it just shy of the fibre ceiling tiles. All sound had left the room, it even seemed as though the oversized wall-clock – the twelve-hour clock that Grayson doubted half the bozos in attendance could tell the time on – had stopped ticking for this moment. Multiple pairs of eyes were squinting nervously, awaiting… awaiting what?

Kerenza's scream, along with those of a few others, pierced the already ringing ears of the classroom's inhabitants, having had zero chance to recover from initial deafening sound. The ruler's flat metal face connected perfectly with the hard laminate surface of her desk, emitting an almighty slam. Her phone leaped from her hands, performing an acrobatic flip before hitting the floor and spilling its SIM card and SIM tray guts.

Grayson bent and picked up the debris. 'So glad to see you're still with us, young lady.'

'If you've broken that…'

'If I've broken it,' Mr Grayson took over, 'I'll remind you how it should be kept switched off and in your bag during lesson, at all times. What's so important, hmmm? So important that you haven't listened to a word I've said all lesson?'

Kerenza looked from the phone in his hand, over to her friend's empty chair, and back to the phone again.

'I'm waiting,' Grayson pushed.

'Nothing,' Kerenza replied sheepishly. 'Please can I have my phone back, Sir?'

Grayson handed the phone and its components back to the girl. 'Put it in your bag. You can reassemble it later.'

As Kerenza reached for the phone, the bell signalled that the school day had finally come to an end. After several texts throughout the day and a number of attempts to call Grace, there had been no response.

Kerenza slid the tray and SIM card back into her phone, stood and grabbed he bag from under the table. She then threw Grayson a look so scornful it forced him to recoil. Turning away from him, she left the room. Next stop, Grace's house.

Arms comforting herself as she stood on the doorstep, panic filled Kerenza's head. She had been knocking for a full two minutes after realising that the bell showed no signs of life. Like the bell, the dark hallway behind the etched glass also seemed lifeless.

Come on, where are you?

Grace never took days off school, and she certainly did not ignore Kerenza's texts or calls. Something was seriously wrong and Kerenza was becoming an agitated mess. Deciding to shout through the letterbox instead of knocking, she bent and lifted the flap with one hand, using the other to part the hard bristles that lay inside the opening. As she peered through, two feet appeared and made their way tenuously down the stairs within.

A key gave a rattle from the other side of the door, before it opened slowly inwards.

'Grace, thank God! You look like shit. What's the matter?'

'Nice to see you, too,' Grace mumbled. 'I've got a banging headache and I was throwing up all morning. And thanks very much by the way, you look great, as usual.'

'Ahh, come 'ere,' said Kerenza as she reached forward and gave Grace a hug. 'I was so worried something bad had happened to you. I've been trying to get hold of you all day. You gonna let me in?'

'Sorry,' said Grace, stepping aside and granting access. 'I dropped my phone in the bog when I was puking. I've got it sat in a bowl of rice. Hopefully Jack wasn't just winding me up when he said it dries it out.'

'Well, I've heard it before, if that helps.'

They went through to the kitchen. Grace delved into the fridge and pulled out a couple of iced coffees. She shook them and handed one to Kerenza, before prompting her to take a seat at the glass-topped table.

'So, what brought this on?' asked Kerenza.

'I don't know,' Grace replied. 'I had a bit too much to drink yesterday afternoon, but I didn't think I was *that* drunk.'

Grace gave Kerenza an uneasy glance, realising she had already said too much.

'Getting drunk in the afternoon, without me?'

'Uh, yeah. Sorry.'

'No problem,' said Kerenza. 'So, who was the lucky guy? I'm guessing it was a boy.'

'Yeah, it was.'

'Well, who?' Kerenza asked, grinning. 'Come on. Don't keep me waiting.'

There was an uncomfortable moment where the room seemed to be closing in on Grace; the corner she was backed into was getting tighter with each passing second.

'Uh,' she twisted in her chair uneasily. 'It was Cameron.'

Kerenza sat hushed for a moment, this revelation sinking into her ears and setting like wallpaper paste.

'*My* Cameron?' she eventually brought herself to ask.

'Well, a funny way of putting it, but I suppose, *yeah*.'

'How did that come about? Why didn't you tell me?'

Grace started from the obvious place, at the side of a dual carriageway on a miserable afternoon two days ago. She watched closely, trying to read the features on her friend's face. What did she expect to see? Acceptance? Disappointment? Maybe anger?

Kerenza listened, nodded, asked questions where the detail seemed sketchy. There was, however, the occasional smile, but Grace sensed a trepidation just beneath the surface at the mention of Hell's Mouth.

'Well,' said Kerenza. 'I'm just glad you're okay.' She stood to take her leave. 'Though why you couldn't've told me about you and Cam sooner, I don't know.'

'I don't even know if there *is* a me and Cam. And anyway, I didn't want it to get in the way of me and you,' Grace replied, standing herself.

Kerenza leaned forward, lightly embraced Grace and placed a kiss on her cheek. 'Never gonna happen!'

They said their *goodbyes* and Kerenza left, contemplating the most fitting angle to use when accosting her darling stepbrother over this deceitful betrayal.

CHAPTER TWENTY-FOUR

Stepping onto the flat grey cobblestones, legs aching and a little short of breath from the steep walk up Stippy Stappy, Andrew composed himself. Hitting a local pub alone was a big step for him.

The evening had that chill to the air that warned of winter's approach, nonetheless he still felt beads of perspiration from the exercise, on his forehead. Using the back of a hand to wipe them off, he deliberated the need to get back into shape. *Maybe later,* he thought, entering the bar.

Wiping his forehead dry soon proved fruitless, as the heat inside brought back the sweat with renewed vigour. To his left, logs blazed on the open fire. Although the place was alive with noise – many of the chairs and stalls occupied by drinkers and diners – Andrew could still hear the crackle and hiss of the logs, fizzing over like fireworks on a November evening; a sound to be cherished.

Having taken the decision not to eat before he left the cottage, the stirring aromas of delicious and substantial pub meals instantly had him salivating and regretting that decision. Staring greedily at a pair of passing dishes, one consisting of steak and chips, the other, mussels and bacon swimming in a creamy sauce, Andrew's stomach gave a low groan. He pulled his eyes away from the passing plates of food and scoped the surrounding area for familiar faces.

None.

Once upon a time, he would be able to walk into any one of the village's plethora of pubs and recognise almost every punter. Now, with copious amounts of houses being flung up around the place, coupled with the growing number of second homes, a true local was becoming a rare bird indeed.

'Hi, Tribute, please,' Andrew said, sliding onto a vacant stool at the bar.

'Coming up,' the curly haired barmaid replied pleasantly. 'Haven't seen you for a *long* time,' she said, with an enquiring air about the statement.

'Feels like I haven't seen *anyone* for a long time,' he replied absently. *Please don't ask how my wife is.* She wouldn't. Everyone knew that *that* question was not applicable anymore.

'Well, it's nice to see you now,' the young woman said, placing the pint of ale in front of him and wiping the frothy overspill trickling down her fingers on a towel.

'Cheers,' said Andrew, raising his glass in a chinking mime.

'Cheers, yourself,' she said, turning away. 'Yes, love, what can I get you?'

Andrew reduced the ale in his glass by one third on his first visit. He laid it on the towel in front of him and watched the disturbed creamy head resettle. A cackle of laughs erupted from an alcove at the far end of the room. Looking over, he saw a table of women sharing anecdotes, enjoying their evening. He scoured his mind, in search of memories of when he last went out with a group of mates. Disheartened and a little embarrassed, he could not bring it to mind.

Turning back to his pint, another burst of hilarity arose, recapturing his attention. This time, looking back to the party gave him a staggering sense of unease. All of the joyful faces around the table were riveted in his direction. Andrew looked to his right, in the hope that something beyond himself was the source of their amusement. All that he saw was the red and black chequered lumberjack shirt stretched across the back of the guy next to him. The rugged-looking bloke sat with the bar at his side, deep in conversation with a middle-aged woman, eyeing him in wonderment at whatever impressive tale he told.

Me it is then. Thanks, ladies. One thought imprinted itself on Andrew's mind in that moment. The People of this village would never forget his past, and never refrain from surmising their own apocryphal and unfavourable theories. He would always be the target of questioning stares and idle gossip. It was time to get the hell out of Dodge.

He returned his attention the clucking crones (as he now rather unfairly thought of them), pondering whether to flip them the bird and leave the pub, or finish his pint in melancholy solitude, mentally erasing every other soul from this scene.

Laughter, again. On a more scrutinising inspection, Andrew found his initial observation was incorrect. Not every face around that table eyed him directly. One face, and a familiar one at that, was looking uncomfortable and focused her attention on the girl sat at her side. She was elbowing the side of the girl's torso in a *stop-it* plea. The head of golden-brown curls then turned to him, locking eyes. Andrew gave a smile and raised his hand in a *hello* gesture. She did the same, shaking her head, embarrassed.

Andrew turned back to his beer, pensively studying the amber glow of the liquid. Moments later he felt three light taps of a finger on his shoulder.

'Miss Sanders.'

'Aw come on, I thought we were passed all that. Especially on *my* time.'

'Sorry. *Alycia*,' he corrected as he turned to look at her, enjoying the view, he had to admit to himself.

'Andrew,' she replied, smiling. 'Sorry, the girls said that I was daft if I didn't come to say 'hi'.'

'And why would they say that?'

'Because you looked so sad and lonely, and I didn't like you looking all sad and lonely.'

'Well, that's very nice of you, telling me I'm a sad case. But maybe I'm just a sad person.' Andrew stated with a snigger.

'I don't doubt it,' she laughed. 'But I'm hoping you prove me wrong.'

The two singletons looked at each other for a few seconds, before Andrew broke the short-lived silence. 'Drink?'

'G and T, please. Large?' Alycia smiled.

'Of course,' he grinned. 'It's the only way.'

After the drinks were ordered, poured and presented, Alycia spotted an old greying couple making to leave. The chap lifted the old bird's jacket from the back of her chair, placed it over her shoulders, and pecked her on the cheek. As they ambled languidly away, Alycia looked at Andrew and nodded over to the vacant table.

'What about your friends?' he asked.

'I think they'll be fine without me,' she assured.

They made their way over, squeezing past other diners trying their best not to disturb them too much, and sat themselves down opposite each other. To Andrew there was a cosy yet unsettling nostalgia to this situation, sitting at a table in a warm and comfortable pub with a good looking – actually, great looking – woman. He had struggled to believe it would ever happen again.

Alycia noticed him eyeing her in quiet consideration.

'You okay?'

'Yeah, perfect,' Andrew said. 'So, single parent out on a night out with the girls. Who has the honour?'

'My mum,' Alycia replied, a strange look drawing over her face. 'Well, I say my mum, when it's actually *his* mum.'

'Oh?' Andrew raised one eyebrow, invited more details.

Alycia decided it couldn't hurt. 'He chose to leave, but she wanted a part in my baby's life. Liz. She's been awesome. *And* she's given me a roof over my head. Can't afford to buy on a teacher's wage.'

Andrew laughed.

'What's so funny?' she asked, looking slightly cut.

'Nothing,' he said, still laughing and taking a swig of his beer to stifle it. 'I was just thinking, the most commonly used phrase by teachers, *"on a teacher's wage."'*

'Shut up, cheeky git!' Alycia jested. 'What do you do, High-flyer?'

Andrew thought for a second before answering. 'Not a lot, I suppose, now you come to mention it.'

Alycia let that go without pushing for further explanation, sensing that the topic may spoil the mood.

'Anyway, it has its benefits,' she defended. 'I'm allowed out late to play, as long as it's not a school night. Plus, I don't have to do any cooking. I pray you never have to sample my cooking, there are people in prison for lesser crimes.'

Andrew was enjoying the natural ease with which the conversation flowed, and the squint in Alycia's eye as she placed her round fishbowl gin glass to her lips.

'Any other benefits?' he asked, pushing for what, he did not know.

'Mmm,' she continued, placing the glass back on the table. She wiped the cool moisture from her bottom lip with the back of a hand. 'I can go wild swimming in the mornings and know that Mum's there to wake Darcy up.'

'Wild swimming?' he asked in surprise.

'Yeah, it's amazing. Most mornings I'm down the beach, six, six-thirty, stripped and ready to jump in.'

'At Trevaunance?' Andrew asked, struggling to get the image of this dark-skinned beauty *'stripped'* out of his head. 'You're nuts! It's like the Bering Sea down there.'

'Not *that* often, it isn't,' she replied, amused by the over exaggeration. 'Besides, the pros far outweigh the cons.'

'What pros? All-over numbness; blue skin; ingested raw sewage?'

'Better circulation; stronger immune system; boosted metabolism; happy hormones; reduced stress___'

'Okay, okay,' Andrew cut in. 'I get the picture.'

'Good, when will I see you down there?' She raised her eyebrows at him expectantly.

'Uh, no, I don't think___'

'What have you got to lose?'

That was a fair question. What *did* he have to lose? In fact, the sight of Alycia in a bikini could only be a huge gain. But scolding guilt chastised him internally, as foreboding as a walk along death row.

Alycia sensed his hesitation.

'It's just a swim,' she said. 'A bit of exercise with the company and encouragement of someone else. It doesn't have to be anything else, if that makes you uncomfortable.'

'Al,' a tall woman with a torrent of dark blonde curls said as she arrived at the table. 'We're off to The Drifty, you coming?'

Alycia looked to Andrew. He raised his eyebrows in a *your call, I won't be offended* gesture, or so she read it to be.

'Do you mind if I give it a miss?' she said back to her friend.

The tall, leggy blonde looked from one to the other, smiled, and assured that wouldn't be a problem, and to head on down there if she changed her mind. With that it was just the two of them again, left to mull over the unfinished conversation that was hanging over them like a bulging black thundercloud.

'You could've gone with them, you know?' Andrew finally offered, relieving the oppressive quality of the air around them. 'I wouldn't've been offended.'

'And leave you sat here on your tod like that sad, lonely old man again?'

'Oi, less of the old, I've only got ten years on you, max, surely?' Andrew replied, wounded.

'Maybe. I'm twenty-seven,' Alycia challenged.

'Okay,' Andrew shook his head. 'Eleven years.'

Jesus, twenty-seven, as if it wasn't bad enough people thinking I drove my wife to suicide, now they're gonna think I'm a paedo as well. Andrew fought to erase the thought. He was enjoying the way the evening was panning out.

Alycia raised her glass, stopping it just before it touched her lips. 'Is that what you wanted?'

'What's that?' he asked, confused.

'For me to go with them?'

Andrew shook his head. 'No. Definitely not.'

The rest of the evening passed in a flash. After doing the *gentlemanly* thing and walking Alycia home, it was now clear to Andrew that he was missing certain connections: the vital connection with other people of not too dissimilar an age to himself – yes, eleven years is nothing. Connections with people outside of his own fortress that life events had imposed around him like an invisible but very real force field. And, importantly, connections with the opposite sex.

That said, he could not help but walk down the pitch black Beach Road with a tonne-weight of guilt hung around his neck. In a world that could leave a young woman so inexplicably broken as to walk herself into extinction, what right did he have to happiness, even if it was just for one evening?

Another wave of remorse washed over him, intensified by the accusations of the heaving trees overhead, and the turbulence of their wrestling leaves. Their scratching voices told him they knew his secret. They knew that he wanted more than just the one evening.

And he was going to get it. As crazy as it felt at the time and still did, one dull half-lit morning next week at an hour he would not normally be conscious to witness, he was going to inch into the freezing cold, clutching waters of Trevaunance Cove. And then, who knows? If the world really was his oyster, he was sure to find it in salt water, right?

CHAPTER TWENTY-FIVE

Thumping to within an inch of its throwaway digital-age life, the cylindrical smart speaker screamed of sleeping with one eye open with a distortion it may never fully recover from.

Cameron lay sprawled on the sofa. Feet up and trainers still on, he lounged in defiance of the rules; something many people allow themselves in times of blissful solitary. His fingers listlessly fluttered the pages of this month's Total Guitar magazine. Nothing of real interest to him: Slipknot – *low budget horror costume-wearing bullshit;* AC/DC – *overrated screaming flat-capped old duffers;* Fooies – yeah, they were pretty good, but this particular featured track? *No ta.*

Silence smashed into the room, obliterating the crunch of Kirk Hammett's *ESP* guitar, as loud and unexpected as a gunshot in the dead of night. Cameron looked sharply towards the speaker, his ears buzzing with a tinnitus quality.

'What the fuck are you doing?' he snapped.

'What are you doing, more like? You'll break the speaker, especially with that shit!'

'I'm sure James Hetfield wouldn't be offended by that if he heard the crap you listen to,' Cameron said, impassively.

'I have no idea who that is,' said Kerenza.

'I wouldn't expect you to. You're a loser.'

Kerenza stepped forward and lifted Cameron's legs off the arm. Dropping onto the cushion next to him, she lowered them across her lap.

'No shoes on here,' she said, starting to untie a lace and slipping one trainer off.

'It's not a shoe,' Cameron helpfully pointed out.

'Oh, you're funny today.'

Kerenza slipped off the second trainer and lightly traced her finger over his foot and up the lower leg, before tentatively running it back down again. Cameron kept his eyes shielded by his magazine, not succumbing to her pathetic attempt at seduction. Feeling miffed and a little burned at the lack of interest returned by the boy who normally acted like a dog with two dicks around her, Kerenza upped her game. Sliding her hand up over his quadriceps, she stopped just short of his groin. Here, she gave a gentle squeeze of intent.

'Can you not, dear sister?'

'Come on,' Kerenza pushed. 'We both know I'm more than that.'

'Sorry, *step*…sister.'

Kerenza ignored the dig and shuffled closer, leaning over his outstretched torso.

'Where've you been the last couple evenings? I've missed you,' she teased.

'Night shift,' he replied deadpan.

'Hospital cleaners don't do the night shift,' she stated doubtfully.

'Who said anything about cleaning?'

Kerenza ignored his efforts to shroud himself in mystery and worked her hand a little higher over his jeans. Instantly she could feel that this was having more of a physical impact on him than he was letting on. She smiled triumphantly to herself. *Like putty*, she thought.

'What are you playing at with Grace?' she asked, taking Cameron aback.

He lowered his magazine. Kerenza's face was so close that he could feel her warm, steady breath on his skin. Her long blonde hair lay in swirling pools over his dark tee shirt. A golden sheen danced in her eyes from the lamp behind him as they darted from one of his pupils to the next at warp-speed, a thing that had always freaked him out.

'What are you playing at with Jack?'

Touché, she thought bitterly. 'Is that why you made a move on her? Because you think there's something going on between me and Jack?'

'Don't think. Know,' Cameron replied with a sharpness in his tone. 'I saw you both when he picked Grace up. On the night of the barbeque.'

'I don't know what you *think* you saw. I only went over to say hello.'

'Normally stick your tongue down people's throats to do that, do ya?' asked Cameron, maintaining a blindingly dispassionate performance. 'Is he the reason you didn't put out when you practically dragged me to your bedroom the other night? Didn't even get to take your knickers off. Prick-teaser!' He raised his eyebrows at her, goading.

'Dragged? I seem to recall you didn't need dragging,' she snapped back in retort.

'Answer the fucking question.'

Kerenza was struck into a momentary silence after being so brutally sworn at. Cameron raised his magazine once again, surveying the pages without taking any of the words in, leaving her to absorb his words in quiet remorse. He was not supposed to find out about her and Jack, and as the seconds passed slowly and uncomfortably by, one thought came to the forefront of her mind. Regardless of the relationship status between Jack and herself, she had to block any potential relationship between her stepbrother and her best friend. One-handed, Kerenza plucked the magazine from Cameron and dropped it onto the living room floor, before touching his hair and looking at him intensely.

'It wasn't the right time,' she said, simulation a vulnerable nervousness.

'Really? A bit predictable, don't you think? I bet that cock-knocker's had his *right time*.'

'He's nothing to me, and no, actually, he hasn't. I'm not a complete slag you know,' she replied, indignantly.

'So, if there's really no you and *fucknuts*, would now be the right time for us?'

'Don't be an idiot, Dad's upstairs.'

'No he's not. *My* dad is at the pub,' Cameron said a little childishly. 'Do you really think I'd have Metallica thumping out like that if he was home?'

'At the pub?' asked a put-out Kerenza. 'Who with?'

'On his own, not that it's any of our business.'

'Since when did he go to the pub on his own?' A sense of concern crept into her voice.

'Since stop changing the fucking subject,' Cameron smarted. 'So, the question remains.'

Kerenza removed her hand from Cameron's hair and slumped back into the cushions.

'No,' she sighed. 'Time of the month.' Possibly a bit too much information, but she was no longer in the mood for games. Circumstances beyond her control were changing, and she did not like it one bit.

'That's cool,' Cameron grinned. 'If the river's red, take the dir___'

'Don't you *dare* finish that sentence, you disgusting little boy!' Kerenza warned.

'Your loss,' Cameron shrugged. He tipped her a wink, connected the tips of his thumb and index finger to form an *OK* signal, and stuck his wiggling tongue through the opening.

She looked at him, unsettled. 'You make me wanna puke. If I find a film, will you snuggle up with me?'

'As long as you don't leak menstruation fluid all over the settee,' he toyed with her.

'Stop being so vulgar,' Kerenza chided, reaching for the remote.

She hit the red circle, rousing the television from its slumber and flicked through the guide, finding nothing of interest in the huge list of channels. No surprise there, television seemed to work to a simple rule: the more channels offered, the less choice afforded. Cameron watched as the library popped up on the screen, and the blue line flashed down through a list of the family's favoured films and programmes. It settled on a title and the menu disappeared, replaced with opening credits.

'Gnomeo and fucking Juliet!' Cameron exclaimed in incredulity.

'That doesn't happen in the film,' Kerenza mocked. 'But I bet you've searched for that online.'

'Show me someone who hasn't,' he grinned.

She leaned in, laid her head on Cameron's chest and looked up at him amusedly. He pulled his arm around her and lowered it down her side before looking back at the TV, wondering what the hell he was sticking around to watch this for. One inaudible sniff of her fragrant golden hair reminded him exactly why.

Kerenza, on the other hand, ruminated over how to keep a rival female's greedy claws from clenching him; and just what Andrew thought he was doing, attempting to socialise and sculpt a life of his own.

CHAPTER TWENTY-SIX

A fountain of orange-hot metal droplets rained down as flame in excess of three-thousand degrees roared from the torch, the mixture of oxygen and acetylene cutting through the old exhaust pipe with devastating effect. Miniature firemen bounced off the heavy steel platform of the ramp, hitting the painted floor and scattering in a multitude of directions like crowds from a plummeting plane. The torch wielder shuffled and cursed as the occasional glowing drop found its way through the neck of his overalls.

Two silent feet appeared in his obstructed line of vision, moving closer and displaying the bottom half of what appeared to be a male.

'Be with you in a minute,' Jack's voice acknowledged the latest customer from behind his scratched and cracked face shield.

The rear silencer of an exhaust fell from toward the mid-section and hung from a rubber bracket behind the rear bumper. It dangled ominously like a murderer from the gallows. Jack killed the flame and grabbed the hot end of the pipe with a gloved hand, working at the bracket with the other until the lump of metal broke free of its host. He lowered the section of exhaust to the floor, stooped his way out from under the soaring vehicle and removed his shield.

'Cameron,' he said in confused recognition.

'Long time,' the visitor stated.

'What are you doing here?'

'That's no way to greet an old friend.'

'We were never friends,' Jack retorted.

'True, but we were never really *not* friends either. I just figured it might be a good time to change that.' Cameron saw the look of irritation in Jack's eyes. 'Not the "not friends" bit. I just thought it was probably time I made an effort. You know, now that you're shaggin' my sister and that. And with me and Grace getting, uh, more familiar, we're practically brothers-in-law.'

Jack presented Cameron a distasteful look. 'I'm not___'

'It's cool,' Cameron cut him short. 'Good luck to ya. Not sure why you'd want to, though. Her fanny's got more of a crustacean infestation than Christmas Island. Honestly, mate, *I* wouldn't touch her with *yours*. But, each to their own.' *And more to their own than you could imagine, dickwad.*

'Don't talk about her like that,' Jack warned, face set.

'So you are then.'

Cameron headed around the back of the car, looking up, inspecting the lines of the bodywork, disappearing around the side, continuing his surveillance. Jack watched, unable to see his eyes and gauge the intent gearing into action behind them. Turning his head away, Jack looked over his shoulder towards the half plastic panel, half Plexiglass box of an office and waiting area. Gary, the stand-in boss on a Saturday (a man who's once-weekly awarded power – obtained by a blitzkrieg assault of brown-nosery on the true and more bearable boss – had gone completely to his stupid flat-topped nineteen-eighties military-haired head), stood behind the main desk. Giving Jack a stern look, Gary tapped impatiently at his watch.

Man, I'd love to take a shovel to that ridiculous head of yours, Jack thought sourly.

Cameron reappeared from the front of the car above, noticing the look of contempt that Jack was trying to hold back from Top Gun dude in office.

'Get to the point,' Jack demanded, returning his attention to the matter at hand.

'Finish early on a Saturday?'

Jack pulled up a sleeve and checked the time. 'Twenty minutes. What of it?'

'Good,' Cameron beamed. 'Pub. I'll wait in the car park, and we'll head over town.'

Sensing that opposing him would be to no avail, for now, Jack turned his back and proceeded to collect the new exhaust section from the other side of the ramp. He set back to work without another word to the skinny prick.

Cameron left through the open roller door and strutted across the tarmacked forecourt, marvelling over Jack's formidable shoulders. My, how he had evolved from the scrawny little shit Cameron remembered from school. This development may have created an inconvenient obstruction. The size difference between the two of them did not worry Cameron. It purely meant that he would have to devise his intentions from a new perspective; come up with something a little more creative than just going head-to-head with the man.

Half-an-hour later, the two sat at a table fashioned from an old whisky barrel. The place was already near full, though the clock had not yet struck one in the afternoon. Laughter broke out here and there. Shouts of amusement mixed with shouts of anger as people either swapped stories from their week, or just simply fell out because someone who had been drinking since opening time had drunkenly stumbled into them.

Wood shavings, added deliberately for some unknown reason, swirled over the dusty floor as the door opened, allowing access to another lunchtime drinker, along with a fresh gust of autumn breeze.

'You look like you're eyeing me up,' said Jack as he took a swig of his lager. 'Didn't have you down as the type.'

'Just admiring your physique,' Cameron said, nodding to Jack's extensive chest and shoulders. 'Heard you'd become a bit of a scrapper, but Jesus, boy.'

'I've filled out a bit,' Jack understated.

'Speaking of eyeing you up,' said Cameron, gesturing towards two girls – late teens, maybe early twenties. They were sat at a table close by, casting the odd glance over.

'I'm not interested,' Jack said plainly without looking over. 'I've got everything I need.'

Fuckin' prick, thought Cameron. 'Piss off. The dumpy one's got tits like fuckin' shot puts pushed up there.'

'You said it,' Jack sighed, bored. '*Pushed* up. It's all false promise.'

'Granted,' said Cameron as he gawked lecherously at the squat chassis. 'Get that over-the-shoulder boulder holder off and it'll be less *shot put*, more *sack race*. But by that time you'll be too up to your nuts in guts to give a shit.'

Jack stared back with growing disinterest.

'Anyway, back to *your* hot bod, Action Man. Could use some muscle at the moment,' Cameron said. 'I owe someone. He's big. Dopey fucker though. Probably soft as shit but I'm not gonna take that chance.'

'What's he done?'

'Taken something from me. Got handy with a guitar string.'

'The cat? Kerenza told me.' Jack spotted an intensely irritated look pass over the face opposite him. 'How d'ya know it was him?'

'I don't,' Cameron revealed. 'But someone's gonna take the flack, and it's his lucky day. Another pint?'

Jack nodded the affirmative, accepting he was stuck with this company for the time being. Cameron grabbed his own empty glass and headed to the bar. Jack stared into the dregs of his glass, mulling over the conversation so far. If Cameron wanted to sort this guy out, why did he want to involve him? Kerenza had spoken of the bloke up the road from her before, though the tales she told spoke were of an unfortunate recluse that wanted nothing more than to keep away from people. He hardly sounded like the kind of person to go around hanging people's pets. There was more to this. Jack did not know what that was, but what he did know was that the lad walking up behind him carrying the drinks could not be trusted.

'You know, you really should drink cyder,' Cameron said, placing the drinks on the table and returning to his chair. 'Lager's for poofs.'

'And cyder's for fourteen-year-olds,' Jack countered. 'Anyway, what would I get out of this arrangement?'

'Knew you couldn't resist,' Cameron grinned.

'I haven't agreed to anything yet.'

'Your boss,' continued Cameron. 'Don't like him much, do ya?'

'He's not my boss,' Jack defended.

'Whatever. Boss or not, you wanted to walk into that office and put his flat head through the window. I could see it.'

Jack could have retorted with a false statement to counter this loser's theories. Instead, he decided to hold his tongue. He looked at his watch and pushed himself out of his chair.

'I need a piss,' he informed Cameron, before heading towards the back of the barroom.

Pushing his way through a heavy black painted door, Jack looked back towards the bar area. Cameron remained sat at the table and tapping away at his mobile phone. Satisfied that he was not being watched, Jack entered the toilets. Stepping up onto a raised terracotta-tiled plinth at the foot of the long, once white urinal, he unzipped his flies. The stale smell of urine drifting up from the yellowing, pubic hair strewn trough forced him to turn his nose up in disgust. The heavy door behind gave a long and agonising creek, compelling him to turn around. *For fuck's sake!*

'So, this is where all the pricks hang out,' Cameron laughed.

'They do now,' Jack muttered under his breath, unamused by the predictability of Cameron's banter.

Cameron hopped on to the plinth, gave a disapproving grunt at the puddles of piss under his feet, made himself ready and leaned forward. Keeping his gaze low, he turned his head steadily towards Jack.

'STOP TRYING TO LOOK AT MY COCK!' Jack yelled.

'*Woohoo,*' Cameron almost howled, flashing a wink. 'I wondered what she saw in you, king ding-a-ling. You could choke a fuckin' hippo on that bleddy-gate wanger.'

Jack stopped urinating before he was completely spent. shaking himself dry, he tucked his bits back into his jeans and stomped off towards the basins. Cameron stood in self-triumph as the tap stopped and the door gave its coffin-lid creek at an excelled pitch. After sorting himself out he made his way back to the table and sat opposite what he hoped was his new partner-in-crime. Rejoicing, he took in the cheerless countenance staring downwards and idly thumbing at a soggy beermat.

Keeping his voice as low as his head, Jack spoke.

'So, when you gonna sort my *esteemed* colleague out?'

'You first,' Cameron smirked.

CHAPTER TWENTY-SEVEN

Sitting on the stony ground, Dryrobe draped over her shoulders to fend off the biting air, Alycia studied the incoming waves. An ensemble of pebbles major and minor churned and tumbled to the beat of the ocean a score of metres in ahead. Rocks, shaped smooth over thousands of years of frenetic activity, clacked loudly as the sea spewed them towards her, chattering lower as they were once again dragged helplessly away.

A lightness grew lackadaisically far away on the horizon, transforming the dark steely clouds that blanketed the sky to pale aluminium over the steadily rolling anthracite Atlantic. Stubborn, murky blackness still loomed behind her lonely figure. Sporadically, the white flash of a seabird stood out in contrast to the dense covering above, whilst others offered low guttural tattles as they huddled among the recesses and shelves of the substantial rockface.

At last, footsteps fell onto the beach behind her.

'I thought you'd gone chicken,' said Alycia, to the new arrival. 'Another five minutes and I would've given up on you.'

'I'm no chicken,' Andrew said as he lowered himself down onto the wet stones next to her. 'I still think you're Bodmin though. So, what's the plan?'

'Well,' Alycia said. 'You've got to get out of that, for starters. Unless you plan on going in fully clothed.'

Andrew untied his boots, pulled them off, and stood unbuttoning his shirt.

'I haven't got a wetsuit,' he informed her.

'Good,' she said. 'Me neither. Not for today, anyway. Won't be long 'til I drag it out, mind.' Alycia looked at him as he unbuttoned his trousers. 'I hope you've got shorts on under those, though.'

They shared a laugh and Alycia stood and faced him, lifting her Dryrobe up and over her head. Andrew did his best to look elsewhere, though it was a challenge that he failed. Alycia spotted the fleeting glance but feigned otherwise. Boys will be boys, after all.

'See that orange buoy out there?' she said, pointing to where Andrew could see only a rising and falling cobalt blue.

He strained his eyes and eventually observed the fleeting appearance of a little ball in the distance.

'Uh, yeah,' he answered dubiously.

'Good. That's where we're headed.'

'There and *back*?'

'Well, there won't be a taxi waiting when we get there,' she mocked.

'Jesus,' Andrew said, with a lousy attempt at hiding his consternation. 'How far is it?'

'Don't know,' she admitted. 'Never taken a tape measure with me.'

'Mouthy little sod, aren't you.' It wasn't a question.

'I'll pretend I didn't hear that.' Alycia gave a look of upset. 'It wasn't gentlemanly. Come on.'

She started to walk gingerly on bare feet over patches of pebbles, sand, seaweed, shells, and scraps of old rope; debris that the ocean had not gotten the taste for. *Maybe I'm not a gentleman*, Andrew thought, diverting his unobserved attention to intrude on her pert bikini-clad rear. He removed his trousers and stumbled awkwardly after her.

By the time he reached the edge of dry(*ish*) land, Alycia was already waist-deep, apparently unaffected by the bitter coldness of the water. She waited, watching as his eyes widened comically in shock. Plodding warily on, he stopped several metres away from her, the water rising and falling from knee to mid-thigh.

'What are you waiting for?' she smirked.

'It's alright for you,' he huffed. 'I've got a seriously sensitive part that's about to make contact with the Arctic. And when it does, it may well disappear inside me.'

Laughing, Alycia said, 'I think that may be a little dramatic.'

'Yeah whatever. But when I'm being fished out of the water later, if you catch a glimpse, just remember it's normally bigger.'

'I'll keep that in mind,' she said, amused. Turning and stretching her arms, she dived into the water.

Andrew watched the small splashes sent showering by her kicking feet, and the alternate arching of her arms as she made her way into the rolling water. After a deep breath he took the plunge himself. The initial submersion was overwhelming, like a thousand serrated icicles slashing into his vulnerable flesh – and not just in his *seriously sensitive* areas, either.

Soon, however, his brain and lungs rekindled their previous relationship, allowing his body's automatic need to breath to kick in again. It was just a shame that the brain did not have the same relationship with the mouth, allowing it to stay open and ingest a large amount of sickly salt water and whatever else might be floating in it at that precise moment.

Andrew thought about the majestic giant basking sharks that, like thousands of human beings each year, also decided to take a beach holiday in Cornwall. He wondered just how the hell they could swim all day with their colossal mouths open. I mean, I know it's their food, right, but it tastes like shit.

Tastes like shit.

He recalled Surfers Against Sewage.

Maybe that was *shit. Happy place, happy place.*

Raising his head, he was temporarily unable to see anything other than a deep blue wall in front of him. Within seconds the foothills of the wall reached him, giving rise to his body as the wave bullied its way underneath him. From that short-lived vantage point, he was able to see his swimming companion. At a guess, he would put her about thirty metres ahead. Bobbing around next to her was the spherical orange buoy. She hovered majestically, looking back in his direction. The sight of Alycia waiting filled Andrew with a keen desire to join her. Redoubling his efforts, he kicked resolutely.

'Well done, you,' Alycia said, as he reached her. 'That's halfway. Did you see the size of that jellyfish?

'What? No,' he panted, drawing himself alongside her and treading water.

'Shame, it was beautiful.'

'*Shame?*' he blurted out. 'If I'd seen that I would've either had a heart-attack or shat myself. *Or both!* Where was it? Is there a different way back?'

Alycia chuckled. 'It won't hurt you, landlubber.'

'Won't hurt? It's a lethal bloody killer.'

Alycia laughed at this monumental overreaction. Her infectious joy encouraged Andrew to join in, even if it was at his expense.

The sky had started to lighten over a wide area of the cove. Small pockets of dusky blue could be seen above, and the clouds started to thin and break away. The sea waltzed and whirled around them, bringing its only visible human inhabitants to within a foot of each other. They did not fight against it, only held each other's attention as the cold started setting in, causing their chins to tremble in a shiver. Andrew studied the salted liquid drops glistening on Alycia's lips, wagering that they would taste exquisite compared to the mouthful of salted liquid that he had sampled on the way out to this point.

'What are you thinking?' Alycia asked, sensing his fixation.

'I'm thinking, shit it's cold. I'm thinking, how did I let you rope me in to this? I'm thinking, I'm glad you did. And,' Andrew paused, contemplating. 'I'm thinking, how soon is too soon?'

'Too soon for what?' Alycia asked, a nervous anticipation building at the pit of her stomach.

'To feel ready to move on.' Andrew lowered his head in self-reproach. Each word that escaped his mouth felt damning, like the merest whisper of them was an unmitigated betrayal. If the sea could swallow him now, he would not have to live with the accusatorial weight of them.

Alycia placed her cold, delicate fingers to his cheek, a spectral caress from beyond the grave.

'You never will,' she breathed. 'So, the question isn't how soon you'll feel it. The question is, how soon can you forgive yourself and allow yourself a life again?'

Andrew lifted his hand and brushed the back of hers, flowing with the dunes of her metacarpals. Another wave of guilt compelled him to drift back from her and he dropped his hand back into the water once more.

'Come on,' Alycia said, disheartened but understanding. 'Let's head back.'

Andrew watched as she once again took the lead, swimming slowly away from him, the chance of happiness drifting away with her. The shivering had stopped, the cold temporarily forgotten as her words sunk in. Deep down he knew that she was right, and after a short time berating himself for so unceremoniously constructing a briny gulf between them, he headed back towards the shore; jellyfish forgotten.

Scrambling over the difficult terrain, with sticks, stones and bits of discarded plastic digging into his feet, Andrew watched Alycia. She was bent facing away from him, picking up her Dryrobe. Holding it to her front, she reached stealthily back to the tie of her bikini top, loosening and removing it in one swift action. Another pang of remorse compressed on his chest as he watched. Swallowing hard, the huge ball of guilt slid down his throat like granite block. Andrew pressed on. Alycia turned as she heard the plunging scrunch of his footsteps draw nearer, pressing her Dryrobe tight against her chest, protecting her modesty.

'Feel invigorated?' she asked, with regards to the wild swimming that Andrew originally seemed so averse to. Her face radiated red from a mixture of cold water and the exertion of the return journey.

Without a word Andrew did what he now knew he should have done whilst treading water and swimming in her dark and non-judgemental eyes at the buoy. Stepping up close to her, he placed a hand on the side of her neck, letting the fingers curl and find purchase around the back. He moved his face towards her and placed his mouth gently upon hers.

He was right.

Her salt speckled lips did taste exquisite.

CHAPTER TWENTY-EIGHT

As darkness had taken hold over the county, streetlights cast an orange domelike safety net over the rarely quiet drive-through burger establishment, reflecting dully in the black windows of a closed carwash.

A moonless sky did little to offer sanctuary to anything that strayed outside the perimeter of the electric glow. The dearth of clouds had caused a temperature drop severe enough to display a tangerine veil of warm breath (mixed with cigarette smoke) around the small gathering of boy racers. Leaning against their budget impersonation sports cars with tarted up, over-elaborate body kits and chrome alloy wheels that were too big for the arches, the crew *shot-the-shit*: who they had done over this week; who they had fucked; who was up for it if they themselves could be bothered; which girl takes it up the shitter. Like *they* would know.

Low and distinctive, the warble of an Impreza's big bore exhaust reverberated from the passing road. The silver vehicle left the mini roundabout with no indication. Slowly, methodically, it headed towards the herd of parked cars. No members of this group had seen the car before, scoping by them at a snail's pace, either eyeing them up to pick a drag opponent, or on some shady errand.

Whoever was behind the tinted driver's window had clearly lost interest in the group, speeding up and making a beeline for a lone black Golf, planted idly in a darkened far corner of the car park. The kids with the boy's toys all knew who was sat in the shadowy interior of the VW, though very few of them ever ventured to interact with him. This brought on a unanimous loss of interest in the newcomer as he reversed up close to its side.

A front window of both vehicles opened in synchronicity.

'You muss be Jack,' a rat-faced guy behind the Golf's steering wheel stated aloof.

'And you must be Chris,' came the reply, from a voice permeating a false confidence. 'Lucas says you can help me out?'

'Yeah, I owe him a bid of a favour.'

'And you don't mind getting your hands dirty?'

'All the bedder, for me,' Chris answered, an unnerving smile displaying two crooked rows of yellow teeth.

'And you're okay for tomorrow night?' asked Jack.

'Depends what time.'

'That's the bit I don't know yet,' Jack admitted. 'How much notice do you need?'

Chris sighed in mild frustration. 'Hour.'

Jack nodded.

'So, big chap like you, not shord o' muscle. Why ain't you sording the wanker out yourself?' Chris asked, twirling his ginger pube-like chin hairs between his thumb and index finger.

Jack paused for a moment of thought. *None of your fucking business*, is what he wanted to say. An unpredictable menace lurking in Chris' hazy grey-green eyes advised him otherwise.

'I can't be anywhere near there,' he went with instead. 'His stepsister can't think I had anything to do with it.'

'Ah,' said Chris, reading between the lines. 'Rootin' the bitch, are'ee?'

Jack let the crude comment slide. You don't poke a honey badger with your finger. 'I want a good job doing, if you get me.' *Course he does, that's what people like him get involved for*. 'Prick's moving in on my sister, too. I can't let that happen. If you end that, it would be perfect.'

'Sounds like you wan'im dead,' Chris considered. 'I don't owe Lucas *that* big.'

'I don't want him dead,' said Jack glassily. 'Just sort it so he has nothing left to offer anyone. Ever again.'

CHAPTER TWENTY-NINE

Cameron gazed out of his bedroom window, gauging the diminishing quality of the light. It was now ripe for approaching and entering *Raymondo's* unobserved. Leaving the cottage unseen shouldn't prove much of a challenge: Kerenza was in her room listening to her shit music (thankfully with her door closed). Andrew was at the pub (again). And Merryn was out for tea with the old farts, Judith and Angus.

Cameron had waited for long enough. He got up, rifled through his top drawer and pulled out a plain black snood and a pair of black gloves. Throwing on a dark jacket, Cameron stuffed the snood into the side pocket and donned the gloves, before silently opening the bedroom door. Tiptoeing across the landing, he alighted the stairs. All was as he expected to find it downstairs; completely abandoned. Slinking through the darkness of the downstairs rooms, Cameron left via the front door.

The grass area that skirted the driveway became his new best friend. He halted to give one last glance back. No stepsister at her window.

Good to go.

Beach Road was perfect in its abandonment. Yellow lights behind the windows of neighbouring properties awarded him with reassurances. He would be hard to distinguish for any roaming pair of eyes within; just a nocturnal animal scouring the hedgerows; maybe an earie shadow playing tricks on the mind.

Cameron stopped at a small iron gate, reddened with age and hanging crookedly from its bottom hinge only. Turning his back to it, surveying the area for one last time, he drew a cold, deep breath of late October air.

Not a peep, not a squeak. The snood an unnecessary precaution, remaining in his pocket.

Putting Beach Road behind him once more and focussing on the task ahead, he crept through the gate.

The pathway was cracked and suffocated by weeds and brambles, the latter of which scraped at his jeans, giving an audible scratch. The dark form lowered, and at some risk of alerting somebody of his presence, removed the mobile phone from its pocket, flicking on the device's torch. Feeling a deal of relief in finding that there was no fabric hanging from the barbed tendrils, he killed the bright white light and moved cautiously on.

Passing a dilapidated summerhouse, Cameron reached the old and forlorn cottage. The two were barely affixed, the skeletal structure hanging crudely from the stony exterior like a discarded Siamese twin. Reaching out, Cameron felt for the ancient paintwork, running his fingers along its cold, moss-slimed surface for balance.

The broken path came to a junction at the rear of the old cottage, giving two options: to advance onto a perforated course of slabs running further into the unknown undergrowth, or skirt to the right and continue around the property's footprint. Cameron strained his eyes into the blackness of the brush in the direction of the slabs. Occasional flurries of breeze moved leaves and long grasses just enough for a distant speck of light to be seen. At a guess, the light would be emitting from a burning oil lamp, given the hermit's disdain for electrical items.

So, you're home, ya stupid old bastard. Where else would you be?

Equipped with this valuable information, Cameron decided to follow the grimy wall of the cottage around to the right. He had no idea what he would find on this course, but he prayed that it would be sharp, or heavy, or better still both. Thickets black and brown in the disintegrating conditions barred most of his passage. They crossed the walkway and climbed the rear wall of the property. There could be a hidden arsenal through there. Getting there stealthily, however, would be nigh on impossible.

That said, the boy had to do something.

Crouching low, Cameron edged cautiously into the thicket.

Three laborious steps in, a dry cracking sound split the evening's stillness. A person could be forgiven for mistaking the sound of the snapping branch for the breaking of a human bone, such was macabre quality of the noise in this desperate setting. Two factors occurred to Cameron in instantaneous succession: one, he did not feel a cylindrical obstacle underfoot; and two, the sound came from a yard or two behind.

As he turned rapidly in abrupt understanding, a faceless shadow loomed large above him. Immediately there followed the deadly flash of a flat, metal object.

***

Jack stared restlessly at his phone as he sat in the bucket seat of his silent Subaru. Something was wrong. Very wrong. Cameron should have made the call by now, summoning who he thought was his new skivvy, a pawn in his pathetic little battle.

Not going to happen, my friend, thought Jack.

Chris whatever-his-name-is, however, was a man that Jack did not want to keep waiting. Taking a psychopath like him for granted could result in untold damage, and Jackie did not intend to be on the receiving end of it.

He could wait no longer. The possible ramifications of the situation threatened to engulf his airways and cut off his oxygen supply.

Pressing a rousing finger to the side of his phone, he tapped in his security code. He hit the *'contacts'* icon, scrolled down to *'Cockron'* and padded the *'call'* button.

Straight to answerphone. This did nothing to steady his feeling of unease.

Looking back to the portion of house visible in his side mirror, Jack saw the shaded silhouette of his younger sister, Grace. She watched him mistrustfully from the front room window. Guilt started to swell and churn deep in his gut.

You're doing her a favour, a convincing voice of reason in his head aided. *Soon, there'll be nothing else to see in him, and that can only be a good thing.*

But first, Jack needed to be sure that everything was going to go to plan. He hit *'call'* again. Same result.

***

Solid stone impacted on Cameron's face as he was knocked sideways with extraordinary force. Striving to scramble off his front, he spat grit and earth from his copper-tasting mouth. A throbbing pain spread from his shoulder with all the devouring fury of a gorse fire. If the object had struck just a few inches higher he would have been worm feed. Instead, the face that narrowly survived the arching swing of whatever it was, hit the floor when he fell. His lip burst and one side of his face scraped on the jagged concrete floor.

Gingerly turning his aching neck to look up, his blurred vision was once again met by the phantom shape, raising its chosen weapon high. Cameron rolled hurriedly away from the wall and onto spongy uncomfortable ground. Landing on his back he felt perforating scratches from brambles and thorns across his exposed neck. The heavy clang of steel on stone blasted beside him, deadening his left ear and leaving him feeling like his head was stuck inside Big Ben.

The blade of the shovel (as Cameron could now identify the weapon) soared skyward again.

Fuck me, he's not giving up, Cam thought, still stranded on his back, a helpless tortoise overturned and belly-up to the baking sun. All he could do to at least stem the flow of the onslaught, was raise his leg and thrust his foot into the midriff of the assailant. It was a good contact, enough to send what Cameron could now confirm as Raymond back a few steps. Sprawling over an entanglement of clutching foliage, the old tramp dropped the shovel. As his back hit ground with a hollow *doof,* the old bastard's wind was knocked out of him, causing him to wheeze desperately.

Determined not to let this chance slip through his fingers, Cameron sprang to his feet and leapt towards his dazed and gasping opponent. Raymond rolled his head sideways, eyes battling with the murkiness of the night. To Cameron's dismay, Raymond espied the fallen shovel. It lay in the brush, within reach of his crawling fingers. With no time to react, the lethal flat surface was skimming towards him again. The contact was agonising, its keen edge impacting with the outside of Cameron's right leg, surely breaking the fibula bone.

Struggling to his feet, Raymond walked wearily towards the fallen boy, the boy that had the audacity to trespass on his property. Cameron looked up to the livid sepia eyes. *The demented cunt's actually laughing*. His murderous demeanour spoke in volumes: the teenager lying at the will of this madman had to find something, *anything*, to defend himself with. His very survival depended on it. Of that, Cameron was sure.

Casting a desperate survey of his surroundings, his acclimatising eyes stumbled upon another long wooden handle, much like the shovel's, protruding from the undergrowth to his right. Raymond approached. Cameron dug both feet into the grit and pushed. *No break then,* he had time to think, as his legs managed to shove him the small number of inches he needed to get within reach.

The dishevelled man stopped, his open trench coat hovering ominously above Cameron's shins, like a hospital sheet all set to cover a deceased patient's face. The arms lifted slowly, the shovel held in the air, a guillotine ready to fall.

'Die you fucking piece of shit,' Raymond sneered, drool creeping from the corner of his mouth like a rabid dog.

Raymond vented a growl and arched his back, a venomous cobra about to strike. With predatory speed Cameron lunged his arm at the forlorn wooden handle. Obtaining a firm grip, with a colossal effort he attempted to ply it from the unyielding tangles of vegetation. Roots raised the earth as their clawed talons refused to let go. With an inspiriting tear, the garden tool broke free of its shackles. Cameron thrust his weapon forward.

As Raymond firmly planted one steadying leg before him, striking the perfect balance to exact maximum force, he felt a crippling pain to his gut. Looking down in stupefied horror, the old man saw the four black prongs of his very own pitchfork piercing his khaki shirt. Blood leaked from holes where the implement had penetrated the shirt and imbedded itself into his stomach. Saliva foamed red from between his flaky lips, cutting a tacky claret gorge through his wiry chin hairs before dripping onto the dark tee shirt worn by the youth below him.

Unaware that he was holding his breath, and with a dying man's still-warm blood soaking through his clothing, adhering it to his trim middle, Cameron lay transfixed by Raymond's eyes. The menace and determination they had burned with moments before had grown dull, vague, and denunciatory.

***

Jack's phone pitched sharply into the nervous tranquillity of the Impreza, so sudden that he almost dropped it in surprise. Fumbling awkwardly, he finally managed to accept the call before his answerphone intercepted.

'Yeah.'

'Thirty minutes.'

The line went dead.

Jesus, thirty minutes! Jack felt a heat burning from under his skin. *Chris is going to be pissed.* He had a word with himself. Every moment he wasted through stress would infuriate the maniac more. He fished the scrap of paper from the door pocket – after all, he did not want this guy's name in his contacts list – and punched in the number that was written upon it.

'Furdy fuckin' minutes! Whad 'appened to an hour?' Chris reprimanded.

'Sorry. I'm really fuckin' sorry.' Jack grovelled.

'Whadever. We'll talk aboud it layder,' a warning voice came back. 'I godda ged a move on. Prick'

For the second time in as many minutes, Jack had been hung up on.

***

Cameron ended his brief call and stuffed the phone back into his pocket. He looked at Raymond for a moment, slumped in a rickety old dining chair. Fuck, he was hard work to get here. Cameron resorted to the good old fireman's lift that worked so efficiently on his father, but the smelly old bastard weighed a ton. His shithole of a jungle made the going even more onerous.

Cameron eyed the surrounding features: bits of old wood, soggy and bowed and propped together, reliant on bits of branch and crudely tied rope to keep them from dropping to the rotting floor. A tarpaulin roof sagged in the middle with the weight of pooling rainwater on its upper face. The makeshift shed harboured few items. The possessions of Raymond's recluse and secretive life: the chair his lifeless body was currently slouched in; a square wooden table, scratched and splattered sporadically with faded paint in a multitude of colours; a wicker basket of perished and yellowing novels (Cameron felt a rare penetrating sting of remorse as he spotted a thin Thomas the Tank Engine book nestled in the pile of more adult material); a camping stove complete with tin kettle; and a glowing oil lamp on the floor in the corner, the burning flame that caught Cameron's attention while the old tramp was still alive.

'Back in a minute,' Cameron said to the dead man.

He turned and left trough a dirty, fraying sheet door. On his return, he wielded the bloody bane of Raymond.

'Sorry, old boy,' he said. The slack-jawed face stared back at him, no longer concerned with life's trivialities. 'I didn't want this, but you had to have a go, didn't you? Had to start something you were never gonna finish.' Cameron smiled at the memory of the struggle. 'Gave it a fuckin' good go though. Tough ol' bugger.'

Disinterested, the cadaver offered no response, opting instead for silence and staring back absently through fading irises.

169

Raising the pitchfork, Cameron lined its killer tips up with the weeping holes in Raymond's shirt. Circling the tines of the fork delicately around the slick bloodied surface of the belly, the weapon sank slightly as it found the four puncture wounds. The youth looked into the old, dead eyes for the last time.

'Sharp scratch,' he said, unable not to enjoy that little quip, even if only for an infinitesimal moment.

Leaning forward, Cameron pushed two-handed on the handle and the shaft. The bloody squelch sounded like a boot falling into fresh snow as the tines plunged into Raymond's torso for the second and final time.

Cameron unclasped his gloved hands, pulled his hood over his dark hair, and turned his back on the corpse. Walking away, he meticulously retraced his steps, erasing any hint of his presence.

***

Purring lowly, the sound of a lone engine muffled through a calm serenity of Beach Road. Navigating from shadow to shadow with only the sidelights to display the rise of the verges, a black hatchback prowled like a slinking lynx on the hunt for prey. Spotting a rundown cottage hidden behind a forest of twisted bushes, the car crawled past.

Godda be the one.

The car turned in an abandoned driveway, returned to the plot, and came to a stop.

The cottage's upper level consisted of a singular diabolical glass eye, spying down like the cycloptic villain of a nineteen-fifties Sinbad film. Below this, a ramshackle timber-framed summerhouse confirmed with near certainty that this was indeed the place. That somewhere beyond this dilapidated dwelling, an unsuspecting Kray-brother-wannabee was awaiting his twin, preparing to exact a brutal revenge on some hapless pikey loser that had supposedly played curiosity and killed the cat.

Cutting the motor, Chris exited the vehicle, clicking his door gently to in an effort to avoid rousing the neighbours. As he alighted the pathway, he was stunned motionless. Straining in the dark, his slowly adjusting eyes failed to point out the wrought iron gate hanging askew on one old fixing, partially obstructing his passage. His booted foot struck the metal, sending it grinding backwards with an excruciating howl that made his skin crawl. Time stopped moving abruptly as Chris slowly rotated his scrawny head, owl-like, scoping the area to his vulnerable back.

Just as he was beginning relax, satisfied that his clumsy actions had not attracted the attention of every living soul on the road, a scampering scurry erupted from the brush on the far side of the rundown property. Chris darted his ferret muzzle towards the estimated location of the sound.

I hear ya, buddy. And I'm comin' for ya, you liddle fuck. You'll find id 'ard bonin' that sister of 'is when I cut yer cock off.

Reaching into the pocket of his tracksuit bottoms, Chris' hand wrapped around a smooth, elongated metal barrel. It felt like unfathomable power between his nasty fingers. After removing the object, one incy-wincy press released its strictly-business interior with a cold *schink*.

Step after feather light step, Chris skirted the outer wall of the decaying death-trap. He could vaguely make out where the building ended. At that point, no more than five meters ahead, the narrow path rounded a corner. That's where he would be, the jumped up prick, hunkered down low anticipating Jack's arrival.

Man 'ave you god a treat comin'. When I'm done slicin' yer liddle pecker off I'm gonna shove it down yer throat. You'll have to tell that sweet piece o' jailbait 'ow it tasted, mind. Cos she'll never gedda gobble on it.

The narrow figure threw his sinewy frame around the corner, flick knife extended like the stabbing beak of a heron, hunting a small, defenceless fish.

To his dismay, Chris' found no hunkering youth, but just more weeds and brambles.

Where are ya, prick?

Chris took a moment to survey his surroundings.

Started without me, eh? He mused, spotting a dim glow deeper into the entangled garden. *Thought ya didn' do yer own dirdy work.*

Chris plodded his gangly legs meticulously over and around the scrub, careful not to snag any of his clothing. If he was going to do this youngster over here, he was acutely keen to leave nothing to track him by. Arriving at the source of the light, he could see that it was creeping through the cracks of a bivouac type structure, erected with old wood and rags. A tatty off-white cover stirred in the gently swirling air, apparently a crude entry way.

Chris listened closely at the hanging cover, confused and somewhat wary that no human sound emanated from beyond. Teasing with his left hand, knife poised in the right, he discreetly forged an opening big enough to obtain a view through.

'What the fuck?' he whispered in horrified bemusement.

Throwing the makeshift curtain back, the whole interior revealed itself. A pool of blood spread as black as pitch under an old chair. The chair housed a sole occupant. Slouched backwards, mouth agape. Drying blood caked on his chin. Soulless eyes staring bewildered at the new arrival. The body seemed to be fixed in place by a pitchfork. It protruded grotesquely from its stomach in a Satanic slaughter.

Covering his mouth with the knife-wielding arm, Chris urged into his sleeve. Swallowing instinctively, the sour taste vomit trickled down his gullet.

CHAPTER THIRTY

The trek down Rocky Lane was steep and cumbersome under the cover of night. But with the buzz of a few pints rapidly streaming to his brain, and the echoes of the live band still ringing in his head, Andrew felt he was walking on marshmallow.

Disappointingly, they had to leave before the night barely got started on account of Alycia's stand-in mother texting to say she had one of her migraines again. Evidently, she needed a darkened room more than she needed to look after her wonderful-but-hyperactive granddaughter. So, the two newly-acquainted...*friends? Lovers? Well, we haven't done it yet,* thought Andrew. So, if society insisted upon categorising them, then he guessed *'friends'* was what they were. Either way, the pair were begrudgingly forced to cut the night short.

'Gotta keep ba ba da ba...'

An owl hooted from within the dense thicket of trees to his left, hidden in some remote corner of the swishing canopies.

'Whoo-whooh,' Andrew replied. 'Vibrations a-hap'nin' with... Gotta keep them, ba da ba'

He stepped awkwardly on an unseen stone, going over on his ankle. 'Shit. Asshole!'

Laughing at himself foolishly, he plodded on. 'Naa na na na ba-dup-a, vibrations ba-da da dada.'

Reaching the bottom of the long descent, Andrew passed the microbrewery and bore right where Rocky Lane met the lower end of Beach Road. There was a good crowd of drinkers outside the Drifty, enjoying a cool, dry evening in the company of good people. None of whom, however, were good enough to pay Andrew the slightest notice. Or was it, he wasn't good enough for them? *Still the outsider,* he thought morosely. *But that doesn't matter one iota,* he reprimanded himself. Outside of his little bubble there were only three people that mattered in this judgmental village now: his *'friend'*, her young daughter, and the built-in babysitter in the form of an ex's mother – unless she had another migraine and rendered herself useless, of course.

Almost home. Grabbing the splintery top rail of his garden fence for support as he stood on the passing road, Andrew looked to the stars and inhaled lengthily. He was by no means drunk, but the effects of the alcohol he had consumed were definitely in evidence. This large intake of air would hopefully straighten him out enough to hoodwink the hoity-toity Judith (who he had almost certainly not been out long enough to avoid) into thinking that he had not touched a drop all night.

Deciding to test his level of soberness out for himself, Andrew let go of the fence, straightened his posture, and looked dead ahead up the road, commencing a count to ten.

As he counted, an unusual sight caught his attention. A small hatchback was parked to one side of the road. Nothing unusual to the average passer-by, maybe, but *where* it was parked would raise suspicion to anyone local to this quiet corner of the village. Andrew had not known a soul to visit Raymond for as long as the Tredinnick's had lived in St. Agnes. The scene was made all the stranger by another niggling factor. Something Andrew had seen before, but could not figure out what. Still unknown to him what brought on the potent feeling of déjà vu, he scanned the ethanol clouded depths of his mind.

Compelled to step closer, Andrew made his way sceptically up the road. The very position of this car – at the gate of a recluse who had no known living relatives as far as Andrew was aware, and unquestionably no friends – was enough to demand further investigation. There was also a familiarness about the car, something taking him back to a previous chapter in his life.

As if a sudden cloudburst had washed the alcohol away, he got it. Two white stickers on the dusty black boot, blurry at first, came into sharp focus under the dullness of the night sky.

Clunge Magnet.

No Fat Chicks.

'Get to fuck,' Andrew murmured to the apathetic night air.

Audible from his position now only ten meters or so down the road, the sound of thrashing bushes and leaves came scurrying frantically through the air. Peering hard, Andrew caught sight of a shadowy apparition, distorted by its flailing and falling motion but unmistakably human. It fought through Raymond's disordered forest of a garden, bursting from between the two granite gateposts and catching their hip heavily on the top corner of the leaning ironwork. The rugby tackle from the defending gate threw them off-balance, causing them to slam against the side of the stationary car.

Andrew saw this as his chance. He sprinted forward on clumsy, alcohol-fuelled legs. Hearing heavy footsteps approaching at a rapid pace from behind, the figure arched over the rear quarter panel of the ironically stickered Golf blindly swung an arm backward. A dazzling flash of lightning bolted through Andrew's head as the elbow, moving with breakneck velocity, connected squarely with the bridge of his nose. His legs gave way at the knees, gravity pulling him gracelessly backwards to asphalt.

With the slam of a door, a drawn-out choke of ignition, and a noisy roar of a revving engine, a shit-shower of loose stones and roadside debris fizzed over Andrew as he lay helpless. Watching from under a shielding arm, he saw the black Volkswagen snake, overcorrect, and snaked again onto the main drag.

Remiss of the fact that he had been enjoying an evening on the suds, Andrew clambered to his feet, wildly feeling for keys in his jacket pocket. If hindsight afforded him a glimpse at the scenario that was about to play out, he would have wished the keys weren't there.

Grabbing them hard he ran towards home, determined legs pounding at the floor, eyes streaming and blurred from the elbow to the face.

The white walls of Sea Glass Cottage illuminated orange as two pulses flared from the hazard lights, signifying that the doors were cooperating fully with his urgency. Andrew piled in hurriedly, hit the 'start' button and reversed the crossover skilfully around the angle of the drive, before forcing the gearstick into first and screaming up the road. He took a slight right-hander at nearly fifty miles per hour. Despite this being a ridiculous speed for such a tight minor road, he pushed harder at the accelerator pedal. Emerging onto a short straight, still unable to get a visual on the taillights he was chasing, Andrew dropped a gear and floored the power. He reached a treacherous sixty as he approached the next bend.

Stabbing hard on the brake pedal and twisting the steering wheel a split second too early, the rear tyres gave out and sent the back end of the vehicle drifting out to the centre of the road. Andrew yanked the wheel back to counteract the spin, landing near the opposite verge.

In a flash his vision became an impenetrable mist of bright white. A screech of rubber engulfed the night sky, followed by a monstrous crumpling of metal and shattering glass. The last fragment of Andrew's awareness was to feel the forceful sucker punch of the Qashqai's airbag, the world's most lethal bubble-gum, blowing into his chest and his already excruciatingly painful nose.

CHAPTER THIRTY-ONE

Laying stretched on his bed in dark seclusion, hands behind his noggin and headphones blaring out Placebo's "Scene of the Crime", Cameron thought of the how the universe selected the most appropriate of tunes at the most opportune moments.

The initial shock of the night's events, which were executed completely and inexplicably against plan, petered out, fizzling away like the dying embers of the last joint that had sent him sinking into nirvana. The tunes acted as a sonic catharsis, through which his feeling of apprehension was replaced by the sensation of euphoria. Euphoria at knowing how meticulously and methodically he had retraced his every movement through the garden that witnessed the last mortal actions of one Raymond...Whatever his name was.

Realising that he did not even know the surname of his latest victim, a man whom he had lived just down the road from for a number of years now, Cameron also realised he could not give a shit.

No point getting sentimental, now. Ain't anyone on Earth gonna miss that smelly old fucker.

What did matter is that, to the best of his knowledge, he had left no trace of himself at that literal scene of the crime. And he was near certain that Kerenza had not noticed him leaving or returning home. This meant a rock-solid alibi. *No sir, didn't see or hear a thing. Yes, I was in all night. Ask my sis.*

Jack, on the other hand. Well, he would have shat himself as assuredly and explosively as Vesuvius once dropped a massive steaming turd on the population of Pompeii. There was no way on this planet that whilst leaving a shitstorm in his wake through

Raymond's neglected oasis, Jack would have thought to erase every last evidential indication of his presence.

With a bit of luck someone would've seen that twatty car of yours too, Jackie lad.

As unwelcome as a cockroach in a kebab, light impeded the perfect blackness, showing a startling pink through Cameron's closed eyelids. Before his brain could register the sudden change in conditions and draw the heavy lids open, a groping hand clawed and shook at his shoulder. Forcing his eyes open, ready to shout abuse at whomever had the nerve to disturb his stupor, Cam saw a clearly distressed Kerenza hunched over him. He ripped off his headphones. Before he could ask what was wrong, she burst into tearful hysterics.

'*THEY'VE BEEN IN AN ACCIDENT!*' she screamed at the stupefied boy on the bed.

'What? *Who?* What you on about?'

'*ALL OF THEM, THEY'RE IN HOSPITAL.*'

'Whoa, simmer down,' he urged. 'You're gonna deafen me in a minute. Who's in hospital?'

Kerenza took a deep breath, before exhaling slowly and gaining some composure. 'Dad___'

'Dad again?' Cameron interrupted in bemusement. 'What the fuck's he done this time?'

'A crash. He hit them head-on.' Kerenza was visibly shaking now.

'Hit *who* head on?'

'Gr,' Kerenza struggled. 'Gran and Grandad.'

Aw, fucking brilliant. 'What the hell was he doing driving?' Cameron asked. 'He was out on the piss.'

'Merryn,' Kerenza said slowly. 'She was in the car, too.'

This is great. The way that prick keeps on screwing up, it'll be just the two of us in no time, thought Cameron conspiratorially.

'And,' Kerenza swallowed and paused, seeming unable to utter the words she needed to get out next. 'Grandad had a heart attack. He's okay. For the minute anyway, but…' She trailed off. They both knew what the *'but'* meant.

Now that's unfortunate. He doesn't deserve that. But it's not the end of the world, if he pegs it that stuck up old bitch will be all alone and demanding custody of Mez from my incompetent liability of a father. One night I'll just be able to leave a bottle of scotch and a handful of strong pills lying around and he'll see to the rest. Won't even need to get blood on my hands. The perfect ending.

In a rare, warm show of sincerity, Cameron reached out and took hold of one of Kerenza's hands.

'I know you won't realise it yet, not when it's so raw,' he comforted. 'But this could all be for the best.'

'How do you mean?' she asked in a sobbing whisper.

'Well, we both wanted it to be just the two of us,' he smiled intently.

CHAPTER THIRTY-TWO

Leafless trees glowed ossein white in the advancing headlights of the Subaru, their elongated fingers ranging and pointing condemningly. Corner after corner came and went with only a cursory attention paid. A whirlwind of thoughts circulating turbulently inside of Jack's head stole all but one small part – the autopilot part – of his concentration from the dizzying country backroads.

He had to get away from the house. The constant reappearances of Grace's shadow at the window scrutinised through the black tinted glass of the Impreza. She knew something was up. The longer he sat there with his thumb up his ass, the more her surmising would seem justified. So, in compunction Jack fled.

His phone pinged. A text message had come through. He slowed down a touch as he retrieved the mobile from the centre console.

Treliske ind est. Last
left b4 hospital 15 mins.

Why couldn't you just phone me to let me know how it went? The not knowing was toying with Jack's sanity.

He did not relish the prospect of another meeting with the unsavoury Chris. The job was done. Make a phone call and move on. Unless Chris wanted something in return. Money? He can go screw himself. Favour for a favour? No, he owed Lucas that one. That was between the two of them. The slate was wiped clean.

Jack had a dismaying feeling that *his* slate was maybe not so clean, that this could be the start of a very ugly friendship. Having asked this deed from Chris, had Jack now installed himself as some kind of proletarian pawn for the ginger psychopath to use at his disposal? Checkmate, asshole.

He threw his phone anxiously onto the passenger seat and headed for the road to Truro at a reckless pace.

Pulling into the industrial estate no more than ten minutes later, Jack was relieved to see that a run of streetlights cast a series of misty hemispheres from one end of the stretch to the other. No dark alleys, nowhere to hide.

How wrong he was.

No living thing stirred as Jack purred the Subaru slowly through the line of industrial units, not even the wild comings and goings of nocturnal creatures sharing his space. Arriving at the last left on the estate he locked the steering anticlockwise. Nothing greeted him.

Must be early, he thought, nearing the end of the short side road. That was when he spotted the black Golf tucked neatly away in the shadow of the last shuttered industrial unit.

Shit.

The silver Subaru thudded down at its offside as the driver failed to navigate a large pothole, near the entrance of the small customer parking area. As it pulled close, an inconspicuous, capped figure slunk from the gloom in a slender weasel-like manner. Pulling into a nearby space, the driver of the Impreza killed the thrumming motor and stepped out arrogantly.

'Wagwan?' he asked, sauntering up.

Chris paid no mind to this lame show of bravado, turning instead to the boot of his car and popping it open.

'*WHAT THE FUCK?*' Jack shrieked, pitched highly enough to make anyone in earshot believe that his balls were years from dropping.

'Keep the fuckin' noise down, idiot,' Chris said calmly as he turned his sharp features back over his shoulder.

'*YOU…*' Jack checked his volume. 'You brought him with you?' Panic oozed through with every terrified syllable.

'Did I fuck, numbnuts,' sneered Chris. 'You godda come see whod I did bring though.'

Chris listened to the tentative steps approach nervously from behind, waiting for them to tread upon what he calculated to be the perfect distance away. Clasped firmly in his obscured hand was the fat end of a snooker cue.

One crumble of discarded glass on the concrete floor told the little hand it was time to rock'n'roll. Spit flew from Chris' mouth as he spun snarling. Gloss black ash wood cut through the air like a sword, connecting with a deadened thud on Jack's neck. The unsuspecting target hit the ground like a fallen tree, writhing in agony, clutching his neck and gasping for air.

Casually, Chris hunkered down on his haunches next to the struggling kid lying on the forecourt.

'Didun tell me there'd be a dead guy waidin for me, did'ee?'

'W_w__what?' Jack asked, bemused and barely able to breathe.

'You fuckin' 'eard!' Chris hissed, lunging a boot into Jack's helpless ribcage.

'I don't__I don't___'

Boot.

'No…cunt…takes…me…for…a…mug,' his attacker persisted, slinging a forceful kick at the defenceless form on the cold ground between every teeth-gritting word.

A barrage of swings came raining down, the snooker cue carrying out a bloody business as far from its intended purpose as a butter knife in a jousting duel. More kicks to the ribs and chest followed, the pain becoming so complete that every inch of his body was numbing itself out of existence. Through one shocked, scared and squinting eye, Jack could see the long, black shaft cruising towards his skull. At long last, darkness became all-encompassing.

***

Jane stepped out into the cold night air, made even more perishing from her long hard slog in hectic, stuffy and suffocating Accident and Emergency department. She sparked up a cigarette and took a long, hard drag.

This evening had proved to be a total bitch. Arriving at work almost five-and-a-half hours earlier after a blazing argument with her boyfriend, which ended with him instructing her not to bother coming home – to her own house! – she felt like a trooper for even turning up tonight. Take one for the team. Her head told her that it would be best if the lazy, sponging cockroach would be gone by the time she got home; her heart told her that she would forgive him (again) because she needed him around.

'For what, though?' she asked the patchy stars, as she exhaled a streaming plume of smoke into the night sky.

Since arriving for her eventful shift at just after seven that evening, Jane had been thrown up on by a drunk with a broken nose; had her ass pinched by his equally drunk friend, of whom she suspected from the tell tail drying claret on his knuckles, had been the one responsible for the broken nose; and she had been spat at by a rough little slapper in a strappy lace top and leopard print miniskirt, neither of which doing a great job in the flesh coverage department. The face-full of phlegm was issued because Jane refused to give her *something a little stronger* for the pain.

It's a twisted ankle caused by a combination of ridiculously high heels and too much cheap wine. Get over it, trollop.

Turning her face away from the stars, accepting that the solution to her problems was not staring down at her, Jane took another soothing drag. As the illuminated cloud of exhaled smoke dispersed, she caught sight of an unusual thing. A large shape lay dormant on the tarmac towards the entryway to the hospital. A shape that was worryingly human. Forgetting the smouldering cigarette between her fingers, Jane darted back into the foyer, ringing out shouts for security.

CHAPTER THIRTY-THREE

Cold, wet beads soaked into the seat of his dark rinse jeans from the hard, metal bench. The curved glass overhead, coupled with practically futile side panels, did little to stop the heavy, stirring Cornish mizzle from plastering him top to toe. Fine droplets congregated over his face, running in streams, amassing and exiting in larger drops from the tip of his nose and the five o'clock-shadow that besmirched his chin.

He was unable to muster the strength to look up. Looking up would be to stare longingly in the direction of the hospital where he had last seen his little girl. Sure, the immense bundle of buildings was shielded by trees, and therefore unviewable from this low roadside vantage point, but just knowing it was there, lurking like a prowler behind them, was enough to rob him of his fortitude.

The endless *swoosh* of continuous traffic forcing treaded rubber through the saturated surface echoed though his disorganised mind, persisting like a swarm of murderous wasps. Turning from reflected cloud to flat green, the puddles lying still before his wet shoes signalled the arrival of a bus. Following this vision came the hiss of air brakes and the flap of concertina doors, prompting Andrew to look up.

'Eighty-seven?' he asked the chubby driver, sat squeezed into his cosy compartment, like a Yorkshire pudding rising over the baking tray.

'That's what it says, pal,' said the Yorkshire pud, completely devoid of charisma.

Happy chap, Andrew deduced.

He stood and stepped onto the double-decker, needing the assistance of the grab bar to help pull his weary body up from the pavement. Luckily (or possibly not so), Andrew had escaped the collision without so much as scratch. Previously sustained broken nose excluded, the airbag proved to be worth its weight in gold.

The occupants of the other vehicle did not escape so lightly. The airbags deployed as they were supposed to. That deployment of the lifesaving bag compressed into a compartment in the centre of the steering wheel, however, unwittingly became a direct contributor to the big man's myocardial infarction. And then there was the smallest of the occupants, sat in the back of a vehicle that was not equipped with such luxuries as rear airbags.

Andrew could not recall the last time he had set foot on public transport. Therefore, he could not hazard a guess as to the price of a ticket. Opting for the route of putting the happy driver out as much as he could, he removed his wallet from his jean's pocket and proceeded to empty every scrap of change onto the driver's cash tray.

'St. Agnes. Single.'

The driver looked up from his double chin and raised a flabbergasted eyebrow.

'Pleeease,' Andrew smirked sarcastically.

Shuffling though the pile of loose change and counting in his head, the driver took what he needed, printed the ticket and handed it to Andrew without further correspondence.

Grabbing the ticket and scooping up the leftover coins, Andrew headed to a spare seat halfway down the double-decker's centre aisle. He studied the faces, deep in thought looking out at the grim day and not paying the drenched man with the chip on his shoulder any consideration. This suited Andrew down to the ground. Idle chitchat was number one on his list of things he could not tolerate right now. Stay under the radar.

He shoved himself gracelessly into a vacant seat, adjacent to the row of condensation covered windows that looked on in the direction of the hospital. This calculated move would avoid the gaze of the building's accusing façade should the trees open out. As the noisy diesel chugged into the flowing traffic, leaving last night's accommodation dwindling away behind, Andrew's frayed emotions buckled.

The rest of the agonisingly sluggish trip was spent with a finger and thumb pressed deep into his eye sockets. His head fought to stay above the surface in a turbulent bath of thick, cloying liquid regret: what the hell had happened last night? How to tell the Cam and Krenz? He wanted out. That was surely the easiest way. Head to the cliff. Walk to the edge. Look down the deep throat into Shona's last known resting place. Fall to her. The end. What could be simpler? The most effortless element of life has to be death, provided you make the act of dying brisk.

The swaying green machine rolled downwards along Town Hill, heading towards the pub and the Chinese restaurant. Andrew pressed the red STOP button, lifted himself from the seat and staggered towards the front of the bus as it mumbled to a halt.

Waiting for the hiss of the doors, Andrew said his thanks to the driver. Hitting a button, *Yorkshire pud* never spoke. Andrew alighted the vehicle, shaking his head in despondency.

He headed around the back of the Chinese and was greeted by a heavy fog. The white wall crawled its languid way from the cove, consuming everything in sight. Walking headlong into it had an ominous feel as ghostly white tendrils lunged towards him like limbs of the dead, evaporating to nothing before their icy fingers could impress upon his skin.

Carrying on in the direction of home, Andrew walked near-blind in the thick damp air. Shallow lost steps delayed his progress. He stopped completely, his heart sinking at the sight of a series of markings on the surface of the road, markings that all the fog on Earth could not shield. Savage slashes of black rubber scarred the aggregate. Fragmented glass lay cast aside along the saturated verge. The leftover debris a poignant reminder of the previous evening's devastation.

Standing forlorn, drenched and pitiful, Andrew visualised phantoms of his little girl, sat smiling her unbeatable smile, and two vehicles coming together in a cataclysm of imploding metal. The smile obscured by steel crushing in around it.

Images of baby Merryn's first ever trip down this road eclipsed those of crumpled metal and shattered glass. Tucked so snug in her car seat in the back, her beautiful mother sat beside her. Andrew had aimed continuous glances in the rear-view mirror. Unable to see the newest member of their family, he instead marvelled at his wife's unfaltering smile, a resolute joy on her face that this world could not conspire to extinguish.

With his head remembering the good times, Andrew encouraged his feet to leave crash site behind and head for the shelter of home, yet still sticking to his lackadaisical pace. I mean, even the very best memories of a happier time were hardly going to inject a spring in his step, were they? There was not exactly a sunset to skip off into.

Rounding the corner that gave a partially concealed vista of Sea Glass Cottage, a hypnotising azure glow pulsated in the coastal fog. The blue light penetrated the fog's enveloping cloak, intensifying with every step forward. Shapes proceeded to materialise from the monochromatic disco, first one white car with Battenberg markings, then another. An ambulance with similar colourings; a third car; and a gunmetal grey private ambulance. All of which were stationary and within close proximity of Raymond's front entrance.

Two uniforms stood in Hi Vis vests before the recluse's crookedly hung garden gate. Their hands were clasped at their fronts, their faces set in grim seriousness.

Slowed by apprehension, Andrew approached them.

'What happened?' he asked, a lump in his throat going down like the stone of a large fruit as he swallowed.

'We can't give any details at the minute, sir,' the taller of the two officers offered, the silent officer looking Andrew up and down sceptically. 'It's best that you just move along and leave us to do our work.'

'I chased someone from here last night,' said Andrew. 'I spoke to your guys at the hospital about it.'

'If that's so, we may require further assistance from you soon. I trust you don't have plans for the rest of the day?'

'No,' Andrew answered, confused and a little concerned. 'I'll be at home, down the road.' He pointed in the general direction. 'They took my address.'

'Thank you,' the officer returned. 'Now, if that's all?'

Andrew nodded confirmation and turned homeward again.

Hitting the gravel drive at Sea Glass, his feet abruptly became cumbersome. Through an unwillingness to enter the cottage, or through sheer exhaustion, Andrew could not discern. A cocktail of both possibilities seemed the likely. Before he could make it the whole way to the front door, it burst open and Kerenza came running out. Throwing her arms around him, she hugged him tight.

'Why aren't you at school?' Andrew asked, voice deep and struggling with the pressure his stepdaughter exerted on his chest.

'I couldn't face it with all that happened last night,' she replied. 'Anyway, that's not important now. Where is Merryn?'

He gave her a look that said *let's not do this out here;* or so Kerenza interpreted.

'Let's get you in. You change into something dry while I make you a coffee.'

'Think I need something stronger than coffee,' he sighed.

'Well, that's not happening,' she said turning to lead him to the house. She stopped short of saying the next line to come into her head: *That's how this whole thing started.*

Soon after, Andrew came downstairs refreshed and in drier attire. He still appeared downcast. This was understandable, Kerenza supposed. She nodded to his steaming cup of coffee on the side table. Seating himself on the sofa next to it, he picked it up, more to warm his tingling fingers than anything else. He spotted Kerenza eyeing him intently and promptly returned his attention to the coffee he was nursing.

'Well?' Kerenza asked impatiently.

'Your grandads doing well,' he started. 'He's still in for observation but he's awake and talking. They think he's going to be okay. Probably making the most of being away from the dragon.'

No laughter came.

'And Merryn?'

Andrew placed his coffee back on the low table and put his face into his cupped hands. Kerenza joined him on the sofa and placed a soothing hand on his shoulder.

'You should see her bruises.' He shuddered under her hand. 'Purple. Blue. Black. All over her neck and down her little chest.

He paused, striving to regain some composure. Tears welled in the corner of Kerenza's cool blue eyes.

'She's taken her,' Andrew went on hesitantly. 'Your gran. Says I'm not fit to be a father.'

'She can't___'

'No. She's right,' he said, cutting his stepdaughter off. 'I go from one screw up to the next. I'm incapable of looking after anyone.'

Kerenza slunk back into the cushions, pondering his words. 'That's not true,' she said after a brief pause. 'And you know it. Considering all that's happened, you're holding together as best you can, and that is good enough. The important thing is that Merrs is with family, and not with complete strangers. We need to pull together, convince Gran that you *are* fit to be a father, and that as a unit we are strong. It may take time, but we'll get my baby sister back.'

Portraying a confidence that was older than her years, Andrew dared to believe that she may be right, though somewhere in his mind, that nagging voice persisted, he was just not cut out for this, and therefore a danger to his children.

After sharing an edgy silence, Andrew realised that someone was missing.

'Speaking of *"as a unit"*, Cam not want to stick around for when I got home?'

'You know him,' her smile a despondent line on her face. 'I left him in his room last night, then came back down and fell asleep. He was gone before I woke up.'

'Shit,' Andrew clapped his hands to his knees and leaned forward urgently. 'I haven't told Alycia.'

The involvement of an outsider annoyed Kerenza. 'That's not impor___'

A knock at the door stopped the young girl from going any further. They both shot a glance at each other, vacated the sofa and headed for the kitchen. Through the etched glass panel of the front door, the outline of two figures could be seen. Andrew opened it to see two uniformed police officers by the step.

'Mr Tredinnick?' a tall, dark-haired man asked.

'Yes, that's me.'

'We'd appreciate it if you would accompany us to the station to answer some questions.'

'I've already been through this,' Andrew replied looking confused.

'There has been a development,' one of the officers said flatly.

'Okay, what kind of development?'

The officer who had been doing the talking looked to the female officer at his side.

'The property that you claim to have chased a suspicious person from last night,' she spoke with confidence, 'We found the body of a man in the garden. We believe it to be the owner of the house.'

'Raymond? Dead?' Andrew asked, dizzying with shock.

'If you'd like to accompany us, sir,' the male police officer persisted.

'Wait,' said Andrew. 'Are you saying I'm a suspect?'

'Right now,' the authoritative brunette woman continued with conviction. 'Your admission of being at the scene is all we have.'

CHAPTER THIRTY-FOUR

Salty tears streamed over Grace's freckled cheeks, mimicking the conditions outside. The usual shallow paleness surrounding the clusters of brown specks, akin to that of a body dragged from a lake on any normal occasion, was now a deep, smouldering rouge.

She turned her phone over in her hands, staring out at the threatening black clouds. Of the dozen or so attempts to call her friend, whom she was desperate beyond comprehension to speak with and pass her heart-breaking news on to, not one click of the call icon had proven successful.

Flicking the screen back to life with a finger, Grace beat the button yet again.

'Grace?'

Finally.

'Krenz, something's,' she sobbed. 'Something's happened, I don't. I__'

'Grace, I don't want to upset you, but I've had a really shitty day. Can you just spit it out?'

Grace was taken aback at her friend's bluntness. 'It's Jack. He's, he's,' she sniffed back through her clogging nose and licked salt water from her top lip.

'What about Jack?' Kerenza's voice started to exhibit the first signs of worry. 'Get it together!'

'He's been beaten up,' she finally managed. 'Badly. Really badly. He's in hospital.'

Another one? Kerenza felt her stomach twist in knots, unsure of whether she may pass out or puke up.

'Grace, I can't do this now. My grandad is in there, too. They were in a car accident with my dad last night,' her throat crackled with emotion. 'Gran's taken Merryn and the police have got my dad 'cos the guy up the road got killed.' Tears were fighting their way from her own eyes now.

What the hell is going on, thought Grace. 'I'm on my own,' she whimpered. 'Is… is Cam with you?' she asked nervously.

Bitch. 'No. He disappeared early hours of this morning, we don't know where he is. Grace, I'm sorry but I gotta go. We'll speak later.'

The line went dead. Grace sat cross-legged on her bed, once again with the sound of grim winter outside her window in soggy battle with her own snivelling. Ten minutes went by, with her static on the bed. A torrent of questions flooded her mind, each followed by an explanatory mental image more confusing and disturbing than its predecessor.

Why had her best friend been so dismissive? How could these completely separate incidents happen to them on the same night? Why had Cameron gone AWOL when her brother had seven bells of shit beaten out of him?

Her phone beeped loudly, making her jump near out of her skin. One new message, Kerenza:

> *Sorry I was so short babe, idk y,*
> *just stressed. Be on next bus in 40.*
> *We'll go see Jack xx*

Grace grabbed up a handful of her bed covers and padded her puffy eyes before throwing on more-suitable clothing.

Skittering to the bus stop she raised her head to the unforgiving sky and prayed to God that Cameron had nothing to do with whatever that landed her brother in hospital.

God's failure to answer did little to convince her otherwise.

CHAPTER THIRTY-FIVE

A colossal roar issued from the dirty engine, resonating around the enclosed space and drowning out all competing sound. Its diesel stink hung in the air like a plague. The old saying *'wait ages for a bus and then two come along at once'* rang true today, loosely. For the second time in a matter of hours, Andrew found himself watching a depressing world roll by. On this occasion, he headed straight for the backseat without giving any other passenger even a fleeting glance. Sitting practically in self-isolation, he contemplated his time in the nick, answering the same questions a hundred times over.

Springing into his mind, a thought caused him to snigger.

Quick enough to drag an innocent man in. Don't give the fucker a lift home, though.

The bus sopped and idled at a set of traffic lights, the engine quieting just long enough to hear a tune playing out from his pocket. Fishing his phone out, the illuminated screen informed him that Alycia was calling.

'Hey' he said mellowly, the conversation just about audible. Watching the flashing amber light, Andrew wondered why the bus remained motionless.

'Hi,' came a meek reply. 'The office just told me why Merryn wasn't at school today. Bloody hell, Andrew, are you okay?'

His observations deviated from the pulsing amber to an old lady crossing the road, listlessly pulling her tired looking shopping trolley behind her. A Cornish tartan scarf wrapped around her slumping head fended off the late afternoon mizzle.

Hurry up you daft old bat. 'No, not really. On a bus to 'Druth at the minute, God knows how long I'll have to wait there for one for Aggie.'

'Why are you over that way?'

Andrew spoke up as the engine grew from a whisper to a din, lurching away in first gear as the old woman vacated the crossing. 'Been at Camborne Police Station. Someone's___'

'About the accident?' Alycia interrupted, sounding a little rattled.

'No,' Andrew resumed. 'That old hermit up the road, Raymond. He's been murdered. They thought it might be me cos I told them I was outside there last night. Think I'm okay though.'

'I'll pick you up.'

'What?' Andrew asked, struggling to hear her on the other end of the line as the bus noisily gained momentum. 'I can't hear you.'

'I'll pick you up,' she repeated, her voice echoing around her in the empty classroom as she raised it; not the first time such vocal force was called for within those four walls. 'Get off at the train station, I'll be in the car park.' Her voice came through loud, clear, and non-negotiable.

Andrew listened to a silent phone as the call was terminated. His dazed attention returned to the passing terraced houses, one thought on his mind: a murder suspect. *I'm a murder suspect.* Well, *that* was an unexpected reality. He was an artist; he had a deftly touch with a brush, but with a…what? A knife? A gun? A lump hammer? He didn't even know the identity of the item that inflicted the mortal blow. And there he was, a *suspect.*

As the bus grumbled to a stop, Andrew descended onto slick granite paving slabs. He crossed the road to the railway station. Entering the small triangular car park that served the travelling customers, he viewed his surroundings. No one familiar was there to greet him. Having no idea what car Alycia drove (in honesty, he didn't even know that she could drive), he presumed that if she had made it already, she would be standing where he could see her. Letting his feet do the talking, he ambled slowly over to the cast iron fence that served as a defensive barrier between the assembly of parked vehicles and the unforgiving train line. Grabbing an iron spear in each hand, Andrew rested the soft flesh of his submental triangle on the rounded black spike between them, heavily enough to leave an indentation.

Eyeing the gleaming friction polished steel tracks, he thought about Shona. More unspoken phenomena. Often, the local travel reports would inform you of delays between so-and-so and blah-blah-blah. Rarely would they mention the dismembered body lying in state on the lines. Much like the jumpers at Hell's Mouth. Yes, it happens; of course it does. But respectable civilians do not need to hear about it.

A car horn gave out two short toots behind him. Rubber scrunched tiny fragments of stone to the ground as the vehicle slid to a stop, like the driver had not thought to apply the brakes until the last second.

Never had her down as a girl-racer, Andrew thought, impressed. He turned his back to the tracks, frowned, and walked towards the car shaking his head.

Alycia leaned over the passenger seat and popped the door open. 'Taxi for Tredinnick!' she stated.

Andrew bowed towards the open door, resting a forearm along the roof. 'You've got to be joking, right?' he asked mockingly, referring to the flamingo pink Fiat *500* that his new interest was sat in triumphantly, smiling away and looking like the fat cat that not only got the cream, but the whole frigging dairy.

'Hottest ride on the road,' she said, grinning from ear to ear. 'Think yourself lucky I'm even letting you in.'

Andrew gave a doubtful expression, though he conceded the fact that Alycia most likely knew more about this pink Italian miniature stallion than he did himself. He squeezed into the vacant seat. Without giving him the time to close his door, Alycia spun the steering wheel full lock and zipped a clockwise one-eighty in the centre of the car park, nearly toppling Andrew straight back out of the void he came in through.

'Whoa, you trying to kill me?' he blasted, finding the handle and yanking the door shut safe and tight.

'Trying to put a smile on your face,' she said. 'You look as bad as I expect you feel.'

'Funny way to cheer someone up.'

Alycia tipped him a wink, poking her tongue out from the corner of her mouth and screwing her face up shrew-like as she did so.

Okay, an inner confessional voice instructed as he sniggered to himself, *a tad unconventional, but I guess it worked.*

They left the sanctuary of the car park and hit the streets. Conversation came as a struggle. In fact, it was at a complete stop for a time. The flamingo stop-started through the convoy of traffic lights that spread like a plague of locusts around the town. The heavy populous of vehicles and the dense air weighed in unison with the seismic events of last night, crushing Andrew's spirits and sapping his resolve. How can a night that started so well end with such a catastrophic chain of events?

Oppressive buildings thinned out, giving way to lines of trees, broken sporadically by pastures of grass and scrubland. The air quality changed in an instant as country approached and town receded. Andrew thought of all the times that he had found a spider in the house at night and could not be bothered to throw it out until the morning dawned. He did not want the spider in question to find another hiding space, so he would grab a jar, trap the creepy looking arachnid inside, and screw the lid on tight overnight. Now he finally got a sense of how the poor creature might feel, striving for breath in the stale air, escape seeming an impossibility, then suddenly, boom. The fresh outdoors.

The thought process of any human being can leave another totally bamboozled. For all the mental torment his brain had to deal with at this extraordinary phase of his life, Andrew had made a decision: he would never trap another spider in a jar again as long as he lived.

'Penny for 'em?' Alycia broke the silence, also sensing the change in atmosphere brought on by the more scenic surroundings.

'Hmm?'

'You look lost in thought. I wondered if you wanted to share.'

'Oh. Spiders.' Andrew looked across to her and smiled.

'Spiders. Okay.' Alycia glanced at him a little bewildered, before returning her attention to the winding anthracite ribbon ahead. 'Anything in particular? About spiders I mean.'

'Not really.' Andrew turned to his misting window, lowering it fully to clear the condensation before flicking it back up to half mast.

'Well,' Alycia replied. 'That's good. Horrible little freaks. I didn't want to talk about them anyway. We can talk about anything else though. I know you've got more to get off your chest than your cryptic thoughts of creepy crawlies.'

'Will you come in with me when we get home?' he asked, taking her completely by surprise.

'I don't know. I___'

'I'll tell you everything,' he said turning his head and looking her in the eyes, pleadingly. 'Please?'

Alycia mulled over the request briefly. 'What about your ki... Sorry, that was stupid of me.' She lowered her left hand to the gear stick, shifting down for a bend whilst chastising herself.

'It's okay,' Andrew said dropping his hand on hers. Its warmth was the antithesis of the cold and miserable afternoon. 'Obviously Merryn isn't there. And the other two, they'll just have to deal with it.'

Andrew clocked Alycia as she glanced down at the hand enveloping hers. To her disappointment, he lifted it away.

'Don't worry,' he said. 'You don't have to.'

Invisible bricklayer's hands proceeded to build a wall of uncomfortable silence between them. Alycia's words soon left it in demolished ruins.

'I want to,' she said. 'I'll phone mum when we get there, she won't mind sorting Darcy out with some tea.'

CHAPTER THIRTY-SIX

Threatening murmurs rumbled distantly from some point over the depths of the Atlantic. Precursory undeviating rain tapped a monotonous beat against the leaves and sodden ground of the cottage.

Alycia studied the intricate map of scratches permeating from Andrew's knuckles as he sat with both hands resting on the dinner table. His own eyes stared vacantly through them. Averting her attention from the backs of his battle-scarred hands to his face, she noticed for the first time the darks lines and greying shadows beneath the lost eyes. Andrew looked defeated; undone. And why shouldn't he? Just how could so many terrible incidents happen to one family? And in such a short period of time?

He had relived the whole excruciating sequence of events, reciting every detail in robot fashion. In the minutes since the burden had been partially lifted from his chest and placed on another's – at least that is what Alycia hoped had happened, a problem shared and all that – he had not uttered another word. He just sat there, staring at or through whatever it was he thought he saw.

A delicate touch on the backs of Andrew's hands brought a sudden flinch out of him. Realising that the contact came from Alycia's subtle fingers as she laid them comfortingly down, he relaxed back into his chair, letting his shoulders drop slowly.

With the accompanying sound of a notification, the dormant screen of his mobile phone jumped into life. Andrew shifted his eyes to its glossy illuminated surface and spied the opening line of a text message in a rectangular blue box. He looked thoughtfully at the phone whilst forbidding his hands from revealing the rest of the message. They were just fine where they were, thank you very much, his rough knuckles safe in the caress of Alycia's soft palms.

'Anything important?' Alycia asked, sensing his reluctance.

Shaking his head, Andrew returned his attention to the nothing on the table. Alycia twisted her head around to where a low ticking had been in constant supply since they had arrived. It had gone seven, and outside lonely night had cancelled out dreary day.

Another rumble of thunder, closer than its predecessors. Running torrents of rain smothered the glass of the kitchen window. They did little to motivate the young woman, who at this point had absolutely no idea where this chapter of her life was taking her. She did however feel that she had served her purpose here. The low levels of response from the troubled man across the table spoke volumes.

At home, Darcy would be impatiently awaiting her return, homework most likely done and out the way thanks to Nanny, and a game at the ready. If Andrew's mournful tale had taught her anything, it was that the littlest human beings in our lives held the highest level of importance, when all things came to the crunch.

'I'd better be getting home,' she said, not yet bringing herself to let go of his hands. 'Time's getting on.'

Andrew spoke quickly. 'Stay the night.' He looked her in the eyes for the first time since starting his account of the last couple of days.

'I'm not sure,' Alycia said, feeling in a quandary, a conflicting mixture of *wants* and *should-nots* swirling around her brain like a confused shoal of fish under predatory attack. 'Kerenza will need you tonight.'

'She's staying at a friend's house. That was her then.' Andrew tilted his head, gesturing towards his phone.

'Cameron then. I don't think he would be impressed.' Alycia was aware that this reaction may suggest she was desperately searching for a viable get-out clause, which was far from her intentions.

'I doubt he'd even notice. If he bothers to come home, he'll probably go straight to his room.'

'If?' Alycia sounded concerned. 'Have you seen him since…you know?'

'Nope,' Andrew stated bluntly.

'Are you worried?' Uneasy feelings started to muster in the pit of her stomach.

'About Cam?' Andrew quizzed. 'Nah, he's an elusive creature. Comes and goes like a shadow. Never around for long. And God help anyone that tries to make conversation with him.' Andrew gave a little laugh to insinuate that this last part was simply jest.

The constant ticking in Alycia's ears petered out of existence, replaced by the silent sound of her own thoughts. Mere seconds seemed like an age as the room around her fogged out of focus and her mind twisted in turmoil. This man had serious complications, and she had monumental doubts that he was anywhere near over his dead wife enough to commit to a new relationship. Yes, she had kissed him, and enjoyed the feeling of being so close to another human being; especially this one. But staying the night? *That changes everything.* Once done, that cannot be undone.

Looking up, the world around her blossomed into sharp clarity once more. Alycia found Andrew's beseeching eyes. She removed her hands from his and reached down to the kitchen floor, retrieving her handbag.

***

Pushing his motorbike through the darkness, a saturated Cameron strolled casually down Quay Road. Patches of slick black glowed and faded like beacons as clusters of cloud collated and broke under a watchful moon. The heavens had opened as Cameron had arrived in Saint Agnes. A thunderous downpour soaked him to his very core. A biblical cleansing.

Dismounting from his bike at the beginning of Quay Road had been a decision made almost without consciousness, as if the intensity of the shower had been sent purely to aid his sudden desire for purification. Within a minute however, the rain had stopped as instantly as someone shutting off a tap. Cameron had cursed at the sky but remained on foot for the rest of the journey.

Exiting the solid road surface onto shifting ground, he was afforded the view of a car roof, glimmering in the moonlight as it sat dormant in Shona's parking space. Drops of water clung in hoards to its metal surface, a sweet scattering of pink hundreds and thousands. No light emanated from the front portion of his home. Making his way around the side of the property to store his motorbike away for the night, Cameron could see that the same could be said of his dad's bedroom window.

He skirted the building back the way he came, until he reached the front door and tried the handle. Locked. Fishing for his keys as quietly as he could (although in the surrounding unoccupied darkness every sound seemed unhelpfully magnified), he laid his hand upon them. Lifting them out of his pocket, he fumbled for the correct one and slid it into the keyhole.

Avoiding the need to flick on any interior lights, Cameron pulled his mobile phone from the other pocket of his soaked jeans and powered up the built-in torch. Nothing out of the ordinary in the kitchen. Through to the living room. Two wine glasses, both empty; one wine bottle, also empty.

'Sly old dog,' Cameron whispered to the sleeping walls.

He shone the dazzling bulb onto one of the wine glasses, noting the smear of lip gloss on the rim. Picking up the smeared glass and raising it before his face, Cameron licked the greasy residue.

'Tasty, girl,' he muttered. 'Here's hoping you haven't got herpes.'

He put the glass back down with a chink. Cameron cleared the lustful thoughts. In all seriousness, although he would like to sample a slice of this unknown pie, the entrance of a new contender to the field of play was a concern that had to be dealt with quickly and efficiently.

CHAPTER THIRTY-SEVEN

A distant beeping pinched its way through unconsciousness. Louder, louder still, land grabbing from another realm. Eyelids heavy with sleep flickered and split, allowing entrance to a white glow accompanying the invading noise.

Cameron reached out a heavy hand and hovered over the source of the illumination. One long, lazy finger slid across the light, silencing the beeping as it did so.

He raised his upper body, yawned a long intake and exhalation of air, and flexed his bony shoulders, hands clasped together above his head. Rising awkwardly onto his knees, his first inclination was to crawl for the bedroom window. The clouds that brought so much rain yesterday had now completely dispersed, and the departed moon left only faint stars on the deep blue backing. Looking down, dew-laced gravel twinkled back at him from where an abandoned pussy-pink car sat during the night.

Who are you, Barbie Girl? thought Cameron, genuinely intrigued. *Scampering off in the wee small hours like a dirty little secret.*

In the shadows of the unlit room, he pulled on his uniform. His mind was preoccupied with other concerns, his body simply programmed to complete this task with as little disruption to his calculating brain as possible. Shoes on and laces tied, Cameron grabbed his identification badge, grimacing at his lost younger self photograph. Closing the door stealthily behind him, he left the room. Passing the empty bedroom that belonged to his little sister, Cameron smirked cruelly at the silence creeping out though a gap in the door as it stood ajar, before entering the bathroom to brighten his crocodile smile.

The lone headlight of his KMX displayed slick but empty roads. The air was fresh and dry. What a world. Everything was peachy: his youngest sibling was out of the way with her detestable grandmother, and she had taken that stinking piece of vermin, Harvey, with her. Plus, his father had provided him with a new subject to challenge his beautifully menacing creativity. The only thing bothering Cameron right now, what had happened to Jack a couple of evenings ago?

Was he stupid enough to turn up at Raymond's? If he did, was he in the frame? Cameron had laid low since the morning after what he now thought of as *Judgment Night*. Attending to other matters elsewhere, the disengagement was leaving a sour taste in his mouth. All he could do for now, however, was wait. It was out of his control, and that was the worst part of the whole sordid situation.

***

Suffering in the sweltering stuffiness of the room, its cold and clinical appearance did little to lift the weight of oppressive air. Grace sat next to her brother's complex looking bed. Its guard rails were raised into position as if it harboured some frail old codger in danger of rolling out and crashing to the floor, and not the strong brother she remembered. Tears left red tracks down her blotchy face as she coupled Jack's hand in hers. The magnitude of what he had told her left her feeling as crushed and broken as he looked.

'They could be wrong,' she said, sniffling hard through her running nose. 'They could. They have been before.'

'They're not wrong, sis,' said Jack, forcing a poorly fabricated smile. 'I can feel it. Or, I can't feel it, more like. Either way it's the same shit result. But look on the bright side, at least I can sit on my lazy ass for the rest of my life. Don't ever think you're pushing me around though. I'll die before I trust you to do that.'

It was painfully difficult to laugh, but Grace recognised that if ever her brother needed to hear it, now was the time.

'Has Dad been in yet?' she asked, fearing that she already knew the answer.

Jack coughed out an airy laugh, shaking his head. 'You know him.'

'I'm sure he___'

'Don't.' Jack looked at her intently, the same fabricated smile still on display between the myriad of coloured bruises and swellings. 'I'd rather see that chair empty than look at him not wanting to be here.'

A clatter came from somewhere between Jack's open side room door and the nurse's station. Grace flinched and looked out at the communal area, seeing a tell-tale mop discarded horizontal across the linoleum floor. Its dripping head balanced perilously on the edge of a bucket next to a long and untidy, paper strewn desk.

'Sorry,' a familiar voice came unseen from around the corner. 'My bad.'

Oh no, Grace thought, sensing her brother tense under her hands. *Please, not now.*

Tall, skinny and dark-haired, the owner of the recognisable voice came into view. Bending to pick up the mop and looking over to the side room as he did so, Cameron saw the young girl sat looking back at him from a chair beside the patient's bed. She looked small and vulnerable as she bowed forwards, elbows on knees. He smiled, both at the girl and this interesting development.

'Hiya,' he said, arriving at the door. His eyes switched from Grace to the person occupying the bed. 'Jack?' he asked confused. 'What the fuck? What happened to *you*?'

'Get, the fuck, out of here!' Jack snarled.

Grace looked from one to the other, wishing the biscuit-coloured floor would open up and swallow her whole.

'That's no way to talk to a mate,' Cameron replied coolly. He looked to the left of Jack's bed and noted the syringe driver. 'Don't worry, I'm not offended. I'll put it down to that. Some good shit goin' into your system there, boy.'

'We're *not* mates.' Jack fixed Cameron with his hardest stare, perfectly aware of how unproductive it would be from his current predicament, yet unwilling and unable to stop himself.

'Well, we need to be,' Cameron persevered in his calm manner. 'Especially with what me and your sister here have got goin' on.' He tipped Grace a nod. 'I think it might be serious.'

Pushing down on the fire that ignited in his gut, Jack kept the emotion in his face dulled down to a passive expression. He would get even, but not from a hospital bed.

Grace cut in, meek and mousey, 'Not now, Cam.'

'Okay,' Cameron conceded. He looked at Jack. 'I'll ask her what happened later, save putting you through whatever it was again, buddy. I will come back to see how you're getting on though, *bro*.' Bowing down, he kissed Grace lightly on her prominent cheekbone. 'See ya later, sweet cheeks,'

Looking after him as if in a state of hypnosis, Jack understood that he not only *wanted* to do something to the gangly streak of piss, but he needed to for his sister's sake. She was falling for a charlatan. Every characteristic played out to her was an act. Jack knew what Cameron was like, the *real* Cameron. He was dangerous, and Grace's predisposed delusions would render her useless against him. Jack would have to use his solitude to decide on a course of action. But that was okay. He would have plenty of that, after all.

Obviously, there was no way on this planet that he could go along with her fairy-tale fantasies, but for the sake of a final outcome in both his and his baby sister's favour, he would at least act indifferently in regard to the relationship between the two of them. If dragging the process out until he was in a stronger position would hurt her more, then so be it.

CHAPTER THIRTY-EIGHT

Judith sat across the table from Andrew, looking down her pointed shrew-like nose at him. Her disapproving face was puckered up like she was chewing on a turd.

Struggling to find any words to say, Andrew opted instead to shrink into his chair, a clown goby before this leviathan of self-righteousness, chewing his fins down to what he knew would lead to torturesome levels of pain come the evening. Acting as a defensive barrier between predator and prey, the table lay dressed in a red gingham vinyl cloth, adorned with a pair of white ceramic salt and pepper shakers, a bowl containing a mixture of brown and white sugar cubes – prompting Andrew to believe he had just taken an unrequested trip back to childhood – and a slim white bud vase with a single dried (*or dead, if there's a difference?*) dark burgundy rose protruding from its top.

There was a light *tink* as Judith caught the sugar bowl with a pair of polished steel tongs, fishing for a second lump. Andrew watched as the steam rising from her teacup parted and drew back together, allowing the cube passage with a *plonk*. He had no wish to share a cup of tea (or any other drink for that matter) with this stuck-up old boiler, but *needs must*, as they say.

'Pathetic!' Judith spat. Stirring her brew, she kept her voice low, as not to air her accusations publicly. Commoner's behaviour.

'Sorry?'

'Look at you, sat like a cowardly rabbit hiding from the world.' She drummed her false, lacquered nails on the glossy surface. 'I honestly don't know *what* my Shona ever saw in such a feeble waste of space. If you ask me, she's better off now.'

'What?' Andrew's voice came as a whispering wind through a cornfield. 'How can you say your daughter is better off *dead*? You spiteful bitch.'

'How *dare* you talk to me like that you horrible little man! You will hold your vulgar little tongue when I am talking.'

Her voice was raised a notch now, prompting disapproving looks from the other tables as the pair stared intently over the chequered battlefield at each other. Each willed the other to make the next catastrophic move. Andrew pushed a probing pawn forward just one space, testing the water.

'What's with the table décor?' he said, nodding toward the dried (*dead*) rose. 'I'm surprised an upstanding person with your reputation to uphold can bring yourself to set foot in here.'

'This happens to be a very fine establishment,' Judith replied with acidity in her tone. 'I do, however, expect that to be poo pooed by somebody on your level. Anyway,' she went on, raising her cup to her lips and giving a gentle, cooling blow. 'There is nothing wrong with dried flowers.'

'Dead.'

'I beg your pardon?' she asked, turning her head slightly to the right and squinting one measuring eye at him.

'The flower. It's dead. You said "dried."'

'Don't be foolish, it was dried deliberately.' Judith turned to the rose and gave a fond smile, her eyes glazing over.

Spotting the look of sentiment and expecting a story, Andrew rolled his eyes in bored anticipation.

'We've had a rose bush for a long as I can remember. Since before my Shona was born.' Andrew felt a pang of annoyance at the '*my* Shona' part. He let her continue, regardless of his disapproval. 'Every house we have lived in. And early summer, every year after my Shona was born…' there we go again, 'I'd eagerly await the blooming of the first rose, for her. I would cut it from the bush and place it in water beside her bed. When it started to wilt, I'd hang it from her curtain rail and dry it for her. I have boxes full of them now.'

A tear rolled down Judith's puffy, powdered cheek. Andrew recalled Smokey Robinson and the Miracles' "The Tears of a Clown", thinking of maybe recording his own version, "The Tears of a Dragon."

'So,' he opened his mouth, knowing instantly that he would come to regret what would tumble out of it. 'Every year, you'd gallantly murder a rose for Shona?'

More uneasy faces looked over.

'What?' Judith sounded bewildered and wounded at the denunciation. 'Don't be preposterous! I watered them and preserved them.'

'Well, would a *dried* flower drink water?'

'Obviously not. What's your point, man?'

'My point is, it's dead. You killed it, water or not.' Andrew was starting to enjoy this outrageous conversation. 'I mean, if you really think about it, as soon as you take those lethal secateurs to it, you're murdering it. Putting it in water is just providing *end of life* care.'

There was a pause as the old woman thought of a way to swing this exchange. The creature in front of her was a dirty little fly, and when dirty little flies avoid the spider's venomous fangs, well, they just needed swatting.

A small brass bell above the door gave a tinkle, signalling the arrival of an idea in Judith's calculating mind every bit as much as it did the arrival of another patron.

'Good morning,' came the delicate voice of the elderly café owner, addressing the latest customer. 'Please take a seat and I'll be with you in a jiffy.'

Judith smiled wistfully, pushing herself back into her chair, contented. Folding her arms over her substantial bosoms, she eyed Andrew with a keen osprey glare.

'You know, I think I may just start cutting the first rose for Merryn, now that she's in my custody.'

The probing, water-testing pawn that Andrew had cast forward, initiating that little repartee, had not just been captured and held. It had been captured; chewed up; spat out; pissed on; shat on; stamped on; and had its tiny little pawn bollocks cut off by the secateurs of the opposing Queen of Roses.

'Is everything okay?' The dainty voice of the aging café owner weakly broke the strained silence as she passed by.

'Everything is fine,' Judith looked up and smiled. 'Though another pot of tea would be wonderful.'

'Coming right up.'

'Lovely. Thank you, Rose.'

Rose, Andrew thought, amused. *That figures. Just as dried out as the table décor, too.* He turned his attention back to whom he now preferred to think of as his *former* mother-in-law.

'That's only temporary,' he declared with a stern glare. 'It's only until___'

'It's until I know my granddaughter will be safe,' Judith cut in with the speed of a striking peacock mantis shrimp. 'And given that you could have *killed* her, and you very nearly did kill her grandad, I think it's going to be a lengthy time indeed!' Leaning forward, she placed her arms on the table. Her bulky shoulders thrust forward, like sacks of flour being flung from the back of a bread van. 'Look at yourself, Tredinnick. You're a long way from having her back.'

'You can't stop me.'

'Oh yes I can,' Judith replied, a cold and uncompromising look burning in her eyes. 'Take me on, by all means. But know that I can *and will* break you.'

Breaking the stale void between their eyes, Rose lowered a tray towards the table. A porcelain rattle from the teapot lid was accompanied by the higher pitched tinkling of teaspoon on a saucer. Rose's thinning, veiny arms tremored noticeably as she wished to make a hasty retreat from the pair sat at this table.

Judith thanked the older woman and set about pouring herself a fresh cup. *I hope it's laced with arsenic*, Andrew thought, looking down at his untouched brew on the table.

'Cat got your tongue?' the snooty old cow said.

'Nope,' said Andrew, still not looking up. 'Just sat here minding my own business, wishing you were dead.'

Judith emitted an airy laugh. 'Well, despite your best efforts, I'm not. And I don't intend to be either. Not for a long time, at least.'

'When can I see her?'

'A supervised visit. Next Sunday. Our house. Ten o'clock, sharp.' Judith sipped her tea without the cooling blow. Andrew delighted in seeing her expression change as the piping hot drink trickle down through her oesophagus.

'Supervised? *Really?*' Andrew looked up in annoyance.

'An absolute necessity.'

Behind Judith, through the café window, Andrew saw the unmistakable pink of Alycia's Fiat appear and draw to a stop.

'Fine. Your call.' He picked up his cold tea and threw it down his parched throat, noticing a winner's satisfied expression of pride on the face of his nemesis. 'My lift's outside. I'll see you next Sunday.'

He threw a wave at the window. Judith turned to see a young woman waving back from behind the wheel of a parked car.

'Who's that?' she snapped, still looking out at the stranger.

'Oh, that's Alycia,' Andrew said, the smirk on his face creeping through in his tone.

Judith turned to look up at him. 'Since when did *you* have a female friend?'

'Since I started having sex with her.' Andrew felt butterflies turning somersaults in his gut as the old bat's jaw hung open. 'Lots and lots of filthy, fabulous sex.'

Childish, yes. He knew that. But that feeling of delight beat the shit out of trying to please that haughty bitch.

Andrew headed for the exit, his grinning face the antithesis of the simmering boiler's.

CHAPTER THIRTY-NINE

Waking this morning had brought feelings of melancholy and isolation. Wind sighed sombrely against the windows and leaves scratched as they sprinted their way across hard surfaces of the pavements and the road outside; a bustling marathon of discarded foliage, echoing through windowpanes of a house devoid of activity.

Sharing a birthday with Halloween had always been a bit of a novelty for Grace Searle. It had certainly led to some amusing parties when she was little, like when her dad caught a trailing Egyptian mummy bandage on fire whilst lighting the candles on her cake. Luckily for Tony, Grace's real *mummy* had still been around to pour the nearby jug of bloody squash over his arm, quenching the flames.

There had also been some pretty gross moments, like only a couple of years ago when Jack had jumped from the porch roof of the nearby church in an attempt to scare the life out of his younger sister during a late-night ghost hunt. To Grace, one spirit still haunted her from that expedition: the sound of her brother's ankle fracturing and dislocating as he hit the ground awkwardly.

Now, not one of those people recalled in those events were present to share in the memories. Her mother had been gone for years: disappeared for a life in the sun with some boyfriend from the past, never to look back. Grace had come to accept that a long time ago. Accept, not forgive. Jack was still in hospital, and her dad was away *'on business'*. She knew this was bullshit. He was away because he didn't want to face up to the fact that his son was in hospital. For a father who had all of the responsibility of bringing two children up, he had very little to do with them. Maybe he resented them both, resented being burdened with them while his wife was swanning about God-only-knows-where, with God-only-knows-who, doing things he really couldn't bear thinking about.

Maybe, but Grace didn't care. If that was the case, they were his demons, not hers.

She had spent the whole day at home on her own. Skipping school, she ignored the landline on the few occasions that it chimed into life. It was the only means of contact that the school had with her dad, so she did not need to dial 1471 to find out who was calling.

Darkness was creeping in now, however, and the school office would be closed. No more unwanted interruptions. Sitting on the spongy carpet underneath the living room window, Grace's back started to numb against the cold, painted wall. Outside, sounds of wind and rustling leaves were replaced with sounds of laughing children and scuffling feet, roaming the streets in small ghoulish groups and knocking on doors for sweet treats. No one was knocking on her door. Keeping the lights off and hiding from the world put paid to that.

Upon hearing the unmistakable sound of a motorbike nearby, she allowed herself her first smile of the day. Standing as the engine grew louder, Grace made her way towards the front door. Upon opening the door, she found Cameron lowering the stand of his bike with one foot. He disembarked with a struggle, wobbling unbalanced by the weight of his bag bulging on his back, before limping towards her.

'What's wrong with your leg?' she asked, concerned by the way he moved.

'That?' Cameron bought some time. 'Oh, it's nothing. Stupid, really. Fell off my bike.'

'Okay,' Grace said, doubtfully. 'And what the hell have you got in there?'

'Essentials, why the hell are your lights off?' Cameron replied, blocking her answer by planting a heavy kiss on her lips. 'Couple of four-packs, wine, stuff for the kids.'

'Kids?'

'Yeah, trick-or-treaters.'

'They're the reason I've got the lights off,' she said, sounding unimpressed. 'I don't want them here.'

'Come on, you miserable git,' he stopped to kiss her again and squeeze her tight to him. 'They're what Halloween's all about! I mean, I know it's *your* birthday and all, but think about the kiddies.'

'Okay,' she accepted defeat. 'So, what have you got for 'em?'

'That's the best part, Mini Heroes and fruit for the ones with parents, and...' he took the bag off his back, groaning as he lowered it to the ground. Fishing around inside, he pulled out a black object. 'This fake gun for the ones without parents. Trust me, they won't stick around for long, and they'll be too shit scared to pull any dumbass tricks.' He smiled, raising the gun alongside his head and pulling back the hammer.

'You evil shit,' Grace laughed, grabbing the front of his jacket with one hand and pulling him in through the door.

After eating a tea of bung-in-the-oven pizza and onion rings, the pair sat on the floor of the living room. Grace leaned with her back against the sofa, and Cameron lay between her legs with his back resting on her belly. The curtains were now closed, and all but the small gangs of older kids with no interest in trick-or-treating had been dragged from the streets and been sent to bed, tired but restive on account of all the sickly-sweet junk.

Both Cameron and Grace were nearing the end of another glass of wine. The television was lit up with false personalities in a so-called reality world.

'I dunno why you watch this crap,' Cameron said. 'If I wasn't in such fine company and so comfortable between this delectable pair of legs, I would've bolted a long time ago.'

'Shut up,' Grace snapped, slapping him on the shoulder. 'It's entertaining.'

'*Entertaining* is watching grown men running an assault course full of charged tasers. Or checkin' out what else can be shoved through the head of a walker.'

'Maybe we're both wrong.' Grace tapped her empty wine glass on his shoulder. '*Entertaining* is filling this up and taking it upstairs.'

Cameron craned his neck around and looked at her in surprise. Seeing her cheeky smile and raised eyebrows, he threw back the last of his wine. Springing from the floor, he grabbed her glass and headed for the kitchen. Grace picked up the remote, killed the television – and therefore the only light in the living room – and made her way up the stairs, nervous yet eager.

CHAPTER FORTY

Water sprayed and splattered from dirt and debris clogged guttering that skirted the two-story house. Mist had turned to mizzle during the early hours, before the heaven's eventually opened; albeit briefly. The thunderous downpour had lasted no more than ten minutes and now, in the darkness of the bedroom, Grace lay in Cameron's enveloping arms listening to the aftermath. Her mind ticked over as rapidly as water cascaded past her window.

She had no regrets on how the evening had panned out; that was not the issue. Maybe doubts would seep through the pleasurable bubble in time, like liquid through an overloaded coffee filter, but that was for time itself to decide. What unsettled her was thinking about the contempt that Jack had shown towards Cameron in the hospital, of how he had reacted when the boy she lay with first dropped her home on that rainy afternoon. She remembered how cocky and assured Cameron had acted in return in that foreboding hospital room.

This constant ticking and travelling of her brain took Grace to a place that she did not want to be, her imagination conjuring up a scenario that brought with it a chill.

Were the arms that held her in any way involved with what had happened to her brother?

Shuddering a little at the thought, she let out a wavering sigh.

'You awake?'

The suddenness of a deep voice entering through the gloom made Grace jump.

'Sorry,' Cameron said. 'I didn't mean to scare you.'

'It's okay. I just thought you were asleep.'

'Just woke up.' He lowered his head, burying his nose in her hair and taking in the sweet scent of her shampoo. 'Something troublin' you?'

Grace paused in thought, unsure of how to answer. Eventually she braved a response.

'I was just thinking about Jack.'

'In bed?' said Cameron. 'That's a bit weird.'

'Grow up,' she berated in jest. 'Why…Why does he hate you so much?' The words stumbled from her mouth with a lack of confidence she hoped would go unnoticed.

'I wouldn't say he hated me,' Cameron answered with a hint on naivety.

'He does,' said Grace. A bit of a blunt reply, maybe, but it was out there now.

'He'll come around, as long as I keep up the niceties.'

'I'm not sure that'll be enough.'

'Come on. I was a bit of a dick in school, and we were never bezzie mates; but we're both older now. Different people.'

Grace went quiet again, feeling Cameron's grip tighten.

'What's really on yer mind?' He struggled to hide the fact that he was now talking through gritted teeth.

She let out a whispering breath. 'What do you think happened to him?'

'I think some asshole beat the crap out of him, which is exactly what we *know* happened.'

'Yeah, but who would do that?' Grace ran her fingers gently along Cameron's bare arm, hoping her tone came across more inquisitive than accusive.

'Can't imagine there are many people who would go as far as they did. Fuckin' psychos. I'll try to find out, shouldn't be too hard. And when I do.' Cameron felt no need to continue.

'And when you do, what?'

'I'll sort it. That's all you need to know.'

Grace had ambivalent concerns, this latest admission both easing and fuelling her anxiety in equal measures. She rolled and lifted herself partially on top of him, found the reflective glint of his eyes through the greyness, and placed a kiss on his lips.

'Don't do anything stupid,' she whispered. 'I kind of need you around.'

He sniggered and she leaned in to kiss him again, slower and longer this time.

***

Closing the front door behind him, Cameron filled his lungs with moist morning air. An icy coolness spread from the centre of his chest outwards. The ground was still saturated as a result deluge during the early hours, but the clouds had mostly departed, leaving the sun to shine low and unencumbered in the sky.

Swaggering to his bike, he raised the stand, rolled it the few metres to the road, and threw a gangly leg over. Looking up at the bedroom window, no figure was present, just the celeste sky reflecting from the glass. He knew this would be the case. Grace was heading for the shower as he was about to leave. But he smiled at the window anyway, happy as a pig in shit with how the previous night had turned out.

Firing up the KMX's engine, Cameron trundled down the road before opening her up and speeding off the estate.

Today was his day off, and it was still a good while until visiting hours. That was all for the good. He had things to do. Dark errands on such a bright morning. He would have taken care of things late the previous evening, had it not been for the very beneficial alternative that presented itself. Cameron's uniform was rolled neatly in his bag. It would not do to have Jack think that it was a special visit; Cameron just hoped that none of his supervisors would spot him at work, in uniform, on his day off. That would be awkward.

Having everything he needed meant that he had no reason to go home. Heading west along the North Cliff's coast road, Cameron knew that completing this particular chore in daylight was running a high risk. But needs must, and all that.

CHAPTER FORTY-ONE

PE. *Not the best way to start the morning*, thought Grace, her head heavy and her gut performing acrobatics. Zipping in from the left, the hard, rubbery oval ball came spinning towards her. She plucked it out of the air and aimed for a gap between two opposing girls closing in on her. Grace had barely made it two paces before a heavy slap from the stocky girl to the right panged her hip. Simultaneously, a forearm belonging to the girl to the left impacted on her midriff.

Touch rugby my ass, the thought practically knocked out of her on impact.

Being the skinny kid, Grace had always been an easy target in contact sports. As a result, she spent most of her time trying to avoid the ball like it had become contaminated with a deadly pathogen.

No such luck of avoiding it on this occasion though, the ball a guided missile homing in on her. Gagging as she stumbled from the double impact, Grace dropped to her knees.

'Get up, Searle! It was just a tap.' Miss Parkinson's broad frame stood, legs slightly parted and hand on hip, like some butch female rendition of the *Green Giant*.

'Fuck off, you old rug muncher,' Graced moaned, lowering her head to the floor and speaking quietly in the interest of self-preservation.

A pair of trainers appeared under her nose, causing a stab of fear to penetrate her chest, assuming her obscenities may not have been quite quiet enough. Having a split second to restore rationality, Grace recognised the trainers and slim legs (not chunky *ho-ho-fucking-ho Green Giant's* legs) to be Kerenza's.

'Come on,' Kerenza said, stretching out a helping hand.

No sooner had Grace clasped the offered hand and struggled to her feet, than she let go again. Covering her mouth with a hand, she ran for the side of the pitch. Barfing up the remains of last night's overindulgence. The poor girl's face turned crimson with embarrassment as other girls started to point and laugh.

Kerenza came running over and rubbed her friend on the back.

'Let's get you in,' she said. 'Ignore them. Stupid bitches.' Kerenza cast a look of condemnation over the crowd, assuring them that *they* were the bitches aforementioned.

After entering the main school building, the pair made their way to the changing rooms and dropped themselves onto the long, unoccupied bench. Grace sipped water from a bottle that Kerenza pulled from her bag, took a series of deep breaths, and tilted her head back against the cold, interior wall.

'Better?' Kerenza asked.

'For now, I think,' said Grace, subdued.

'Something you've eaten, maybe?'

'Don't think so,' Grace laughed nervously. 'More like something I drank. Or how much.'

'What? You told me you didn't want to do anything for your birthday.' Kerenza was incensed.

Grace rolled her head to face her friend, who looked hurt and betrayed.

'I didn't,' she replied, placing her hand on Kerenza's. Why she did this, she didn't know. Maybe to protect herself; a way to create a tranquil atmosphere before she disclosed the next piece of information. 'Cameron showed up. Said he was just popping in on his way home from work. Checking how I was.'

'Oh,' said Kerenza quietly. 'Funny. Just popping in. He didn't come home last night.'

Grace felt her stomach turn again and tried to disguise the composing breath she took. Striving to stay the tremble she felt working its way down her arm, she willed it not to reach her hand. There, her friend would surely feel it.

'No,' Grace finally responded. 'He pulled out some drinks, and that was that.'

'So, he plied you with alcohol?' The question was rhetorical. 'Did he___'

'He didn't do anything that I didn't want him to.'

There was a tense moment as Kerenza sucked in news, refusing it as if she had merely misheard the words. Taking on a vacuum-like quality, the stale changing room air squeezed in on Grace, tightening her chest.

Laughs and shouts began to resound in the corridor, bouncing from the cuboid walls as the others approached the changing rooms. Their rugby session was over. And perfectly timed.

'So, you and him are…' Kerenza couldn't decide on how to finish the sentence.

'Yeah, I guess so.' Grace anticipated what her friend was hesitantly asking. She could see no reason why they would not be friends after this revelation, but something about Kerenza's behaviour bugged her. She seemed standoffish.

The changing room door slammed back against the hard wall, cranking the echoing voices from outside up to a roar. Grace snatched her hand back from Kerenza's with the speed of a chameleon's elastic tongue, hoping to avoid the rumour mill spinning into life, thanks to one or two overactive imaginations misinterpreting the scene that met them upon entering room.

They made eye contact. Kerenza got up to get changed, grinning.

'Don't even think I'm calling you sis.'

CHAPTER FORTY-TWO

Incoherent sounds muffled their way through his hazy, semi-consciousness world. Feet shuffled; voices mumbled; paper rustled, like litter in a steady breeze.

Jack eased his eyes open, the consistent morphine supply hampering their progress. Corn yellow painted walls morphed into focus, along with other objects developing from the blur: window; screen hanging from the ceiling; equipment with gently pulsing LED's and readings (where the newly noticed beeping must be originating from); a figure in the chair.

Jack tried to pull himself to sitting. His useless legs offered his weakened arms no assistance, reminding him of just how unattainable the completion of that simple task had become.

'Hey, buddy,' the figure in the chair said, noticing Jack's shoulders lift slowly and his head roll to the side. 'Don't push yourself.'

'What,' Jack coughed gently, but hard enough to shoot a stabbing javelin of pain down through his ribcage. Composing himself, he wheezed, 'What, the fuck, are you doing here?'

'Chill, dude. Brought you some gifts. Lucozade; grapes. Kind of stuff you'd take yer gran, like, but.' Cameron raised his right hand, showcasing the item he was flicking through. 'And *Top Gear Magazine*. Not my cup of tea. Two wheels is better than four. Mind you, don't spose you'll 'av' much choice now. Hey, look on the bright side; at least you'll get Motability.' Cameron gave a remorseless smile.

Jack sighed a harsh obscenity which Cameron could not make out, but he believed the C-bomb was dropped in there.

'Shit! Sorry pal, the magazine was insensitive. I should've looked for a copy of *Able*, or something.'

Jack rolled his head to the opposite wall, hoping to hide the moisture that was forming in his eyes.

Cameron sprawled backwards further into the chair, crossing his legs and analysing the specimen before him like a psychiatrist.

'So, Jackie-o, how d'ya think you ended up in here? Most people know the reason they got the shit kicked out of 'em. What's yours?'

'I don't have to tell you anything,' Jack murmured.

'That's not how conversation works, Jack,' Cameron teased. 'So, I'll tell you something first, then you respond. I fucked your sister last night.' Cameron saw Jack's left hand clench, fingers squeezing the ruffled bedsheet. Response adequate. He allowed himself a satisfied smile. 'Man, did I ever! She's a little firecracker, eh? I just thought of her all alone. You in this shithole. Your old man AWOL just to avoid having to visit you. On her birthday as well. Don't worry, mate, I made sure she had fun. She'll be walking funny for a while, fucked that girl six ways from Sunday.' Cameron said this last line wistfully.

Jack turned his head to Cameron, face reddening with through a cocktail of exertion and anger. 'This'll end in one of two ways,' his voice growled. 'Either I tell the cops what you did,' Jack took in an element of surprise on Cameron's face. 'Yeah, that's right. I know. It's either that, or I kill you when I get out of here.'

For the first time since being carried into the building, Jack smiled. *Knowledge is power, as they say, and I have the upper hand now.* He held the killer cards that would rid him and his sister of this freak forever.

'Hmmm,' Cameron raised his hand to his chin in mock thoughtfulness. 'Only problem with tellin' the pigs, they're hell-bent on finding some chap who fled the scene in a black Golf. I mean, what reason would he have to shoot off like that if he wasn't involved in whatever happened. Want me to pour you a Lucozade? No? Fair enough. He must be a bit dodgy to have been involved in the first place, right? Wouldn't surprise me if he's already known to them. Guy like that, when they find him, they won't believe a word he says.

'And then there's the other thing,' Cameron continued, audience of one gripped. 'Killing me when you get out of here? Down behind the morgue there's often a little black ambulance. For the stiffs; not sure if you knew that?' Cameron uncrossed his legs and leaned forward with intent. 'Anyway, with the state you're in, anythin' could happen. Who says you won't be *getting out of here* in one of those?'

'Is everything okay in here? Can I get you anything?' said a young, cute looking healthcare assistant poking her head in through the door. Cameron recognised her as one that he had shared some banter with from time to time, as well as the odd innuendo.

'No, thank you,' Jack replied, unsmiling.

'And you?' she said, turning her attention to Cameron. 'You plan on doing any work today?'

'Unless you can think of somethin' better we can do.' Cameron replied, lifting himself up out of the chair and casting her his best roguish smile.

She smiled back, raising her eyebrows before turning and heading off down the corridor.

'Jesus Christ, you don't know how lucky you are, watching those hips thrust all day,' Cameron said to Jack, studying the healthcare until she disappeared around a corner. He turned back. 'Oh, and about that other thing. Not a word to Grace, yeah. She knows it's you with the problem. Not me.'

CHAPTER FORTY-THREE

'Well? Are we going in, or are you just gonna sit here staring at the place?' Kerenza asked leaning forward between the seats.

'Staring at the place sounds good,' Andrew replied, as the last of surviving autumn leaves finally let go of their hosts and scratched their way down the windscreen.

'You've got to go in sooner or later,' Alycia chipped in from the driver's seat. 'And your daughter's in there. Seeing her has got to be worth any consequences.'

'I almost killed the guy.'

'Alycia's right, Dad. Merryn's waiting for you, you can't let her down.' She placed a reassuring hand on his shoulder. 'If it helps, you couldn't have picked a more laidback person than Grandad to try to kill.'

This caused the two in the front to let out a snigger.

'I suppose you're right,' he said, unfastening his seat belt and opening the door. 'Let's do this.'

Andrew pulled himself out of the car awkwardly, making a mental note that one as lanky as he should not consider purchasing a Fiat *500* when he eventually got his license back. Popping the seat forward, he let Kerenza out and leaned in.

'Thanks for the lift,' he said.

'Thank you,' Kerenza almost sang from behind.

'No, problem,' Alycia replied loud enough for both to hear, and then quieter to Andrew, 'You sure you don't want picking up?'

'Nah, you're alright, ta. I'm not sure how long we're going to be, so we'll get a bus or something.'

Having said their goodbyes Andrew shut the door and gave the roof a couple of taps. The engine ticked into life and the pink machine pulled into the road, moving away steadily.

Facing each other and sharing a look of trepidation, they wrapped themselves up against the cold morning: Kerenza winding her woolly scarf around one more loop and Andrew clasping the open fronts of his jacket together with a white fist. All was dry and bright, though the temperature had slumped noticeably overnight.

'Nice of Alycia to drop us off,' Kerenza said, a vaporous cloud forming from between her moving lips.

'Yeah, it was,' Andrew agreed. 'She's a handy friend to have around. *Friend.*

Kerenza said, 'Shall we do this, then?'

Andrew's chest heaved. 'Come on.'

A little over three hours later, the duo remained at *Chez Ballantyne*. Or rather, were *back* at chez Ballantyne. It had been a pleasant morning. The five of them: Andrew, Kerenza, Merryn, Angus, and Judith, had gone to the nearby woodland for a walk in the early November sunshine – equipped with an old takeaway container full of monkey nuts that Judith now kept stocked at all times, for Merryn to feed the squirrels. The ground was soggy, even boggy in places, causing Merryn frequent giggle fits as Andrew and Kerenza (not having received the memo about appropriate footwear) took wide and unbalanced tippy-toed steps in grey deck shoes and white trainers respectively, failing miserably to keep their original colours.

Even the two opposing forces, Andrew and Judith, had managed to act with a magnanimous civility towards each other.

In the living room, Andrew and Merryn lay on the carpeted floor colouring in an underwater-themed picture. Angus caught up on a programme about the world's most scenic railway journeys that had started a week or two before.

Giving his arm a short break from colouring, Andrew looked up at the screen. Spruce trees and mountain lakes whizzed past, with snow-caps looming in the hazy distance. He looked from the screen to the old man sitting slouched back with a hand on his chest.

'I'm sorry about your car,' Andrew said, sounding mournful. 'And…for everything else.' He gestured towards Angus' chest with a tip of his brow.

'It happens.' *What a moronic remark*, Angus berated himself. 'Fancied a new car anyway. Last one was a piece of shhh,' he spotted Merryn's eyes dart up at him and expected a Supergirl-type laser to blast from them, searing and turning his flesh to dripping lava. 'Shh…ugar honey iced tea.'

The sound of Merryn's laughter travelled through every room in the house. It burst into the kitchen like the dawning of summer, filling every corner with golden rays.

'God I've missed that sound,' said Kerenza as she picked up another plate from the drainer. She ran a tea towel over it in neat circles.

Judith stopped mid-task, pink gloved hands submerged into an ocean of suds.

'You don't have to stay with *him*, you know.' She looked earnestly at her granddaughter. 'We have room for you *and* your sister, now your mother is.' Judith paused as if unable to allow the word admission to the room. 'There's no need for you to have any connection to him at all. It's not like he's blood.'

Kerenza stopped whirling the towel around, a little taken aback by the woman's casual dismissal of the man who had been there for her for the best part of a decade.

'He's my dad, or at least the closest thing I've ever had to one.'

'He can't offer you what we can,' Judith persisted, sensing that she had overstepped the mark. But, lacking that filter that tells a considerate person when to shut up, she had always been hungry to keep the argument rolling. Jabbing away at others until they were railroaded into her way of thinking had always been a super-power that Judith possessed. Something her long-suffering husband knew only too well. So many differences of opinion over the years, all with one thing in common: the inevitability that Angus would eventually feign agreement just to stop the constant hen-pecking.

'Safety; stability. A home where you know someone will always be there for you, rather than not knowing when, or even *if* they'll come back.'

'That's a bit drastic, Gran,' Kerenza protested. 'He always comes home. And I'm practically an adult now anyway. I grew up fast. I had to.'

'Yes. Too fast. If you live with us, you can experience the freedom a girl of your age should take for granted, instead of being forced to keep house for a feckless alcoholic.'

'Whoa, hang on a____'

Judith placed another plate on the dishrack, a heavy-handed clash exposing her frustration.

'Lord only knows what effect it's having on your schoolwork.'

'My schoolwork is fine, thank you very much.' Kerenza was trying hard to contain her own frustration. 'Anyway, he needs me.'

'Hmm,' Judith smiled smugly. 'I don't believe he needs you at all. Not now that he's got that *floozy*.'

Kerenza was glad that the steel object clutched in her hand was nothing sharper than a teaspoon. Not that she would have done anything. Though she did take some sick pleasure envisaging gauging her gran's eye out with the spoon.

Kerenza pushed the image to the back of her mind. 'What exactly are you talking about?'

'That, that woman he's fornicating with.'

'If you're talking about Alycia, they're just friends. I take it he's allowed to have friends of the opposite sex?'

Judith stopped what she was doing and turned to look Kerenza sharply in the eye. 'You said you were practically and adult, but you're just a naïve little girl. I heard from the horse's mouth exactly what they get up to.'

'I don't believe you,' said Kerenza, holding her gran's stare.

'She picked him up when I met him the other day. I asked who she was, and he took delight in telling me in lewd detail.'

'And you believed him? God, you preach to me about being naïve.'

'I have no reason not to,' Judith nipped, returning to the laborious task of dishwashing for five.

'You were desperate for it to be true, more like.'

'Remember whom you are talking to, young lady.'

'I know you can't *wait* for him to screw up again,' said Kerenza, 'But on this occasion, he's winding you up. Nothing's going on between them, but if he can use her to get under your skin like you get under his, then that's what he'll do. And I don't blame him.' Kerenza placed the spoon and the tea towel onto the worktop as Judith gaped in horror. 'Finish up yourself.'

CHAPTER FORTY-FOUR

Lasting no more than a few days, the early November sun had tipped his hat, disappeared behind a more common blanket of cloud, and hushed the hip-hip-hip hoorays.

Kerenza stood with the school building – one that always reminded her of a US State Penitentiary she'd once seen on a death row programme – to her back. Drips fell from high above and the earthy smell that often comes with new rain permeated the air around her.

She checked her phone. No messages.

Riled by the fact that Grace had given Kerenza's stepbrother the nod over her own brother, she headed down the steps and off the school premises. Alone, and literally under a dismal cloud, she made her way to the hospital.

She found Jack lying in bed (of course he was) but awake. He smiled as she walked in, but Kerenza could read the emotional anguish written in blotted ink behind it.

'You don't need to put a brave face on for me,' she said, settling into the chair beside his bed and reaching out for his hand.

'It's probably not as bad as I think it is,' he said with a twisted optimistic woefulness.

'Well, that's probably the most positive view you've taken recently.'

Jack smiled at that, and Kerenza was glad to see a genuine quality to the façade.

'You don't have to come here, you know.' He turned his head and looked at her with pleading eyes.

'What d'you mean? I want to see you.'

'You didn't sign up to this.' Jack nodded towards his motionless legs further down the bed. 'You've still got a life. Get away from me while you've got the chance. I can't bear seeing you every day if you're only sticking around cos you think you have to. You don't.'

'Stop talking like this, Jack. I'm with you cos what we have is real.'

'*This* is fucking real!' He pulled his hand away from hers and slamming it down on a blanket-covered leg. 'See? *Nothing!*'

'You don't know it's going to stay that way,' she said, knowing it was bullshit. 'It could___'

Jack grabbed her hand again and placed it on his left leg.

'Pinch it,' he said. 'Punch it. There's a pen on the table, stab it for all I care, I won't feel a fuckin' thing. And that's never gonna change.'

Pools formed at the bottoms of Kerenza's eyes, one spilling over and leaving a glossy trail down a red cheek.

'Sorry,' Jack said, voice full of regret.

'I think we both need a coffee,' the distressed girl said with unconvincing calmness. 'I'll pop to the café. Back soon.'

She stood leaning over and kissed the boy on his forehead, like his mother may have once done in a time he could not remember. Then she headed out of the room. Jack watched her walk away, before closing his eyes and processing the prospect that he may never see her again.

'Okay, that's long enough,' a female voice echoed through the darkness.

Slowly opening his eyes, Jack looked around the room. 'I didn't think you'd come back,' he said as his eyes settled on a blonde head.

'I told you,' Kerenza said, sounding surprisingly upbeat. 'We're real.'

'How long was I out for?' Jack dug his elbows into the bed and heaved himself up onto his pillow.

'Long enough for this to cool down a bit.' Kerenza stood with a takeaway coffee cup, complete with straw, and extended it towards his mouth.

'Ugh,' Jack blurted after taking a long drag. 'No sugar?'

'Stop moaning and drink.'

He did as commanded, screwing his eyes up in disgust until the last drop slurped up the cardboard straw.

'That's a good boy.' She put the empty cup on the bedside table and climbed up next to him.

They shared a few minutes of silence, made uncomfortable by a detectable weight in the air: a weight of words that needed saying.

'If you're serious,' Jack eventually managed to squeeze out.

'Which I am,' came a quick-fire answer.

'Well, if you are,' he tried again. 'Then there's a problem we need to get over.'

'And what's that?' Kerenza asked, intrigued.

'Your brother.'

'*Step*…brother,' she corrected, wondering if somehow word had reached him that there may be something going on between the two of them. 'What, exactly is the problem?'

Jack took a large breath and exhaled. His chest visibly rose and fell as he composed himself.

'I'm pretty sure he did this to me.'

Kerenza let the weight of the incrimination settle. 'Wait a minute, surely you would've caught enough of a glimpse of the guy to know if it was Cameron?' she asked, managing to disguise the relief in her voice.

'Not *actually* him. No offence, but he wouldn't be capable. But I think he had something to do with it, like maybe he arranged it or something.'

'I don't get it,' said Kerenza, thinking hard. 'Is this about him and Grace? I'm taking it she told you?' She struggled to accept that Jack could be so bitter about that as to try to implicate Cameron in his assault.

'She didn't have to. He did.' Jack's mouth clenched in annoyance. 'Took great delight in coming in here braggin' about it.'

Kerenza shook her head, not knowing what to say.

'You think I'm wrong.'

'Yes, I do.' She put an arm around Jack's neck, causing him to wince in discomfort. 'I know you're angry, and you need someone to blame. God knows Cameron's guilty of a lot of things. But this?' She let out an exaggerated sigh. 'I get it. I really do. You're protecting your sister. You've never liked Cameron; you've made that clear from the start. But trying to blame him for something he had nothing to do with, it's only gonna end in tears.'

'You really think he had nothing to do with this?'

'He wouldn't.'

Jack could see the determination in her clear blue eyes. She would never think badly of that scrawny wanker.

'Okay. If you're that sure. I'll let it go,' he lied.

***

Kerenza leaned over, pulled the cord tight on her bag and shifted to the outer seat, preparing to jump off the double-decker that lurched its way down the steep decline past Stippy Stappy.

Trancelike for most of the journey home from the hospital, her mind battled in a tag team partnership – neocortex and thalamus combining forces to act as tormentor against prefrontal cortex: her imagination devilishly teasing her rationale.

Cameron orchestrated this
No, he wouldn't
He's obsessed with you
That doesn't mean he could…
He's capable of worse
Yes, he's capable of worse, but…
He's done worse.

Kerenza knew that her stepbrother was obsessed with her. He had made little effort to hide this from her even in the early years. His forwardness had escalated ever since. Now, he practically pounced on her at every opportunity. Oftentimes she had used this fact to her advantage – a knight in shining armour on tap.

There was the time when this spotty little ginger kid, Joel Pitt, constantly snuck cringe worthy poems and love letters into her school bag back in year seven, along with the occasional Turkish Delight (an acquired taste that through some stalkerish means, Pitt had found out Kerenza loved). Yearning for an end to the unwanted attention from Pitt the Zit, she told Cameron that he had put his hand up her skirt in the lunch queue. This nugget of fabricated information had the desired effect – only with Cameron's unique touch. The next day, Pitt the Zit was found bound to one of the school fences with a bike cable lock around each limb, shorts lying on the ground nearby, cacks stuffed into his mouth, and *PERV* printed in black permanent marker pen across his soon-to-be acne scarred forehead.

The Zit never did say who did it.

Kerenza made her way down the centre aisle of the bus, slapping her hands alternately on the handrails as she went. The slowing vehicle rolled past the bottom pub and ground to a stop. Accompanied by the usual hiss and a clumsy flapping sound, the double-doors opened.

Jumping off and casting a glance towards the pub, two familiar faces sat across a table from each other.

They're always bloody drinking, Kerenza thought, deciding at the same moment to pop in and say *hi*. As she stepped forward Andrew stood, empty glass in hand. He and Alycia shared a laugh about some unheard chatter, then he bent down towards her. At the same time, Alycia stretched her smooth, brown neck up, and their lips briefly met.

Gran was right, stupid old bitch, Kerenza thought, suddenly losing all interest in joining them.

CHAPTER FORTY-FIVE

It had been a long and draining day, both physically and mentally for Katy White. The single mum of two was an hour into her third twelve hour nightshift in a row, but she had had both children home from school all day, demanding her attention in their infirm state. Technically, she should not be here at all, what with the little darlings firing from both barrels (or ends, to be more precise.) But those bills were not going to pay themselves, as we all know.

Confident that she was not ill and spreading any major diarrhoea and vomiting bugs herself nonetheless, she dragged herself into work, soldiering on even though sleep was a distant memory.

Tonight, the kids were with Katy's wonderful mother, Eileen, as they were last night when the doting grandmother cooked them a prawn curry. As it turned out, Eileen had also been unwell. Her tummy letting go in volcanic proportions confirmed what Katy had assumed from the start: that her mother had not cooked the prawns to the required standard, leaving the three of them slightly poisoned. Luckily, all three of them were much better this evening, and hopefully not planning on eating shellfish, or chicken, or any other damned food that Eileen may inadvertently screw up.

A safe distance away, avoiding attention, an inconspicuous domestic observed a redheaded nurse remove and replace the narcotic contents of a syringe driver. She clicked the clear plastic case shut and turned a key, before dropping the bunch into a deep pocket on the front of her cyan blue tunic. Turning back to her drugs trolley, the nurse wheeled it slowly out of the room. She stopped the rolling pharmacy outside of the door, pulled a clipboard from its side, and proceeded to study the print.

Ideal, thought the domestic, absently twisting a mop head into a bucket. *A fully loaded one-way ticket to oblivion.*

He was not stupid; he knew that this on its own was not going to be enough. He had done his homework. Thanks to the modern world of internet search engines and video sharing sites, budding psychopaths around the globe could access all sorts of information to aid and convert of their twisted fantasies into devastating reality. The keys to destruction at their very fingertips.

Just this week, he had learned that it generally takes a minimum of two-hundred milligrams of morphine to result in a fatality. However, this figure could be as low as sixty milligrams if an intolerance to morphine is unknown or goes unnoticed. Fingers crossed, eh?

For the previous twenty minutes on the ward where he was not supposed to be working (all the other cleaners on shift had packed up and gone home, thankfully. Though who notices a young domestic minding his own business, keeping his head down and just getting on with the job?), he had done a quick bin change of every bay and side room, counting as he went the number of other patients with this type of driver placed on slim, chrome poles next to their beds.

Two more. A total (including Jack's fresh batch) of ninety milligrams. Not enough, but knowing that this drugs trolley served the adjacent ward of similarly smashed up patients, Cameron hoped for the best. This drug trolley could still contain the motherload.

How to get the keys? This was the next hurdle. The complete set that the redheaded nurse held in her custody would not only give access to the trolley, but also to the syringe driver. The rest, a piece of piss. Cameron could not believe his luck when his internet searching returned a video of how to *actually* use the exact model that was now intravenously hooked up to the lad who had threatened to muzzle in on Cameron's comfortable life – everything from opening the casing; to changing the syringe; to (last, but most definitely not least) silencing the alarm in the event of error or malfunction. I mean forget the do-gooders trying to heal the world and make it a better place for generations to come. With hidden figures of the cyber realm incumbent on facilitating evil to untold levels, shielded by untraceable IP addresses in sordid basement rooms and dishevelled tower blocks, sporting bushy beards and Benny hats and wanking off to bestiality videos (or at least that's how Cameron imagined them), this planet's course on its macabre downward spiral would only ever gain momentum.

A juddering slide of rubber on vinyl sounded out from beyond the deserted nurse's station, attracting the attention of both Cameron and the redhead.

'Alright, Mr Johnson?' she asked this old dude in brown check flannelette pyjamas, who was exiting the bay to the left of the station.

'Yes, my bird,' he replied cheerily (and loudly, largely down to his age-impaired hearing.) His flimsy aluminium walking frame gave another rubbery shudder. 'Off to spend a penny.'

'Well, you mind how you go,' said Katy, trying not to laugh out loud at the thought of the whole ward now knowing Mr Johnson's business.

He waved a frail hand. Smiling, Katy returned her attention to the clipboard she was holding.

Yeah, old man, mind how you go. Cameron scoped the area and, being as certain as he could be that he was still unnoticed, he skulked behind the crenellations of the station, a Ghost Mantis safe in the withered jungle of papers, pamphlets and folders.

The rub-clack, rub-clack of the walking frame seemed to take an age before it crept into view from Cameron's low vantage point, though judging by the muffled voices, the rest of the nurses on duty were still busy in the bays. All of Cameron's eggs were in one basket now, a basket shaped like a nice juicy pear and wearing a blue tunic, hopefully still staring intently at her clipboard. As the rear support legs of the walking frame slowly passed, and the scuffed toes of an old pair of moccasins limped into view, Cameron thrust the aluminium handle of the mop forward between frame and feet.

A sudden clatter of metal and the slapping of thinning flesh and bone on hard floor snapped Katy away from her ticks and scribbled notes. Running past the desk, she threw her charts aside, shouting for assistance. Peering from floor level, Cameron could see black tights charging from the nearest bays, like the many legs of flocking sheep being shepherded to their pen. With the commotion beautifully executed, he crept-crawled to the far side of the desk, feeling like the one-man-army-Arnie in that one where the body count rose from incalculable to inconceivable.

Rising and looking at his creation – a blue and green tide of arched backs jostling in a sea of support – Cameron turned his attention to the abandoned trolley.

Jackpot.

Gleaming like the bright lights of the dodgems he rode once as a child (one of the few occasions his father had taken him anywhere), the set of keys sparkled temptingly as they hung from a hole in the cabinet's thin metal top. Katy had unwittingly saved him the hassle of having to bust the lock by removing the keys from her tunic in preparation for the next patient's fix. Cameron had not seen her do this, but what a sign it was!

Things are going my way.

A look back at the huddle of medical professionals confirmed what his alert ears were one step ahead with; everybody was still preoccupied with the unfortunate old duffer lying partially broken on the floor. After gloving up, Cameron grabbed the handle and wheeled the copious drug supply, slick with the movements of hunting tiger, into the sleeping Jack's room. Pushing the door to leave a small gap, he was now completely hidden from the otherwise engaged staff.

Turning the key and popping the lid, Cameron ruffled through the hidden wonders. His hands shook slightly with adrenaline. Such power at his disposal: boxes; syringes; needles; bottles containing pills; bottles containing liquids. And there it was. The silver tuna. Morphine sulphate. One, *shuffle*, two, *shuffle shuffle*, three, four, five.

It might do.

It might.

Sneaking a peak out through the fractionally open door, he could see that the ruckus continued. In fact, the busy crowd was growing.

Two doctors had now joined the medley. *Shit, maybe I've killed the old duffer,* Cameron thought. How Jack had slept through all of this, Cameron had no idea, but he looked to the ceiling and thanked God, amused at how such a heinous act could seem to gain the reward of divine assistance.

Finding the correct key for the syringe driver took three attempts. Once found, it slid readily into the underside of the lockbox. With a click, it fell open. Cameron hovered a thumb over the *silence alarm* button. He knew it would not sound at this disturbance, but he was loath to invite unnecessary complications. At the sound of blissful silence from the machine, he flicked down a plastic clamp that held the current syringe in place. Pulling a lever and unlocking the drive, Cameron removed the vessel, careful not to alter the position the drive-stay on the machine. With the syringe in his right hand, Cameron lightly applied pressure to the plunger, shooting the liquid into Jack's body until the tube was spent. Removing the cap from a fresh syringe, he disconnected the empty tube from the line and replaced it with another thirty milligrams.

Smiling sardonically, he repeated the process. Squeeze. Replace. Squeeze. Replace. Repeat. All the while, the mumbling from the hectic nurse's station area thrummed though the door in low pulses.

After slotting the last syringe of morphine back into the driver with extreme caution, lifting the drive locking lever, and clicking the lockbox closed, Cameron returned to the door.

Outside, the unfortunate Mr Johnson still lay on the vinyl floor. His moaning suggested he was still alive. The crowd of helpers continued to busy themselves and offer reassurances.

Cameron turned to look at Jack, still unconscious on the bed. He wondered if the liquid overdose was taking effect. Thankfully, there were no other gadgets hooked to the patient to let him know for sure, but noticeable tremors shaking the bedsheets indicated that it most likely was. He tipped Jack a nod, an unfamiliar feeling of regret coursing through his veins. Pulling the door open, Cameron wheeled the trolley back to its original position, still unnoticed. Walking behind the nurse's station to avoid the crowd and retrieve his mop – which lay hidden by stacks of drawers – Cameron returned to his cleaning trolley. He quietly sat the mop in the bucket and wheeled his kit off the ward, apparently invisible.

Mr Johnson was eventually returned to his bed, heavily bruised and cut, but no more broken than before his fall. The traces of blood and the pool of piss were cleaned and disinfected.

By the time Katy noticed the catastrophic anomaly in the drug trolley's stock level, Jack was already dead.

CHAPTER FORTY-SIX

Rain. Always rain. The dismal Cornish autumn refused to die. Even when it inevitably did, winter would be no different. Many people romanticise about a mythical county surrounded by coastline and sunshine. The stark reality, nevertheless, was that thick blankets of cloud collected unfathomable amounts of moisture from their lengthy travels over open ocean, before dumping it on this tinpot scrap of land. This remained an isolated realm jutting from the foot of the country like the scuffed toe of an old boot, forgotten during the rainy season, remembered and descended upon by armies of emmets when summertime showed its beaming face.

Droplets of that moisture splattered now, against the outer face of the darkened window. They lit like fireflies in the glow of the *evil eye* print shaded lamp that stood on Kerenza's disorganised dressing table. Sporadic gusts of wind rolled the saturated air like sea spray from the crests of waves, bringing a shamble of cold sounding crackles into the room.

The reflection looking back at her applied black mascara to its opposite eyelash, brush held delicately with surprising composure. Behind the girl in the mirror, a vertical black line appeared at the edge of the door. The floor behind Kerenza creaked, followed by a couple of light knuckle taps on wood.

'I saw your light was on,' Andrew's voice crept quietly into her bedroom. 'You're up early. Is everything okay?'

'It's Jack's funeral this morning,' she said, turning and placing an arm over the back of her chair. 'I'm getting an early bus to Grace's and going with her.'

'Oh, shit. I'm sorry.'

'What for?'

'The fact I can't drive you myself. Sorry that Jack's,' he trailed off.

After not getting a response from Kerenza he asked the stupid question that everyone asks at a time like this. He waited to receive a variant of the same awkward and erroneous answer: *I'm fine,* or *I'm okay,* or *not* too *bad.*

'I'm okay,' and after a pause. 'I think. I'm not sure how I'm supposed to feel.'

Andrew came fully into the comforting glow of the room and made his way over to her. He put his hands on her smooth blonde hair and drew her head against his hip.

'There's no rule about how you should feel,' he said. 'No script you have to follow. It's yours to deal with in your own way. But know that, just because no one can tell you how you should be feeling, doesn't mean you're on your own.'

'Thanks,' she said, holding back the tears that would leave tragic black tracks down her cheeks.

Andrew lowered one hand and rubbed her shoulder in a chummy *nice one sport* kind of way, then, letting go, he took a seat on a corner of her bed.

'What about you?' Kerenza asked, returning her attention to the mirrored version of herself and getting busy on the other eye. 'It's a bit early for you too, isn't it?'

'Hmm, me? Oh, I set the alarm for a swim down at the beach.'

'The beach? In this weather?'

'A bit of rain doesn't get you any wetter than the sea does.'

'Fair point,' she said, looking at him in the glass. 'With Alycia?'

'She may be there,' he said, the familiar feeling that he had willingly entered an interrogation room. 'Anyone could be there, it's not exclusive.' Andrew was babbling now, a touch flustered. 'It's quite casual. There's a group of people who go. Some on some days, some on others. And no set times.'

His tee shirt started to tighten like a noose around his neck and he could feel the superficial temporal artery start to kick in his head like an unborn child in the womb. He needed desperately to change the subject.

'Don't you youngsters wear bright colours to funerals these days?' *Shit, not* that *subject you dick!*

'What?' Kerenza asked, looking down at her black cotton dress with black lace sleeves, accompanied by black nylon tights. 'Is there something wrong with what I'm wearing?'

Another wave of raindrops broke against the windowpane, louder than any of its predecessors. Andrew looked into the gloom, thinking that swimming this morning was a bad idea, but worth it just to get him out of this hole he could not stop digging.

'Hello-*oh.*,' said Kerenza.

'What? No. No way, you look g... very passible.'

'Passible?' she said baffled. 'Thanks. It's not an interview, but thanks.'

'I didn't mean that,' Andrew protested.

'It's okay, I'll take g...passible,' Kerenza teased. 'There's no dress code though, Grace's dad didn't set one. He's *set* very little,' she said ruefully, locking eyes with the man in the mirror.

'I'm sorry to hear that.'

'Don't be. It's no more and no less than Jack would've expected from him.' Kerenza leaned forward and plucked up a bullet-shaped plastic tube from the table. 'I will be wearing something bright though. Red lipstick, especially for Jack.'

She pulled off the clear plastic sleeve and twisted the stick. The smooth glossy red interior arose, a periscope from dark waters.

'He always had a thing for the blonde hair and bright red lippy combo,' Kerenza remembered fondly. 'Always trying to get me to wear it for him but, not being a fan, I never did. According to Grace, it's the only reason he watched *Dancing on Ice,* though he would never admit it. She said she could actually see his shoulders drop whenever that presenter's Cheshire cat grin was painted anything less than crimson.' Kerenza started to trace the curve of her lower lip, still eyeing him in the mirror. 'Still, he gets his wish today.'

'Well, I hope it goes as well as it can do,' Andrew said, getting up. 'I'm off. Don't want to be late.'

'I thought it was *casual*.' Kerenza did the American finger-quotes thing as she spoke the last word.

'It is,' he said. 'I'm in no rush. I just thought I'd better…You know.'

He walked out onto the landing, plunging into darkness as he pulled the door shut behind him.

Kerenza stared at its plain white surface momentarily, before returning her attention to the girl in her mirror.

***

Grace answered the door. Her hair was dishevelled, and red streaks charted a map over the freckles on her puffy cheeks. She snivelled a *'hi'* and ran her hand forcefully through the short mop on her head, disorganising the scorched cornfield of strands and stalks even more.

Kerenza reached over the step and took her friend in a warming embrace, finally breaking to head inside and out of the cold, damp, late November morning.

'Car's gonna be here in ten minutes,' Grace said as they headed into the kitchen. The room was dull due to the absence of electric light. 'D'you want a drink?'

'No, thanks,' Kerenza said. She could hear Grace's dad pottering and moving things around upstairs. 'How is he?' she asked, flicking her eyes towards the ceiling.

'He hasn't been down this morning.'

A loud thud issued through the floorboards, followed by a growling *fuck's sake* that seemed to scramble down the stairs and charge menacingly from the building. The two girls stood uncomfortably silent in its wake, a sympathetic glance issuing from Kerenza to Grace.

Heavy footsteps bounded rapidly down the stairs and Grace's dad appeared through the door.

'Car's 'ere.' Tony Searle said, flatly.

'He's early,' Grace exclaimed.

'Good.' He eyed Kerenza up and down, making her feel like a jarred specimen in a freak show tent.

'Mr Searle,' she said timidly, nodding acknowledgement.

'Oright?' he grunted. 'Right. Let's get this over with.'

Tony turned and headed outside, the girls following obediently like ducklings behind their mother.

The cortege sat on the roadside, motionless apart from the occasional wobble caused by irregular gusts of sharp wind. The train consisted of one hearse, and – the Searles being a small and private family – just one tailing limousine. The black box-like vehicle tasked with bearing a recently fit, active and popular young man on his final journey (aside from the short roll from the car to the crematorium chapel, and then its final destination: the committal chamber), shed veils of morning drizzle which congregated in slick oily pools within its shadowy underbelly.

Grace shifted to Kerenza's left as they reached the front car, using her as a human shield to protect her from the sight of the yellow flowers that spelled out her brother's name. From behind the rain-specked rectangle of glass, every letter seemed to frown accusingly upon the two girls. Kerenza retched acidic air as she studied them and the wooden box behind.

Reaching the second car, a top and tailed man with thick greying eyebrows and comically long legs opened the rear kerbside door. He gestured like a footman in an old black and white film, his arm swinging towards the opening with a marionette motion.

Grace's father hunched himself in, followed by the timid frame of his daughter. Kerenza watched on, thinking that a hand on the shoulder could break the girl's serpentine back. Finally, she steeled herself to follow. The sound of several doors closing in quick succession startled sparrows from the hedgerow. As they flew off in confusion, the engines came alive, and the procession rolled gently forwards. The crumble of heavy rubber on the stone chip road lagged behind like a haunting entourage.

Arriving at the grounds of the crematorium, the cortege headed down a tree-lined drive. The vehicles slowed to a stop at a pull-in, killing time due to their early arrival.

Straggling mourners from the previous service evacuated the chapels in slow droves, their last goodbyes complete and an agonising realisation hitting them: their lives must continue, albeit slightly hollower than when they arrived.

'Queuing up,' Tony Searle mumbled, nonchalantly. 'Mass dispatch.'

Grace gave him a hard stare, prompting Kerenza to take her hand and give it a gentle squeeze. The return squeeze was one of anguish, but at least her attempt to comfort the grieving girl was acknowledged. As Grace returned her attention to the road ahead, the modest caravan lurched back on to the main drag.

They pulled up alongside a broad-fronted building. Tall, slim windows doubled up at either side of a large entryway, crowned with a towering gable. After her door of the limo was chaperoned open, Kerenza hoisted herself out and looked upwards at the dominating structure. Its walls of immaculate white, aiming to offer the impression of a serene and sympathetic refuge, appeared grey under the thick fabric sky. Thus, the complexion offered instead a dark, lurking intent.

The hearse lay stationary in the murky shade of a portico. Colonial pilasters held the structure aloft. Hairline fractures and flaking paint ran their lengths, apparently the only parts of the oversized furnace that had failed to defy time.

A group of Jack's friends loitered close by. Some Kerenza knew by name, some by face, some she didn't know at all. You never understand how many so-called friends you have until they contemplate the guilt of not seeing you off. As they hovered and milled about in the gloom of the portico, a large wooden bier was wheeled from within a gaping pair of gloss black doors.

A moment later, Grace emerged from the back of the car. Kerenza placed a steadying hand on her shoulder as she arched out, unstable. Straightening up as the coffin containing the remains of her brother was transferred from hearse to wheel bier, she watched as it was mournfully rolled into the chapel. Her father followed, and side-by-side Grace and Kerenza fell in line. A *v* formation of flying geese was created as other mourners took their lead.

The service was cursory and impersonal. At the beginning we are pushed into the world in a series of forceful breaths and screams through clamped jaws and gritted teeth. At the end we are ushered out with a meaningless and exhausted prayer that has been murmured a million times over, a listlessly mumbled hymn, and a puff of incinerator smoke.

The ceremony was as unremarkable as it was impersonal. There was no real praise for a life lived, no anecdotes of how Jack had achieved this, and how he had gone on to become that. The fact is, he had died too young. There was little time for him to put a real stamp on the world, to reach that celebratory accomplishment that everyone should at least have a shot at.

He was too young, and nobody, not family, friend, nor even guilt-quelling supposed friend, should had to have witnessed the events at the chapel to begin with.

In the sombre bar area, Grace sat looking at the half empty glass of beer her dad left on the table. Traces of leftover creamy head clung to its inner top half in a confusion of intricate snail trails.

Grace spoke miserably. 'He's not coming back, is he?'

Her father had exited through the back door fifteen minutes previously, expressing the need to relieve himself.

'Don't think so,' said Kerenza, before drawing more blackcurrant and lemonade through a straw.

Grace had not touched her drink. At present, she didn't feel capable of keeping anything down if she wanted to. She even screwed her nose up in disdain at the mouth-watering smell of the carvery, drifting through from the restaurant in the larger area of the pub.

Partially thinking aloud, Grace said, 'I'm surprised Cameron didn't turn up.'

Kerenza gave her an uncomfortable look over the top of her glass.

'What's that face for?' said Grace.

'I didn't want to tell you…'

'Tell me what?'

'I haven't seen Cam since you told him you couldn't be with him.'

'I didn't mean permanently,' Grace defended. 'It was only for a few days while I sorted my head out. He knew that!'

'Well, he took it to mean that you didn't trust him,' said Kerenza. 'That you were suspicious of him, because of…you know.'

'And he told you this, did he?'

'He didn't have to.' Kerenza gently placed her glass on the tacky surface of the table and leaned forward. 'I know him better than you do. And I know how it looked.'

'Are you saying you think I blame him? That's ridiculous, Cameron was trying to get on with him.' Grace shook her head in consideration, her wavy fringe dropping to cover one eye before she blew it up out of the way again. 'So, you haven't seen him for, what, three weeks? Three weeks! How d'you even know he's okay?'

'Because he's Cameron. He's always okay. I texted him this morning,' Kerenza said looking down at the table in regret. 'I told him to stay away today.'

'How could you do that?' Grace croaked out.

'You didn't want to see him, so I made sure he wasn't going to upset you.'

'And did he answer?'

There was a moment where neither of the girls spoke. Laughter drifted towards them from various parts of the small bar that was mostly populated by other funeral-goers. Mixed in with the laughter was a loud clack of pool balls, a moan, and some jibing remarks. Grace felt something hard come to a stop against one of her shoes.

'Sorry,' a tall, dark haired, athletic lad said as he bent to pick up the ball. He stood and gave her a compassionate look and ruffled her hair. 'You were lucky to have a brother like Jack. We're all gonna miss him.'

Grace smiled a reticent reply. He smiled back before returning to his game.

'Who was that?' Kerenza asked.

'Did he answer?' Grace persisted, not allowing the diversion.

'Who?'

'Who do you think,' Grace said curtly.

'Yes, he did.' Kerenza picked up her glass, sucked, and swallowed another mouthful. 'He told me to F off.'

'So how do you know he's really alright?'

'Don't worry, he will be.' Kerenza's attempted assurance sounded lame. 'He'll just be dossing on a mate's sofa licking his wounds. We'll see him soon enough. You can be sure of that.'

They sat reserved for the next fifteen minutes, observing if not digesting what was happening around them. Kerenza had drained her glass, Grace had still not touched hers.

'Stay mine tonight?' said Grace, finally diluting the cloying atmosphere.

Kerenza hesitated, not wanting to be in the same house a Grace's dad. Given the disconnected way he had taken his son's death and his disconcerting behaviour since, she no longer felt comfortable in his company.

Grace sensed her hesitation and pleaded. 'Please.'

Kerenza looked into the girl's tormented eyes. 'Yeah. Course.'

CHAPTER FORTY-SEVEN

If awarded the privilege of an aerial view over this gateway between dimensions, one would see its dramatic, theatrical beauty; the decisive divide between two opposing worlds, with two opposing agendas. On one side: land. Melpomene's tragic frown, sympathising with the souls of the tormented. On the other: sea. Thalia's amused smile, calling for those same souls to feast on.

Sitting at the summit of Hell's Mouth with his arms cradling his shins, Cameron rocked in unison with the torrents of Atlantic wind. Sweating from what felt like an oncoming fever and shivering from the cold, he fought the urge to shuffle closer to the cliff's rugged and crumbling face. To remove his shoes and socks and hang his feet into black emptiness. To allow the ghosts of the past to reach up and tickle his vulnerable soles.

Had he moved to the edge, he had an unequivocal notion that even in such darkness he would see the face of his dead mother looking indignantly back at him from the rocky floor, incredulous to his actions.

And he may be okay with that. It had been a long time since he had seen her broken body spread out for the gulls to feast upon in a greedy frenzy. And besides, the bitch deserved it.

But then there was Jack. What if it was his face looking up from the watery grave? Cameron had left Jack for dead without a second thought. Jack, whose only crime had been to get with the wrong girl. Was that enough of a reason? Well, they do say 'all is fair in love and war,' right? And he must have conspired to stitch Cameron on the night at Raymond's. Why else would the Golf be there, and not Jack's Subaru?

Shit, Raymondo. There's another one.

A flash lit up the horizon. After a several seconds had elapsed, a deep rumble rolled in from across the ocean. Waves crashed at the bottom of the cliff ferociously, Hades' underworld accepted a dance-off with Elysium veraciously.

Cameron struggled precariously to his feet, reaching behind and clutching the single wooden rail for assurance. Another flash illuminated the horizon with a white divinity as he turned and surmounted the fence. Teetering on the slippery lip of the devil was not a perfect place to be in a storm. Navigating the narrow and uneven foot-worn pathway in the darkness was near impossible, until another burst of electrical discharge came into force. The earthy path lit like a dewy thread of silk under its brilliance. The brief glimpse burnt onto Cameron's retinas, a map etching his route back to the road imprinting on his memory.

Once at the layby, he clutched his motorcycle and flicked back the stand. Opting to roll the bike east, towards the dilapidated farm building that acted as his temporary refuge, he traipsed his way along the cumbersome coast road.

By the time he had completed the laborious trek, the storm had rumbled closer, pushing and shoving the clouds in a cacophony of vapour and spray. Sparkling grass waltzed and swayed with sickening fluidity in the fitful flares of moonlight.

Tussling his motorcycle though a narrow gap in the ramshackle Cornish hedge, tyres bumping over lumps of rock long since tumbled, Cameron wheeled the hulk of metal off to one side and let it fall into the tangle of brambles and nettles. From here he looked across the vast open space, flat for a distance before descending towards the symphonic sea.

The upper section of an old granite structure could be seen peaking above the roll of the land, its charcoal skeletal trusses breaking through a series of jagged holes in the roof; the ribs of a decaying corpse through torn and maggot eaten flesh.

Crossing over the open expanse, Cameron stopped short of the building and looked back, assuring himself that he had travelled unnoticed. Anyone would have to be missing a few marbles to still be out on this desolate stretch tonight. His heavy footprints had left a weaving series of black holes in the grass, like fertile craters of old volcanoes caught via drone photography. Sporadic yellow lights glowed from the scattering cottage windows in the distance. Nothing moved other than the fabrics of nature.

Upon reaching the dilapidated structure, another crack of lightning transformed the sky, proceeded by a deafening crash. Cameron pulled at the partly collapsed security fencing. Stumbling through the thorny gap, he let the mesh fall behind him to its default position; angled like a headstone marking a partially sunken grave. Stepping across the threshold and into the darkness, he grimaced, clutching at his side. The last remaining shard of door, clinging stubbornly to one rusty iron hinge, took a penetrating bite at him.

'Home, sweet fucking home,' he thought out loud.

Wiping the sweat from his forehead with one sleeve, reaching into his pocket with the free hand, Cameron animated the screen of his phone. No messages or missed calls from Grace, likewise from Kerenza. Swiping the menu down, he silenced the alerts and thumbed the torch icon. His black rucksack came into view and he made his way over. Splashing through the interior puddles – *yes, sir, it's a wonderful property, lovely sea views, well ventilated, scope for an observatory, indoor plunge pool already under construction* – he reached the rear of the building, put his back to the slimy wall and slid down next to the bag.

On the menu, dry Pot Noodle. On the damp floor, cold creeping into his rump and sure to give him piles, Cameron peeled back the foil lid and pulled at a lump of noodles that seemed set in mortar. Crunching away, he contemplated moistening the snack with the sachet of hot sauce provided. One taste of it not watered down was enough to inform him that occasionally, and only very occasionally, his brainwaves were shit.

Once his meal was finished, he looked out at the barren, single room. The trapdoor lay brown on black like a doorway to Purgatory, keeping a lid on the dank and musty cellar. His dark work down there was completed earlier that evening, before his jaunt to Hell's

Mouth, but still he crawled to where the large planks lay. The draft through the uneven and woodworm-eaten edges of the slats would be a bitch. But on the whole, it would surely be an upgrade on a bed of sodden earth for the night.

Outside, the storm was frantic. Strobe lighting battered its way through various entry points in the decrepit ceiling above, and moisture seeped through the blanket that covered Cameron's head and body. Voices kept sleep at bay for several hours: voices in the wind; voices from the sea; voices from withing the aching bones of the aging building. It was as if everyone he had ever wronged in the past had come back to haunt him, carried in on spectral winds to the present.

Constant quavering sapped his energy. Crestfallen faces floated in front of him, staring him to sleep, or to death. He could neither tell nor care which, but finally one of them took mercy on him.

CHAPTER FORTY-EIGHT

The driveway lay deserted as Kerenza stepped onto its gravelly bed. She wondered how long this would take to become the norm, not seeing Andrew's Nissan hauled up behind her mother's vacated space. It had taken long enough for the expectancy of seeing her mum's Ibiza to wear off. Now, she could not hazard a guess as to the moment it finally did.

One good thing though: no pink Barbie car.

She had left Grace's an hour earlier, after preparing her a light lunch and hanging around to eat with her – or more importantly, to make sure that Grace ate. Kerenza doubted very much that Grace would eat for the remainder of that day, or even the following day given the emotional car crash she resembled at this point in time.

Unfortunate as it might be, Kerenza had to leave her unsupervised at some point. For one, she needed to see if Cameron had finally come home. He had seemed uncharacteristically sentimental after having the metaphorical door slammed in his face by Grace, leaving Kerenza to wonder just how unhinged he may become. Furthermore, somebody had to make sure that a certain young lady's feet were not becoming rooted under *her* table.

My god, it was hard work, looking out for everyone.

Kerenza poked her head around the far corner of the cottage. No sign of the KMX.

The front door was unlocked, though upon walking into the kitchen, the only sound that greeted her was the ticking of the wall clock. Listening momentarily to the otherwise silent voices of the old dwelling, she placed her bag on the kitchen table, pulled a glass from the drainer and ran herself a drink of water. After drawing a few sips whilst looking dreamily out of the window, wondering who had gone out last and left the front door unlocked, a single heavy thud sounded through the ceiling above.

Placing the glass down carefully, Kerenza turned and headed into the living room. She paused in contemplation as she was about to mount the stairs. There was no way of knowing who or what had made the sound. Logical thinking would suggest that it was Andrew. Or maybe it was Cameron, having drunkenly left his bike somewhere and stumbled home to sleep it off. Worst case scenario, an intruder. *Logical* thinking however, had been blurred and compromised after the morbid and unsettling events of the last few days. Visions of a scrappy and milky-eyed Exit Wounds rounding the top of the stairs and growling lowly at her came into her mind.

Total nonsense of course, but…

Not knowing which would be worse – the intruder or the walking dead feline – Kerenza did know that neither was a good thing. Her eyes surveyed the room for something heavy or sharp. Just in case. Scanning desperately, they fell upon the fireplace. Bingo. The wrought iron fire poker. Creeping over, she plucked the poker from its stand nervously, returned to the stairs, and started to climb.

Almost all the way up now. Still no other sound broke the tense stillness. At this altitude Kerenza could peer through the gaps in the top set of railings. Just one bedroom door hung ominously ajar. If this was a horror film, Kerenza would be shouting at the dumb blonde for even considering going to investigate.

She raised the poker's lethal point to head height and tip-toed to Merryn's open door, edging one dilated pupil past the wooden frame.

'What are you doing in here? And how drunk are you?'

Sprawled out on Merryn's bed, lay Andrew. One bottle of wine was in hand, and another (the source of the bang, presumably) was lying empty on the floor.

He sluggishly rolled his head to the door. 'Well, I'm here because I'm depressed, and in answer to your second question, not drunk enough. Why are you holding a poker?'

'It's more of a case of *where am I going to stick the poker*, not why am I holding it!' she fired back in annoyance.

'Bit touchy,' Andrew said, rolling his head away again.

Kerenza propped the poker against the frame of the door and made her way over to Merryn's bed. Andrew, a grown man, spread out on a pink duvet cover embellished with a unicorn, a rainbow, and stars (the latter two an unlikely combination), swigging straight from the bottle, gave every impression of someone deeply consumed in a total mental breakdown.

'Budge up,' she said kneeing him in the hip.

He shuffled over with a groan and Kerenza lay down next to him, taking the bottle and reaching over to put it on the floor.

'What gives?'

'It's all gone to shit. Ever since your mum went,' Andrew whimpered with all the heartache of the last kid to be picked for either team in the big game down the park.

'Well, you're clearly being a dick.'

'What?' Andrew looked at her with hurt in his eyes. 'Thanks very much. I thought if anyone would sympathise, it'd be you.'

'Grow up, Dad,' she said, but not in a nasty way. 'Sympathy's thrown around too freely, usually by people who actually have no idea what you're going through. I know that as well as anyone. We cremated Jack yesterday, remember?'

'It's not the s___'

'Not the *same*? Why? Because we're young? Because we're incapable of experiencing or understanding love at our age?'

Andrew felt a tonne weight of shame fall onto his chest. 'You were?'

'Yes, we were in love.'

'I'm sorry,' he said, able to look her in the eye again. 'It's just, since your mum died, I've burned down my studio, lost Merryn, lost my driver's license, driven my son away. Oh, and I nearly killed your grandad.'

'Okay, it sounds bad when you reel it off like that. But. You *will* get Mez back. Cam, too. He's got his own demons to face, but they are not down to you.' She raised her eyebrows, in hope of ascertaining if this was going in. A curl of his bottom lip confirmed he was listening. 'The studio was an accident.'

'A deliberate accident.'

'But an accident all the same. It was just seriously poor execution on your part,' Kerenza persisted. 'As for Grandad, you *didn't* kill him, and you were trying to do the right thing. You just went a stupid way about it.'

Kerenza waited for a counterargument. There was none.

'Plus, you've got Alycia now.'

'Huh? There's nothing happening there!' Andrew dismissed.

'There is, I saw you kiss her in the pub. Unless that's what you do to everyone. But don't worry. It's all good.'

'Sorry. I guess I didn't tell you cos I don't really know what I'm doing.'

'Moving on,' she suggested.

'I'm not over your mum. It's too soon.'

'You'll never stop grieving for Mum,' she said, delicately moving his falling fringe away from his eye. 'Nine months; nine years; nine lifetimes. Part of your brain will always try to convince you it's too soon. Fact is, time is meaningless. You have to get on with your life at some point. So, just give it a chance.'

There followed a drawn-out period of silence.

'You could be right,' Andrew finally conceded.

'I am right,' Kerenza assured, leaning over and kissing him on the forehead like he was a hurt infant. 'Start believing that and things will go your way.'

'Okay,' Andrew sighed. 'Can I have my wine back, please?'

'Nope,' Kerenza said rolling off the bed and picking the partly-drunk bottle from the floor. 'You've had enough. This is mine now, I've had a shitty couple of days and I'm off to my room to mope and chill on my own. Besides, getting drunk and sobbing on your kid's bed is seriously uncool.'

She turned to leave. On reaching the door, she craned her head over her shoulder. 'Night night, Old Timer. Love you.'

'Nu-night. Love you too, cheeky sod.' *And don't worry, there's another bottle where that came from.*

CHAPTER FORTY-NINE

I need to see you x

Cameron read the line over and over again. No explanation. Not even a hint as to why the sudden change of heart. It had been five weeks since Grace had so unceremoniously dumped him Then a couple of days ago, this.

The phone's screen dulled before turning black. He tapped the button on the side once more.

I need to see you x lit up, as it had countless times during this moment of deep reflection.

Women! He thought exasperated.

The door handle dropped and a heavy thud came against the wood.

Kerenza's distorted voice rang through. 'For fuck's sake, Cameron. Unlock the door!'

Clambering lethargically from his bed, Cameron made his way over and slid back the newly fitted, heavy duty steel bolt.

'What d'you want?' he said, fractionally opening the door.

Kerenza pushed, forcing entrance.

'What the hell is that?' she said.

'Duh, it's a lock. Dipshit.'

'And why exactly have you put that there?'

Cameron sighed and raised his eyebrows, as if the answer to her question was glaringly obvious. 'Because I don't like people, and I don't want them in my room.'

'Not even me?' she said with a teasing smile.

'Are you gonna get yer tits out?' His expression was blank but conveyed seriousness.

'No!' said Kerenza.

'Then no. Not even you.'

Cameron closed the door and squared up to Kerenza, pinning her against the wall and pressing his pelvis into her.

'You will one day, though,' he said, his face close now, green eyes devouring her blue.

'You'd better believe it.' Her breath warmed his open mouth as she spoke.

He kissed her ardently on the lips. Kerenza went with it, reaching her arms around her neck and pulling him tight. His caress felt insanely good as he gripped her. She could feel his excitement growing, pressing against her groin as he toyed with her skirt and lifted her to a more suitable height. Lifting her knees, she wrapped her legs around his middle. Cameron grabbed a handful of each ass cheek and carried Kerenza across the room, dropping her on the bed and running kisses down her neck and chest between the open *v* of her crop top.

'Okay, stop,' she breathed out heavily, pushing him from on top of her. 'Now's not the time.'

'Fuckin'ell,' Cameron exclaimed. 'It's never the time with you. Fuckin' prick-teaser!'

'Dad's downstairs, you idiot. And I only came in to ask why you were ignoring Grace's text.'

'How do you know I even got a text?'

'That's as good as telling me you did.'

Cameron thought about it, accepting defeat. 'She dumped me. So why would I give a shit?'

'You don't think she might have been in a bad place?' Kerenza reasoned. 'That she might not have known what she was doing?'

'Maybe. Never really thought about it.' Cameron started absently picking at the cuticle of one thumb.

'That's because you only ever think of yourself. Like right now. Grace is less than two hours away from leaving Cornwall and you're here trying to get in my knickers.'

'What?' he said, getting up in a flustered state. 'You never said.'

'No, but Grace tried. That's why she wanted to see you, but like the child you are you chose to ignore her.'

'She could've let me know. Where the hell's she going?'

'She shouldn't have to chase after you. You needed to be there for her, and you weren't. It's obvious she wasn't in her right mind.' Kerenza was angered by Cameron's ignorance.

'But.'

'She's moving to Buckinghamshire. Her uncle's place is big enough to put them up for a while.'

'A while, so she's coming back?' Kerenza was irked by the look of hope in his eyes.

The bastard's just tried to bed me, and now he wants her *back all of sudden.* In one fickle instant her best friend had become *the other woman* again.

'No. She's not coming back,' she said bitterly. 'As soon as her dad's sorted another job, they're getting their own place up there.'

'She's at home now?' Cameron pleaded.

'Yeah. I was about to go and see her.'

'Right, I'm off,' Cameron said grabbing his helmet from the bedside table.

'Can I jump on the back?' she said swivelling over the edge of the bed.

'After pushing me off once already today?' he said. 'You can fuck right off. Get the bus.'

***

It was tense, awkward meeting: Grace at the edge of her garden, Cameron on the pavement outside, and her old man passing to-and-fro between house and van with boxes of old tut strained to bursting point. He cast disapproving glances at the boy talking to his daughter with every trip.

'No removal van, then?' Cameron murmured, noting the small Caddy van parked up onto the kerb.

'He's only taking the small stuff,' Grace said, looking back to the dark doorway, a distant demeanour about her. 'Records, CD's. Folders of who-knows-what. Clothes. Bedding. He's spent the last few days taking everything else to the dump. Furniture. Beds. Even the dresser unit; and that was vintage. He smashed that up with a sledgehammer first just to get it in the van.' She turned back towards Cameron and frowned.

'D'you think he's losing it?' Cameron asked.

'Maybe,' she said.

'Maybe you shouldn't go with him.' Cameron suggested.

'What are you on about?' she laughed. 'I've got to.'

'I just mean, if he's going off the rails then maybe you shouldn't be around him.'

'He's my dad,' she reminded. 'And what else am I supposed to do?'

This was met with silence as Cameron stared down at the floor, feeling stupid. Was he going to put her up? Him, Grace and Kerenza all living under the same roof? Talk about shitting where you eat.

Tony squeezed through the door again and alighted the garden path with two ballooning black bin liners in his hands.

'Still fuckin' 'ere then?' he aimed at Grace.

'A bin man with Tourette's,' Cameron said cockily.

'Ged'im gone,' Tony snapped back to his daughter. 'Don't need you mopin' over 'im when we need to get gone'.'

He passed by and started stuffing the bags into the back of the van, swearing with every forceful shove.

'Come on,' Grace said to Cameron, stepping over the low border of plants and walking away.

She led the way to a patch of green around the corner. They sat on a bench in the shadow of a trio of tall fir trees, huddling and warming each other against the cold. Neither knew what to say, but the silence was by no means uncomfortable. Both seemed contempt with just being together for the last time.

Grace checked her watch every couple of minutes, hoping to string out the inevitable.

'That's time,' she said, eventually.

They stood and embraced each other tightly.

'Keep in touch,' she said.

'Definitely,' said Cameron, whilst knowing he would never commit to a long-distance thing, no matter how he felt about her.

He looked over Grace's shoulder and spotted Kerenza rounding the corner.

'Here she comes,' he sighed. 'I'm off then. Any way I can get back to my bike without passing her?'

'Yeah,' Grace said with tears rolling down her speckled cheeks. 'Down that lane, left, and left again.'

'Cool. Another time, sweet cheeks.'

He kissed her cold forehead and squeezed her bum cheek with a teasing right hand. More tears streamed from her eyes as she let out an anguished laugh. Cameron turned away, and just like that he was gone.

'Nice of him to stick around,' Kerenza said, with a gallon of sarcasm swishing in her mouth.

Grace erupted in a balling torrent of tears. Reaching out, Kerenza wrapped her arms around her, pulling her head into the crook of her neck.

'Okay. It's okay,' said Kerenza. 'Hopefully it won't be forever. Your dad needs time, but he *will* come around. Deep down he knows you both belong here.'

'And what about him?' Grace pulled her head back and tilted it towards the empty lane.

'Cam? Don't you worry about him. I'll keep him close.' She fought to keep the underlying smirk from her lips.

'He'll soon get bored and move on,' Grace snivelled, returning her face to the hidey-hole of Kerenza's neck.

'No way,' she assured her. 'You're the first proper girlfriend he's had in like, forever.'

The sound of Cameron's bike cracked into life over the rooftops, sending a flap of pigeons scattering in fright. The engine revved high, echoing along the alleyways and ricocheting through openings between the numerous semidetached houses, before dwindling and eventually dying out in the distance.

'GRACE! GET YOUR ASS IN GEAR. WE'RE OFF.'

The two girls looked towards the blaring voice. Standing back at the corner was Tony Searle. The hands cupped around his mouth drew away in a puff of cigarette smoke.

'He gave up five years ago.' Grace looked lost in her own thoughts.

Kerenza felt a sting of sympathy pierce her heart. Berating herself for recently saying that sympathy was thrown around too freely by people who didn't have a clue, she reached a hand forward. Grace immediately threaded her icy fingers through Kerenza's, closing her hand as if to make an unbreakable bond.

Walking back with promises to keep in touch and one day meet again, they had no idea that life's grand and callous scheme would ensure that their reunion would never materialise.

CHAPTER FIFTY

A din of shrill, overzealous voices bellowed towards the rear of the classroom where a door exited onto the playground. Trying her best to block them out, and failing miserably, Miss Sanders pulled at her reading glasses with a thumb and a forefinger and placed them on a stack of papers. She rubbed her eyes and the bridge of her nose before resting her head in an upturned hand.

Positioned between the door and the outside world, Chloe – a teaching assistant Miss Sanders had been awarded the help of for a massive two afternoons a week (a token gesture from the powers that be) – endeavoured to calm the fractiousness and pair the appropriate adults with their corresponding children.

Home time was always chaos, as was the case when arriving at school.

Make up your minds, kids, do you want to be here or not? Alycia wondered; a light throbbing starting to potentiate above one eye.

'If you wouldn't mind just waiting a couple of minutes,' she heard Chloe saying over the ruckus, 'I'll be able to let you in once the way has cleared.'

There was no audible response.

Replacing her glasses, she returned her attention to the student's progress reports on her desk.

Students. Some of them aren't even seven yet. Give 'em a break. No chance of that, though. SATs coming up in six months for these lucky little people.

'Miss Sanders,' Chloe interrupted timidly. 'Mrs Ballantyne's here to see you.'

'Mrs Ballantyne?' Alycia looked up, struggling to relate the surname to a child. Sorry, *Student.*

'Thank you, young lady. I'll take it from here,' Judith said sharply, issuing Chloe a *'scoot'* warning with a single raised eyebrow. 'Judith Ballantyne, Merryn's grandmother.'

'Oh,' said Alycia, evidently caught off-guard. 'Hello, I'm___'

'I know who you are.' Judith snapped. Raising her voice to the young assistant who clearly struggled to read body language, she barked, 'Thank you!'

At this unmistakeable instruction, Chloe scurried to the back of the room and busied herself tidying trays of colourful mathematics cubes. Merryn stood at the door with the loop of her rucksack in both hands, the bag swinging gently back and forth. She offered Chloe a surprisingly adult smile as she passed – a smile that reassured her, *don't worry, she's like that with everyone.*

'I assume you're here to talk about Merryn's schooling?'

'You assume wrong,' Judith scowled. She placed her podgy fingers on Alycia's desk and lurched forward, her doughy shoulders rolling forward like an incoming tsunami.

'You know, I wondered how he could have met you.'

'He?' Alycia questioned, knowing full well whom *he* was, but wanting to be awkward and hesitant in her cooperation.

'My son-in-law. The man who married my daughter. The man who has parental responsibility over my granddaughter and has no room, or purpose in his life for *you*.' Judith gave a cocksure smirk. 'I came to pick my granddaughter up. That's when I saw that stupid little car___'

'That's unnecessary.'

'That *stupid* little car out in the staff car park. So, I put two and two together, and decided it must be the car his floozy was driving.'

'Chloe,' Alycia called. 'Would you like to take Merryn to the library? She's doing so well with her reading now, I think she should take an extra book home as a treat.'

Judith glared at Alycia, 'My granddaughter is very grown-up for her age. Shielding her from anything I have to say is not necessary.'

'Unfortunately, Mrs Ballantyne,' Alycia coolly returned, 'You're not acting very grown-up yourself. Someone of your age really should know better. Chloe, take Merryn to the library.'

Chloe had already taken hold of Merryn's hand and gotten partway to the door, before stopping and awaiting further exchange. There was none. A nod from Alycia told her now was a good time to leave, with the young girl.

'How dare you belittle me in front of my own___'

'Sit. Down.' The dull throb in Alycia's head had now turned into a full-scale assault. The time for being spoken to like a bitch had come to an end.

***

The sound of feet pounding down the stairs came like a drum roll through the open doorway behind him.

An out of breath Kerenza burst into the room. 'Heads up!'

'Yep. I know.'

Andrew's hands turned from pink to red in the hot, soapy dishwater. On seeing the pink Fiat pull onto the drive he felt that teenage kick of excitement in his chest. On spotting the shiny new electric hybrid saloon that followed, he completely forgot himself.

'Shit,' he said, pulling his stinging hands from the bowl and turning the cold handle. It took a moment for cooler water to flow, igniting the pain even more before the sensation of a thousand icy needles stabbed it away.

'So, what do you think this is all about?' Kerenza asked.

'I don't know,' said Andrew. 'But d'ya think I could sneak unnoticed out the side door?'

'Get lost,' she laughed. 'You're not leaving me here with her.'

'Why not? She's *your* gran.'

Beyond the window, car doors swung open. Alycia appeared, standing confidently and looking back at Judith with all the resoluteness of a hostage negotiator.

Andrew's spirits lifted further as the back door of the second car sprung outwards and two little feet crunched to the floor below it.

So, this is a hostage negotiation, he thought.

Last out of the two cars was Angus. Andrew's first assumption was that he had been delayed whilst savouring the comforts of his new motor's lavish interior: sinking into the soft heated fabric of the moulded driver's seat; stoking the veneer of the dashboard; flicking switches he knew nothing about, like an old-age pensioner newly appointed as pilot of Airwolf. Further inspection however, indicated that Angus' delayed emergence was more down to physical deterioration. His movements more cumbersome than Andrew remembered, his steps more circumspect.

Turning off the cold tap and drying his hands on the tea towel – one of Shona's pet hates – Andrew made his way to the front door. His body felt top-heavy and sluggish, thanks to the thought of what he had turned the big man into. Guilt was no stranger to gravity.

Andrew clutched at the handle, pulling the door open.

'Jesus Christ!' He jumped back in alarm as Judith's colossal face filled the frame. 'How did *you* get there so quick?'

'Yes, well it really is wonderful to see you, too,' Judith quipped. 'But I'm not The Lord Jesus; slightly less facial hair, you'll no doubt observe.'

Yeah, on Jesus, Andrew thought. 'Thank heavens for small mercies,' he smiled.

Judith leaned forward, worrying Andrew into thinking she was going in for a kiss. Instead, she drew a series of exaggerated sniffs. 'Sober. Thank heavens indeed.'

Touché, bitch, he thought, irritated by the sour breath invading his personal space.

He moved aside for the juggernaut to enter, hoping her sizeable hips didn't brush up against his nether regions. That would be a mental image that would never dissipate.

'*DADDY!*' an excited scream rang from along the drive. Merryn darted towards him, throwing her arms around his legs.

Andrew clamped a hand under each armpit and heaved her up to his level. 'Hey, squirt. This is a nice surprise.'

Angus gave him the complementary clap on the shoulder as he got to the door. 'Sonny.'

'Come on in,' said Andrew. 'What's going on?' he whispered to Alycia as she brought up the rear.

'Later, honey,' she said, nodding towards the back of Merryn's ruffled head.

The anticipated negotiations were tense. As afternoon turned to evening and the skies transmuted blue to grey, the atmosphere became that of a high-stakes poker match. Heavy air was flavoured with a sour mixture of accusing glances and speculative stares. Judith glared at Alycia through the dim light of the room. Alycia aimed prompting looks at Andrew. Andrew leered at Judith. Angus looked absently at his hand, picking at some imagined something under his thumbnail and wishing he was in the other room, from where there drifted the joyous sounds of children's television.

'I don't see why *she's* a part of this,' Judith finally fired at Andrew.

'I'm here,' Alycia cut in faster than Andrew could respond – not that he had a response within his grasp, 'Because *you* brought this feud to my place of work.'

Judith thrust a disapproving look at Alycia, finding herself, however, utterly without retort. It was one of the few times in her confrontational existence.

'Ultimately,' Alycia took up the reins. 'A man needs to see his children. Equally, a daughter needs her dad. And as good a job as you may be doing____'

'We're doing an exceptional job!' Judith interjected defensively. 'And I will not have a young *madam* like yourself, with your limited life experience, tell me how to raise a child.'

'As good a job as you *may* be doing,' Alycia reiterated. 'You have no legal right to keep Merryn away from her father until you see fit.'

Andrew and Angus simultaneously receded into their outer shells as a battle of female personalities snowballed.

'I am not prepared to leave my granddaughter with a tragic waste of skin like him.' Judith laid a full house of honesty onto the table.

'Whoa! That's a bit harsh,' Andrew whined, like a wounded puppy.

'That is a bit unfair,' said Alycia. 'He's been through so much. You all have, so you all need to pull together and help each other through. Grief has made Andrew, unpredictable, maybe. But he'd *never* put any of his children deliberately in danger.'

'Grief?' hissed Judith. 'He wouldn't know grief if it came up and biffed him in the face. Just how quickly he shacked up with you is testament to his susceptibility to grief.'

'I agree,' said Alycia.

'I beg your pardon?' Judith was shocked, trumped by an unexpected royal flush.

'In part,' Alycia said. 'It might have happened too soon. But we're good for each other, and Andrew's life *will* turn for the better, and much sooner with me around to help.'

Andrew was flummoxed. 'I'm not a stray dog that needs either rehoming or putting down.'

'Shut up, Andrew,' Judith barked. 'Adults are talking.'

'Hang___'

'Judith's right,' Alycia certified. 'Best leave this to us.'

Bloody hell, he thought. *One minute they hate each other's guts and the next they're a flippin' tag-team.*

'So, what do you propose? Miss?'

Don't pretend you've forgotten my name. 'Please, call me Alycia.'

Silence from Judith.

Alycia continued. 'There's no sense in rushing. Pushing Merryn from pillar to post could cause her to have security issues.'

'Quite so,' said Judith. 'And I would need visual proof that he is capable of being a father again. I won't be convinced overnight.'

'Okay,' said Alycia. 'But I think we'll come to mutually beneficial solution sooner without the mudslinging. He's always been a father, and a good one at that.'

'Thanks,' Andrew contributed.

As the two women fired silencing looks at him, he wished he hadn't. He felt like a cricket between two stealthy chameleons: one unintentional twitch and he was lizard lunch.

Alycia spoke. 'Why don't we all get together here on Christmas Eve? It's only a couple of weeks away. We can make a day of it. Go for a walk; watch movies?' Eyes darted around the table, weighing up the pros and cons of the suggestion. 'I can even cook for everyone. Or at least get mum to. That would probably be safer.'

Andrew and Angus laughed mutedly at the joke. Judith only looked at Alycia in that disdainful way which she had perfected over years of acrimony.

Alycia probed, 'It's got to be worth a shot, right?'

Standing on the doorstep soon after, Andrew put an arm around Alycia. 'You're amazing. How on earth did you manage to strike a deal with that ghastly woman?'

Alycia turned her head and kissed him on the cheek as the flashy car pulled off the drive. 'An abundance of experience with awkward parents. They're worse than the kids, sometimes.'

They both raised a hand as the car disappeared between the trees. Merryn's smiling face and erratically waving hand was just visible through the tinted side window.

'What will it take for Wonder Woman to stay the night?'

'Not gonna happen, Batman. Way too much prep to do, and my own little treasure I need to spend some time with.'

They turned to go inside as the sound of a motorbike entered the valley.

Judith fidgeted in the seat that had not yet become acclimatised to her girth. 'I forgot about that creature,' she said of the boy on the death-trap that hurtled past them. 'No doubt he'll be there.'

'Don't be too concerned with that,' Angus said, pleased to be behind the wheel of his new automobile again. 'He may have to work. Hospitals don't close for Christmas.'

'Let us hope,' she said.

'You may enjoy it,' Angus said optimistically, trying to disguise the doubt in his voice.

After a moment of quiet contemplation, Judith spoke again. 'I'll tolerate her while I have to, but I won't have that woman saunter into our lives and smother every trace of our daughter's existence.'

Angus turned his head to the side, spying a mist forming in his wife's one visible eye. 'That's not going to happen, love,' he said, taking one hand from the wheel and placing it compassionately on hers.

CHAPTER FIFTY-ONE

Sea Glass Cottage had never been so busy. Every room seemed alive with ebullient voices, as the glass of every window turned from white, to grey, to black.

Trampling feet echoed bumps and thuds through the ceiling as Merryn and Darcy were entertained by Harvey (also allowed home from the *old boiler's* for the day), upstairs.

One half of Kerenza's conversation muffled through the door of the downstairs toilet – a strange place to go for a telephone conversation, when she had a perfectly comfortable bedroom upstairs.

Through in the kitchen Judith and Darcy's nan, Liz, chewed the cud, to all appearances getting on like a house on fire.

In the living room Andrew had dug out one of Cameron's old *Ice Road Truckers* DVD's and started it up for Angus. *Not quite relaxing train journeys,* Andrew thought, but a worthy substitution, nonetheless. He, Angus and Alycia put the world to rights as the cameras rolled through a frozen wilderness, panning down at the odd corpse of a truck fallen irretrievable from a precariously high mountain pass.

'Sod that for a living,' Angus muttered looking at the crumpled shell of the doomed rig.

'Couldn't have been much easier for you?' said Andrew.

Some long years ago, Angus had taken his engineering skills, nurtured and honed in Scotland, underground when he moved to Cornwall. Earlier that day, they had all intended to take a clifftop walk from Trevaunance Cove to Chapel Porth. Instead, after stopping for a lengthy rest at Towanroath Pumping Engine House, Judith's ankles had taken enough. The poor woman would be lucky to make it back. As they sat on a hulk of granite at the side of the coast path, looking up at cawing jackdaws and crows shouting their abuse from the top of the structure's towering chimney, Angus had gone into stories of old. Stories of how bal maidens wielding heavy hammers, processed and shifted ore sent up from hundreds of feet below; of how boys as young as twelve lost their lives in underground explosions, or drowned in flooded tunnels.

'Ah worked at Wheal Jane, ya dippit!' Angus laughed at Andrew's lack of understanding. 'T'was a wee bit hairy, sometimes, but nuthin' oan that scale.'

'Sorry,' Andrew said abashed. 'I just thought…those stories you were telling…'

'They were back in the eighteen-hundreds. How auld d'ya think ah am, pal?'

Alycia laughed at the light-hearted ridicule aimed at Andrew and stood. 'Another drink, boys?'

'Please,' said Andrew.

'Aye,' said Angus, raising his glass and tipping Alycia a wink.

She made her way to the kitchen. As she entered, Liz was coming the other way.

Alycia asked, 'You okay?'

'Yes, sweetie. Just popping to the loo.'

Liz was a youthful sixty-four, slim and athletic (to her, the amble across the clifftops was a mere walk in the park), with thick flowing hair of pure white. Polar opposites with Judith Ballantyne, yet they interacted as though they had been friends for years.

'Okay,' Alycia said. 'Krenz is in that one. Bathroom's up the stairs and to the left.'

'Thanks, hon. See you in a tick.'

'You two seem to be getting on well,' Alycia said, turning to Judith as Liz disappeared from the room.

'And *you* seem to have too much knowledge of the layout upstairs,' Judith fired back sourly. 'Just because I have no ill feeling towards your mother, or whatever she is to you, do not think that you and I are suddenly bosom buddies.'

'I wouldn't dare,' Alycia said, with feigned pleasantry.

A flavoursome Wild West stand-off ensued, Alycia with a satisfied smirk, and Judith with a set countenance failing to hide the boiling blood beneath her skin.

As the impression that these two gunslingers were all chat and no trigger grew, Kerenza walked into the firing line.

'Ahh, that smells awesome,' she said, sensing that the atmosphere needed slicing. She sniffed deeply, taking in the warm sweet smell of a ham hock slow roasting in the range cooker. A rainbow of vegetables sat cold in the steamer, awaiting later cooking: carrots, runners, red pepper. Corn cobs were wrapped in foil on the worktop, and wine bottles, red, white, rosé, and even mulled, sat temptingly next to them. 'I'll pop a couple of those in the fridge,' Kerenza said. 'When do we get to eat?'

'We're___' Judith and Alycia started at the same time.

'We're going for a walk around the village soon,' Judith resumed as Alycia conceded, an imaginary slug firing through the air and embedding into her forehead. 'The girls want to look at the Christmas lights.'

'Sounds fun,' said Kerenza.

'Yeah, well good luck motivating the boys,' Alycia put in. 'They're glued to the telly.'

'Angus will do what I tell him,' Judith said assertively.

'Well, Andrew's welcome to have his own mind,' Alycia snarked.

A look of fury screwed Judith's face like clingfilm on a flame.

'Shall we go sooner rather than later?' Kerenza mediated with haste, fully aware that the war of words would soon boil over into an ugly, irreversible conflict.

'Sounds good to me,' said Liz, oblivious to the fact that she had just entered a wrestling ring. 'I'll go back up and get the girls, one of you three can go and gee the boys up.'

***

A fine mist settled over the village, turning the hanging miniature lanterns of red, green, yellow and blue to glowing orbs as they bobbed gracefully in the breeze. The watery roadway and pavements radiated a warm orange under the lining streetlights. Clouds of breath emitting from sporadic groups of villagers enjoying the cool festive evening swelled with the same hue.

Christmas songs poured from the steamy windows of the top inn, and through the large open doors of the old institute building.

Descending further down into the square, forming a crescent around the eighteen-foot-high illuminated tree, the village band blew their brass instruments and banged their drums.

'Can we go in the pub, Daddy?' Merryn asked excitedly.

'Um,' Andrew thought out loud.

'Pleeease?' she pleaded.

'No, I don't think so, squirt,' said Andrew, much to his daughter's dismay. 'Not this time.'

'We have to get back and finish sorting the grub out,' Liz intervened. 'It's nearly time to stuff our faces.'

Oh, how common, thought Judith. *I could go off this woman yet.*

Alycia noted the contemptuous raise of the old battle-axe's nose and stored it in the bank for safekeeping. She never would need to pull that one out, but who could possibly be privy to that information in advance?

Darcy cupped a hand over Merryn's ear and whispered something secretively.

'Well, can we go down Stippy Stappy instead? Merryn jumped up and down as if the anticipation would soon cause her to explode.

'Dark, wet and muddy? Don't think so Merz.' Andrew had spent most of yesterday making the cottage presentable for the guests it was due to accommodate. The last thing he needed was the dirt and sludge of eight pairs of feet trampled across his clean floors.

'You're not fair!' Merryn seethed. 'Nanny let me and Pappa look for hedgehogs in the woods one night. It was dark and wet then.'

At this point, the honourable Judith Ballantyne could have magnanimously defended Andrew, encouraging her granddaughter to see reason. At this point, however, she thought *to-the-Devil with honour.*

Alycia had her hand around Andrew's arm. She gave it a prompting squeeze and hinted with a flick of her eyebrows.

What the hell, thought Andrew. 'Did I say no?'

'*YES!*' Merryn and Darcy shouted in unison.

'Didn't you know?' Andrew smiled. 'Today's Opposites Day?'

'What's ossopites day?' asked Darcy.

'Yes means no and no means yes,' answered Alycia, stifling laughter at the mispronunciation.

The two youngsters cheered and ran around the corner hand in hand.

'Wait up!' Andrew called after them.

Kerenza said, 'Don't worry, I'll catch them up.' She set off at a jog, disappearing into darkness beyond the church.

By the time the oldies had caught up, the three girls were standing at the narrow entrance of Stippy Stappy, all casting exaggerated looks at imaginary watches on their wrists and tutting; a gesture clearly orchestrated by the comedic teenager.

Andrew ruffled Merryn's hair. 'Very funny. Let's do this.'

Past the quaint row of cottages, the firm ground petered out, becoming a sliming mess of mud and fragments of stone. Heavy wet drops fell tapping onto their heads from the leafy canopy above.

Full of acrimony, Judith pulled her lips tight over her teeth. She turned to Andrew. 'If I fall and break my ankle, I'll never let you forget this,'

'Well, you seemed up for Angus breaking his in the woods,' Andrew smiled.

Angus chuckled, until he received a silencing dart from his wife's eyes. Alycia and Liz looked away, hiding any suggestion of amusement from view.

Around five treacherous minutes later they were back on terra firma. Andrew sighed with ambivalence – relieved that Judith hadn't fallen on her fat ass, and disappointed that Judith hadn't fallen on her fat ass. Turning towards the roaring sound of the Atlantic, the troop headed down Beach Road in near pitch black, closing in on the homely promise of wholesome food, and enough alcohol to dupe even the most sceptical into thinking the company may not be so unbearable after all.

***

The open fire was ablaze. Bellies were full, and wine bottles were diminishing in content at the same rate as the drinkers were of self-awareness. Relaxing lips jested toward others, though strangely, the talk was kept largely in the safe zone.

Two little cherubs, one big Jock, one boiler and one failing artist sat around an antiqued oak coffee table, playing Monopoly's Cornwall Edition. Judith had managed to by the Eden Project and build a hotel. Andrew's motorcar was careening right for it, signalling a pitiful and premature end to his game.

Money goes to money, he thought, proceeding to total the mortgage values of his small property haul. 'Amazing how in a game that nobody ever finishes, I never even make it to the part where we all give up.'

'Ahh diddums,' Angus laughed.

'Sorry, Daddy, I wanted to help,' Merryn comforted.

'You. Help?' Andrew teased. 'How were you gonna do that? You spend most of your time in jail.' He got up and drained the remains of a bottle of pinot into his glass, chuckling to himself.

Through in the heat of the fragrant kitchen, Liz leaned over a steaming saucepan. Botanicals swam in a lazy whirl as she stirred gently: orange; cinnamon; star anise; cloves. The warming blend of aromas drifted up in twirling misty wraiths, teasing her senses.

'That'll do nicely,' she said. 'Even if I do say so myself.' She removed the pan from the range's simmering plate and cagily headed over to the worktop, careful not to allow any of the deep red liquid to spill over. Popping the pan onto a heatproof rack, Liz slid a preloaded tray of crystal tumblers closer. After filling them one-by-one with a ladle – spillages unfortunately not averted this time – she plucked two of them from the tray.

'Ladies first,' she said, handing one each to Alycia and Kerenza, who appeared to be forming a firm friendship already. 'Oh, actually,' Liz retracted one of the tumblers. 'Is your dad okay with you drinking?'

'Don't be daft, woman,' Alycia said, raising her eyebrows in a dismissive manner. She took the glass from Liz and handed it to Kerenza. 'She's not a child.'

Liz frowned at her, dubious.

Kerenza spoke up. 'Don't worry. He's cool with it.'

'Okay. I believe you. Thousands wouldn't.' Liz tipped Kerenza a wink, picked up the tray of vaporous beverages, and headed for the living room singing, 'Mulled wine's a coming.'

'She is *so* nice,' Kerenza said.

Alycia considered. 'Yeah, she's a godsend. I mean, she can be a right pain in the arse, too. But can't they all?'

Kerenza did not answer, instead choosing to raise her glass and lower her head in an attempt to conceal her eyes.

Alycia sighed at her own insensitivity. 'Shit! Sorry, I didn't mean to___'

'It's fine. Don't worry.' Kerenza forced a smile, but the sadness lurking behind the brave façade was plain to see. 'You're lucky you have her.'

'Yeah, you're not wrong there. She does so much for me. Happily, too.' Alycia smiled in reminiscence. 'Well, apart from last Christmas at the staff party, when I came home and threw up all over the porch carpet.'

They both shared a jubilant laugh at that little snippet from Alycia's past.

Kerenza caught her breath and said, 'Isn't that the sort of thing people my age should be doing?'

'Oi you, I'm not over the hill yet,' Alycia argued, jocularly. 'But you're right, girls your age *should* be doing that.'

'Sounds good to me, though maybe not with Gran in the other room.' Kerenza took another sip of the spiced wine. She could not admit to actually liking it, but alcohol was alcohol. 'She doesn't need any more ammunition to take my dad down.'

'That's fair enough,' Alycia said, her dark eyes full of mischief. 'After Christmas then?'

'After Christmas then, what?'

'You and me. Girl's night out. Couple of drinks, catch a chick flick, couple more drinks then puke through our noses.'

Kerenza laughed loud. 'Spoken like a true, responsible teacher. You are aware I'm only sixteen, right?'

'That's a whole year older than I was.'

'Yeah, well, I've heard it was different in the eighties.'

'It was the nineties, cheeky mare,' Alycia chuckled. 'And the late nineties at that.'

'Whatevs,' jested Kerenza. She raised her glass in agreeance. 'After Christmas it is then.'

They chinked to the pact.

'Cheers!'

'Cheers!'

As the two of them toasted their plans the front door swung inwards, dragging a vortex of chill night air with it.

'Wosson?' said the tall, dark-haired newcomer, shutting the clawing darkness away behind him.

'I didn't hear you pull up,' said Kerenza.

'What, d'ya want me to ring a bell or summin', like a fuckin' town crier?' the young man said, with a dry astringency to his tone.

Alycia said, 'I'm guessing you're Cameron.' She held out a hand.

'Then I guess you must be Miss friggin' Marple,' he quipped.

'Cameron!' Kerenza reprimanded.

'What?' He raised his hands, palms held upright protesting his innocence.

'Don't worry about it,' Alycia said to Kerenza, retracting her hand.

'Just messin',' said Cameron, this time offering his hand.

'Alycia,' she said, after a moment of hesitation.

They shook, Cameron immersing himself in her liquid gold smile.

Father, you jammy prick.

Sensing Cameron's mild obsession already blooming, Kerenza broke the stare. 'Where have you been?'

'Work,' said Cameron, with a *where else?* flatness.

'You don't normally finish this late.'

'Yeah well,' he said aloof. 'In demand, ain't I.' He repositioned his rucksack on one shoulder and left the room without another word.

Alycia said, 'Always this pleasant, is he?'

'Nah,' Kerenza said with disparaging grin. 'He's not always this tolerable.'

'Well, I'll look forward to getting to know him.'

'So, you and Dad are going to make it a thing then?'

'We're just playing it cool at the minute. Nothing too formal, keep the pressure off a bit.' Alycia tried reading the young girl's face and couldn't figure out whether the eyes were duplicitous or honest. 'Unless, of course, it's upsetting anyone else. Your gran aside. If it puts you three kids out, then I'll back off.'

'Don't be silly!' Kerenza said. 'Merryn thinks the sun shines out of your backside. Cam's, well, Cam. And it'd be good having some mature female company around.'

'You're sure?'

'Deffo,' assured Kerenza. 'Shall we go through and see what that lot are up to?'

As the hour grew late, Cameron lay on his bed in near darkness. The only light was in the form of red, white and sepia pulses from his laptop. YouTube was bringing him an old Placebo gig, live at Paris Olympia, a personal favourite – one of two reasons why his headphones were at set to *ear-splitting*. The other was to drown out the fun and games from downstairs.

Happy fuckin' families.

Five green bottles sat empty on his bedside table. One rested half-finished in his palm. Too many cyders at six percent ABV. Their slogan was right, it bites.

Gig finished, he threw down his headphones, swung his legs around to the floor, and glugged the last of the cloudy liquid. Arm swaying drunkenly from side-to-side, he plonked the empty onto the table to join the other castoffs. He stood unsteadily, before heading downstairs to see what the Waltons were up to.

In the living room Andrew, Kerenza and some older woman were laughing at an apparently amusing scene in a Christmas film. Merryn and a friend of hers had crashed out on a fluffy white bean bag. Angus and Judith had apparently left.

'They're letting her stay over?' Cameron asked Andrew.

'Yeah,' Andrew said, not taking his eyes off the telly. 'Wasn't expecting it.'

'Must be going senile,' said Cameron.

He wobbled his way through to the kitchen. If he didn't get some water down his throat soon, he was going to have a stonker of a headache.

Daddy's new squeeze stood at the sink washing dishes, her back presented to him and her perfectly circular ass looking chewable in tight black jeans.

'Not watchin' the film?' he slurred slightly.

'Thought I'd better chip in,' Alycia said, turning to give him a smile. 'Do my bit.'

I'd do your bit, Cameron mused.

'I'll dry,' he said reaching the sink and picking up a tea towel.

'Thanks,' she said.

With each item he dried, Cameron made his way unsteadily around the *L* of the worktop and placed it aside. After each trip, he edged a little closer to Alycia on his return. This didn't go unnoticed. Alycia started picking up the pace with the washing and scrubbing, eager to be back in the living room with the others.

Another plate, another trip, another inch closer.

This time he stumbled into her. Alycia was forced to grab the edge of the worktop for support.

'Sorry,' Cameron said, still too close for her liking. 'I'm feeling a bit dizzy.'

'Maybe you should go and have a lie down,' she suggested, turning her back so she didn't have to look at him.

Big mistake.

Alycia felt hands on both of her hips and a light press of his groin on her rear.

'Good idea,' he whispered. 'Are you gonna come with me?'

His mouth tickled her slender, brown neck; warm breath sending alarming tingles down her body.

'You're dunk,' she said. 'And you don't want to do this.'

One hand searched around to the front of her jeans and nestled in the V where her thigh met her private region. Cameron applied firm but tender pressure. She grabbed at the hand, halting its progress but struggling to pull his fingers away.

'I *am* drunk,' he agreed. 'And I *do* want this. You're so fuckin' hot.' Applying further pressure, his fingertips could feel her warmth through the denim.

Refusing to enjoy the potential ecstasy his probing fingers could provide, Alycia steeled herself. Inhaling deeply, she yanked his arm away, spinning to face him. Instantaneously, his lips were on hers, his tongue desperately seeking access to her tightly closed mouth.

'No,' she breathed hard, pushing Cameron away. 'This is *not* gonna happen!'

He was back on her, fast, raising one hand to her chest while the other fumbled at the bottom of her shirt. Alycia tried to block his kiss. Clamping her fingers on his neck, she forced him off again. This time she was successful. Away from his groping grip, she took off for the downstairs toilet in a fluster. Cameron was left standing solitary at the sink. A trickle of blood secreted from a small puncture wound under his chin, leaving a short, weaving evidential track.

Dabbing the wound, Cameron sucked the coppery blood from his fingertips.

CHAPTER FIFTY-TWO

Throwing on his uniform and grabbing his rucksack, Cameron bounded down the stairs, hoping the frigid bitch from last night was at her own house for Christmas.

Had she told his father about his little indiscretion?

Actually, so fucking what if she did. Cameron tried to envisage the immensity of the shit he could not give. It was unfathomable.

Merryn was alone in the living room, sat cross-legged on the oak floor in front of the twinkling tree, head submerged in a novel. *A bloody novel!*

'Ain't that a bit big for ya, brat?' Cameron asked.

Merryn looked up with a beaming smile on her face. She jumped up and flung herself at her big brother. 'Merry Christmas! Nanny and Papa gave me the box set. Do you want to see?'

'No thanks,' Cameron said lowering her to the floor. 'Not my thing. I didn't know you could even read.'

Merryn slapped him on the belly. 'Meanie!'

'Whatever.'

'You're not working?' Merryn asked, noticing the uniform for the first time.

''Fraid so, mizzle. We can't *all* sit 'round stuffin' our faces and playin' happy families.'

'You're coming beach with us tomorrow, though?'

Devious ideas started to formulate in his head. 'You're goin' beach? In this weather?'

'Dad said we can get hot chocolates.'

'Did you know, when the water's this cold we get sea-unicorns?' Cameron saw a confused excitement brew on his little sister's face.

'Sea-unicorns?'

'Yeah,' Cameron teased. 'They're like seahorses, but horny. Some of them even light up.'

Merryn doubted his sincerity. 'If they were real, wouldn't I have seen them on TV?'

'Don't be a div! We only get them here, and since when have they ever filmed something here?'

Merryn guessed he had a point.

'They only show themselves at the very end of the harbour wall,' Cameron continued.

'But the wall fell down.'

'I know, but when you can only just see the tops of the stones, you can step across them. And that's when they come. No sooner, no later. Be *really* careful, though. Like I was.'

'You've seen them!' Merryn's eyes nearly popped out of their sockets. 'Maybe Dad can take me across.'

'No,' Cameron warned. 'He'd never let you. And he doesn't believe in them, so they won't show themselves for him. You have to do it without him even knowing. Without *anyone* knowing!'

Merryn lowered her head, the contemplation torturous.

'I promise you it'll be worth it,' Cameron assured.

He ruffled her hair and left the room, heading for the kitchen, leaving the young girl swimming deep in deliberation.

Tears of condensation tracked down the inner window as the cold outside conflicted with the warmth of cooking cuisine inside. Andrew and Kerenza were busying themselves with pots and pans; wine on the go already.

Kerenza spoke first. 'Decided to get out of bed then?'

'Duty calls,' said Cameron. 'For those that bother, anyway.' He walked over to a kitchen unit, dumped his open bag on the floor and started filling it with items from the cupboards: Crisps; bread rolls; plus fruit from the bowl.

'Bit much for work, isn't it?' said Kerenza.

Andrew chirped in, 'He's a growing boy, aren't you, soldier?'

'Get lost,' Cameron mumbled.

'He can't eat that much,' Kerenza said to Andrew. She turned to Cameron. 'Why *do* you always take so much with you?'

'Why do you always take your ugly face with you?' Cameron said bitchily. 'You should be made to cover it up.'

'Cameron, play nice,' Andrew jested. 'What time will you be home?'

'What do you care?' said Cameron.

'We're eating about two. Judith and Angus are joining us. Will you be?'

'I hope not.' Cameron tussled with the zip on his rucksack, slung the bag over his shoulder, and headed out.

'We're celebrating,' Andrew called after him.

Cameron stopped in his tracks. 'Celebrating what?'

'Police came around a couple days ago. They got the guy who killed Raymond, so it wasn't all for nothing.'

'Got your license back?'

'No.' Andrew looked hopeful. 'May get it back quicker, though. All being well.'

Cameron stared motionless. 'They say anything else?'

'Like what?' Andrew asked.

Cameron was quiet for a moment. 'Dunno,' he said eventually. He closed the door on the conversation and walked off into the crisp Christmas Day sunshine.

Kerenza watched his silhouette diminish, his long spindly shadow stretching out in front of him. 'He's up to something.'

'You think?' asked Andrew. 'What *sort* of something?'

Kerenza picked up her wine glass and held it thoughtfully. 'I don't know,' she said, taking a sip whilst still looking slyly out through the window. 'I just don't trust him.'

***

Clouds bustled overhead, clashing with the wind like demonstrators and the law as the protest turned not quite so peaceful. Above Hell's Mouth they puffed their chests a heavenly golden yellow in the setting sun. Further to the west where the land gave way to things unseen, they burst in livid greys and charcoals.

Late Christmas afternoon strollers walking off their excess dinners headed back to their vehicles at a pace, holding their heavy clothing close to them in the swelling air. They could see the blackness rolling over from St. Ives. Their cars and camper vans lay in wait; temporary safety before the true sanctuary of home, a log fire, an advocaat Snowball, and more excessive stomach stretching.

Cameron made no attempt to move. His green eyes in another land, ignorant of the coming storm. He barely even recognised its existence while his third eye played out possible variations of the future. A future with just himself and Kerenza.

Grace was already gone.

That was a good thing. As she jumped onto the back of his bike on that rainy afternoon, his intentions towards her had been purely sexual. Fucking her would be a laugh. Kerenza was playing hard to get. But all red-blooded males need to get their willy wet, right fellas? He could tell by Grace's nervy persona that she was a nut that may not prove hard to crack. Developing feelings for her, however, was as unintended and unexpected an outcome as that of a particular night in February, right at this very spot. Grace was the one person who could have genuinely gotten in the way. And maybe that would have been for the best? Only the outcome of the next few weeks could answer that.

As the wind played violently with his hair, the barren land became devoid of all other human life. The last van had pulled away, leaving Cameron alone. Alone, but for the ghost of his mother. She often moaned to him when he sat at the top of this beautiful creation, crafted by nature over millions of years. He loved hearing his mother cry. Her salty tears splashed and sprayed upwards from the rocky bottom with each alluringly agonising wail of self-pity and desperation. Had the little Cameron not tested Mummy's flying capabilities those years ago, he may never have met Kerenza, putting that fatal shove firmly in the category of *The Best Things Cameron Tredinnick Has Ever Accomplished*.

With the sun a memory and the sky darkening, his thoughts grew brighter. Tomorrow should be Merryn's turn. Surely his ridiculous little sister could not resist the thought of seeing a sea-unicorn. She knew spoilsport *Daddy* would never let her go out onto the tumbled rocks that were once the stronghold of the harbour. Merryn would be peering through her mousy-brown hair almost bursting with anticipation. Just at that moment when the water was not-too-high, not-too-low, she had to make her secretive move. Cameron just had to hope that a freak wave (which were virtually too regular to be described as *freaks* at this time of year on the north coast of Cornwall), would jump up and drag her away. Or that she would slip on the green algae surface of the boulders. Either way, Daddy would be too far away and too wrapped up in his new piece of ass to save his little girl.

Bon voyage.

Hell, Cam might even have to grab a pint and sit out on the terrace of the beach bar. Ringside seats for the main event.

The downpour was closer now, maybe only a mile or so away. It was too dark to gauge. Far below, his mother let up another howl.

Back to the piece of ass. Why the bloody hell did he try it on with her? Less people, less complications. She needed to go. Then his dad would surely crack. If not, more dirty work. Cameron licked his lips, remembering how she tasted. Had he been wrong to place all his eggs in one giant, Kerenza-shaped basket?

Grace? Alycia?

No.

Kerenza was the answer to everything.

Cameron convinced himself that he had only tried it on with his dad's new girlfriend for *JOPO*: the Joy of Putting Out. Plus, she was black. In the romance department, that was uncharted territory for him.

'Maybe she still will put out,' he thought aloud.

An icy rain splattered the side of his face. Cameron forced himself up, joints aching from the cold. Bending hands on knees, stretching the muscles on the backs of his legs, he grabbed his bag and helmet from the moistening ground. He walked away and left the clifftop to the fate of the elements, his ghostly imprint on the grass the only sign he was ever there.

CHAPTER FIFTY-THREE

Fresh, still air wrapped like film on Andrew's face as he opened the door and crunched his feet down onto the glistening gravel.

Why he had opted to step outside and greet the old boiler, being followed loyally by her old collie dog of a husband, he could not answer. Maybe the festive spirit had softened his addled brain. Or maybe (he would find when he had time to take stock) he was grateful for being allowed Merryn over for a second night.

Allowed.

And here she came now, running out from the front door behind him, nearly knocking him to the ground as she wrapped one arm forcefully around him and waved frantically with the other.

'Morning,' called Andrew, a mushroom cloud of steam issuing from his open mouth as he spoke.

Angus replied after looking left, right, and left again, 'It didnae snow here either then?'

'It did. Lots and lots,' Merryn fibbed.

'Well,' said Angus, reaching them and bending to give Merryn a peck on the top of her head. 'I guess this sunshine melted it all away. But it shewer does beat the rain.'

'Coffee here first, or down there?' Andrew asked. 'The horsebox should be there. Better coffee than I can offer.'

'*Should* be?' Judith's upturned nose pointed out the possible flaw in Andrew's plan.

'*Will*, be. Boxing Day's no different from a weekend, right?'

'You had better be right,' Judith warned. 'Well, if everybody is ready, we may as well head down there.'

'Shall ah fetch yewer stick from the car?' said Angus.

A stick, Andrew thought. *Well, if that isn't a dig about our last walk.* He had not known Judith to use any walking aid in her life.

Judith gave a wordless commanding nod and the big guy tottered off.

The walk down to the beach was a pleasant one. All were gloved up, hatted up, and wrapped up in warm coats. The clear skies did little to amplify the bright but weak winter sun. Merryn skipped and sang several paces in front of the group as the descent intensified. Kerenza and Judith chatted about how school was going – mainly how she was preparing for her exams. Angus walked quietly, looking up at the rise of the valley on either side, ostensibly lost in thought.

Much to Andrew's delight – or relief – as they rounded a corner and the sea opened in front of them, there, positioned to the left and smelling divine, was the horsebox.

'*DARCY!*' Merryn's shrill scream was akin to fingernails on a blackboard.

'Dad, Darcy's down there!' She pointed at a run of rocks sat just beyond the slipway.

'Oh, silly me,' Andrew smiled. 'I completely forgot to tell you we were meeting them.'

'Can I run down?' she asked excitedly.

'Yeah, but go careful. You know how nervous I get when you run downhill.'

Without even a false reassurance of *I will*, she was off down the slipway as fast as her little legs would carry her, the pompom on her head bouncing up and down like a basketball.

Andrew watched after her, his heart pushing its way up his throat.

Kerenza grabbed his arm, sensing his unease and attempting to distract him. 'Come on, let's get the coffees now, so we don't have to come straight back up.'

'We'll be straight back up, taking her to A&E if she's not careful.'

Laughing at him, Kerenza pulled at his arm, leading him away from those worries.

Merryn leapt from the slipway and came to an abrupt halt, feet sinking into the small, exposed area of wet sand.

The sea-unicorns. How could she go and see them without telling Darcy? Cameron had strictly told her that she couldn't let *anyone* know about it.

But Darcy wasn't just *anybody*, was she? She wouldn't try to stop her. Surely, she would want to see them for herself.

'Are you coming over?' Alycia asked, snapping Merryn from her daydream dilemma. 'We're not going to bite.'

Merryn got a jog back on and clambered up the rocks. She sat next to Darcy and held her tongue temporarily, battling the desire to blab about her little secret.

Soon after, they were joined by Andrew and Kerenza. Andrew hauled himself up next to Alycia and handed her a paper coffee cup. Steam spiralled upwards from a small rectangular cut-out in the plastic lid, like sprouting foliage viewed via time-lapse photography.

'Where are the in-laws?' Alycia asked looking up the hill.

'Judith decided, if she made it down here, she probably wouldn't make it back. Arthritis still playing her up from the other day.' Andrew took a sip of his coffee and looked out at the choppy ocean. 'They're okay. On the bench, part way up.'

Seagulls scavenging for crabs, snails and other salty treats in a run of seaweed took flight as a wave broke high up the beach. It brought with it a clattering cacophony of rocks, pebbles and shale as it tumbled up the cove, echoing from the surrounding cliff-faces. Hovering clumsily in the air, the gulls eagerly awaited the right moment, before dropping back to their business of squabbling and fighting for scraps once the water's edge drew away.

Merryn and Darcy had agreed on some unheard plan of action, both sliding down the sloping rock and landing on the sand. Merryn looked thoughtfully out to the left. The derelict harbour wall was not yet in sight, but swirls of foam in chaotic flurries told her it would soon raise its head.

Andrew looked at Alycia. 'We should've checked the tide times. There isn't much room for the girls to spread their wings.'

'Isn't that a good thing?' Alycia asked, with a pleasant smile. 'Less space for them to disappear. Anyway,' she said turning her attention to where the girls played. 'It's on the way out.'

'How do you know that, mastermind?'

'Close your eyes and concentrate *real* hard. You can feel which way the vibrations are running through the rock.' She placed the palm of her hand flat on the cold surface on which they sat.

'Shut up!' Andrew said. 'You serious?' His face displayed a genuine awe at this absurd revelation.

Alycia looked at him and sniggered. 'No, you plank!' She pointed to the base of the rock they were perched on. 'The sand's wet. Tide's already been up here.'

'Oh,' said Andrew, feeling silly.

Alycia gave him a gentle nudge with her elbow to show she was only teasing.

'You know, no one's called me a *plank* since I was twelve,' he jested. 'What decade are you stuck in?'

Kerenza joined in with, 'I've never heard anyone called a plank, ever.'

'Alright, so I'm outdated,' Alycia said. 'And I know he's family, but you should be on *my* side. Us girls've gotta stick together.'

'Another time,' Kerenza laughed. 'Right now, I'm gonna split. Give you two some privacy. I'm gonna check on Gran and Grandad.'

'Privacy?' Andrew smirked. 'No chance of that with those troublesome tykes there.' He nodded at the two youngest girls piling pebbles one atop the other in decreasing increments. Not long from now, his head buried in a bottle, he would chastise himself regarding being careful what he wished for.

The morning wore on. The low sun continued to offer its cool brightness. More seabirds gathered as the beech shook off the tidal waters. Dog walkers gave their four-legged friends a runout, throwing balls into the shallows from plastic launchers for their excitable hounds to retrieve.

Merryn eyed the emerging harbour wall from the body of sand to the tip of its tail. No gaps. Now was the time. She looked back to her dad. He lay back supported by the natural formation of the rock, all alone. His eyes were closed. Merryn looked to the slipway and saw Darcy's mum walking away from the beach, maybe to the coffee trailer, maybe to see Nanny, Papa, and Kerenza. Either way, her back was to them.

'Can I tell you a secret?' she whispered to Darcy.

'Yes.' Darcy looked suddenly curious.

'Promise not to tell? Anyone.'

'I promise!' Darcy whispered, barely able to contain her excitement at the prospect of shared secret knowledge with her bestest friend.

Merryn cupped her hand to the frizzy, dark hair skirting Darcy's ear and whispered covertly.

'*SEA-UNICORNS!*' Darcy exclaimed, springing to her feet.

'*Shhh!*' Merryn jumped up, her crazy Jack-in-the-box, head swinging from side-to-side surveying for eavesdroppers.

She saw her dad lift his head, give them a funny look and an intrigued smile.

Poohsticks!

He lowered his head, eyes closing once more against the brightness of the day.

Phew. 'You have to be quiet, Darcy,' Merryn whispered.

'Sorry.' Darcy managed to control her volume. 'I just didn't know they were for real.'

'Well, they are. And they're over there now.' She gave one last look at her dad. The coast was clear. 'C'mon, let's go.'

The two girls meandered to the start of the fallen wall. Just a couple of kids having fun at the beach. Nothing to see here.

Andrew was unsure how long ago he had let his head drop, but he woke with a start to the sounds of young screams. Lots of panicked shouting voices joined the commotion. He never even realised he dropped off. Jerking up to sitting, his back aching from the hard surface he had unwittingly chosen as a bed, Andrew rubbed his hazy eyes. A hectic crowd of people gathered at the water's edge to his left. Looking directly in front of him, two pebble towers leaned precariously on the uneven sand. The girls were gone. The rough swell of the sea commanded his attention. Spotting something small in the water, his heart plummeted like a diving bell.

Without the luxury of thinking time, Andrew slid down the rock, feet bursting into a frenzied gallop as soon as they hit the sand. His ankles rocked and twisted as he trampled over beds of pebbles, the pain overcome by adrenaline.

Out to his left, the athletic figure of a young man leapt in splashing bounds along the ruin of the harbour wall, a feat of man turned Mother Nature's steeplechase.

Looking to its end, Andrew could see the small brown hands of a child, clinging to a boulder. Slick dark hair stuck to a head, submerging and re-emerging in the volatile current. Fifteen yards further out, maybe twenty, no safehold or lifeline to cling on to, pair of pale hands waved frantically. Their owner's head and face were nowhere to be seen, swallowed alive by the dark, greedy Atlantic.

Nearing the scene, Andrew pushed through the crowd, bodies flying everywhere, like the desperate, crunching start of a fourth-and-goal play in the dying seconds of the Superbowl. His feet hit shallow water as soon as he broke free of the crowd. Pulling his knees high, looking comically like a marching soldier in jittery old black and white footage, he ran until heavy waves slapped at his belly. Unable to run anymore, he arched his outstretched arms and disappeared, diving under an encroaching wall of water.

Isaac had been on his usual coast path run, starting at his home in Porthtowan and reaching St. Agnes, where he would turn back again. It was an idyllic but demanding four-and-a-half miles each way, over rough, rubbly ascents, and descents whose gradients ranged from severe to stupidly severe. They hugged the extremities of the Cornish landscape as intrinsically and accurately as the pen of a polygraph machine follows the jumps and starts of a pulse rate.

Today's run was scheduled to include his customary drop down the precarious steps to Trevaunance Cove beach, before skirting the waterfront to the far rocks, and returning home after using the flight of steps as a torturous alternative to hill sprints.

Stopping for breath on a large stony platform that bridged a chattering stream, Isaac saw an unlikely site. Two young girls, alone and apparently unobserved (but for him), leaning over a large, rectangular boulder. The unpredictable and sinical sea swirled with intent on three sides of their tiny bodies.

Isaac jumped down from the platform, his feet cooling instantly in the quick-flowing water. Another look around confirmed that the girls were indeed unsupervised.

Holiday makers, he assumed. No locals would harbour such a blatant disregard for the power of the sea, especially here on the north coast.

A sharp scream ripped his mind from its observations, ricocheting hauntingly from steep walls of land behind him.

All it took was one second. One second, one erupting wave engulfing the surface of the boulder.

Both girls were in the water.

Isaac was away, determined feet striding fast and hard along the wall's algae-clad remains. Instinct controlled his rapid legs, his eyes never leaving the two desperate figures being thrown about like sweets in a jar. It was by sheer luck rather than judgment that he didn't fall and crack his skull, or worse, break his neck.

Nearing the end of the land, Isaac saw that one of the girls had managed to grab a chunk of rock as a new surge of water assaulted her. Her grip would be hard to keep up, another hammering wave would likely rip her free again, but for now the other girl was in greater peril. All but her hands and forearms had been consumed by the unforgiving ocean.

End of the line. He sprang from the last visible rock, soaring over the first sodden and exhausted looking child whom, God willing he had made the right call, would still be clinging there like a limpet when he swam back with her cohort. The leap, the soar, the perfect entry, probably looked more spectacular than he had intended: *one for the cameras*, as they say in the goalkeeping world. But damn it, after running the gauntlet when it seemed no other living soul was willing to help in the struggle to save two precious little lives, he deserved to look the hero, didn't he?

Bloodless hands and forearms slowly sank as he swam, edging down as if being excruciatingly digested by quicksand. Now just one bleached finger broke the surface, a fishing float that had lost its vividness. Then it was gone.

Plunging under the surface, Isaac could see the murky outline of girl number two hovering in the low-gravity gloom. Bubbles leaked from her mouth and nose. Her eyes, big and round and horrified, stared at him, despondent.

Conscious.

He wrapped his powerful arms around her and hauled her upwards to bright daylight. The girl gasped for air, crying with fear but very much alive. Isaac spun her around and leaned back. Swimming with one arm, he called out words of encouragement to the girl he hoped would still be at the rock.

As his knuckles scraped on slimy rock Isaac turned. The girl was still there, being pushed up by a man in the water.

'Daddy,' the girl in Isaac's arms said, weak and trembling.

'Oh my god!' The man's emotions came tumbling out. 'You're ok.'

He took the girl from Isaac.

'Thank you. Oh my god, thank you.'

'No worries,' Isaac panted. 'It was nothing, really.'

The girl's father embraced Isaac tight along with the girl.

'Alright. Calm down, dude. Let's just get out of here, yeah?'

Isaac climbed out of the water and reassuringly stroked the other girl's jet hair, before turning back and reaching down to the water. He could tell the man was reluctant to let his daughter go – probably ever again – but he eventually managed to raise her out of the water. Isaac grabbed her around the waist and lifted. She landed safely on the rock. Telling her to watch her step, he turned his attention to helping the man out of the water.

The foursome took timid steps, carefully heading back to the safety of the beach. Fixated, the onlooking crowd stared with hungry interest. A group of them kicked off an applause. Cheers; shouts; claps and whistles. Some just wanted to indulge in what could provide them with aeons of gossip. *Did you hear*…and, *aww yeah, I was there…*

Andrew spotted Alycia alighting the beach from the slipway at a frightening pace, Kerenza hot on her heels.

Oh fuck!

The ailing Judith had made it down the steep slope after all.

CHAPTER FIFTY-FOUR

'So,' Cameron said with a snidey smile demonising his face. He popped the cap off a beer bottle with a short, sharp *psssst*. 'Favver's really fucked up this time.'

'Don't,' Kerenza replied. 'It was horrible. They could've been killed.'

'Where is he now?' Cameron drew back a chair and sat opposite her.

'Upstairs. He hasn't been down all day.'

'The old bat got Mez again?'

Kerenza placed both hands flat on the wooden tabletop and leaned back, stretching her back out and drawing a deep breath through clenched teeth.

'If you're talking about my gran,' she said. 'Yes, she has. And I don't think she'll be giving her back for a *long* time. Not after this.'

'Awesome,' said Cameron. 'And that tart up the road? She dumped the sad twat after this?'

'You actually look happy about it,' Kerenza scolded.

'Best Christmas I've ever had. Or it will be, when you drop your cacks.'

'Keep your voice down!'

Kerenza got up and made her way to the fridge. As she opened the door, the glow gave an angelic tinge to her skin and lit her tight, white tee shirt. Cameron took in the view, resisting the strong urge to touch himself.

'And you're wrong, actually,' Kerenza said as she sat back at the table with a freshly poured glass of wine. '*Alycia* hasn't been here since, but I think you'll find they're still very much together.'

Cameron screwed his face up in disbelief. 'As if.'

Kerenza studied his expression. 'Did you have anything to do with what happened?'

'Don't be a dick,' he protested. 'I wasn't even there.'

'You didn't have to be to plant a stupid idea into Merryn's head.'

'Look, if that dipshit wants to go drownin' her dumb ass, that's up to her.' Cameron picked up his bottle and took a large swig. 'Why did she do it, anyway?'

'She won't say.' Kerenza eyed him with mistrust, like she was trying to mentally crack open his skull and see into his brain.

With a dislike for the way she was trying to read him, Cameron stood and made his way around her. Standing behind, he lowered a hand to each of her shoulders and massaged his fingers into the upper fibres of her trapezius muscles. Kerenza gave an unintentional groan of pleasure and leaned her head submissively to one side.

'She'll ditch him,' he said, lowering his face to her head and taking in the honey scent of her hair. 'He'll lose the plot.' Cameron dug his thumb in, causing another low moan. 'Then he'll fuck off. This place will be all ours.'

Lowering his head further, Cameron placed a light kiss high on her cheekbone. She reached up and wrapped her fingers around one of his sensually working hands, pulling it lower down the smooth cotton of her front.

Finally, he though, his gut a stirring feeding frenzy.

The moment was shattered agonisingly by the grinding of gravel outside. The security light pinged into life, revealing a pink Fiat.

Shit on a stick! He straightened up balefully, lips pursed.

Kerenza pulled away from him, hoping that the person behind the wheel had no chance of spotting the encounter through the window. She shot up and headed to the front door.

'Hiya,' said Kerenza, opening the door as the new arrival got out of her car. 'Stupid question, but are you okay?'

'I think so,' Alycia sighed. She looked tired. Dark crescents under her eyes added years to her age. 'Is your dad in?'

'Come in,' said Kerenza. 'I'll give him a shout.'

'Just go on up,' Cameron interjected. 'That's where you'll end up anyway.'

'Cameron!' Kerenza blurted, a shocked countenance reaffirming her disapproval.

'It's fine,' Alycia said, looking down at the floor and shifting her feet nervously. 'I just need to speak to him.'

'Whatever,' said Cameron, boredom flooding through his voice. 'We're going, anyway.'

'Going?' said Kerenza. 'Where?'

'Pub. Come on.'

Before Kerenza even had time to grab a jacket Cameron had his hand clamped around her arm and was pulling her firmly out through the front door.

They sat in the beer garden just a hundred yards or so down the road.

'You were so rude to her,' said Kerenza, her ass frozen on the wooden bench.

Cameron swigged his cyder, unperturbed. 'Give a shit.'

Kerenza huffed in frustration, picked up her half full wine glass and knocked it back in one mouthful.

'Get me another,' she said, placing the glass firmly down on the old top. 'Then you can tell me what your problem is with Alycia.'

'My problem, sweet sister, is that I don't want *him* being encouraged to stick around. Not when he's the last thing standing in our way.'

'They're finished,' Kerenza replied. 'Trust me. A girl knows the signals.'

'*Signals* my ass ya muppet. *"Very much together"* is what you said?' Cameron drained his glass and puckered his mouth against the bitterness of the strong alcohol. The fresh breeze ruffled his fringe as he stared at her, his icy green eyes moonlit shards of glass piercing her skin. 'He'll be sat with that stupid grin on his face, satisfaction full and sack empty.'

'Lovely image. Thanks for that.'

He stood and picked up her glass, leaving her sat alone in the dull electric glow.

Kerenza called after him, 'I think you're wrong. She only came around to end things amicably.'

Cameron's dark figure raised an arm as it headed back to the pub, extending his middle finger at her.

Fact was, Cameron was right.

The stupid grin was there for all to see.

Andrew was even meeting Alycia for a swim in the morning.

Everything was back to fucked-up normality.

CHAPTER FIFTY-FIVE

In the unbroken darkness of his bedroom Andrew slept heavily, wrapped up in the duvet with only his small unseen mop of hair poking out.

There was no sound as the bedroom door eased open. The dark landing revealed nothing of the entity that allowed itself entry and lowered itself to the floor.

It crawled, hidden from the world by the early hours of a winter's day. Rounding the bed in total stealth, no sign, no sound, until the screen on Andrew's mobile phone lit, penetrating the darkness in an inverted cone. The figure stilled momentarily, phone in hand.

No movement from the bundle in the bed.

A finely covered finger swiped downwards, opening a menu.

'Upcoming alarm 05:00.'

The finger swiped to the right.

'Upcoming alarm cancelled.'

The entity reached out to the bedside cabinet, resituating the phone without even the slightest tap upon contact. Waiting statuesque for the screen to time out, blackness once again filled the entirety of the space.

Able to breathe again, the crouching body crawled back across the room and out onto the landing, silently drawing the door shut behind them.

***

Alycia sat on wet sand, watching charcoal clouds waltz across a purple backdrop. Faint stars appeared and disappeared like an illusionist's trick with the clouds' coming and going. Her wetsuit had kept her body from freezing so far, though she could feel a slight tremble emanate from her core. Her bare feet were more than feeling the bite.

She looked back towards the rising slipway. No movement was visible, save for the odd flap of tarpaulin fastened to one of the small sailboats lined up at its side, catching in light wafts of air. No padding of heavy feet could be heard. The only sounds were that of lofty gulls calling, steady waves breaking rhythmically, the flap of the tarps, and hollow *ting, ting, tings* of halyard and downhaul ropes tapping against metal masts.

Sighing, Alycia hauled herself to her feet, wobbling gently as they sunk into the soft, wet ground. She hadn't given up on Andrew turning up, but she had given up on waiting. He would just have to swim fast and catch up. She started down the beach. Waving her arms like an aerialist as she struggled over the pebbly patches, Alycia reached the water's edge. The temperature of the foamy seawater felt like a welcoming hug on her feet compared to the bare elements of the morning air. It urged her to keep moving forward, to submerge herself in a perfect watery world.

Head down, arms reaching and legs kicking she let the sea raise and lower her body. Making her way out, she spied the marker buoy in the distance, its bright orange sphere a beacon in the shadowy surroundings.

By the time the floating target was in reach, the sky had lightened to a steely blue. Gulls bobbed up and down on the glassy top of the water, eying her with confusion, as if asking exactly what she thought she was doing in their domain. Looking back across the abyss there was no sign that any other human had joined her in the water. Her gaze found the big white frontage of the bar above the beach, though the beach itself was temporarily concealed by the bloated waves.

As another rolling swell lifted her tingling body, the new vantage point afforded her a better view. On the dark beige belt of sand, the grey outline of a lone figure could be seen. Alycia could vaguely make out that its head was fixed in her direction. Feeling herself lowering in the heavy sea, another wave pulled away in front of her, once more blocking the view of the beach. Alycia waited.

Finally rising again, the grey figure was still there, only closer to the shoreline than before. Alycia raised and waved a hand in greeting, hoping it wasn't taken for a signal that she was drowning. The greeting was either unregistered or ignored.

Being forced to concede that it was either not Andrew, or that he simply had not seen her in the early morning gloom, she levelled herself out. Placing her face back in the salt water, Alycia began her slow swim back to shore.

After a few minutes she brought herself to a stop, treading water whilst waiting for the beach to open up in her view. As it finally did, Alycia could see that the beach was as empty of people as a freshly dug grave. There was also no sign of human occupancy between the sand and herself. Shivering, she resumed her lonely journey, cursing Andrew and assuming he had overslept.

A series of splashes beside her broke her from mentally berating the new interest in her life. Looking to her right, Alycia could see somebody swimming past no more than six feet away. Head to foot in black: black swimming cap; black goggles; wetsuit; boots, the ninja of the sea passed without a glance.

'Hello to you, too.' Alycia muttered. 'Miserable sod.'

Starting off again, she wanted nothing more than to be out of the water. Her mind wandered to home, with a hot drink and waiting for Darcy to get out of bed and brighten her day.

Within seconds of the restart, Alycia felt a sharp tug at her left leg. Whatever it was that grabbed at her, it had a firm grip. Her first thought, totally irrational, was *Shark!* Kicking as hard as she could proved inadequate; try as she might, she could not shake it off. Alycia tried to turn but suddenly the unknown body had a hold of her hips and was clambering up her.

Definitely not a shark, then, she thought during the struggle.

As she wrenched her head around, the heel of a hand caught her hard on the soft flesh below her chin. Her vision flashed white as her face was knocked towards the water's dark face.

This was no marine animal. The attacker was on Alycia's back, legs wrapped around her slim waist and hands over her head, pushing forcefully downwards. Frantically, Alycia shifted her body. One thrust of her elbow caught the person in black violently in the ribs, compelling them to let go.

The reprieve was temporary. Mid-turn the hands landed on her head once more, driving Alycia below the surface. Legs stamped at her from above, connecting painfully with her lower back, bearing her deeper and deeper.

Alycia took a powerful stroke downwards, aiming to evade another blow. Rolling over to check her position, she could see the human shape above her, totally black against a decayed green ceiling.

Not far enough above her.

The partially covered face glared down at her. There was a moment of shock recognition when the underworld seemed to stop, before the dark hovering shape raised one foot in slow motion.

Piston-like it slammed down, contacting with the centre of the loved mummy's, popular teacher, and doted over girlfriend's stomach. The air was kicked out of her. Her body's instinctive reaction: to refill her deflated lungs.

Rancid ocean permeated her mouth, an overwhelming assault on her tastebuds. Water cascaded into her lungs. Excruciating pain flaring up in her chest, feeling like she had swallowed a blowfish.

Alycia looked up at the floating figure, realising that this known assailant was the last person she would ever see.

Knowing she would never get home for that hot drink.

Knowing that her beautiful daughter would never brighten her day again.

Scanning the shoreline, the attacker saw no one. They peered back into the iridescent waters, watching in fascination as the limp body hovered a few feet below them, suspended in time.

Gradually, with the expulsion of air and the admission of brine-laden fluid, the dead, macabre eyes staring in vacant disbelief back at the killer receded. Fading from view, Alycia's body drifted through the gloomy obscurity to the seabed.

CHAPTER FIFTY-SIX

The pub was quiet for this time in the evening. Two blokes at the pool table, bigging themselves up after every pot no matter how average a shot it was. They strutted and peacocked around the table, arrogant and desperate to attain the attention of a group of girls sat having a laugh and a drink in front of one fairy-lit window.

There were seven of them in all, aged somewhere between eighteen and twenty-two, at a guess. Through having one eye on the girls and another eye on the television high up in the corner, Cameron could see that he was winning more looks and hushed conspiracies than the losers at the pool table.

Why not? He felt no need to show off playing games or puffing his chest out. They had all seen him looking at them through his sharp, green eyes. Those eyes commanded attention, and the dark liner he used added an extra dose of intrigue to his character. Couple that with his sly one-sided smile that he had already cast at one or two of them, and Cameron Tredinnick had more than enough alluring mystery about him to get by.

A few old men – the regulars with nothing (or worse than nothing) to go home to – huddled along the bar, moving aside pleasantly whenever a female needed to squeeze in to order a drink, yet requiring a gentle shove when a male attempted the same.

Other than that, the place was empty.

On the television screen, opening music from the local news hummed out. Two newscasters then informed viewers of what was coming up on tonight's programme. Cameron struggled to hear with the low volume and the background noise of the scattering of patrons, though he picked up enough of the detail to steal his attention away from the group of young women.

Cameron picked up his drink and moved to the small vacant table next to them. This did not go unnoticed by the pool players. They had already noted the exchanged smiles – smiles they were not getting themselves. Now, the pair huddled together talking in secretive plotting voices, staring at the youth in the guyliner.

The screen cut to one of the presenters, a fit piece of ass with flowing auburn hair; eyes sweet pools of spiced rum; thin glossy lips with seductive curls at the corners, a vibrant maroon to match her lace dress.

Stay on the subject, Cammy-boy.

'*A date has been set for the trial of a man accused of murdering another man in St. Agnes, Cornwall,*' the newsreader announced.

The screen cut to the mugshot of a rough looking guy. A raw-boned face; scruffy ginger hair in disarray; vulturelike hook of a nose; a confusion of wiry orange-white hairs sprouting from a pointed chin; tattooed crucifix on his scrawny neck. *Proper ugly bastard!* Cameron thought, wondering how anyone who had ever been photographed by the fuzz looked like a murdering psychopath.

'*Christopher Michael Wright, a thirty-seven-year-old from West Cornwall,*' the hot newsreader went on. '*Has been accused of killing Raymond Clay, fifty-six, in his garden in St. Agnes, back in October this year. The trial is due to start on the tenth of March. Mr Wright will remain in custody pending the trial.*'

Excellent news, Cameron thought with butterflies whirling excitedly in his stomach.

'*Staying in St. Agnes,*' the camera cut to the nerdy looking male presenter, before cutting to an all-to-familiar coastal scene. '*The body of a young woman has been found on Trevaunance Cove Beach earlier this morning. The woman, thought to be in her mid-to-late twenties, is believed to be local to the area. Police have confirmed that the family have been informed, and they are awaiting formal identification. A police spokesperson also stated that they are not looking for anyone else in connection with what is believed to be a tragic drowning.*'

Cameron had had a ton of missed calls and text messages while he had been at work, though he had no desire to checking whom they were from, or what they may concern. Now, reaching into his jeans pocket, he pulled out his mobile. Kerenza's name flashed up above numerous alerts. He sighed and threw his phone down onto the sticky mahogany surface of the table.

'What's up?'

Cameron looked to where the voice was coming from. It was the girl closest to him at the next table. Straight titanium blonde hair; dark eyeshadow and lipstick. A small black heart high on her left cheekbone stood in stark contrast to her porcelain skin.

'Well,' Cameron replied with his razorblade smile. 'I was just about to let you know everything I plan on doing to you.'

'But?' she asked with nervous stimulation in her eyes.

'But, family just fucked that up,' he said grabbing his phone from the table and standing. 'So, I'll just take yer number and *show* you instead. Another time, obvs.'

Cameron unlocked the screen and headed to *'Create New Contact'*. He typed the words *'EMO CHICK'* and lifted his gaze.

The titanium blonde reeled off a series of digits, finishing with, 'And it's Grace.'

Fuckin' would be. 'Whatever. Cameron,' he said.

'Whatever,' she replied, grinning.

Cameron bent down, sunk his fingers into her cool, silky hair, and placed a long, sensual kiss on her dark lips.

A chorus of teasing *ooohs* rang out around the table. Cameron turned to leave, smiling on the inside.

As he headed for the back door, the two douches at the pool table stopped their game, moving side-by-side and barring Cameron's exit.

'C'mon guys,' Cameron said smirking.

'Think you're really something, don't ya,' the shorter of the two said, folding muscular arms across his barrel chest. 'Fuckin' li'l ponce!'

'Look, I need to get past, and I intend to,' Cameron said, sounding bored. 'So why don't you two get back to playin' with yer balls, and just leave me to it.'

'Or,' the other one cut in, his shaven bald head shining under the artificial light, 'We could just pick you up, bundle you in the back, and take you for a little drive.'

'That's really nice of you, seriously, but I don't think I'll fit in the boot of your hairdresser's car.'

'Gobby shit,' hissed the guy with the billiard ball head. Does *that* look like a hairdresser's car to you?' He nodded to the window, where a monstrous, gleaming black pickup truck sat just beyond the glass.

'That's yours?' Cameron asked in surprise. 'Spot on. And I do really appreciate the offer, but I still have to decline.'

'You're acting like you've got a choice.' Baldy leaned his face close enough for Cameron to smell the stale alcohol on his breath.

He turned his head to downwards in hope of avoiding the smell. That's when he noticed something about the big guy.

Lifting his head to look him in the eye again, Cameron said, 'Look. It's pretty clear you could beat the shit out of me. You're three times my size, you're boyfriend here's two of me.' He nodded to the other meathead, who was clearly angered by the reference. 'See that redhead?' Cameron asked the bald one and nodded to the table of girls. They were deep in amusing conversation and laughing loudly, oblivious to the dispute taking place towards the rear exit. 'She was eyeing up your package.'

The big guy looked down, the reflection of light moving from the front of his great melon to the back. When he lifted his head, he was wearing a moronic smile.

'Don't look so proud,' Cameron continued. 'That wasn't a compliment. No offence, but those jeans are so tight they could make an acorn stand out.'

'One more comment 'til yer dead,' the guy warned.

'Anyway,' said Cameron unperturbed. 'She reckons she's gonna get that out by the end of the night. So, stop fuckin' around wastin' time on me and starin' at them. Go over there, get yer little chap out, and let me get the fuck on with my day.'

The smaller dude looked at the bigger one. The bigger one looked back, gave him a stern nod, and took a step to the side. Cameron stepped between them and patted Baldy on the shoulder.

'Fill yer boots, cue ball' he said, and left through the back door.

Kicking tiny stones across the carpark, Cameron thought back with amusement at the confrontation. He made his way to the rear of the plot, where his bike stood quietly next to a rocky flowerbed. Bending down to analyse his options, he scooped up the biggest rock available and clambered onto his trusty steed. One handed, he held the rock against the handlebars. It had a good weight to it, maybe three kilos, with angular, sharp edges.

Kicking his KMX into life, he used his feet to roll him down the carpark. Stopping at the window closest to the pool table, Cameron leaned over and give it a tap.

The pair of useless assholes must have decided to finish their game before chatting to the girls, if they were man enough to do that at all. At the tapping sound on the glass, Baldy looked up from taking his shot. Short and muscly turned his broad shoulders in the direction of the window.

Satisfied that he now had their full attention, Cameron gave them his best *winning* smile and held up the rock triumphantly. Confusion painted the faces of both men, before Cameron pivoted a quarter turn, pulled back his catapult arm, and launched the rock hard. The pickups screen burst into sound. From its centre, a fulmination of jagged spider webs spread instantly throughout the expanse of the glass. The rock rebounded, leaving a tearing streak in the paintwork as it slid down the bonnet.

He turned back to the window, delighted with the anguished looks of disbelief and fury at his creation. Cameron continued to smile, finding just enough time to raise his middle finger at them, before they scrammed through the pub's back door.

Opening the KMX's throttle, Cameron raised his feet from the floor. With a celebratory lift of the front wheel he was gone before the two chumps made it outside.

Arriving at home less than ten minutes later, Cameron was still unable to quell his laughter. This was in part due to the rock and the windscreen incident, but also because his helmet was still strapped to the back of his motorbike. Luckily for him, the only fuzz he had seen en route were preoccupied with filling up on pasties in the bakery parking area – a regular haunt for the local law enforcement, rare it was indeed that a marked car or four were not on the premises during open hours.

As the KMX scrunched onto the drive of Sea Glass Cottage, Kerenza came bounding out through the front door.

'Cameron, why the fuck haven't you been answering?' she screamed as he brought the bike to a stop, close to running over her foot in the process. 'Dad's gone!'

'And?' he asked without concern.

'And we need to find him,' she panted. 'Haven't you heard?'

Cameron toed the kickstand down and lifted a leg over the seat. 'Yeah, that Chris guy's goin' down. Whoopie doo!'

'Alycia's dead!' exclaimed Kerenza. 'She drowned this morning.'

'I wondered if it was her,' he said passively. 'Shame.'

'Shame?' Kerenza was exasperated. 'Is that all you can say?'

Cameron met the question with a shrug of the shoulders. 'She was cute.'

'You're sick,' said Kerenza. 'We've got to find Dad. He stormed off when he found out and hasn't been back since. Where would he go?'

'Fucked if I know,' said Cameron.

'That's not helpful. Where is your spare helmet?'

'Round the side.'

'In your shed?'

'Well, it's not really a shed,' Cameron said, unhelpfully.

Kerenza turned and ran around the side of the cottage, small chunks of gravel kicking up behind her as she went. When she returned she was struggling with the neck strap.

'Hold up,' Cameron said. 'Let me.'

Fiddling with the clasp until satisfied, he retracted his hands.

He looked into Kerenza's frightened eyes. 'You know, this could be a good thing.'

'In what way could this possibly be good?' she asked in disbelief.

'*Uh, hello*. He fucks off, we get what we always wanted. Just me and you.'

'Not like this, we don't,' Kerenza scolded. 'Get on the bike. We'll start down the beach.'

A roaring tide soared high, waves breaking violently against the wall of the slipway. Below the veranda of the beachfront bar, flowers with letters of condolence had already begun to amass along the rocky wall. No formal confirmation of identity had yet been released, but word had spread like a virus through the alleyways and opened doors and windows of the village, as it has a tendency to do in village life.

A small crowd was gathered nearby, tearfully hugging those who needed comfort as much as themselves. Alycia was a great teacher. Adored by children and warmly admired by parents, the loss of her life would leave its mark on hundreds of people. The morning's events would devastate the community for many a dark year to come.

Andrew was nowhere to be seen among the small clusters milling around.

'I'm going around the head,' Kerenza said raising her voice to carry across the breaking waves. She pointed to the coast path rising steeply west. 'You take the path next to the Drifty. Don't stop 'til you get a view back to Trevellas.'

Cameron muttered under his breath and pushed the bike back up the steep incline. Dumping it against a hedge at the foot of the path, he started to scramble up the rubbly track. Looking across the cove, he could see Kerenza, navigating similar terrain at running pace. Her blond hair flew in torrents with the shifting winds. Paying less attention to his footing than his stepsister, Cameron tripped over a partially submerged rock, landing heavily on one knee. Cursing every obscenity that came to mind, he scanned the area to make sure nobody had seen his embarrassing fall.

All apparently clear, he strained his eyes, hoping to pick up the swirling blonde hair. He caught its movement a split second before she vanished around the rugged veil of landscape.

Right, that's enough of that.

Convinced his journey would prove utterly futile, Cameron turned to make his slippery, stumbling way back down to where he started. There was no way he was going to make himself look foolish again for that stupid old prick. Duplicity would come easily, as it always did. His stepsister would never know he did not bother.

Yes, Krenz, I went all the way around. No, Krenz, he wasn't anywhere to be seen. Probably drowning himself in a whisky glass rather than the ocean.

The air's blustery currents picked up a notch as Kerenza rounded the head. It played havoc with the frothy surface of the water down below. Spray whipped up from the crests of breakers, and spectrums of colourful light darted in daggers as barrelling waves slammed the cliff face. Balancing precariously in the unpredictable wind and insecure terrain, Kerenza edged closer to the brink of the land and leaned slowly over. She hoped to see nothing but rock and water. She expected to see a body being thrown about and torn apart by nature.

The bottom of the cliff was devoid of human presence.

That was good, but still not enough to settle the girl's apprehension. Was she already too late? Had the devious sea already hidden the evidence in its vast belly?

Kerenza could not allow herself to think like that. The sun was sinking. Hopeless night would soon arrive. She needed to concentrate solely on Andrew being alive, and where she might find him. Taking a deep, composing breath, the air cold on her lungs and salty in her mouth, she turned cautiously and headed back to where she and Cameron had parted ways.

When she finally arrived, she found Cameron sat on a bench outside of the pub, cyder bottle in hand.

'Well I'm glad you're taking this seriously!' she scorned. 'Did you even go up there?'

'Chill the fuck out,' he replied. 'He ain't there. He'll be in some pub, mopin' over a Scotch.'

'He left his wallet on the kitchen table.' Kerenza's face started to redden with rage.

Cameron got up and guzzled the remainder of his drink. 'Come on,' he said when he was finished. He headed over to where his motorbike lay abandoned.

'Where are we going?' asked Kerenza, breaking into a jog behind him.

'Hell's Mouth.'

'Don't be stupid,' she panted. 'How would he get there?'

'He's got legs, hasn't he?'

'It's miles.'

'And how long ago did he leave?'

Kerenza stopped and thought about it. She could not imagine Andrew walking all that way, but what other option did they have?

The pair donned their helmets and mounted the bike. Cameron stamped it into life, relishing the feeling of her hands around his waist, and they shot off up Beach Road under the cover of twilight and the canopy of trees.

The winding coast road passed by in a blur of dull greens, browns and blacks. Leaning this way and that into each bend, Kerenza felt that she was on the world's worst rollercoaster, with the world's most untrustworthy theme park attendant at the helm. As her stomach lurched repeatedly, the relief that she had not eaten all day was immeasurable.

They descended upon Hell's Mouth. Parking up, the echo of the stirring waters, coupled with the heavy blanket of dusk clutching the landscape, conjured an oppressive apprehension.

CHAPTER FIFTY-SEVEN

The scrunching sound of rubber on asphalt grew distant as Kerenza watched a trio of taillights dwindle and disappear over the farthest crest, heading for the small village of Gwithian. Soon after, the sound petered to nothing, leaving once more just the lonely whistling of wind through grass and the calling of the sea.

She cast a look back at Cameron. He was sat on the top of a worn old wooden picnic table, feet on the seat, and absently chewing a fingernail. He looked back at her through faint light under a cobalt sky and nodded for her to keep moving.

Kerenza did as was bade with trepidation. Neither of them needed to clarify whom the outline slumped against the single thick, horizontal rail belonged to. It could only have been Andrew.

Taking a deep breath, she placed one foot onto the firm surface of the coast road. Several steps more gained her access to softer ground. Stepping lightly, Kerenza made her way up the mud and sand scattered pathway. Nearing the figure, she took one last glance back towards her stepbrother, hoping for more reassurances from him. Instead, all she saw in the distance was his pale face light up a haunting orange as he took a drag from his joint.

Don't let us stop you. A feeble smile gave her a melancholy countenance.

Reaching a hand forward, she tentatively placed it on the person's shoulder. In her mind, she prayed that her assumption of the character's identity would be vindicated.

It was.

The man started ever so slightly under her touch, but the face that turned slowly to inspect the intruder was that of her stepdad.

His dark eyes looked defeated and distant, yet he tried his best to smile. All that came however, was a slight tremble of his upper lip, before he turned his head away once again, settling his gaze on some point of emptiness on the horizon.

Kerenza lifted herself cautiously over the wooden rail and lowered herself down next to him, feeling both scared and strangely stimulated at being this close to potential death. Leaning into him gently, she watched a line of moonlight reflecting on the ocean, running all the way from the horizon to the dark hole below their feet. Narrow at first but increasing in width as it worked its way closer, the white light danced and flashed like a million fireflies above an unknown world.

Andrew raised an arm around her slight shoulders and Kerenza nestled in some more. Both trembled as the cold fell from the open sky above them, but neither felt the need to leave in search of warmth. They just sat looking out to sea, lost in their own thoughts with a unifying tragedy. Neither felt compelled to speak for a long while.

'Well, this is fuckin' boring,' Cameron exclaimed, appearing from nowhere.

The huddling figures on the clifftop craned their necks around synchronously to view the new arrival. His pasty face turned to shadow as the moon crept behind a rogue cloud, extinguishing the searchlight beam across the water.

'Only got room for one at a time. If you're coming, that is.'

Andrew said, 'Hi Cam, buddy.'

Buddy? What the fuck? 'Alright?'

'Yeah, ta. Take Krenz first, if you don't mind coming back for me.'

'No probs,' Cameron said. 'Just make sure you're by the road when I get back. I ain't comin' lookin' for ya.'

'I will be. Just go steady.'

Cameron held out an assisting hand to Kerenza as she prepared to step back over the barrier. As she grabbed the hand, he gave her a short shove backwards, before jerking her back violently again.

'You prick!' she panted, slapping him around the head.

Cameron lifted her clean off the floor to safety, laughing at his own hilarity. Andrew made his own way back to the safe side of the fence and halted, watching two of the only three people in his life walking back down the rutted path, Kerenza punching Cameron several times on the arm whilst he continued to air his amusement.

The bike's engine cracked into life, shattering the sombre tranquillity of the night. Andrew watched with Hell's Mouth at his back while the single light wound away into the enveloping darkness. He dared not turn back. Hell's Mouth's taunting calls continued to rumble on invitingly behind him. To turn and look upon it again tonight was sure to welcome surrender.

CHAPTER FIFTY-EIGHT

Time had become meaningless at Sea Glass Cottage in the days since the grim discovery of Alycia's body. The world outside span on its axis, just as it ever did. Although life's ceaseless pestering and pushing forced the inhabitants of the old dwelling to potter and mope about – all but the insouciant and emotionally bankrupt Cameron, who could seem to wash off each disastrous development like shit from the pan, continuing blissfully from one day to the next – the dwelling itself struck as quiet and motionless as the grave.

New year came and went without recognition. Kerenza had not returned to school with her peers. And the funeral was due in three days' time.

Andrew had not left the house since Cameron brought him back from Hell's Mouth. The very idea of attending the service tortured him. He was devastated inside, emotions torn like a leg of beef in a lion's enclosure.

He should have ended it up there that night. Taken the plunge before his kids had got to him. The questions as to why he never went through with it played over and over in his head like a depressing track stuck on repeat.

Was it his responsibility to his youngest, Merryn? Hell, he didn't even know when he was likely to see her again. And what sort of father was he? She would undoubtedly be better off without him.

The same went for Kerenza and Cameron.

Being a man without religious belief, he gave no credit to the afterlife. In disillusion however, his mind teased him. What if there was a God? If so, would Andrew's scepticism be punished by his two wives and his girlfriend awaiting his arrival to the spirit realm? The three of them. Together. Three women who all perished under his watch. Was he somehow to blame for all of this?

Kerenza sat alone at the kitchen table, a cold cup of coffee between her pale hands. Her stepdad's listless feet could be heard above, making their slow and monotonous steps across the landing, from bedroom, to toilet, and back to bedroom again.

Letting go of the cup, she headed for the front door, pulling down the handle and stepping outside. The January air was fresh, the sunshine bright enough to force a squint as her eyes adjusted. As her lungs filled with revitalizing morning oxygen – the atmosphere inside had become so stale, leaving a bitterness in her mouth that was hard to swallow – she stood on the step, placing the fingertips of both hands on the doorframe behind her to steady herself. The hit of oxygenated air went to her head like a tonic, energising her soul, making her dizzy, heightening her senses to a level she had not felt for as long as she could remember.

Kerenza had always known that something would have to change. In her current clear and alert state, the comprehension that the time had arrived hit her like an invigorating slap in the face.

Leaving the door open to cleanse the musky decaying air from inside, she breezed back to the table and picked up her mobile phone. Hitting the 'messages' icon, she scrolled down to Cameron:

> Fancy riding out to HM tonight?
> Just u, me and a bottle of voddy? xx

How can he resist?

The reply came almost instantly, igniting a mischievous smile on her face.

She sprang up in euphoria, carried her cold coffee over to the sink and poured it away. Picking up a clean glass from the drainer, Kerenza poured herself a water and headed upstairs to her bedroom, where she would lie on the bed with headphones on and volume high, dreaming, prospecting, and craving the future.

Tonight was the night.

***

Under a greying sky, Cameron arrived home at just after four that afternoon. Kerenza strolled out with a bag on her back and the spare helmet already in hand, explaining that Andrew still had not been downstairs that day, and that they would talk more about him when they were away from *'this place.'*

Cameron was thrilled at that news. The wheels were fully in motion, as they were on his KMX.

After stopping at a local shop for a bottle of spirits – and being asked for proof-of-age for what felt like the thousandth time by the same assistant – he guided the bike easily along the coast, indulging in the comfort of Kerenza's warm hands around his flat stomach.

By the time the couple pulled slowly to a stop, the tyres losing traction on the fine gritty stone momentarily and coughing up white clouds from the ground, the grey sky had deteriorated to a dirty sepia. The dry scrubland had a shady feel to it in the brown haziness; a place where conspiracies were formed, where the sea mumbled and the wind whispered responses, working in cahoots to draw desperate souls from their desperate situations.

Delighted to see that they were on their own, they made their way up to Satan's gaping mouth.

The yawning jaws widened ominously as the pair closed the distance. Arriving at the wooden barrier, Cameron asked, 'On the fence?'

'Sounds good,' Kerenza confirmed.

She lifted out a hand, which Cameron took supportively, helping her to balance as she lifted each leg over in turn. Having both legs over, Kerenza sat on the beam, shuffling until she found relative comfort. She pulled the bag from her back, placing it on the ground and pulling out a pair of fleece gloves. The onshore wind carried in a biting undertone that had failed to penetrate further inland. On the bleak coast however, its powers were more severe, cutting through human skin like a knife at the cliff edge, spilling unseen sacrificial blood for the Devil.

Resting a steadying hand on her shoulder, Cameron followed her over, taking his seat next to her.

'You can get a bit closer than that,' she invited.

He looked at her with his crooked smile before shuffling over a few inches, coming to rest against her dark clothing. Kerenza pressed herself into him, encouraging him to relax against her body. Cameron slid his right arm around her back. The beating of his heart accelerated as she lowered her head into the crook above his pronounced collarbone. Lowering his face to her head, the fragrance of sweet raspberry drifted from her lustrous blanket of blonde silk.

They huddled together that way without a word for several minutes, before Cameron lowered his arm, smoothly working his hand around until it touched upon the slight curve of her bottom.

'Time for a drink, don't ya think?' she said suddenly.

Fuck's sake. All that crap and the bitch is still teasing, he thought.

'Course,' he answered with a smile on his face.

He reached down into his own bag and pulled out a litre bottle of clear liquid.

'Jesus, you don't do things by half, do you?' Kerenza laughed.

'Don't worry,' he grinned back. 'This is nothin'. I'll still be able to handle the bike, and I'll still be able to perform.'

'Perform?' she said with raised eyebrow.

'Yeah,' he said. 'As in, I'll still be able to *fuck* you like a train.'

Kerenza grabbed the bottle from his clasping hands, unscrewed the cap, and took a long, glugging swig. She lowered the bottle and wiped the glistening vodka from her lips with the back of a gloved hand, looking him in the eye unrelenting. 'Not if I jump on you first.'

Cameron moved in for a kiss. Kerenza rolled with it. The coldness of the wind and the bitter rampaging of the sea was all but forgotten. She opened her mouth, allowing her ethanol enriched tongue to explore his. He placed a hand on her taut neck. Working it around and down her front, thinking she would surely pull back again, he felt instead a tensing of her body as she arched forward. Her provocative posture enticed further exploration. Taking the invitation with desperate greediness, Cameron lowered his hand further, finding openings at the bottom of her layers of clothing. He edged in, fingers trembling as their tips touched upon soft bare skin. At his gentle caress, goosepimples as traceable as braille invaded Kerenza's flesh.

Finally, the realisation that this was too good to be true became apparent. She backed away giving him a slight push. Opening her eyes, Kerenza stared into his.

Crouching before him, she said, 'We need to talk, first.'.

Fucking knew it, he thought. *Me flippin' balls are gonna explode in a minute. Blast you right off this fuckin' cliff.*

'Well? Talk then,' he snapped.

'I need to know you'd do anything for me,' she said. 'For us. Whatever it takes.' She looked at him as though their entire lives depended on his answer.

'You're never gonna open your legs for me, are ya?' he demanded. 'All this time you've just been stringin' me along, lettin' me scurry around after you like a randy puppy?'

Kerenza grabbed his hand and thrust it onto her crotch, her jeans heating to boiling point under the contact.

'They're open for you now.' With one hand on the vodka bottle, she lifted it and took another long guzzle, before extending it to her stepbrother's lips. She tilted the bottle until clear liquid overflowed from his mouth and ran down his chin. Kerenza leaned and let her tongue follow the line of fluid up his chin. 'I just need to know,' she cooed.

'Haven't I proven that?' he asked. 'With everything I've already done. For us?'

'You've been adequate. So far.'

The sky was dark now, enough so as to leave the pair just able to discern each other's features, yet not to be spotted by the sporadic flow of passing motorists. Kerenza gave a self-assuring glance towards the feint trace of road over the short and gloomy distance of wild scrub.

Unable to restrain himself, Cameron raised his voice. 'So far? Adequate?' He quickly scanned the area, ensuring there was no unnoticed company. He lowered his voice to a hush. 'I killed your mum. For us! Right on this fucking spot!'

Kerenza raised her free hand, gently removing his fringe from over one eye. 'I know,' she said. 'And I don't think anyone else would've done that. Not for me.' She moved her mouth so that her lips touched upon his ear, tickling. 'That's why I want us to fuck right on this spot.'

Cameron squeezed at the crotch of her jeans and fumbled for her zip.

'Not so fast, stud,' she teased.

'For fuck's sake, I'll throw *you* off in a minute!'

'We both know that's not going to happen,' she smirked. 'I'm much better for you alive than dead.'

He kissed her again passionately. Breaking the kiss, he told her not to be so sure. 'Not everyone gets to complete a hat-trick.'

Placing the bottle on the earthy ground, she pushed herself to standing and unbuttoned her jeans. Cameron smiled up at her as she slowly slid the zip down and rolled the waistband over.

'Well,' she said, pulling down enough of the dark denim to reveal the thin band of her white nickers, 'I think Dad's gone over the edge and taken himself out of the equation. So, answer me one more question, and all *this* is yours.' Kerenza pointed both index fingers at her crotch.

'Go for it,' he said leaning forwards, running his hands up her thighs.

'It's not an issue...not anymore, anyway. But would you have killed Alycia for me? If it needed to be done?'

His hands stopped in their tracks, and he looked up, trying to read eyes he could barely make out.

'What makes you so sure I didn't?' he said.

Kerenza got down to kneeling in front of him, spread his legs and moved in tight. Reaching her left hand out to the side, she rummaged in her bag.

'What ya looking for?' he said.

'Protection.' She spoke matter-of-factly before kissing him again, licking his lips as they parted to allow a response.

'So,' he whispered, almost refusing to believe all his hard work would finally pay off. 'It's really gonna happen then?'

'Oh, it's gonna happen alright.'

The sound of an engine whirred somewhere in the darkness. A vehicle's headlights mounted a distant apex, lighting Kerenza's eyes in the piercing brightness of the ice-white beam. They burst into life with a devilish glint that commanded Cameron's attention.

Lurching her face towards his, her mouth found his again.

Pulling back a fraction she breathed, 'But I *know* you didn't.'

'Didn't what?' He studied her expression but in a snap her mouth was on his again. Breaking away momentarily, she inhaled exhilarating air.

'I know you didn't…' she whispered, 'Because *I* did.'

'What the…? Struggling to digest this information, Cameron failed to finish the sentence.

'That's right.' Her smile lit up as the distant motor hit another crest at the perfect angle. 'I did it for us. Just not the same *us* that you might be thinking.'

He looked back at her stupidly. It annoyed her to see such a blatant lack of understanding on this face, having been so calculating and cunning in the past.

'What's the line in that song you like so much?' she went on. 'The one about being wary of your friends.'

'I don't…'

'Course you do, my love. Something about how some hold the rose.'

Cameron recalled the line. 'Some hold the…' Cold realisation hit home. 'The rope.'

The girl's arm that had recently been in her bag made a rapid thrusting movement. Partially numb against the cold, partially numb through bewildered shock, the boy felt no pain. The warm fluid running down his side, however, dancing and dodging between his fine body hair, was all too palpable.

His eyes took on a pitiful disbelieving hue. The act of breathing became almost unattainable.

'See,' the girl said, raising up to standing and recovering her exposed flesh. 'I appreciate everything you've done. You've made everything possible. But you were never part of *my* us.'

Lightheaded through trauma and flowing blood, Cameron slid from the beam.

'*My* us is waiting in his bedroom now. He's waiting for me. He just doesn't know it yet.' She grinned down at Cameron and clambered over to the safe side of the fence. Leaning down behind her stepbrother, Kerenza reasted her chin on the top of his head. 'You know, your dad's going to be so heartbroken, losing you. Especially as he has no chance on *Earth* of getting that little shit, Merryn, back.'

'You, you c, can't___' Cameron stuttered, chocking on air.

'I'll be all he has left in the world,' she cut him off in a cool, composed voice. 'And he's going to have me, any way he wants me. It's the least he deserves.'

'I'm gonna kill you,' Cameron threatened, finding a new strength.

'No, you're not. You'll bleed out soon. Screwdrivers aren't the widest, but the good wiggle I gave it'll do the trick.' She kissed his jet-black hair. 'It's over. Do yourself a favour, brother, and just crawl over the edge. It'll be so quick. You'll feel like you're flying, just like our mother's did.'

Kerenza reached over the fence, retrieving her bag and wrapping the bloodied screwdriver in a bundle of kitchen paper. Returning the evidence to her bag, she sat upon the dry, wiry grass and pulled out her running shoes, replacing the deck shoes she had arrived at Hell's Mouth in.

No sooner had she finished tying the second lace, Cameron came flopping back over the fence, landing hard on the ground a yard short of her feet and desperately reaching out.

Kerenza sprang instantly and backed off a pace. 'Whoa, don't think so, sweetness. Preserve your strength, you'll need it for climbing back over.'

Cameron lay looking up at her. Encompassed by shadowy gloom, her face hovered pale as death while his mind scrambled and gripped for reality.

Without another word, she turned and ran down the uneven turf. Turning for home, Kerenza unceremoniously left the boy who had fantasised about her for years, lying, bleeding, dying on the wintry gateway to the broiling inferno.

CHAPTER FIFTY-NINE

An angry swell cursed and balled over and throughout the labyrinth of rocks at the foot of Hell's Mouth. Large and torn slats of driftwood, caught in the stone entanglement, rattled and clattered in nature's surging saliva; tonsils vibrating violently in a cavernous throat screaming for blood.

Flattened grass on its fuzzy lip voiced the promise of flesh, flesh that the Devil's watery skewer of a tongue failed to strike.

Blood as black as tar clung to wiry blades of grass, presented in spits and spats away from the cavity, befouling this so-called area of outstanding natural beauty.

Nocturnal eyes watched with curious interest as a dark shape scrambled across fine grit, occasionally on two legs, occasionally dropping to all fours in agonising discomfort.

Finally, the form reached a sedentary hulk of metal. Pulling itself up, it straddled the strange unmoving hulk. The beast kicked at it. A pulse of light and a hoarse garble broke the night, before all fell dark and hushed again instantaneously. The beast kicked again, and again. At last, the light and sound burst into life and held its resilient power, forcing the wild nocturnal eyes to act on their natural fight-or-flight instincts. The roar was courage-shattering. Flight won over.

Leaning over his handlebars and breathing deeply, Cameron gained some small amount of composure before slowly edging the bike into motion. The helmet did not seem so important anymore. His body was losing vital fluid and his strength was waning. The sharp, piercing pain in his side was like nothing he had ever felt before, like he had been cut near in half with a rusty sawblade and had neat absinthe poured over the mangled and shredded gash. Once cruising east, however, along the old bootlace of road, the night air ran clean through his waving hair, liberating and invigorating the young man on the cycle.

The prospect of descending upon Kerenza, winding along the coiling blacktop like the snake that she is, encouraged him; kept his juices flowing. He could feel his time drawing to a close, her cold metallic bite his demise. Nonetheless, mowing her down and taking her with him as his last mortal act would ensure he died with a smile on his face.

Rounding a bend, the KMX's single headlight picked out a familiar sight. His destination: a dark and narrow gap in the overgrown Cornish hedge. His place of sanctuary was within reach.

With the deep regret of not advancing on his dear stepsister prior to this juncture eating its way through his sticky, seeping wound, Cameron slowed the machine and cut left. Pain stabbed at his midsection akin to being jabbed by a red-hot poker as he threw the bike over piled rubble. The violence of the terrain did not dissipate once clear of the rubble. The long open field's rutted geography pounded at the motorcycle like a pneumatic drill at stubborn ground, shaking the suspension and smashing the faux leather seat against his backside.

As the outline of a dilapidated farm building swelled against a charcoal canvas, Cameron released the throttle and threw himself from the cycle. He hit the floor hard. Landing on his belly, he urged at the combination of the verdant floor's pungent aroma and the air being body slammed out of his lungs. His beloved KMX rolled on alone, lighting a path across the field before toppling drunkenly on its side. The engine rattled and spat for a small number of seconds, humming out the broken fragments of its swansong.

***

Low smudging sounds, intermingled with exerted grunts, reverberated through the dank, dripping ceiling. A persistent, progressive resonance carried, like that of a plump caiman's scaley body being helplessly dragged across the oozy Brazilian Pantanal floor, clamped between the inseparable jaws of a sovereign jaguar.

A heavy creak issuing from the trapdoor fell through musty air, followed by the sound of a heavy object tumbling down the rotting timber staircase. It landed with a dense thud and more pained moans.

Amid a bout of raspy coughs, the dragging sound resumed. A steel bucket – crudely left for daily defecation – clattered, giving the impression that it toppled over. Blindfolded, it was hard to tell exactly what was coming through the darkness.

Something grabbed at the tied ankles. A hand? The diseased muzzle of some feral beast?

Please, please, please, let it be a hand!

Ropes that were tight enough to burn the captive person's flesh at the slightest movement, loosened.

A hand.

The detainee muffled something into the stinking, soggy gag wrapped tight around their head and mouth; the sound as potent in fear as it was in relief.

Feet free, the body attached to the busy hands shuffled around to the rear of the chair. Aggressively and painfully, the securing bonds around skinny, milk-white (but for the dirt) wrists were being worked at. Panic bit in as the chair's forelegs left the floor, before a forceful shove sent them back to earth with a clatter.

Incredulity, or the simple plain refusal to believe, commandeered. The binding materials fell to the ground. Captive hands were free.

The detainee leapt up to run, though through a combination of unused limbs and light-headedness, they failed to fight gravity. The body tumbled to the floor in a cacophony of rustling, chinking and crunching. Raising an emaciated arm to their head, clumsy fingers hit at the blindfold, before finally finding purchase and pulling the veil from their eyes. Nothing appeared at first, so long had it been since their vision was unimpeded. As shapes began to evolve from nothing, the noise of the rough landing became apparent. The skeletal figure lay in a confusion of rubbish bags and empty food containers.

The stink of rotting leftovers and their own unwashed skin was vomit inducing. Moving rapidly, the detainee lurched to the side and threw up green-brown bile into the gag. It dribbled from the edges, hanging in stringy ribbons. With an effort, they removed the disgusting cloth.

Looking back into the darkness, a human shape could be seen crawling closer through the dirt. Tensing up, the prisoner scrambled backwards, agony igniting their lower spine as it made heavy contact with the wooden staircase.

'Go,' the captor struggled, the voice feeble but recognisable. 'You need...*urgh*. You need to go.'

'Ca...Cameron?' Barely able to comprehend, and as timid as a fieldmouse, Shona asked again. 'Cameron. Is that you?'

After her unfathomable length of time shut away in whatever this was, Shona was certain the familiar face before her was a hallucination, an apparition conjured up by her desperate need for human contact.

'How, how did you find...' Her voice trailed off as realisation dawned on her. 'You?'

Tears welled at the lower lids of her eyes. Shona became overwhelmed as pieces of an inconceivable puzzle shifted and adhered into one horrifying montage.

'You need to get out,' Cameron hissed, spitting on the floor.

'What's____'

'*Go, home!*' he growled, breath steaming.

Shona only looked at him in dazed despair.

Cameron let out a choking cough. Oil-dark liquid trickled down his chin as he edged awkwardly closer.

'Up the stairs. Door's straight ahead.' More coughing. More blood. The iron taste lay rancid at the back of his tongue. 'Turn left when you get out.'

'I'll get you help,' Shona's emotions distorted her voice.

'Forget me!' Cameron commanded. 'You'll recognise the road. Maybe. In case you don't, turn left again. Flag down the first car you see.'

'Cameron, what's going *on*?' Shona's head tore apart as a multitude of scenarios clashed like wayward waves in a storm.

'Kerenza. She did this.' Cameron forced himself to a kneeling position, pushing himself up with one elbow on the seat of the chair. He removed his other hand from his side. Through patchy shadows, Shona's recovering eyes could see dark, sticky fluid on his top and his hand. 'She did this to me. She did this to you.'

'No,' said Shona, refusing to accept the accusation. 'She's my daughter. She put me... Kept me fed. Made me...' she cringed in embarrassment, looking at the steely lip of the toppled bucket. 'Made me use *that* disgusting thing!'

'Not exactly,' Cameron lowered his dark head, black fringe masking his shame. 'We haven't got time for this.'

He motioned forward another few inches. Shona backed away and slip-crawled onto the bottom step.

'I don't believe you,' she whispered.

'It's me that's been here. Every day since...' He did not need to say since when. 'Kerenza thinks you're dead; that I killed you.'

Through the low level of light, Cameron could make out Shona's grey features, her face frozen in shock.

'That's what she wanted. What she planned. When it came to it, I couldn't.' He climbed up and lurched himself clumsily onto the chair, it's wooden surface still warm from its previous occupant. He noticed Shona flinch away at his action.

'I was in love with her. Still am,' he said, a bittersweet smile stretching the corners of his mouth at the recollection of her face; her scent; her touch. 'She made me believe I was doing it for us. All this time I was doing it for her. For them.'

'Them?' Shona had cautiously moved her bottom up another two boards on the stairs.

'Her and my *prick* of a dad.' His face screwed in anger; the smile replaced with a hard, purple scar. 'She's on her way home now. Get there first, or she's gonna 'ave her tits in his face and her ass riding his wrinkly old cock like a racehorse by the time ya do.'

Weak and disorientated, Shona heaved herself up another step. She stopped to look back at her stepson. In the pale underground room, he could just make out her vacant, glazed eyes.

'*GO!*' he shouted with all the conviction he could muster.

Shona started at the outburst. Turning, she scrambled up the stairs on hand and knee. Without looking back, she emerged through the black rectangular whole and stepped onto dirty, sludgy ground. It was her first attempt at standing (other than five minutes ago) since she could remember. Her instability getting the better of her, she fell forward, face scraping through the mud.

Her head a cyclone of nauseating spins, the taste of stagnant slick earth in her mouth, Shona pressed her listless, anaemic arms – arms that she did not recognise as her own – into the dank floor. Exerting all her strength through the veiny white branchlike limbs, she gained her feet once more, wobbling under her own frailty.

Winning that battle after half-a-minute or so, Shona made for an opening where a fragment of door hung on a single hinge. Passing through, the freshness of the air outside hit like a narcotic. She looked to the heavens, drinking in large gulps of the pure outside world. Saltwater particles floating in the misty atmosphere grasped her tastebuds and clawed their way down her oesophagus. The chorus of a raging sea was omnipresent, a symphonic filling of the night sky. Unaware of salty tracks cutting away the grime on her cheeks, her first taste of freedom for time untold induced floods of tears from her chestnut eyes.

Snapping her back to damning reality, the sound of an engine whined across the field Shona found herself stood in. She looked to her left, the direction Cameron had instructed her to take. A beam of light penetrated the sky, coming and going with the short passing of seconds.

In fits and starts she ran, the long grass entrapping her weary feet and pulling her to the soft floor on numerous occasions. Finally, she spotted a blacker shade in the dark hedgerow. An opening. Body, mind and soul invigorated by the discovery, she ran with revitalised determination, her filthy cargo trousers slipping around her bony, angular hips.

Bursting through the bramble-choked opening, the distressed, dishevelled woman hit the road. Turning left, again as instructed, Shona grasped her whereabouts instantly.

CHAPTER SIXTY

Kerenza focussed on the face in the mirror with meticulous scrutiny. Sharp, azure eyes returned their full attention, the deep colour intensified by their seductive copper-bronze shadowed lids. Her cheeks glowed a healthy vital pink, while below them lips of plump strawberry looked good enough to eat.

Her resplendent body reeked of youth and feminine beauty. Every parasitic touch from her abhorrent stepbrother had been scrubbed and stripped clean, like shed skin.

Outside in the quiet sanctuary of Sea Glass Cottage's secluded garden, a refuse sack lay covered by lengths of charred wood in a dark corner of the tumbledown studio. Within it, her incriminating clothing lay in wait of incineration: the top he had clawed at; the crotch of her jeans that his contemptible hand had soiled at her deceptive (and personally repugnant) own bidding. All would soon be reduced to ash.

She thought of his bleached and lifeless corpse. The ceaseless torrent of waves battering the cadaver against tearing scythes of rock. The body that once wanted her, now lying cold, broken, destitute of life.

Her thoughts turned to the body she intended to give herself to. The body lying warm and unsuspecting in a bed of grief and vulnerability just a couple of rooms away.

Giving herself a smile of approval, Kerenza stood and untied her short, silky dressing gown. Pulling her shoulders free, she let it fall to the floor. The mirror gave a silvery look of lustful adulation as it took in her naked glory. Starting at the hollow *v* of her neck, the tips of her fingers gently traced their way down between her breasts and over the ridges of her toned tummy. Her body erupted in goose-pimples at her own tantalising touch.

Returning to the stall before her dressing table, Kerenza leaned sideways to her bottom drawer. She pulled it open and reached in right to the back, finding the tissue paper that concealed her *special surprise* for Andrew. The evil eye of her lampshade hovered close to her lowered face. It watched with disapproval as the duplicitous miscreant removed the package. Easing herself back up slowly, she carefully placed the bundle on the table before her.

Visually taking in the neatly wrapped package, she could with colossal relief assume that Andrew had not noticed the item disappear from his bedroom.

Picking at the edge of a sticky paper seal, Kerenza peeled cautiously, unfolding the top flap of tissue paper as it came free. Unwrapped in front of her lay a neat pile of pure white silk, lace and nylon: her late mother's wedding night underwear. Piece by sumptuous piece, Kerenza adorned herself in the fine garments.

She clipped the last lace-banded stocking at her thigh and stood for inspection. Running her hands over the material, Kerenza pushed at the underside of the bra, ensuring they sat pertly, commanding the attention of anyone lucky enough to get within reach. The fit was close. Not perfect; there were places where she would prefer the fabric to be a bit tighter (especially at the shapely contours between her legs, where the sweet trap would be set to devilishly alluring effect). Although her mother was not a big woman, Kerenza was indeed slighter in frame. This fact however would pale into insignificance once she had *her way*. Her hope was fully invested in the smalls being removed by the voracious hands of the only man in her life in the very near future.

Desperately plotting with the objective of making herself irresistible to a man devasted by the loss of the women in his life – maybe not the first one, from the anecdotes Cameron had told of his own mother, but certainly the latter two – the youth had even considered colouring her hair dark, like her mother's. Time, however, had had massive implications on that possibility. If Andrew could have seen the likeness of his beloved second wife enter his chamber, served on a platter in her wedding underwear, he would undoubtedly have been putty in her hands.

One last look in the mirror filled her with an undeniable self-assuredness.

'Relax, girl,' she told the duplicate. 'He won't be able to keep his hands off you.'

***

Blood soaked into the lower portions of Shona's cargo trousers, her knees torn and shredded after multiple falls to the unforgiving rough ground. The road seemed to wind through infinity. Every once in a while, a house bordered the route. Dishearteningly, all lights were out, and drives were devoid of vehicles. Portreath lay a short distance ahead, though with the rapidity her already fatigued body diminished in strength, it may as well have been on the moon.

Stumbling to her hands and knees again, Shona coughed acrid phlegm onto the dull, sulphurous surface. Her stomach cramped and her head whirred like a toy boat navigating the brutal Bay of Biscay.

Forcing herself to press on, to fight through the pain barrier and deny her need to drift into unconsciousness, her hands crawled forward searchingly like a rock climber on a sheer cliff face. Her frayed knees did not cooperate, suddenly deciding that they spoke a language foreign to the desperately clawing hands. They held firm, ignorant to the message the hands were striving to impart. Levelling out, one side of her face came to rest on the frigid asphalt. Shona succumbed to oblivion, blacking out in the middle of the road.

***

Opening into a dark bedroom, the door silently skimmed over plush carpet. From outside the room the landing light cast a mellow glow across the bed, dimly displaying a man lying curled up and asleep under the covers. Back turned, he was unaware of the surveying intruder.

Clad in her short dressing gown, Kerenza made her way into the shadows. All was silent, but for the light, rhythmic breathing of the sleeping figure. The cool carpet through her stockinged feet had an emancipating effect, like stepping naked onto dewy grass under a fresh, starry sky after years of incarceration.

Reaching the bed, she leaned forward and flicked the switch on the bedside lamp. Positioned on the matching table on the far side of the bed were two empty wine bottles. Next to these was a book. On the cover, a boy and a tiger shared a boat. Its pages were dog-eared and discoloured from multiple reads.

Rousing, the waking individual rolled over, bleary eyed and sensing the weight of another person push down on the bed. With the heal of each hand, he rubbed his eye sockets hard. Morphing from the angelic white outline of a dream, his stepdaughter came slowly into view. Kneeling on the bed, she watched over him intently.

***

A fearsome shriek bellowed from the tires as a heavy foot plunged on the brake pedal. The macabre sight – spotted by chance at the last second as Ben (Benny to his friends, though they were getting fewer seemingly by the day) glanced up from attempting to switch stations on the small Peugeot van's radio – was consumed beneath the line of his bonnet. Too big to be a badger, and having never seen a muntjac deer on this stretch to be sure they graced the area, Ben had to admit that the form had a worryingly human quality.

Killing the engine, along with it his and his wife's *first dance* song, with a mildly trembling hand Ben opened his driver's door and placed one tree trunk leg onto the road. The other followed and he straightened to his unimposing five-feet-eight-inches. Rather more imposing, he carted his forty-eight-inch ass around to the front of the vehicle.

In the brightness of the van's headlights, he could see with sickening horror that the bundle on the floor was undoubtedly human; bloodied, pale, and as dead as a doornail. Turning aside, Benny Brown lurched forward and placed his pudgy fingers on the knees of his long camo shorts. Retching, he brought up the homecooked beef stew his mother had sent around early that evening. Lackadaisically inspecting the chunks: chewed brown beef; bright orange carrot; turnip; spuds, a movement in the corner of his eye caught his attention. He rolled his head to the side as the corpse did the same.

'What the hell?' he blurted, as the dead eyes flickered open.

Benny stepped back and wiped the residue of puke from the corner of his mouth.

'Shit,' he gasped. 'You're alive! We've gotta get you to the hospital.'

'*Ho…*' the bundle struggled.

'What?' He leaned closer, moonlight catching the bald channel between the two flanks of wiry brown hair. 'I can't make out what you're saying.'

'*Home,*' she whispered. 'I need. I need to get home.' The unfortunate thing on the floor closed her eyes, her face wincing, clearly in discomfort.

The man raised his hands to his head deliberating his dilemma, knocking his thick-framed glasses askew in the process. 'I don't think that's a good idea,' he said.

'*Please*. Please.'

Against his better judgment, the barrel-shaped man swung his way around to the side of the vehicle. Shona heard a door creak open. The man returned, picking her up like she weighed next to nothing. Despite the night coldness, the armpits of his tee shirt displayed dark patches, and the stale odour of his sweat plugged her nostrils. He carried her lax body around to the side he had just opened and placed her on the passenger seat with a florist's gentle dexterity. Closing her door, she saw him waddle past the glow of the headlights. Her side of the light van rose as he lowered his bulk into the driver's position.

He looked at her for a moment. This is not right, his expression criticised.

'So,' he said softly. 'Where's home?'

***

'Krenz,' Andrew said, his mind half asleep and half intoxicated from the wine. 'What's the matter?'

'Lonely. Upset. Can't sleep in there on my own,' she said. 'Thought you might be the same.'

Kerenza lowered herself to the *virasana* pose, bottom between her feet, back and neck straight. She knew this posture would have the desired effect on her attire. Without the need to take her eyes away from Andrew's, she was well aware that the short dressing gown had ridden up her strong thighs, revealing the lace tops of her stockings.

Naturally reacting to the situation, Andrew's gaze lowered. He retracted his focus almost instantaneously, but not so instantaneous that Kerenza did not notice. She smiled and slid a massaging hand down the smooth rounded surface of her leg.

'Upset,' he said. 'Yeah, of course. But the wine knocked me out. I was sleeping quite well.'

'That doesn't help me though.' She bit a corner of her lower lip. Innocent. Seductive. 'Only you can do that.'

He yawned, 'Sorry, I don't see how *I* can help.'

'You can be there for me,' she said with BAFTA winning anguish. 'We can be there for each other.' Pulling the cover back further, she could see that Andrew was naked but for a pair of tight, grey boxers.

Either he's well equipped, she thought, looking at the mound, *or I'm making things happen down there*. 'Can I?' she asked, nodding at the opening in the bedclothes.

'Any other time, I'd say yeah,' he assured her nervously.

'But?'

'But,' he swallowed and looked down at himself, pulling the cover back to hide his shorts as best he could. 'I'm not really dressed appropriately for, you know.'

'Oh well,' said Kerenza. She hooked a thumb behind the silk belt of her gown and pulled, letting the robe fall open. Slipping it from her shoulders and slinging it to the floor like some showboating magician, she revealed her heavenly slinky body. 'Guess you're not dressed inappropriately for *"you know"* anymore.'

Andrew was stupefied into temporary silence, not cognizant of how to act in a situation where this semi-naked girl was ostensibly offering herself to him on his bed.

At that moment a spark of recognition set his brain conflagrant.

The delectable underwear (of which he hated himself for categorising as so on his stepdaughter, no matter how fantastic she may have looked). He had seen it before. Not just seen it, but fervently peeled it from this imposter's mother's exquisite skin on the best day of his life.

'Whoa, what the fuck are you doing?' He threw back the covers and started to scramble off the bed.

A leopard leaping on an unsuspecting infant gazelle, her powerful claws settled on his bare chest before he made it to the safety of the savanna's high grasses. Pinning him to the spongy bed, she swung a leg over his middle, straddling him.

'It's okay. You don't have to fight it,' she said as he struggled beneath her, his drunkenness damping his vigour. 'Everything that's happened has been for this moment. For us.'

'What___'

Kerenza cut him short by placing her full, red lips on his. Grabbing one of his hands, she clamped it on her bare ass cheek. She dug her nails into the back of his hand, prompting him to squeeze her flesh. Like a pathetic man with a one-track mind, he worked his hand to the delicate fabric running down the centre of the thong. Wrapping his free hand around the back of her smooth blonde head, he allowed her sweet tongue the freedom to flick unimpeded into his mouth. The venereal act intensified as she scraped her nails down his chest and ran her hand over the mound in his shorts.

Pulling her head from his, she sat upright and reached behind her, feeling for the clasp of the brassiere, sticking her lissom chest forward.

In an act of metamorphosis, the youthful face leering down at him transfigured. It enhanced in maturity. The full lips became finer, the blue eyes darkened to chestnut brown. Shona's face hovered above him, hauntingly real.

Outside in the glow of a security light, a spherical bowling ball of a man burst from the driver's door of a small white van. The man scampered around the vehicle, each headlight flashing against the peaceful façade of Sea Glass Cottage as he passed. He pulled at the handle of the passenger door. As it swung open, he reached in. A slight human shape in the passenger seat looked to refuse his help, before almost falling to the floor and being suddenly appreciative of his presence.

As he led her gingerly to the entrance of the property, he cast glances back towards the passing road. Speeding through tight, winding roads as nimbly as the van could manage, Ben had been fed broken fragments of a staggering story, one suited to prime time television but inconceivable in reality. Through short, gasping breaths and fumbled words, he had deciphered that this woman had been missing, presumed dead, for nearly a year. She had been kept alive – all the while, though she did not know it until tonight – by her stepson. Her apparent death had been orchestrated by her own daughter, manipulating the boy and playing puppet master, keeping her hands clean while he converted her fantasies to reality.

The insidious deviant was at home now, casting her web of deceit over the woman's husband and moving in with arachnid intent.

Hastily and frantically whilst behind the wheel, Ben had grabbed his mobile phone from the driver's door pocket and phoned the emergency services. When asked through a patchy line what service he required, he answered, 'Whatever you've bloody well got.'

Casting another desperate look back, he pleaded for God to let him see blue lights approaching.

Only his own headlights broke the night.

Arriving at the door, the woman reached for the handle. It held firm. Looking through the glass, a key could be seen protruding from the keyhole. Not letting go of the man's arm, she leaned over, groaning in agony as tight muscles in her back stretched into life. She plucked up a rock about the size of a cricket ball and hit the glass. It gave with a loud, mortiferous smash.

'What the...' Andrew scorned, grabbing Kerenza by the arms and shoving her to the vacant side of the bed.

'Come on,' she said rolling back onto him. 'We both know you want me.'

'You're sick,' he hissed, trying to remove her again.

She grabbed at each side of his pillow and pulled herself down, clamping the two of them together in an embrace of writhing flesh. Thrusting his knee up, a chunk of quadricep muscle caught her on the groin.

'Mmm, you can do that again,' she breathed in his ear, rubbing the warm triangle of lace against his leg.

'GET...THE FUCK...OFF!' he shouted. Forcing all his resolve to his arms, Andrew threw her over the side of the bed.

Landing hard at the right angle of floor and wall, her face a mixture of hurt and anger, Kerenza moved a hand to the back of her head. When she brought it back before her eyes, the tips of her fingers were tacky with blood.

'What___'

The sound of smashing glass from downstairs rang through the house, cutting off the remainder of her accusing interrogation.

Andrew sprang from the bed. Grabbing a tee shirt and throwing it over his head, he bounded from the room, leaving a shocked Kerenza propped against the wall under the bedroom window, staring dumbly at her claret fingertips.

Taking the stairs three-at-a-time, Andrew shot through the living room, stopping dead in fear as he entered the kitchen. Standing open-mouthed, all colour drained from him like the deceased.

Looming larger than life before him, resurrected from her watery grave, was his dead wife.

Neither spoke. Tears streamed from her dark, vibrant eyes. As she stood in her ragged, bloodied, soiled state, Andrew had never seen anything more beautiful.

The apparition took a step towards him. Disquietude held him rooted to the floor. Another step, now within touching distance, she raised a hand to his face. Her touch was cold, but it was not imagined. *She's here*, he thought. *She's real and she's here.*

He touched her face. Wiped her tears with a thumb, leaving a grimy smear across her bony cheek. Crying himself, he took her in close.

'What the *hell?*' Kerenza stood in the doorway that opened onto the rest of the cottage. She was made up and adorned in a short dressing gown, and what appeared to be white stockings. A deadly, black cast iron fire poker swung like a pendulum from her right hand.

'Stay away,' Shona warned with unconvincing conviction.

'You were dead,' said Kerenza with a disconcerting smirk. 'You should've stayed that way!'

With a feral snarl, she raised the poker and charged at her mother. As Andrew jerked his wife to the side, the poker swung. A violent swooshing sound like a golf club on a tee shot whipped past her head, ending with a clatter as it scarred the dark stone worksurface.

Pulled by her own body's momentum, Kerenza toppled off balance against the countertop. Straightening up next to her frightened mother she raised the heavy iron weapon again. Andrew made to drag his emaciated and fragile wife to safety once more. Kerenza concentrated on his movement, homing in for the double. She could never trust Andrew after this betrayal.

As the lust for retribution hastened through Kerenza's delirious mind, a man Andrew had never seen before sprung through the open front door. He was short and extremely rotund, yet the agility of his overweight body was mind-bendingly incomprehensible. The hefty bulk of the man shot across the room like a greyhound from the starting trap. Kerenza's unsuspecting eyes bulged in horror as she was rugby tackled from behind. Plummeting, she careened to the floor as if she had been struck by a bus.

Squirming on the cold tiled floor, the girl with dark fluid matting her pretty blonde hair fought in vain under the sweaty, doughy mass that kept her pinned.

Shona collapsed in tears against her husband. The shock of all she had been through, and all that she was now witnessing, overwhelmed her every emotion. Andrew held her tightly, never wanting to let go again. Hell, he might even swear allegiance to God if this was really happening, and not just one deranged fantasy.

As the reunited pair cried together in a protective huddle, and with the startled teenager furiously kicking and screaming in desperation under his weight, Benny lauded himself for the most heroic act of his relatively meaningless life. That the beast beneath him would escape his bulk, was as likely as him owning a Lamborghini and dating Naomi Campbell, yet still the swelling sound of approaching sirens brought with them an intoxicating relief as such that he had never experienced before.

CHAPTER SIXTY-ONE

December arrived with a flurry of late autumnal sunshine. The invigorating clear skies imbued an assured promise of a brighter future, seeking out and evaporating the overcast shadows that had descended upon their lives.

The couple stood, a radiant smile glowing on the face of one, an unamused smile faltering on the face of the other.

'So,' Shona said cagily. 'What do you think?'

A cool breeze toyed with the fine hairs of her dark fringe, the cool air tickling her rosy cheeks like icy fingers.

Andrew sniggered. 'I think you're winding me up.'

'It's the next model up,' she said earnestly, bolstering her campaign. 'And only six-hundred and fifty quid.'

'It's got almost a hundred and fifty thousand on the clock!'

'And still going strong. It's a total bargain!'

Andrew looked at the infantile hope in her eyes. Those irresistible smouldering lumps of autumn embers could have anything they wished for.

Smiling, as love-struck as the day they first met, he said, 'It's perfect.'

Condensation built at those mesmerising embers. She raised her hands to her mouth and screeched like a bird of prey.

'Yay!' Merryn's voiced piped up excitedly from between the two adults. 'So can we go home in it?' Jumping up and down on the spot now, a sentiment her mother shared, only with a touch more dignity.

Andrew looked at the red Ibiza, sighed, and put the back of a hand to his forehead checking for signs of fever. It was cool.

'Well,' he said. 'Let's go buy your car.'

One forgettable hour of paperwork and online insurance and tax purchasing later, Andrew was removing the booster seat from the back of his vehicle and handing it to his wife.

'Go careful,' he said, kissing her lightly on her smooth jawline.

'You too,' she beamed uncontrollably.

'I'm gonna make a quick stop on the way home, if that's okay?' he said.

'That's fine,' said Shona. 'But don't expect me to follow you. You know how I feel about that road.' She knew exactly what he meant by *"quick stop,"* and more importantly, *where* he meant. 'Take it easy.'

'I'll see you back at home,' said Andrew, ruffling Merryn's straw-like hair and turning away.

Sliding behind the wheel of his own car, an overwhelming gratitude hit him as it always did. Having his license returned was a huge step back to normality for Andrew Tredinnick. As for having his wife back? Well, you just can't write that.

Blowing two kisses (one for each of the women in his life, young and not-so-young), he watched as the red hatch pulled off the forecourt. Nostalgia flooded his brain like the opening of a canal lock. He smiled reminiscently, fired up the engine, and headed to his clifftop rendezvous.

Snoring rhythmic and docile sighs, the Atlantic rested at unseasonal ease. The sleeping giant's chest rose and receded in a lazy swell, caressing semi-submerged rocks, shushing peacefully over their slick surfaces with each intake of draughty breath.

Beneath his feet to the left, the right, and directly below, seabirds sat serene in lofty tufts among the crags of Hell's Mouth's vast and ancient face. Chatting their idle chatter to one another, they rested in lethargic stupor.

Andrew inhaled deeply at the crisp, salty air, taking in the rugged tranquillity, and the often unforgiving beauty of Cornwall's wild north coastline. Looking over the precipice, down the vertical landscape of greys, browns and reds falling away from the observer, a lone grey seal pirouetted through the crystal blue waters. Whether hunting for food, or just living the life in the gentle oozing of the current, Andrew did not know.

Cameron's trusty sidekick – the KMX 125 – had been found abandoned in the concealing grass of a field not too far from here. A forensic investigation of the plot's sole property (a derelict farm building where Andrew's wife was held imprisoned – alive and unbeknown to anyone else for just shy of a year), was carried out. Traces of the Cameron's blood were found on the rotting staircase, the floor, and the properties singular piece of furniture: a chair found in the centre of the chilling basement.

Nothing was found of the young man himself.

Andrew had made his peace with Hell's Mouth.

Despite that acceptance, he would often pay a visit here, absently scanning the shifting sea, or the winding thread of coastal path. Expecting to see him, finger raised in a show of boyish charm.

He never truly believed that he would see his son again. But he had never believed that he would see his wife again, either. His soulmate.

This particular giant, however, sleeps with one eye open, and keeps its secrets hidden deep.

About the Author

Kevin Knuckey was born in Cornwall and raised on horror films from an inappropriately tender age, *Horror Express* and *Salem's Lot* particularly esteemed introductions. The first book he ever read from cover to cover, *The Jungle Book* (Disney rendition). The second, Stephen King's *The Shining*.

Inspired whilst working as a primary school teaching assistant, Kevin began to plot his first children's book, though after pulling himself aside and having a serious chat with himself, he decided that the targeted market was not ready for an old folk's home that processed its residents and served them through the sinister owner's freshest business venture, Old Biddy's Burgers.

Experiencing the physical deterioration that comes with Charcot-Marie-Tooth disorder, however, Kevin has streamlined his attention, remaining true(*ish*) to the genre he was born into and thrives in, for the appropriate audience. With his debut psychological thriller "Hell's Mouth" he utilises his keen interest in the macabre, though confining the actions to within the brutal realms of human capability.

CPSIA information can be obtained
at www.ICGtesting.com
Printed in the USA
LVHW032055290722
724733LV00004B/86